NICHOLAS-BEAR

# SIXTH PERCEPTION

(SEXTA PERCEPTIO CUM EXITIBUS)

PART THREE OF NL:2012/2013 TRILOGY

Sixth Perception


tellwell

Tellwell Talent
www.tellwell.ca

ISBN
978-0-2288-7270-2 (Hardcover)
978-0-2288-7269-6 (Paperback)
978-0-2288-7271-9 (eBook)

# SIXTH PERCEPTION

(SEXTA PERCEPTIO CUM EXITIBUS)

***Other books by the same author:***

First Perception (Primam Perceptionem Mansuetus)
Second Perception (Secundum Perceptionem Placidus)
Third Perception (Tertia Percepcio Cum Papilionibus)
Fourth Perception (Quarta Perceptio Aeterna)
Fifth Perception (Quinta Tristis Perceptio)

*This is an invented story about the lost realm of Atlantis reborn as a nonexistent modern-day archipelago. It comprises tales of fictitious weaponry, paranormal abilities, homosexuality, polyamory, and alternate social and family structures as well as direct democracy. Those cringing at their mentioning, or not willing to contemplate such ideas, need not try read it.*

*This is a work of fiction. Names, characters, businesses, places, events, and incidents are either the products of author's imagination, or used in a fictitious manner. Any resemblance to actual persons, living or dead, or actual events, is purely coincidental.*

*Among other themes, the novels about Newlands purport to describe relationships this imaginary state has with the most important countries of our world. To this extent, the political leaders of these countries, their civil servants, scientists, and prominent soldiers appear as characters on these pages, in a completely fictitious manner.*

# ABOUT THE NEWLANDS ENGLISH

*English, one of the official languages of Newlands, is the mother tongue of more than a third of its population, as well as being the chosen language of communication for most Newlandeans. English is therefore lingua franca of the Newlands Archipelago. During the decade-long wars with a coalition of Arab states, English became the only official language of MANATO. Newlands English exists in a form more flexible than any other existing variation of English, as all accents, dialects, phonetics, phonology, vocabulary, grammar, and spelling are equally accepted (and thus used in this manuscript). On Newlands, English also acquired numerous expressions from other spoken languages (you can find the list of some of those in the appendix). Typically, Newlands English relies on the American spelling and British grammar (use of passive forms being common, for example). Some new words have also been coined; others are spelled in a different manner than elsewhere. Hence, in this book can be encountered words like Newlander / Newlandean, Electocracy, Airforce, Coastguard, Firefighters, Cophot, Crabtown, Lobsterville, airboat, fireboat, and waterpolo. Often employed in this novel are words like: defense, color, center, harbor, favor, labor, gray, mustache, and traveling – although defence, colour, centre, harbour, labour, grey, moustache, and travelling may be equally used.*

*It is not this author's intention that my readers continuously flip to book's last pages in order to translate bywords and swearwords used. My hope is that you'll accept them as part of the spoken Newlandean English, and simply go with the flow.*

# AUTHOR'S NOTE ON PERCEPTION NOVELS

Dear reader, if you're leafing or scrolling through these pages, it's probably safe to presume that a copy of one of my novels is in your hand (or on your eBook reader). It might surprise you that Perception novels developed from a book which was never meant to be published. Bear with me, and you'll discover how this came about.

There are two main components to all my six Perception novels.

The first important and invariably present component is the inclusion of gay (especially "bear") and heterosexual erotic (pornographic) scenes, which stem either from my personal sexual inclinations or adopt my main characters' stated desires.

Definitely, my Perception novels are not for children.

The second important and invariable component is the location, my story's background, which is the imaginary Newlands archipelago, the ancient Atlantis risen again, with its mongrel population comprising people from all the countries I lived in or visited (and beyond, from all over the globe). It boasts an unmatched horizontal democracy called Demarchy (a term borrowed from the science fiction, as well as from real-life political theory; it assumes slightly different meanings depending on origin) or Electocracy (to the best of my knowledge, I'm the proud inventor, cobbler, father of that term), which allows its citizens to modify or overrule decisions of their political leaders and assume direct rule in their country's political life. Newlands is characterized by some facets of society rarely encountered elsewhere. As far as I can with my meager knowledge, experience, and means ascertain, even when some of those

aspects are encountered, they are never all found in the same society (cashless or cash-free society, absolutely free schooling and health insurance, all its vehicles connected via a proprietary intranet network to a central authority, legal use of drugs, legal polyamorous relationships, ultra-low crime rate, legalized prostitution and pornography, soft stance towards paedophilia, legalized lack of privacy – a no privacy society, acceptance of nudity and the normal biological body functions, acceptance of death and the right to die, acceptance of cloning and designer babies, universal CCTV camera coverage, ostracizing of religions without an outright ban while emphasizing the freedom from religion.... and one rare prohibition – a ban on tobacco and all smoking).

In the late seventies of the twentieth century, my brother and I, then young teenagers, "invented" Newlands as an entertaining intellectual exercise. It excited us to have a personal secretive land of our own which no one knew about, without a long history to forcefully determine its social structure and customs, yet one which wouldn't change the broader balance of power and political relations of the existing world (thus be fully fitting into it). What we designed was much simpler than the complex society I described above; many of those facets were added along the way. We populated our new land with our chosen people. We drew maps of its most important islands (later in my books transformed into the Main Islands of Newlands, Anan and Dekan), and plans and maps for its four original cities (New Belgrade, Old City, Paloma, Atlantis), designed its mighty armed forces, imagined its wars, devised its sport teams. For fun, against each other, we played off those fantasy teams in table handball, table hockey, and carpet football (soccer), and recorded those scores. As an avid modelmaker, I assembled plastic models of airliners and finished them in various liveries of archipelago's airlines. As we grew older and reached the age of compulsory military service, musing about Newlands was a great pastime during the army life's dull moments. Gradually, our lives moved on to more mature endeavours; Newlands got abandoned to a large box full of notebooks and drawing paper, and the airplane models on their shelves.

I rediscovered Newlands after I finished my faculty courses and became an assistant professor. I faced long and gruesome Master of Science Studies and, later, even more stringent Doctoral Studies, all accomplished to a background of civil war in my disintegrating homeland. By then, computers became part of my life. As a means of pure relaxation,

sandwiched between working and studying, I started digitalizing Newlands maps and stories, constantly adding to the whole. In leaps and bounds, now solely mine, Newlands grew.

Why am I telling you this? To prove that Newlands, despite being an imaginary land, is quite real; it exists. Since its inception, it always existed, first in a big carboard box, nowadays as more than forty thousand files on my computer and a website.

In 2012, by now living in a different country (my fourth in total, albeit officially the third), I was employed in an interesting but stressful workplace, also encompassing an occasional but ubiquitous slow period of inactivity. I decided to combine my erotic daydreams and the unique land of Newlands into a story the writing of which would provide somewhat wicked entertainment (nothing more entertaining than deciding which of my characters will or won't have sex with another). Also, that timeline is the main reason my plot starts in 2011, as I used vivid recollections of recent history for its background.

My efforts resulted in a single novel, sensibly titled "Perception", that took more than two years to complete. It was never meant to be published, as it mostly presented a detailed pornographic vision with a science fiction / alternative history / alternative reality plot. I envisioned maybe gifting it to a gay friend, and nothing more than that. When my husband got to read it, he was delighted, especially with the variety and quality of the erotic imagery.

In the meantime, I grew fond of my story and its characters, compelling me to continue writing. Halfway through my second book it dawned on me that I could just.... maybe.... some day.... try publishing my first novel (I yet knew nothing of the self publishing process, it was all just a vague idea); though, obviously, not in its original form.

That's when the endless revisions of the freshly renamed "First Perception" started occurring, one after another, literally encompassing its every page, requiring almost as much time as it took to write the original version. One obvious step was to delete or radically mute all descriptions of sex, creating space for a more varied plot and copious explanations of the Newlandean society and the everyday life in the archipelago (the first revision of my entire novel).

As I was, from the beginning, forced to blend in occasional non-English words, it also occurred to me that I should try to undertake another daring step and create a slightly skewered form of English language, one

which I could brand "the Newlands English". Easier imagined than done, as concocting that language proved to be quite a chore.

When you start reading my first novel, the lack of articles "the" and some of the "a-s" will immediately become apparent. It's also true that Slavic languages (one of them being my mother tongue) don't use such articles, but that's not the reason for omitting them. "First Perception" lacks its articles because of BBC (or CBC, it's difficult to remember). About the time I was writing my second novel, I listened to a writers-and-books type show, or podcast, which presented some of the (well renowned and serious, I guess, but beat me if I can remember their names) modern English writers who, in their literary work, skip all articles. Delighted by quotes from their works, I decided to incorporate that idea into my writing. I reviewed my "First Perception" from start to finish, expelling almost all articles I dared to expel (its second major revision). I also exchanged as many remaining "the-s" as I could for "that", "our", "this", or the use of Saxon genitive (*the shore of the ocean - ocean's shore*), etc. However, much later, after I in the same vein finished writing my "Second Perception", I felt uneasy with the appearance of my text, as the lack of articles occasionally caused imprecise and dubious meanings right when I wanted them to be precise (such as in military descriptions). So, while proofreading my second novel, I started reintroducing some of the articles (too late to reshape my "First Perception", as it already got published). By the third book, as you'll hopefully discover if you decide to acquire it, almost all articles were back, though I still tried to replace as many as possible copiously using the Saxon genitive and the other gimmicks mentioned (I simply hate those articles!).

"First Perception's" third rewriting happened after another BBC or CBC show / podcast, purporting to prove that the form better accustomed to the structure of British English sentence is "which", while "that" is more an American form (geographically, Newlands is much closer to Britain than to the United States, hence its English should be more under the British influence, no?). Notwithstanding the grammar rules about clause as the determining factor for choosing "which" or "that", you might notice that on the pages of my novels "which" is far more often used than "that". This rewrite proved much more thorough and time consuming than anticipated as it often required repunctuation or rethinking of whole sentences.

The use of specific "Newlandean" bywords in my newly minted Newlands English didn't occur to me while writing the "First Perception" (to begin with, as originally created, most of my Newlandean characters were flawlessly polite, even during sex). The necessity of highlighting a limited "domestic" vocabulary of imported swear words, bywords, sayings, and proverbs, occurred to me halfway through the creation of the "Second Perception", requiring retrofitting those bywords into the "First Perception" as my characters couldn't remain flawlessly polite in one book, while profusely cursing in the next (the fourth extensive rewriting). Frankly, in my first novel, those imported words badly fit into existing sentence structure. I tried to precisely match their assumed or real sense with the meaning of a sentence as originally conceived before their introduction, which was a mistake. In the second book they appear more organically integrated, and by the third novel I developed an instinctive hang of it, avoiding insisting on their literal meaning. Nowadays, while I'm writing chapters of the fifth and sixth sequel, they've become a second nature.

At some later point, inspired by German grammar, I decided to change the order of words in my syntax, to place a person's name, an object, or the temporary article at the end of a sentence. Thus, I changed sentences like "*Dave, are we going to lunch*?" into "*Are we going to lunch, Dave?*" For a while I felt that this newest change gave my sentences an unusual, strange cadence, almost a rhyme, which I liked at first but by the fourth sequel mostly abandoned.

With all those forced rewrites, it's obvious that "First Perception" suffers from numerous issues and lack of cohesion. Some of its early readers, who later acquired other currently published novels, suggested rewriting it in the more homogenized later-novel language. I decided against such additional massive change, instead adding this author's note as an explanation for gradual development of my Newlands English.

I harbor another theory. Though Newlands English presents but a subtle change from the standard English, it requires time to adjust to. Therefore, with each additional novel under my reader's belt, it becomes easier to accept. Hence their preference for language of the later novels.

Last but not the least. Almost everyone is puzzled by the additional Latin subtitles I bestow on my novels, not the least my publishing consultants. First Perception is Primam Perceptionem Mansuetus, Second Perception is Secundum Perceptionem Placidus, Third Perception

is Tertia Perceptio cum Papilionibus, Fourth Perception is Quarta Perceptio Aeterna, Fifth Perception is Quinta Tristis Perceptio, and Sixth Perception is Sexta Perceptio cum Exitibus. Why? If we disregard that their Latin subtitle, once you translate its meaning, actually indicates content of that particular novel (in the case of "First Perception" its Latin subtitle literally translates as "Softened First Perception", alluding to major softening of its erotic content), you need to keep in mind that my academic background is in a medicine-related field of science. In biological sciences, to precisely define subjects, such as species' names, you use the Latin name. Thus, domestic cat is Felis catus, to distinguish from the European wildcat, which is Felis silvestris, and the African wildcat, which is Felis lybica; and so on for every living thing on Earth and (maybe one day) beyond. To me, those Latin names lend a layer of specificity to my titles.

(After the first two novels got published, I switched from Google's English-to-Latin translation to a registered professional translator. It appears that in its translation Google's algorithm made a big mistake. Can you spot it?)

I hope that you'll find my Newlands English and my story as a whole different and kinky enough to warrant following. Remember, after all, that I'm the world's foremost authority on Newlands English; so, trust me, I know what I'm doing....

Nicholas Bear

Discover more about Newlands:
Twitter: "Nicholas Bear" or @nesafred
Facebook: "Perception novels" or @NewlandsArchipelago
Website: www.newlandsgovernment.com

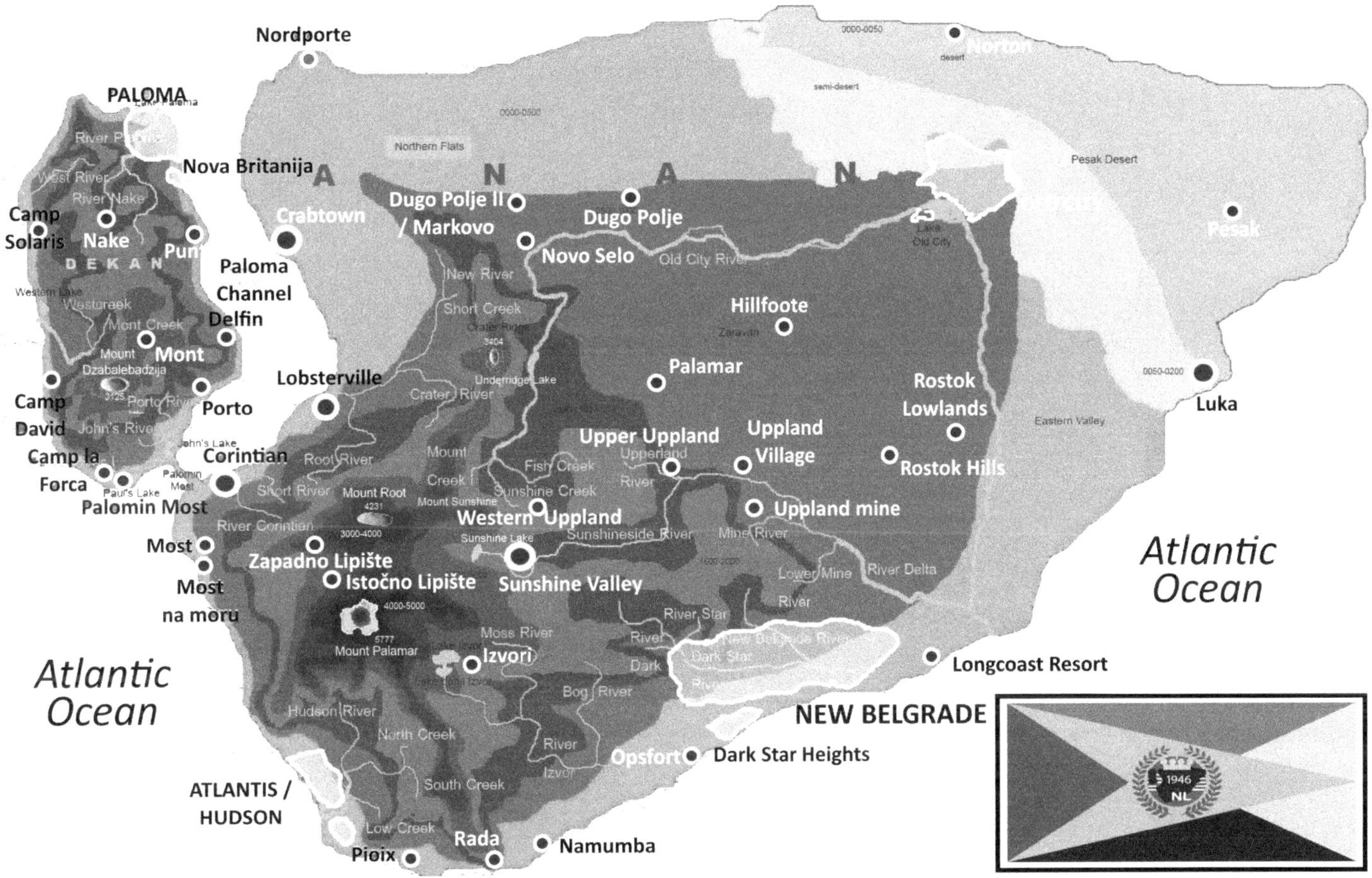
Nordporte
PALOMA
Lake Paloma
Nova Britanija
Camp
Solaris
Nake
Pun
DEKAN
Paloma
Channel
Delfin
Mont
Mount
Dzabalebadzija
3125
Porto
Camp
David
Camp la
Forca
Paul's Lake
Palomin Most
Corintian
John's Lake
Most
Most
na moru
Atlantic
Ocean
ATLANTIS /
HUDSON
Pioix
Rada
Namumba
Crabtown
Lobsterville
Northern Flats
A N A N
Dugo Polje II
/ Markovo
Novo Selo
Dugo Polje
Old City River
Hillfoote
Zaravan
Palamar
New River
Short Creek
Crater River
Underridge Lake
Root River
Short River
River Corintian
Mount Root
4231
3000-4000
Zapadno Lipište
Istočno Lipište
4000-5000
5777
Mount Palamar
Mount Sunshine
Sunshine Creek
Sunshine Lake
Western Uppland
Sunshine Valley
Moss River
Izvori
Hudson River
North Creek
South Creek
Low Creek
Bog River
Upper Uppland
Upperland
Uppland
Village
Uppland mine
Sunshineside River
Mine River
Lower Mine
River
River Star
Dark Star
River Delta
Rostok
Lowlands
Rostok Hills
Lake
Old City
Eastern Valley
Pesak Desert
semi-desert
desert
Norton
Pesak
Luka
Atlantic
Ocean
Longcoast Resort
NEW BELGRADE
Opsfort
Dark Star Heights
1946
NL

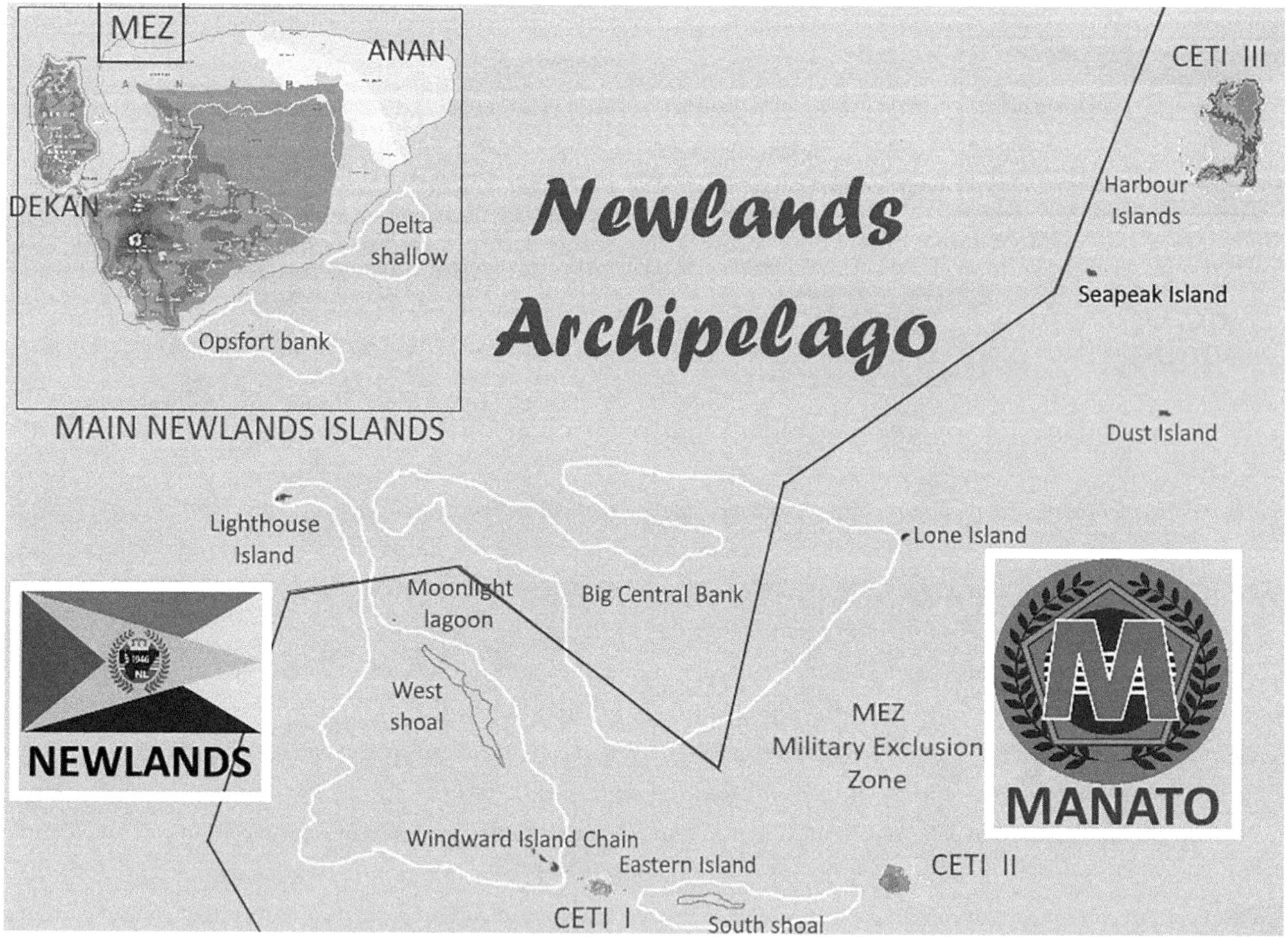
Newlands Archipelago
MEZ
ANAN
DEKAN
Delta shallow
Opsfort bank
MAIN NEWLANDS ISLANDS
CETI III
Harbour Islands
Seapeak Island
Dust Island
Lighthouse Island
Moonlight lagoon
Big Central Bank
Lone Island
West shoal
NEWLANDS
MEZ
Military Exclusion Zone
MANATO
Windward Island Chain
Eastern Island
CETI II
CETI I
South shoal

# LIST OF PROMINENT CHARACTERS FOR PERCEPTIONS:

**David (Dave) A-H Anderson – Lionheart** (originally Major **David Anderson**, US Army and CIA), General of Newlands Army, Commander-in-Chief of MANATO, member of CCofGHQ, member of privilege of twelve, privilege of five, and group of three cliques. This is his story, one of a continuous life change. He arrived as an enemy agent, bent on sabotage and destruction, but soon became one of the greatest Newlands heroes of all time. In possession of considerable supernatural powers.

**Alan Wykes**, Inspector of Newlands Police, Camp Solaris detachment. He developed telepathic abilities after a serious traffic accident in which a young girl got injured. Partially transferred to GHQ to use his abilities in resolving psychic threats to Newlands.

**Alexander Edwards, originally** from Ipswich (UK), deep-ocean oil-field computer specialist, and an agent of DFQL. Though English-born, migrated to Newlands when his future Newlandean wife declared her pregnancy. At first employed by Newlands' oil and natural gas companies, switched to running DFQL's Paloma Embassy. Since student days Taoist by conviction.

**Alisa Tomić – Lionheart**, Komodor of Newlands Navy, MANATO intelligence. A natural empath, able to penetrate emotions of people emotionally close to her, even at considerable spatial distance. Chief

analytical member of the Lionheart intelligence team and later one of the key PsiMANATO members. A secret member of the NSS. Mother of seven Lionheart sons.

**Andrew Lighthouse**, originally a Constable of Newlands Police (Highway Patrol), then an officer of TPB. Possessing powerful telepathic abilities, albeit unaware of those until mid-life. At forty decided to transfer into the ranks of Newlands Marines, achieving widespread renown. His courage and telepathic abilities allowed him to become a co-worker of privilege of five group and to achieve prominence inside GHQ of MANATO.

**Angela Merkel**, German Bundeskanzlerin (Chancellor). One of world's most prominent leaders and one of the most important political friends of Newlands. Merkel's Germany and Newlands are good trade partners, exchange lots of tourists, and work on military cooperation, as well as joint scientific research and space exploration.

**Barack Obama**, the Forty-fourth President of United States. He was faced with the sudden re-emergence onto world political scene of a powerful, albeit tiny Atlantic neighbor. Started his presidential mandate by covertly attacking the Newlands defence systems, to later become a solid friend, though never shedding the core suspicion of truly malevolent Newlandean intentions. Throughout his mandate, the relationship of America and Newlands is one continuous rollercoaster ride.

**Bogdan Petrović**, Petty Officer of Newlands Navy, later speedily climbing through the ranks, the only son of President Nemanja Petrović. Dave's blood brother. He trekked from an irresponsible teenager to a promising young sailor of the Newlands Navy. Married with three wives. Their family includes three daughters.

**Dr. Amanda Ross**, the youngest heart surgeon on Newlands, employed by the Fiona Stanley Hospital in Paloma. Feeling eternally in debt to General Mansur Al-Hammadi, she cared for him until his final day, then transferred that care to the whole Lionheart family and their closest friends. Married to the ex-sex worker Eaton Magnificent.

**Dr. Lenko Zdravkov**, MANATO Weapons Design Bureau. Mover of many astonishing military projects, he's a scientists and designer who's not

afraid to step out into the field and test his creations under the most realistic conditions of use. Supporting member of PsiMANATO.

**Dr. Irena Panj**, chief MANATO's geneticist on Ceti II in the Golden Angel Facility (MARC). General Al-Hammadi's late-life love, she transferred her love and professional care to Dave, General's adopted son, and his family. Supporting member of PsiMANATO.

**Dr. Philip Kieron Pardagh**, chief MANATO historian. After an early start in academia, marred by pedophilia, through Newlands-style justice-imposed redemption became one of its most important secret policy makers. Member of privilege of five and cofounder of the group of three.

**Fanta Lionheart**, MANATO warrant officer with various duties and ranks, and an operator of MANATO intelligence. Later engaged in the office of the Ambassador of MANATO. The most cheerful member of family Lionheart, albeit an independent thinker and schemer. Mother of Dave, Sam's son.

**Fran Lionheart (born Steiner)**, Komodor of Newlands Navy, member of GHQ Intelligence, various MANATO positions and ranks, member of CCofGHQ, privilege of five and twelve. A creative and logical polymath, with considerable ability for remembering details, he's Dave's main support in the Central Command as well as the founding pillar of family Lionheart.

**Henri Deladin**, Major of Newlands Marines, the overall commanding officer of TP Brigade. Member of CCofGHQ and privilege of twelve. Has devoted his military career to solving the primary Newlands military riddle: how to defeat huge numbers of potential enemies with but a handful of soldiers armed with futuristic weapons.

**John František**, the best Olympian in Newlands history. He won nine Olympic medals in biathlon over ten years, while participating in four different Winter Olympic Games. After ending his sport career, he entered foreign service as Ambassador to various Middle East countries. He transferred to MANATO to become the first MANATO Ambassador ever.

**Li Lian**, the Ninth President of Newlands. Her two terms in office were from 2001 – 2011. Next year reactivated as a member of privilege of five. With a voracious sexual appetite, she falls in love with Dave and becomes his pillar of strength in dealings with DFQL and China. Mother of Zhenxiang, Dave's daughter. Married to Major-Pilot Robert Hadži-Janković.

**Leo Hunter**, chief strategist of the National Bank of Newlands. Instrumental in providing financial backing to Newlands Government and MANATO. Dave's close friend. Married to Sue Campbell, Dave's American ex-girlfriend.

**Mansur Al-Hammadi**, retired General of Newlands Army, member of CCofGHQ, privilege of twelve and five. Long-time commander of MASP and MALD. A great friend of Bundeskanzlerin Merkel. Dave's adopted father. Grace to his psychic ability, successfully travelled the path from one of the principal enemies of Newlands to one of its greatest assets. Died in 2011 of terminal brain cancer.

**Marino Marino**, Komodor of Newlands Coastguard, member of CCofGHQ and privilege of twelve. One of Dave's closest allies in MANATO's Central Command and an undoubting friend. Able to carry out various important projects. He's married with three wives and has a teenage son.

**Mario Dražić**, Marshal of Newlands Army, Commander-in-chief of Newlands Armed Forces, the leading member of CCofGHQ for more than forty years. Presided over the rise of MANATO into world's preeminent military power. Died in 2011 of terminal brain cancer.

**Mietje Dobrašinović**, daughter of Robert and Zelda, developed supernatural abilities after a traffic accident in her early childhood which left her a mute paraplegic. Possesses the strangest and most powerful psychic abilities on Newlands, including ability to telepathically interact with computers and the internet. Found a new, exciting field of activity in cooperation with MANATO's telepathic dolphins.

**Miodrag Raonić** (**Miki**), General of Newlands Airforce, Commander of GHQ Intelligence, member of CCofGHQ. Through his work, liaises with NSS and privilege of five. Main coordinator of all secret projects

and services of MANATO and Newlands. Dave's great friend. Married to two wives.

**Nemanja Petrović**, since 2011 President of Newlands. Once Dave become blood-brother to his son Bogdan, Nemanja became his "socially adopted father". While conducting a proactive presidency, he's forcefully thrusting his country back onto the world political scene and into major headlines.

**Nikola Tomić – Lionheart**, second in command of Swift – 1 and all MANATO shock troops, member of MANATO Intelligence and Newlands Secret Service, holding various ranks in the Newlands Army, supporting member of PsiMANATO. Of enormous physical strength, Nikola is the epitome of a soldier able to remain cool and concentrated in any situation.

**Pavel Varina**, center-forward of FC Paloma. Member of a famous wine-producing family. When not battling ankle injuries, one of the greatest football players of Newlands in the 21st century. Though mostly choosing to be gay, married Cleo Novotny, another famous football player, with whom he has a son named Sam.

**Raj Chahal**, Colonel-Pilot of Newlands Airforce and other various ranks, various MANATO positions, member of CCofGHQ and privilege of twelve, a secret member of the Newlands Secret Service. Dave's guardian angel, acting from the Newlands Cosmodrome. When not performing his duties, inventor of useful military gadgets.

**Robert Hadži-Janković**, Major-Pilot of Newlands Airforce, test pilot and commanding officer of 100th GHQ Squadron. Through a chance pregnancy with Alisa, became an associated member of family Lionheart. His special abilities, including his sensibility to telepathy, made him ideally situated to command the elite Newlands Airforce pilots.

**Robert Prosinac**, Pilot of Newlands Airforce. A young flyer whose approach to service got noticed by his CIC, allowing him to become part of one of the most elite squadrons of Newlands Airforce. Demonstrates some paranormal skills of his own which bring him the membership in PsiMANATO.

**Rocco Stelle**, the most famous male Newlands' actor, Major of Newlands Army (Intelligence Branch), member of the Newlands Secret Service. Despite his utter public visibility, the most enigmatic personality in Newlands Archipelago. Unmarried father of seven children. Against all odds, Rocco becomes one of Dave's best friends, as well as Nikola's co-worker.

**Ron Sparks**, Major-Pilot of Newlands Airforce, "Inspector of fighters", commanding officer of 33rd Experimental Squadron "Hawk". Best friend of Sam Roberts – Lionheart. Enjoys major successes in readying revolutionary Newlandean warplanes for service.

**Sam Roberts – Lionheart**, Major – General of Newlands Airforce and other various ranks, various MANATO positions, member of CCofGHQ, member of PsiMANATO. The shadow ruler of MANATO, promoted to such a position to be able to help Dave and take over in case of need. Always ready to sacrifice his limb and life in the service to his country. Possesses minor telepathic ability.

**Sue Campbell**, Dave's American ex-girlfriend, wife of Leo Hunter. A freelance American photographer, Sue delights in embarrassing her own government through exposing American dirty secrets. Partially moved to Newlands and married Leo Hunter, Dave's friend.

**Thom Vigo – Lionheart**, Commanding officer of Swift – 1, and all MANATO shock troops, member of MANATO Intelligence, supporting member of PsiMANATO, holding various ranks in the Newlands Army. The strongest pillar of Lionheart family, man of fast reflexes, tested courage, and swift impulse for action, in his unique way Thom can resolve any problem. Apparently killed in the terrorist Benghazi attack in September 2012, he survives using the android construction and cloning technology.

**Toša Popović**, leader of the Newlands Atlantis Party. As head of the least popular political party of Newlands, through personal courage and character, he becomes one of the leading Newlands politicians and Dave's close friend.

**Yoshi Soga**, Sergeant-Pilot of Newlands Cybercommand, after reform of his branch of service becomes Cyber-captain. Developed and built his Cybercommand from bottom up into an outfit able to monitor the world and its leaders and protect MANATO from all kinds of cyber threats. Has tough time trying to defend Dave's secrets from the prying eyes of the aliens. Supporting member of PsiMANATO.

**Yulia Linares**, Pilot of Newlands Cybercommand, after reform of her unit becomes Cyber-commander. An avid hacker, she transforms herself into the backbone of Cybercommand, protecting MANATO and Electocracy. Dave's lover.

**Zoran Tasić** (**Taske**), Rear-Admiral of Newlands Navy, commanding officer of Nordporte Naval Command, member of CCofGHQ and privilege of twelve. Dave's closest friend in MANATO outside of Lionheart family. Prefers to serve and obey rather than to create military decisions.

# TABLE OF CONTENTS

# INTRODUCTION

*Summary of* ***NL:2011 Trilogy****, and books 1 and 2 of* ***NL:2012/2013 Trilogy***

Though founded on a small, originally lifeless Atlantic archipelago, recently tectonically uplifted from the oceanic depths into the exact place where the legendary Atlantis once stood, the young Newlands state unexpectedly succeeds in developing futuristic materials, industries, and technologies, securing an absolute immunity against nuclear attacks from abroad. Its almost perfect political neutrality shields it from being perceived as a threat to the wider world and its existing political order. However, with every passing day, its MANATO (the acronym for the armed forces of Newlands) is growing stronger.

The infatuation of Newlanders with their direct democracy, which allows citizens to vote on almost all pertinent political questions and thus directly guide their government, their abhorrence of the vaunted rule of law (as defined by the Western world) and the international treaties (in both these cases the only acceptable rule on Newlands is people's democratic choice which trumps any law or treaty), archipelago's abundance of minerals and energy, its immense food-production capability, the cash-free society, legalized drugs and prostitution, an absolute ban on smoking of all substances, massive but benign state surveillance, polyamory, and a nation-wide mustache fetish, though fascinating enough, can't endear this land and its society to the Western powers (except for their tourists flocking to its beaches).

Finally, the American political and military elite decides that it's high time for something to be done about this prickly Atlantic thorn spoiling their righteous sense of appropriate. Hence, among other attempts, the mission of David Anderson, an US Army Major in employment of the CIA, who arrives with sabotage and destruction in mind. Things won't go as planned, though. Major Anderson immediately falls in love with a local woman. Their relationship blossoms into a full-blown romance and is shattered when she mysteriously disappears. When he embarks on his mission to kill General Mansur Al-Hammadi, the lynchpin of Newlandean defense program, and wreck the Labyrinthium Shield, MANATO's preeminent defensive structure, he manages to penetrate to his target only to fail at the very last hurdle.

Convicted by a military tribunal to be terminated by a firing squad, Major Anderson is sent to the National Jail of Newlands, situated on archipelago's furthest, most isolated, easternmost island.

Then his luck changes. He's pardoned and incorporated into MANATO itself. According to the polyamory laws of Newlands, he marries into an all-military family, gaining two wives, four husbands, and two babies. He's instituted as the Commanding Officer of the Newlands Space Program. With one of his husbands, he performs the most heroic deed of the Newlandean history after the end of wars against the Arab coalition. For this feat, he receives the top military decoration MANATO can dish out. Finally, many famous politicians of the Western world, such as President Obama, Prime Minister Harper, and Bundeskanzlerin Merkel, befriend him.

Pretty classic hero stuff, no?

However, nothing is as it seems. In the first place, Dave learns that he wasn't much in control of events which took him to Newlands, those which unfolded since his arrival, nor is he about to start steering any future happenings. Secondly, evidence of his strange abilities starts accumulating, seriously unbalancing his satisfaction with the new life.

Soon, the episodes of premonition, telepathy, and intangibility manifest, allowing Dave to accomplish extraordinary feats, impossible for any other human being. At the same time, he learns the truth about the famed Atlantis of old, becomes a member of the most secretive circle in the archipelago, and meets face to face with DFQL, the apparent secret enemy of the current world order. Surging from one heroic deed to another, now as General David A-H Anderson – Lionheart, he's elevated to

the position of Commander – in – Chief of MANATO, world's preeminent military machine. And, in those tasks, he's no longer alone; he meets other Newlanders with strange abilities similar to his own: telepaths, empaths, and those able to directly connect their mind to the world wide web.

Dave's husband Sam suffers a midair explosion of his experimental fighter jet but survives, paying for it with his left arm, soon replaced by an android implant. Dave re-establishes himself as a nationwide hero when he secures a spectacular last-minute victory for MANATO against the Russian special forces in the grandiose Seapeak Island wargames. He avoids an assassination attempt using, for the first time ever on the Main Islands, a live beam weapon against his would-be murderer. And the number of Lionheart children climbs to the unexpected and unhoped for tally of eight sons when Alisa suffers a miscarriage and is hospitalized in MARC.

An incredibly special person walks into Dave's life; Andrew Lighthouse, whom Dave is convinced represents the future of MANATO. From his job as a highway patrolman, Andy is soon being transferred to one of the most elite Newlands Army units.

Yet, all isn't well. There's a new development concerning a DFQL agent who visited Newlands. His DNA appears very strange, unmatched by anyone or anything on Earth.

So, is he an alien, then?

However unlikely, this hypothesis steadily gains traction.

An unexpected and devastating eruption of Mount Root all but eradicates a mountain village causing more than a hundred casualties. Under Dave's leadership, MANATO fights against volcano's fury, in the process earning Sam an unprecedented second peacetime Gold Star. A new conspiracy between Dave and two important scientists is formed to contemplate the aliens literally living somewhere in the scorching magma under everyone's feet.

PsiMANATO is formed to counteract the alien threat. Almost immediately, the life of Dave's strongest telepath is snuffed out while opposing a telepathic alien intrusion. And an Airforce transport plane is blown out of the sky by the explosive hidden among its electronic equipment five years previously while it was being upgraded in England. Dave loses four important colleagues.

While trying to deliver humanitarian help to the war-devastated Eastern Libya, during their visit to the American Consulate in Benghazi,

a diplomatic envoy of Newlands and his entourage, including Dave's husband Thom as his team's security officer, is attacked by Islamist insurgents. Sensing the grave danger, Dave's aura travels across Africa. Once inside Thom's body, they together fight a glorious rearguard action to protect the survivors. Ultimately, Thom is killed, plunging Dave into a long-lasting turmoil, augmented by a strange malaise diagnosed as recurrent ataxia.

Leading MANATO's rescue mission to Benghazi, Sam earns his unprecedented third peacetime Gold Star, becoming the uncontested greatest hero of Newlands of all time.

A Newlands Airlines Boeing 737 is lost, with only two survivors, after a midair collision with an American spy drone. This episode brings Dave at loggerheads with the American President Obama but allows him to discover MANATO's proprietary pod of well trained super-intelligent dolphins with telepathic abilities.

Just when life seems to have returned to the customary grove, while performing her PsiMANATO duties, Alisa is struck by a mysterious infliction. Then she, a little bit later, miraculously recovers. Dave believes that there's only one agency which could have produced that stunning reversal. The DFQL aliens, dwelling deep below the eternally active Newlands volcanoes, below everyone's feet (and reach). The evidence is accumulating that they aren't such enemies of Newlands (and the rest of the world, maybe the whole humanity) as everyone suspected. On the contrary, they seem to have an ultimately beneficial effect.

Dave decides to, once for all time, resolve his doubts. In desperation, he sends his aura hurling downwards, into the boiling, terrifying ocean of magma.

# PROLOGUE

Alisa's eyes pop open; she whispers, her whisper coming out hurried, with a somewhat desperate note of rushing, as if she wishes to unburden herself before it all disappears again: - "I remember everything! I remember everything; it's such a bloody rush in my head, but I do remember, Marka mu.... I was working on the individual files, updating passwords, putz adding links to personal pages.... I finished all PsiMANATO's original members and next I wanted to turn to DolTeam's MANATO webpage.... As that new window opened, immediately, immediately.... This dreaded certainty: I'm not alone; I'm no longer alone!"

"Not alone?"

"A presence, as if waiting for me on that newly opened webpage. Not a singular presence, though."

(That's crazy.... interesting.... no one ever reported more than a singular presence.)

"How many?"

"I felt.... many. Many. Mrdat, more than two, less than a big crowd. Marka mu, let's say less than a dozen. There, with me, all coexisting for a moment in space and time. Tabarnaque, all looking at DolTeam's data."

"Who are they?"

"It, they.... are strange. I can't seem to visualize their shapes, bre. Or many shapes of one individual it? Who knows, majke ti? I don't know. And I don't recognize them. They don't communicate with me."

"Is it.... are they.... one huge dark monster, gigantic, overwhelming, looming towards you, maybe a frightening feeling like it's extending a black tentacle of despair towards you?"

Alisa shudders.

"No, Marka mu. Nyet; nada. Why do you mention that? I didn't receive that impression. It would be frightening if I did. And what happened wasn't beshoor frightening. My whole experience was anything but frightening, my Mo."

(Alisa seems to have received a different impression than I usually do; than Mietje does on her fantastic online explorations; also, than Akiko did when she detected her imagined Godjira in our depths.)

"To me, they resemble a forest of amorphous statues, statues of no specific sakra shape. It's dark around me, almost pitch black, but their shapes somehow penetrate the gloom. They are statues chiselled out of rock...."

(Living rock, I bet.

As Marc and Kieron predicted, anticipated.

Aliens made of living, intelligent rock.

Whether Alisa felt the presence of the gigantic black monster or not, it all boils down to one thing, one thing only: the DFQL aliens below our feet.)

"My impression is.... they brood, they watch, they study, they absorb information."

They absorb information? Statues of rock absorbing information? Living rock absorbing information?

I shudder.

A thought occurs to me: is this possibly an unforeseen coincidence, an unlucky parsimony, Alisa and those DFQL minds meeting by sheer chance on the same webpage, in the same instant of time? Then, something happens.... their defense, maybe automatically, gets activated? Alisa's computer is wiped clean, and so is her memory, albeit only temporarily?

(I mean, I know that her memory loss was only temporary; maybe the same will be proven right about her computer?)

"What happens then, my moon and stars?"

Alisa turns her head towards me.

She blinks a couple of times.

"I feel.... I'm positive, that's what I feel: an external source of massive surprise. Colossal amount of surprise. Dixi."

It appears that I might have guessed right; Alisa surprised the DFQL agents, they didn't expect her there and aware of their spying.

"They are surprised about.... what exactly?"

Alisa shakes her head, indicating no understanding or knowledge.

"Dave, that's where my memory terminates. In a feeling of surprised warm fuzziness, like a satisfied child holding a giant teddy bear."

Like holding a gigantic teddy bear?

Satisfied fuzziness?

In her interaction with DFQL, Alisa certainly received a different impression than any of us.

Yet why was she aware of those DFQL agents in the first place?

Because of her extraordinary parapsychological empathic ability?

All of us who telepathically touched DFQL are, in some way, abnormal. Hyper normal. Paranormal. Mietje, Akiko, and I had similar visions. Using their telepathy, Alan and Andrew shared those visions with us. Alisa experienced something utterly different. Is that significant at all? And Thom Brdar, before he was killed, what did he experience? What did he see and feel? I never had a chance to find out, but he seemed shocked and afraid.

Not Alisa.

Now, a crucial fact suddenly crystalizes in the form of an all-important question: in Alisa's place, in Akiko's, Mietje's, or my place, would a normal human being detect anything at all? I bet not; I bet not. Was the reaction of those aliens, which temporarily froze Alisa's memories into an igloo construct in her mind, caused by the sheer surprise that she detected their presence?

"My Mo, my memories are warm and friendly. I didn't feel any dread, nor fear. No giant black monsters for me. None, bre."

Suddenly, her eyes widen, as if she's a cat spotting a sudden movement: - "Calisse de merde, I just remembered something else! It simply popped into my mind. I just remembered how I woke up this morning!"

My eyebrows arch in surprise. The way Alisa said those words.... utter surprise, maybe even slight fear?

"Dave, can you.... somehow, go back into my mind, Marka mu? I want to share this with you, I don't know how to describe...."

I immediately nod, though I'm not certain that I can do what she's asking me to do: - "I will try."

And, despite my uncertainty, I do try; gingerly, carefully, very gently. I let my aura drift into my wife's mind. Though, I have my doubts. How can I locate and isolate a single specific memory which Alisa wants to share with me without any directions where to locate it?

Yet, as soon as I'm again immersed in Alisa's dark tropical jungle, a thought rushes me, as if it was waiting for me to show up. Yes, Alisa was right. It is warm, friendly, gentle. Yet, I'm right, too. It's unmistakeably uttered (produced, projected) in the voice of a giant; soft but strong, penetrating, rhythmical, pulsating: - "*Bonjour.... Good morning.... Guten morgen.... Hola.... Bom dia.... Buongiorno.... Hallo.... Dobro utro.... God dag.... Dobro jutro.... Goedemorgen.... Goeie more.... Kaliméra.... Jó reggelt.... Dzien dobry.... Hyvää huomenta....*"

There's no doubt, no doubt at all!

So like the attempt at communication when Thom Brdar (maybe also accidentally) got killed!

DFQL!

DFQL raised Alisa from her sleep, in the gentlest way possible, by wishing her good morning. DFQL was responsible for her "electroshock", whatever it really was (since it wasn't a shock caused by electricity). Now I know that DFQL was also responsible for waking her up from her coma.

Why?

Why?

Accidental detection.

Instinctive, immediate defense, which overwhelmed and paralyzed Alisa's mind.

Then a cure for that, whatever mysterious form it took.

A gentle wakeup call.

Voila.

Unmistakeably, DFQL again at work, both perilous and friendly.

Why?

Why?

Why?

They had Alisa, one of the most important PsiMANATO members, in their clutches. Yet not only did they resurrect her and let her go, they also permitted her to retain her memories. Those memories unmistakeably indicate DFQL's interest in our dolphins. Which, again without any doubt, sometime in the past, they themselves augmented into telepathic beings.

Why?

I can't see the logic in any of their moves.

I can't discern any logic at all.

I can't.

Maybe Fran will be able to tell me more.

Or Alan and Andy, especially when I replay for them all I learned from Alisa.

Another unexpected and unescapable conclusion is crystalizing in my brain: DFQL is not our enemy, not in the pure, human sense of it. It's as if they are trying to.... well, guide us and direct us, us humans (Newlanders, Atlanteans). When we stray too far away, they become harsh and punitive. When we're successful, whatever measure they judge our success by, they help us even more.

Like what Marc and Kieron surmised: maybe they really need us to help them go home.

I smile at my thought.

With my mind's eye, I just imagined an amorphous stone statue furiously pedalling a bike through the air above one of our volcanos.

Silly me.

Yet.

Why did they try to kill me?

Sigh.

I don't know.

I don't know enough.

How can I learn more?

Where can I find additional knowledge?

Blink.

Wait.

I'm not defenceless.

I'm powerful.

Yes.

I'm powerful. I have my weird powers.

Blink.

I know what to do.

I can try....

I know what to do.

It's a frightening thought, but I know what to do.

"Alisa, hold me."

"Why?"

"Hold me. Don't let go."

My words are chilling my wife's enthusiasm and damping her happiness for the resolution of her temporary amnesia: - "Dave, what's sakra wrong?"

"Love, I'm going to try something. Please, don't let go of my body!"

"Don't do whatever you want to do...."

Too late.

My patience is spent.

It's time for answers.

And I plan to do it in a way nobody yet attempted.

At least, I don't know of anyone who attempted this.

The old Atlanteans?

If they did try it, they failed.

Or were destroyed for trying.

Time to....

Time to find out.

Time to find out the truth.

I summon all knowledge and experiences of my intangibility I accumulated; without further ado, I hurl my disembodied mind into the abyss.

Straight under my feet.

Straight under the foundations of MARC.

Straight under the thin layer of fertile soil.

Straight under the layer of volcanic rocks upon which this island was erected.

It's getting warmer.

And even warmer.

It's no longer dark.

I can imagine fires rushing towards me.

It's scorching hot.

Hot!

The solid blackness is suddenly exchanged with a heaving ocean of magma.

I'll burn!

I'll die!

No.

This horrible Hades, this indescribable Hell, can't touch my mind.

I sore.

I sore, but always deeper, ever deeper.
I dive further.
I still rush on.
Deeper.
Deeper.
Now's the time.
Search for the answers.
Then....
Shock.
Fear.
A terrible presence.
All black.
Huge.
Impenetrable.
Gigantic.
Frightening.
Overpowering.
I can't see, but I feel.
I can't touch, but I sense.
A giant black tentacle is extending my way.
I try to slow down my plummeting into the depths of Earth's mantle.
I try to brake.
How do you brake in my intangibility mode?
To my utter horror, I'm not succeeding.
My plummeting accelerates.
The black tentacle rushes ever faster towards me.
No!
I can't!
I don't want to!
Closer, closer, closer.
I scream.
Contact!
Shock.
My aura vibrates.
My aura shakes.
As if shaken out of my soul, a form is taking shape around me.
Like a shadow, but slightly larger than me.

Mu aura, my soul, my imaginary body is completely contained within this shadow as a painting is within its frame. This shadow is framing me.

It hurts!

Pain!

Ache!

Horrible torture.

My brain splits.

My heart splits.

My lungs split.

I feel my imaginary testicles being pulled out of my body in a torrent of unsurpassed pain!

End.

No more.

Pain, such pain as I never felt before!

Such hurt!

Such.... splinted fear.

No more.

Suddenly, I'm rushing back; up, up, up!

The shadow still contains me, frames me.

Up!

Inside me and outside me, a part of me and not part of me, the shadow itself solidifies.

Up!

My being is splitting. In my mind, in my perception, the shadow materializes into a soft, undefined picture of a human being.

Up!

The shadow.... the shadow.... its shape solidifies, gains more detail.... I recognize it.... I recognize it!

Up!

I slam back into my body. My one, intact body, not affected by the splitting of my soul (and still containing my testicles).

I'm wrong.

My words were wrong.

Both my spirit, and the newly formed shadow, together slam back into my body.

I can't move, I can't scream, I'm utterly paralyzed.

I'm in Alisa's tight embrace.

The shadow is still around me, inside me, contained in my mind!

I open my eyes.
I scream.
"Thom!"
Nonexistence.

# PROLOGUE TWO - ON THE PRECIPICE

Hand in hand, Nikola and I stand alone on Ceti II volcano's summit, as close to the fire and heat as we dare.

This simple statement can't in any way convey the violence, trepidation, and tumult of this moment.

At two thousand two hundred and forty-five meters, Ceti II volcano is of a much lesser stature than the imposing mainland calderas and is even dwarfed by Ceti III volcanos I got accustomed to during my stint in the National Jail. But it's still a steep, tall, violent mountain, permanently spewing billowing clouds of colorful but intoxicating (deadly) gasses, daily venting lava into the ocean for three quarters of a century since Newlands rose above the ocean's waves.

Head to toe, our bodies are protected by the best KGZ military clothing MANATO possesses (including shielded darkened visors, gloves, and the above-ankle battle boots). Yet, I feel naked in front of this magnificent / terrifying display of nature's raw power.

In this tortured air, bathed by wafts of toxic gases, it's impossible to breathe and survive. On our backs, we both carry double tanks with special oxygen mixtures and independent failsafe double tubing snaking around both sides of our necks, leading to sturdy masks covering our mouths and noses. Everything doubly and triply shielded in KGZ. (Oxygen is quite explosive, you know? You don't bring unshielded explosives to the lip of a fiery volcano.)

The awesomeness of this moment should be overbearing, dampening our spirits. And maybe it is and maybe it does. A tiny bit, only somewhere

in the background of our thoughts. Our main concern, which brought both of us to this perilous place, is claiming all our attention: how to transfer Thom's essence, residing somewhere inside me, into Nikola.

Why do it at all, you might ask?

What's the difference between me and Nikola?

Dr Irena Panj: - "You're killing Thom!"

This whole sequence of events started with that unbelievable cry of pure horror uttered by my most trusted medical researcher.

"Killing Thom? How?"

Thom: - >You're killing me? You're not really killing me, are you, tabarnaque? How are you killing me? And why?<

>Shut up! I'm not killing you!<

"Nature above, I've no idea, we still have to start formulating a scientific base for this "soul" thing. But there's no doubt, bre. With each passing day, Thom's aura is getting weaker...."

Dr Panj must have seen the shock on my face, prompting her to rush on: - ".... judged by your respective EEGs, General. Yours is daily getting stronger. Thom's is slowly disappearing. Marka mu, it all resembles a putz rejection process, when the body turns against a transplanted organ."

>See, I putz told you so. I feel that I'm drifting away.< - opined Thom.

No!

I can't lose my Thom!

Not again!

"What are we to do?"

>What are we to do, Thom? Any ideas?<

"I mrdat...."

Silence.

We stare into each other's face.

How do you save someone's soul from disappearing?

More silence.

And more silence.

Irena is silent.

Thom is silent.

I'm silent.

Despair.

"What about...."

A ray of hope.

“What about what, Irena?”

>What did she tabarnaque mean?<

“Nikola, tabarnaque?”

“Nikola, what?”

“What I meant is, Nikola and Thom were always like brothers, no? Almost twins.”

Yes!

Yes!

“Yes! Brilliant!”

>Brilliant! Let me transfer into my bro!<

“I sakra meant, they would tolerate two auras in one body much better than you can.”

It was a great idea.

For a while, I enthused like a giddy elementary school student.

Nikola proved even more enthusiastic.

Faced with his final destruction, Thom was the most enthusiastic of all.

Yet, the method how to accomplish this transfer continued to elude us, which is where we started hitting road bumps.

Serious road bumps.

Firstly, we tried to accomplish our task in MARC’s labs. Our researchers connected my brain to Nikola’s, first via an intermediate computer, then directly, as if we were doing some strange form of reciprocal encephalography. I tried reasoning with Thom, coaxing him. After all, it was such a short jump into a willing host. Maybe a yard of wire separated Nikola and me. Couldn’t he just walk, stream, float.... run like the electrical current all the way across?

But Thom couldn’t envisage the path.

To be truthful, neither could I.

(My eyes could see those wires but to my mind they didn’t resemble highways for transferring human auras.)

Being in my mind, Thom could read my renewed despair. And started despairing even more.

There arrived an awful evening when Thom decided to attempt suicide. Not a real suicide, he didn’t wish to endanger my life. (Is it to be called a suicide at all when his body died half a year ago?) His decision was to let himself drift into nothingness – if that was even possible. And

he would have almost succeeded, if I didn't pull him back, infusing and strengthening his aura with my life energy (the whole procedure almost wiped me out; afterwards, I slept more than a day, but when I finally awoke, Thom was still with me – or within me).

Then Cybercommand offered Gaillon's help. For a couple of days our hope was rekindled. But no programmer, there including our supercomputer itself, could conceive an algorithm to facilitate transfer of a soul between two human beings.

Mietje tried direct contact but failed.

So did Andy and Alan, always attempting to construct a telepathic bridge between Nikola and me, one which Thom could hopefully use to "cross over". One of Andy's attempts was extremely entertaining. During that attempt our telepathic foursome somehow released pleasure hormones in all our brains, in an unfathomable way affecting Thom's aura. But an hour of laughter and merriment produced no better result than all preceding attempts; Thom was still trapped within the prison of my being.

There appeared to be no way out.

No way out.

My brilliantly white toga almost blinds my eyes. The irradiating sun isn't helping, either. I lift my left hand and place it above my eyebrows as a shield against all that bright light.

(I need sunglasses. Sunglasses? Strange thought. What are sunglasses?)

I feel pressure under my left sole where a pebble lodged into a crease. I bend my face downward and briefly inspect my left sandal. Worn out hide, no doubt at all. I'll have to ask Alisa to mend it. Or make me a new pair.

Just yesterday I brought home a large chunk of cured hide; she could use some of it.

Thom's recently washed toga swishes as his arms rise in a powerful move: - "How do you escape a prison which has no windows or doors?"

I scratch my forehead: - "Does anyone have any new ideas?"

Forcibly contrasting his dark skin, Alan's toga scintillates its pure whiteness stronger than any other: - "Through the walls, tabarnaque!"

Thom: - "Which hammer may I use, Marka mu? If I shatter a wall, wouldn't Dave suffer?"

"Better not shatter my body to get out of your prison. I'm not ready to die. Or go insane. We need to find another way. Andy, any ideas?"

While we walked from the Plaza of the Temples towards the town, Andy lowered his toga's fold from his shoulder, tying it around his waist. It now resembles a quilt, at the same time proudly displaying his strong chest. Atlantis needs more soldiers like him, able to wield our heaviest weapons: - "None, whatsoever."

Nikola sneaks his hand around his brother's waist: - "Do not despair, bro. We will sakra find a way. Nobody will be allowed to keep my bro in a prison against his will!"

In silence, we walk onwards.

The sun is relentlessly shining.

The wind brings the aroma (stench) of a volcano, vaguely smelling of rotten eggs.

So familiar.

A feeling of wellbeing from being at home spreads through my whole body, immediately dampened by Thom's trouble.

Our sandals clang on the stony surface.

Tall cypresses rustle in the wind, but no one dares to break the silence.

How do you break out of a prison without windows or doors?

How?

> How do you break out of a prison without windows or doors?< - I ask in my telepathic voice.

>Why not ask the man walking in your midst?< - arrives the unexpected answer.

Yes.

The man who's walking in our midst.

There is another toga-clad figure among us.

Another man.

Throughout our debate he kept silent.

Perfectly quiet.

It's strange. Nobody can see his face. Not clearly. He's male and, in a strange way, someone well known to us. A face from the past (or future) comes to my mind, yet I'm far from certain that the mysterious man is that person. Thom Brdar. The dead prisoner Thom Brdar.

>Go on, friend. You kept silent for a long time. Too long, maybe. Don't be afraid to say your piece of wisdom. Do you have any advice about our predicament?<

The stranger: - >Indeed, General. You guys are missing the point; you aren't thinking of the most important question, bre."

Am I a General now?

Maybe I am.

I think that I am.

Thom: - >We aren't?<

I marvel at my husband's beautiful telepathic baritone. I realize that it's the first time I witness him using telepathy. Still, it's marvelous. Certainly not someone who should remain imprisoned.

Nikola: - >Are you implying that getting my brother out of his mrdat prison isn't the most important question?<

Interesting. Nikola can now do telepathy as well. And he's an even more impressive telepathic bass.

The stranger: - >Nyet. It ain't.<

Alan, shaking his head: - >What is the important question you mentioned, then? What kind of twisted logic are you trying to sell us?<

Andy: - >You're right, Alan. Mister here doesn't appear to be on our side, Marka mu. Maybe he's a spy from our barbarian enemies.<

The stranger: - >On the contrary, my friends. On the contrary. I'm not a putz barbarian. I'm not your enemy. No person was ever a bigger friend of you and your country. No one.<

As he's uttering his thoughts, there's majesty in his telepathic voice; a power which none of us can match. Ancient, immensely wise, immensely patient. A power to be trusted. My hope soars.

>Teach us then, friend. What are we doing wrong?<

The stranger stops walking and turns; we all gather around him, like disciples around a teacher: - >My friends. Let's consider the central question of human philosophy.<

I'm definitely puzzled. Philosophy isn't my forte. How does philosophy help to break out of a prison without windows and doors?

(Another disquieting thought: "human philosophy"? Does there exist any other form of philosophy? Is there an inhuman one? Maybe the philosophy of gods?)

>Which is?<

Like a timid student, Alan partially raises his right arm, then professes his answer without waiting for a spoken permission: - >Which came first: the chicken or the egg?<

The stranger: - >Now we're sakra talking!<

Chickens? Eggs?

Andy: - >How can the classic dilemma of the order of events be applied to Thom's unending imprisonment?<

A long silence exposes our collective bewilderment.

Nikola: - >Calisse de merde, I got it! I got it!<

Thom: - >Ochen balshoy bro, great! What is it?<

Nikola: - >It's not how Thom can escape a prison with no doors or windows; it's how Thom got into such a prison in the first place! Certainly not through a door or a window, no? That's what we need to figure out, Marka mu. Presumably, tabarnaque, he can escape the same way he got in....<

Andy: - >Brilliant!<

Alan: - >True, orcae ita; yet do we have any answers to that riddle? Do we have any solid data about that? What did actually happen in Benghazi? Dave, you pulled Thom's aura with you when you abandoned his body, didn't you?<

Everyone concentrates on my face, on what I'm going to say next. But what am I going to say? Did I really do what Alan implies I did? Did I really accomplish the deed which, from the very first moment, the very first day, everyone presumed I MUST have somehow accomplished?

Not intentionally.

Not on purpose.

There's no doubt about that.

I don't remember those events the way everyone presumes they unfolded. When it all occurred, when I somehow managed to pull Thom's aura out of his dying body, I had no inkling it actually happened. For a long time, I genuinely believed Thom dead. I can't claim doing anything to save Thom's essence, unintentionally or intentionally. My being was forced out of his body, violently expulsed against my will, as if his approaching death was relentlessly expelling me, pushing me out. I was utterly powerless to control that process.

I spread my arms in defeat.

I lower my face until my eyes fixate on dirt below our feet.

My body starts shaking with uncontrollable tears.

Suddenly, a great warmth springs in our midst, irradiating outwards as if the sun itself descended into our circle. Stranger's body is transforming, getting brighter and brighter, the unusual radiation visibly streaming out of his figure. His eyes are now brilliant purple. They stare at me. Even

without lifting my head, I'm certain that two purple rays are now directed my way.

I blink.

My crying stops.

I feel a surge of optimism, hope.

I lift my head.

I turn towards the transformed stranger and let the purple beams emanating from his eyes bathe my face. Irradiated in Labyrinthium's purple glory, I remain silent, understanding of solution for our plight slowly dawning.

The stranger: - >General, you do have great powers. You're an exceptional human unit. But when you decided to join Thom in Benghazi, you signed your death warrant if Thom got slain. Great nature above and beyond, you do not possess power to abandon a dying body, not to mention spirit its aura away with you. There was another being present with you in Benghazi, one whose powers vastly outstrip yours....<

Instantaneously, I'm awake!

DFQL!

DFQL, of course!

The moving earthquake, the trajectory they took to rapidly travel from Newlands to Benghazi.

We always wondered what DFQL accomplished in Benghazi.

It appeared they did nothing, professed no help, accomplished nothing.

Now I know better.

Now, I DO know better!

In a hectic motion, I sit up, then jump from our Rad bed (dislodging some books from the adjacent night table and send a Surface, probably mine, clattering to the floor), startling Fanta and Alisa who're tonight sharing it with me. I now know what Nikola, Thom, and I must do (and Thom, being inside me, knows it too)!

Nikola and I are at the lip of the Ceti II volcano.

The awesomeness of this moment should be overbearing, dampening our spirits. But it can't lessen our resolve to carry out what we're here to achieve (and the excitement we all deep down feel). Now I have no doubts that our task is achievable (though I don't yet fully understand the

process), and all three of us (Nikola, Thom, and I) are of one heart and mind (and resolve) to remain here until our goal is achieved.

I have now at the first hand experienced what those scientists, explorers, soldiers, and other chosen Newlandeans encountered before me. Deep in my dream, I received the necessary explanation and an inspiration how to act.

Or were those my marching orders?

Look at it whichever way you wish.

Maybe I'm just a dumb pawn carrying out someone's orders, but if those actions can save Thom's aura from perishing....

Everything is now clear.

DFQL aliens WERE in Benghazi with Thom and me and we did record their powerful underground travel. Fran didn't imagine those earthquake epicenters in straight line connecting Newlands and Libya. They did leave traces of their incredibly swift passage (travelling through magma, they were faster than our fastest fighters travelling through the atmosphere).

The aliens were there, but not to help MANATO's relief force rescue our diplomatic team. It's DFQL, after all. For us, their motives are still opaque. They may not be our enemies, after all, but they certainly aren't our friends. (Newlands prides itself on its neutrality; maybe DFQL aliens feel as much pride in remaining neutral in human conflicts, no?) They went there to prevent ME from perishing, as I unknowingly placed myself into a precarious and deadly position. They saved me, and they did the best they could for Thom.

They saved me.

Why?

Why am I suddenly important to them?

After all those attempts on my life?

The logic of their deeds still fully escapes me.

Yet.

I'm certain of one thing.

When I take my plunge, any moment now, my aura won't be in danger. Not even when it encounters the great black monster under our feet.

I'm starting to trust Akiko's alien Godjira.

>Ready?<

Thom: - >Ready.<

Nikola acknowledges with his nod.

>Nikola, please support my body if it loses its tonus. Don't let it fall into the caldera.<

"Trust me, hub."

I do. But I'm nervous about this whole undertaking.

>Thom! I've no idea how DFQL is going to accomplish this. But if you spot the opportunity, transfer immediately.<

>Do not worry. I wish to go on living.<

Existing inside another person isn't my idea of living but I can't even think that aloud or I'll spook Thom.

"Good. That's it. No more procrastinating." – I say aloud, psyching myself for my attempt. It mustn't fail! It mustn't fail!

>Calm down hub. It ochen balshoy won't fail.<

A deep sigh.

Yep, Thom's right. DFQL would not have sent me that dream if it wasn't the key to unlock Thom's prison.

I close my eyes.

How did I do it when Alisa was sick?

I simply directed my mind downwards.

But I was then angry and terribly afraid for my wife's future. Combination of those emotions made me reckless. Now there's no anger, just fear for the future of my husband.

First think how you're going to do it.

Then do it.

There's to be no jumping.

Gravitation can't influence an aura, a soul.

Therefore, no need to jump anywhere.

I need to actively seek the direction I wish to send my mind in.

Downwards.

Downwards, into the heart of this volcano.

Where the silicone aliens live.

I stare at the hot maelstrom of lava below my feet.

That's where I want to go.

(Ouch. I don't really WANT to go there.)

That's where I must go.

I must.

Then go, finally!

Deep breath.

I go.

# THE ATLANTIS TABLET

Davit Jighauri carefully pushed away his hammer, chisel, and three differently shaped toothpicks; then, after a moment of deliberation, he picked one of his two paintbrushes (the thicker one). He crawled a bit further into the hole which was his workplace. He then smoothed his night-black moustache, removing some of the accumulated grayish volcanic dust, removed his glasses, produced a small microfiber towel to clean their lenses, then placed them back to their customary perch on top of his nose.

Slow, methodical, deliberate moves.

Out of the blue, his often and well-rehearsed exam answer rang in his head - "For an archeologist, excavating archeological material is a slow, careful process. Working from the exposed surfaces to the unexposed areas, archeologist slowly flakes away the sediment and rock matrix which surrounds the object. This may sound difficult, but there's a plane of weakness between the object and the sediment surrounding it...."

Oh yes, said Davit to himself. Or, as they often say here, orcae ita. It's easy to quote my textbook. But its author never imagined the archeologist having to perform in a tight hole, itself part of a narrow tunnel, inside one of the galleries of a vast cave, buried in the interior of a live and quite active volcano, on an island in a tropical archipelago in the middle of the Atlantic Ocean (not really; more like adjacent to the coast of Northwestern Africa).

The twenty-two-year-old student of archeology hailed from Tbilisi, the capital of Georgia, where he studied archeology on the Ivane Javakhishvili Tbilisi State University. The famous Georgian Professor

Dimitri Akhvlediani, currently a senior researcher in employment of the National Museum of Georgia, provided his recommendation for this student exchange project arranged through the Department of Archeology of the University of Old City, after Davit helped with filing of data accumulated during Professor's recent digs.

Davit remembered Professor Akhvlediani talking about difficult environments for researchers: the heat, the cold, the dryness of deserts. Yet, Davit would bet his life that even he couldn't imagine the warmth of this hellhole, its sharp abrasive volcanic dust, its lack of oxygen, and the ever-present cave darkness. Davit was wet from head to his toes, the state of his clothes increasingly deteriorating with absorbed dirt, his breathing labored and uncomfortable, a persisting headache smoldering in the background.

But he wasn't about to complain.

He never complained.

Certainly not now.

Because the promise of what he was doing far outweighed his discomfort. For he was digging out the archeological remains of the mythical, fabulous, notorious (and some say supernatural) Atlantis itself!

Davit was finishing his semestral exams when he got wind of this student exchange project. The offer for three Georgian students to spend a year on Newlands, working on various Newlandean archeological sites under mentorship of researchers from the University of Old City's Department of Archeology, their stay sponsored and paid in full by the Government of Newlands, and a guaranteed Newlands tier two monthly pay during their stay (much more than an average Georgian earns!), their studies in Tbilisi to seamlessly resume upon their return.

How fortunate!

Davit had a distant cousin living on Newlands, in the town of Norton north of Old City on the northern shore, whose name was Giorgi Okriashvili. Once or twice per year (on such occasions as New Year, Christmas, Easter, or maybe their birthdays) they would communicate over social media, mostly Facebook, as it's so difficult for foreigners to register on Newlandean social media apps. It was always Davit's plan to, one day, studies finished and a job in hand, travel to Newlands to spend a week or two with Giorgi on those fabulous gigantic (and mostly empty) Norton beaches, or the scenic Lake Old City where Giorgi has a small weekend home floating on a raft (and maybe manage to watch a football

game or two; everyone knows that FC Old City is one of the most famous teams in the world). Yet, here was a chance to get to visit his cousin much earlier than anticipated (and for much longer than two weeks).

Hundred and nine students applied for the exchange program. To his dismay, Davit found that his academic record was evaluated third from the bottom (why didn't he study harder, idiot!). Yet, armed with Professor Akhvlediani's endorsement and his cousin's guarantee of lodgement (countersigned by the local Norton authorities vouching for Giorgi Okriashvili's ability to host and provide for his relative), Davit was named the second choice for the adventure (they named three students as main choices and two reserves as replacements in case of cancellations).

Davit carefully brushed a rock ledge with his paintbrush, dislodging volcanic sand and pebbles. His excitement was rising. Why, might you ask? Well, because he could see, or imagine that he could see, a straight edge where no straight lines should exist! (The University of Old City gave them a short course on behavior and crystallization of magma; over time, the occurrence of perfectly shaped hexagonal structures was possible, often enough discovered on Newlands; but no one mentioned continuous straight edges.)

The usual archeological excavation would involve the recovery of several types of data from a site, including artifacts (defined as portable objects made or modified by humans), features (non-portable modifications to the site itself such as post molds, burials, hearts), ecofacts (evidence of human activity through organic remains such as animal bones and charcoal.... and, well, excrement), and archeological context (relationships between all previously mentioned types of data). Recording all of this can make a dig immensely logistically complicated. None of that applied on this dig. They knew where they were and knew what occurred here, just a year ago or so. A volcanic eruption inside a cave. All participants of this dig were told that one of the survivors of that tragic event recounted seeing a cave wall collapse, briefly revealing in the chamber hiding behind the wall a multitude of traditional archeological objects (statues, weapons, furniture) before lava covered everything. Therefore, the primary objective of this dig was recovery of those artifacts.

So far, nobody managed to recover any, anything at all, to the point that some senior researchers started doubting survivor's report.

Could he be the first to succeed?

Would he be the first to succeed?

That would be such good fortune that Davit almost disbelieved his right to it.

His arrival to Newlands was a dream come true. He flew directly from Tbilisi to the Newlander capital city of New Belgrade on an Airbus 330 belonging to LUX, the renowned New Belgrade airline. The flight itself went much better than expected, creating life-lasting memories, yet it was but the first of wonders in store for him. Right from the cold, snowy Georgian winter, he jumped into a warm Newlandean one, with temperatures on average close to thirty degrees Celsius. His cousin waited on the airport, and they took a fast bullet train from New Belgrade's Capitol International to the Central train station in Old City (that train runs mostly underground while crossing the capital with its four million inhabitants but the scenery, once they returned to the surface, and all the way to Old City, was stunning). There, on the railway park-and-ride lot, waited his cousin's 2010 Titan - Ford Ka. A small car but minty and perky. Hey, the two of them didn't need anything larger and he brought only one duffel bag (for his return, he did plan to buy a glamorous suitcase in Old City and fill it with gifts for everyone at home). All that remained to be accomplished was a short highway dash northward to the ocean shore.

The tiny town of Norton proved charming beyond his expectations, its beaches spectacular. Giorgi's small one-bedroom home near to Norton's "True Nord" golf course was breezy and comfortable. It may be a tiny house, but it's so modern and lavishly equipped that Davit took a whole day to learn all quirks and quarks of its functioning (its electrical blinds, solar collectors, gray water tank system, a fairly complicated Wi-Fi, cable TV, and intranet access system, the WWW internet access needed to stay in touch with home, and the pertinent applications to his new abode of the sparking new CREDIT he received when admitted to Newlands). At first, exhausted with his new life's excitements, Davit got to sleep on an improvised (and rather uncomfortable) bed in the TV room, but soon traded it for an unimaginably relaxing porch hammock nightly serenaded by the crash of oceanic waves against the shore.

Once he got to Old City, the metropole built where Atlantis once stood (or so they are saying), he was immediately impressed with the sprawling but functional facilities of the University of Old City and the utilitarian Newlander public transport (inside Old City proper, between Norton and Old City, and Old City and the archeological sites all over the Main Islands) which allowed him the full freedom of movement when

Giorgi was at work in Old City's glamorous "Pyramid" shopping center (when travelling alone, Davit refused to drive Giorgi's Ka, fearing a lack of practical knowledge of land, its laws, and its road system). Atlantida, the Museum of Atlantis, shook him to his bones with its novel approach to the legend of the sunken land. If only he could one day work in such an establishment!

Their tutors took them all over the Main Islands, explaining Newlandean archeological finds, visiting all current digs, and teaching how they all fit into the Atlantis saga. They also spent time covering much more recent history, mostly discussing the historical sights pertaining to the Libyan Wars' years.

Four weeks ago, completing his training courses in UNOC and Atlantida and receiving a temporary Newlandean work permit, per his personally stated wish, Davit joined the Optimus Cave dig. Almost immediately he emerged as the most enthusiastic exchange researcher. (In his mind, Davit makes a brief summation: there are twenty-five international students present here, from China, Japan, India, Nigeria, Brazil, Mexico, Chile, Canada.... Is that all? There should be ten countries on that list. One two.... eight. Georgia makes it nine, obviously, though the other two fellow Georgians aren't assigned to this dig as they opted for the Libyan Wars' excavations. Ah, Germany. I forgot Germany. Two girls out of Cologne. Eva and.... I can't remember. That makes it ten.)

By the end of the second week on this dig, he established himself as the most productive researcher of all personnel, Newlandean and international, daily working double shifts and disregarding any time off.

Yet, he achieved no breakthrough....

Wait.

Wait!

Is that a crack in the crystalized lava right there?

Yes!

Yes, it is.

What if he's to give it a tap or two?

Will the crack spread?

Will it allow him a glimpse of whatever is hiding behind?

Davit reached into his pocket for his LED battery light.

He tested its switch.

Click – on.

It works.

Click – off.

Working feverishly, albeit with exaggerated care, his heart beating in an ever-increasing rhythm driven by anticipation (this is it, now or never!), Davit placed his chisel on the (almost imagined) crack he spotted.

Now the hammer.

One tap.

Another tap.

A third....

Crack!

The crack was loud enough that for a moment Davit remained convinced that one of the supervisors must appear running down the tunnel to check what happened. However, after a prolonged wait nothing happened.

Should he call for a supervisor?

Should he call for help?

No.

No; there's nothing here he's not trained to handle on his own.

His heart stopped racing and Davit put his tools away.

What do we have here?

In renewed anticipation of a breakthrough, he shone his LED light into the crack.

Disappointment.

Nothing to be seen, just more lava stone.

Tentatively, he grabbed the separated slab of volcanic rock jammed vertically into the mass of crystalized lava. He tried pushing to the left, then to the right.

Nothing.

Maybe he needs a better holding point and seriously more support for his left arm.

He slightly adjusted his body's position, certain that this new angle allows his muscles to deliver considerably more force.

Then he spent some time searching up and down the exposed ledge, orienting himself as much by touch as by sight.

There.

Enough space for all his fingers to exert pressure.

For a moment, his thoughts floated away from this cave and his research.

There was a reason why he became so workaholic once lodged in the incredibly picturesque Sunshine Valley in a guesthouse belonging to the University of Newlands. By working such long hours, Davit avoided returning to Norton.

The truth was, he wasn't certain about the state of affairs between himself and his cousin.

Almost seven years ago, when the puberty struck full force, Davit became aware of his homosexuality. Being gay in Georgia is rather unfortunate. Yes, last year a law got passed forbidding discrimination against the LGBT community, making offending against sexual orientation an aggravating factor in any legal process. Still, the Orthodox-Church-dominated Georgian society wouldn't easily accept gays, considering them deviant, amoral, against the traditional family, a source of pedophilia, and generally seeing the open homosexuality in a very negative light.

Davit balked at coming out as a gay person.

Instead, he opted to act in public as a butch heterosexual, hopefully for everyone to notice (especially his parents), publicly dating a series of girls (a conveyer belt of girls!), mostly schoolmates, then getting himself settled with a steady girlfriend, occasionally having sex while carefully avoiding making her pregnant (truth be told, that kind of sex left him cold, and he almost never climaxed). He couldn't understand why he bothered at all with avoiding her pregnancy. Starting a family and having a couple of children would be the best protection he could wish for, the perfect cover. Then, once secure, his debt to his nation, his community, and his parents paid in full, he could carefully try to establish contacts with the other likely-minded people.

However, once on Newlands, as Giorgi took him to the beaches and into their shared home life, Davit soon understood the gigantic erotic impact his ten-year older cousin was having on him. Firstly, they looked like twins who didn't age at the same rate, so that one somehow became older. Almost like one person and his slightly distorted mirror image. Giorgi had a larger frame, a fiercer moustache, and hairier body, but otherwise anyone from the outside would easily confuse the two (which happened on a couple of occasions). Even their voices sounded almost identical and couldn't be distinguished in traditional phone calls (unless it was a video call, which Davit here experienced for the first time).

Davit indeed started sleeping in the TV room, then used the porch hammock. But then, four or five weeks into his visit, an evening arrived

when a tropical storm raged outside, strong wind accompanied by bursts of torrential rain. Giorgi offered Davit a place in his king-size bed. Despite feeling trepidation at sharing another man's bed, which never happened before, Davit agreed, mostly hoping for some comfortable rest.

That night, accompanied with the storm's bedlam outside, he never slept a second.

All those weeks Giorgi didn't mention his own sexuality, though Davit noticed no hints of female presence, a girlfriend. Giorgi went to bed nude; Davit kept his undies (just seeing Giorgi naked made Davit's throat constrict and his manhood stir). A few minutes after they turned the lights off, Giorgi's hand touched Davit's belly and slowly slipped underneath his underwear. His heart beating madly, as if ready to jump out of his chest, Davit let it happen.

Giorgi was his first male lover and Davit's appetite, released from the dungeon (or the proverbial closet), proved insatiable. After that night there was no abandoning Giorgi's big bed (and no more wearing of underwear; the offending pair got thoroughly ripped during one of their bouts of passion).

Suddenly, with Giorgi at his side, Davit's life appeared fulfilled.

Yet, he faced a huge dilemma.

What was the worth of his unexpected and unlooked for love affair?

In slightly more than six months he must return to Georgia and resume his life in the closet. Newlands may be amazing, a life with Giorgi would be heaven, but he was sincerely patriotic; he wanted to work for the betterment of his country, nation, and community. He will marry a girl, begat a couple of children (or more), hopefully boys who could one day serve as Georgian soldiers. He would make his parents happy and proud.

Did he love Giorgi?

Oh, yes, with all his heart and soul. He was Giorgi's without reserve.

Yet, what's the future of his love?

What's the long-term product of man-to-man love?

With no progeny to leave behind, its inevitable, ultimate loss, the ultimate sad ending?

When he leaves Newlands and breaks with Giorgi, it will be forever. He could never return to face again the heartbreak of their emotions.

Night and day, while avoiding returning to Giorgi's home, he mused about his options, severely missing Giorgi's passionate touches and kisses

(and much more), yet fearing sinking into a deeper level of hell, one there would be no return from.

What if he immigrated to Newlands?

What if?

If he could accomplish that, he could forget Georgia, his parents, and his girlfriend, and live with Giorgi his whole life and never be afraid to show his love; for in this land gays are truly free. Even their best football player, that renowned and popular Pavel Varina he the other day watched play for the national team, is openly, unashamedly gay. However, Davit knew that immigration to Newlands always takes long years and consists of many hoops to be jumped through; and still, many hopefuls were at the end refused their chance. Giorgi wouldn't wait for him. He couldn't. It's a simple biological truth. Another person would step into Giorgi's life and Davit would forfeit his chance for a Newlandean future.

But what if.... if only if.... if he could make a really big discovery, really really big, something spectacular? And become famous on Newlands before having to return to Georgia?

Then, and only then, apply for immigration?

Would they refuse him then?

Could they refuse him at all?

He didn't think so.

That's the solution.

That's his way out.

I must discover something big.

I must discover something important.

Be there!

Be there for me!

With the strength of desperation Davit's fingers grabbed the volcanic rock and pressed. His biceps curled like never.

Cra....a....ack!

A cloud of disturbed volcanic dust momentarily blocked his view and Davit let go of the rectangular rock. It fell sideways, accompanied with lots of tearing noises. The very next moment something else dislodged from the wall, up to that moment hidden behind the petrified layer of lava Davit removed. At first, the movement was barely discernable, but it quickened fast. Another slab of rectangular rock, greenish grey, with curious shapes impressed into its front, rushed towards the bewildered

archeology student. Davit had but a second to glimpse it, understand what's about to happen, and react.

Oh no, it's falling right toward his extended arm!

It will hit his head!

It appears large and heavy!

Davit tried to scramble backwards but no fast retreat from his hole was possible. Falling rock's sharp edge crashed into his extended left arm just below his elbow, eliciting a wild scream as he felt his bone part. Then the slab hit his forehead.

Then, shock.

Fear.

Naked fear.

A presence.

A dark presence.

Huge.

Black.

Amorphous.

Reaching towards him with an appendage from hell.

Davit tried to shriek, he put all his strength into the movement of his diaphragm and ribs, opened his mouth and....

The sun is shining.

It's murderously shining.

It's hot, very hot.

He feels unprotected.

Behind him is their Sacred Cave's entrance. Nowadays, that cave is their home and their temple. He's looking down the slope. Recent multiple eruptions have eroded and stripped away its previously abundant jungle, leaving occasional buildings, strewn here and there, in shattered ruins. The previously lush and fertile slope nowadays appears yellow, brown, and gray, an abode of poisonous dust.

"Halea, are we finished taking all our temple treasures inside the cave?"

"Yes, my husband. Today I packed in straw our last statue of Ormus."

Satisfied, he sighs with relief.

At least, their gods are now safe.

Whatever happens to us, they are safe.

"My husband, do you think that the cursed Egyptians will be back?"

It's been more than a year since the last incursion of the awful conquerors from the far east, from the Nile delta. How the tables turned! Ten years ago, then still a stripling, Kiron rode the great Atlantean ocean ships into the narrow sea, trolling for slaves. The Nile delta was always their preferred hunting ground. Wherever they went, they would return to that location for more catch. Nowadays the roles are reversed.

As he fights for control, Kiron's fists involuntarily shake. On they last visit, those brown-skinned bastards took Aea, his daughter. She was only six.

"No, Halea. Do not fear the Egyptians. There's not much here left to plunder. They will go where there are fatter pickings."

Suddenly, Halea gives a sharp but subdued shriek. The ground shakes below their feet, then stabilizes.

"Just another earthquake."

"No, Kiron. Look.

(Halea is pointing southwards, over the mountain's shoulder, to a pillar of thick black smoke suddenly rising into the previously impeccably blue sky.)

It's another eruption."

Kiron shrugs his shoulders.

Another eruption.

There have been so many.

They are no longer of interest.

His throat is raw from the endless prayers to Ormus, Kala, Sympack....

None of the gods are helping us.

Why?

What did we do to anger them so much?

We always carried out their orders; always! To the letter!

Ahhhhhhh.

Think happy thoughts.

Leave god stuff to gods.

Think happy thoughts, yes.

When the Egyptians took Aea, Kiron pursued them to their embarkation beach. He was too late. He failed to save his daughter. As he watched the Egyptian ship gaining speed, heading out into the open ocean, he caught up with two of them, standing by a smaller skiff, tarrying on the shore, collecting loot from the ruins of Atlantis. At that time he still owned an electrowhip in working order. Electrowhip is a tool of control,

not really a weapon. Atlanteans primarily use them to control their slaves. To be more precise, they used to use them that way. That day, Kiron didn't want to control. He wanted to kill. He struck and struck. Again, and again, and again. He cut off hands, arms, legs, heads. He opened their stomachs for the screeching ocean birds to feed, then watched as their bodies slowly got consumed.

Only two.

They all deserve to die.

Good memories.

Halea's voice shatters his vision: - "Calisto."

She points.

Calisto.

In Greek, the language of the primitive tribe of his origin, "the most beautiful".

Well, what a misnomer.

That man may be many things (the strongest, the most intelligent, a born leader, a steadying rock in adversity), but he's certainly not the most beautiful.

A strange barbarian, praying to his strange gods.

Calisto is climbing towards cave's entrance, slowly but deliberately threading his way between sharp volcanic boulders, still managing to exude urgency.

Yesterday Calisto still walked naked, a hairy giant with the body of a gorilla and a wild black beard falling onto his chest. Today he's wearing a strange armor concocted from carved wood chips, reminding Kiron of overlapping fish scales. In his left hand he's holding his powerful war knife. Kiron saw it used in battle. Besides being sharp as a diamond's edge (and as strong), it can also deliver a stunning electrical shock.

At least, it could, when Temple's electro-chargers still worked.

Sigh.

Atlantis is falling apart.

Everything is falling apart.

Back to sad reality of the heart-wrenching present. Like Halea, Calisto must be leery that the Egyptians are returning.

"Here, Calisto!" – calls Kiron in a voice he can himself barely recognize. He spent the whole night praying to the powerful gods of Atlantis over the last of his family's votive candles, inhaling their intoxicating, addictive

smoke, alternately sending his mind to the underworld and the star-filled sky hoping to touch them.

No wonder he can't speak.

He'd give his life to help his surviving compatriots.

But the gods remain aloof, unreachable, deaf, and silent.

A frightening thought.

The gods have turned their backs on their children.

And I have no more votive candles, nor can any be made again. How am I going to pray to our gods? How am I going to reach them?

"Hey, Calisto!"

"Hey, Kiron! Hey, Halea!"

"How's your day going?"

"Disquieting. Yesterday Milon spotted a sail on the northern horizon."

"Egyptian."

Calisto shrugs: - "Milon says that it was too far."

"But you're dressed for battle."

"Yes."

Against his will Calisto was brought to the mighty city-state of Atlantis as a teenager taken from one of the wild barbarian islands north of Egypt. A slave. Exposed to the advanced nutrition of the mighty ocean empire, he grew, both in size and stature. Soon, he started demonstrating his worth. Two years after arriving, he won a running competition for slaves. When he was twenty, his master entered him into the wargames, a contest for slaves using real weapons, the favorite Atlantean pastime. Wargames were thoroughly scripted and steeped in formality and tradition. Though not very often, occasionally some slaves would nonetheless perish, but never those really gifted. Calisto was really gifted. Year after year, he won the coveted title of the King of Slaves, skipping only the year when his master took him on a six-month-long raid of the narrow sea. After his fifth win his master adopted him as his legal heir and gave him his freedom. Calisto joined the Atlantean military and rose through its ranks. By the time the calamity struck, he was away on some mission on the African mainland, one of the three generals ruling the Atlantean military, with only the priest-king above them in the hierarchy of power. When he returned to his wrecked homeland, he was the most senior leader alive, the uncrowned ruler of Atlantis. The slave whom fate slated to become almost a king.

"I saw climbing up that you repaired the water collectors."

"Yes, Calisto. I had a dozen people helping me. We finished yesterday. Today I checked; the reservoirs are already filling with drinkable water."

Kiron was a minor priest in the Temple of Ormus. His wife Halea was a junior nun. After the catastrophe, they found themselves the most senior clergy left alive. For four twelve-moons they ceaselessly labored to assemble all surviving Temple property from the numerous shattered buildings across the land. With due reverence and continuous prayer, it was all deposited in Sympack's Sacred Cave high on the shoulders of the restless volcanoes.

Somehow, the Atlanteans made their gods angry and are now suffering their terrible punishment for those sins. But we'll rise again. No doubt about that; with gods' mercy, we'll rise again.

Then, the statues of gods will be needed again.

"Kiron, I spoke with Hul and Damas. They are still measuring the speed with which the ocean is sinking us."

Kiron's heart sinks. Calisto's tone of voice was dire: - "And?"

"Two cubots during the last moon."

Two cubots! That's not good! Kiron is aware that Atlantis is unstoppably sinking. But two cubots?

"If the sinking continues at that rate, in the next twelve-moon our Frasna valley will sink under the waves."

No!

Not the Frasna valley!

The only area of flat land where they can still grow fruits and crops! If it floods, their only remaining source of food will be the merciless, fickle ocean.

"Calisto, when you again see those priests, ask them.... no, order them to speed up the assembly of those additional fishing boats we talked about.... please."

Calisto nods, understanding Kiron's line of thinking. Uncrowned, without any formal recognition, Calisto, Halea, and Kiron, together with half a dozen other surviving noblemen, form the unofficial government of the waning ocean empire. They persuade, coax, order, plead, bribe, and cajole.... whatever is appropriate or needed.... to ascertain completion of necessary tasks.

Delaying what?

The inevitable?

The gods are still sinking us....

We're doomed; why continue fighting?

Suddenly, Calisto appears to lose patience and, with unmistakeable unconscious authority, fires a staccato of quick words: - "I climbed up here to check how your project is faring."

Right.

That's it.

No more dillydallying.

Time for the important report.

Kiron points towards his wife: - "Halea finished securing the last statue of Ormus. Yesterday, Hut and Zelon temporarily closed the hallowed "Room of all knowledge". It will be there, perfectly protected and preserved, to serve many future generations of Atlanteans once we're out of this trouble and our empire rises again. Safe, untouched, undisturbed. I'm putting the last touches to our Universal Temple of Atlantean gods, in the Crystal Hall. We will be...."

The ground suddenly violently shakes; this isn't another minor earthquake. The mountain seems to jump many cubots straight up, right into the sky, then crash down with a bone jarring thump, only to start the whole process once again. They try their best, but none manages to remain standing. Soon, on the ground, crawling in dust, they're desperately grabbing for support.

The explosion, right at the summit of the mountain, when it finally arrives, is a sound immeasurably stronger than anything Kiron ever heard (felt, not heard, as his whole being seems to be vibrating). The mere sound seams to be ripping the skin from his body and scorching his lungs. Then the huge boulders start landing around them, to continue rolling downhill, unpredictable, deadly.

Nowhere to run, nowhere to hide!

A metallic object suddenly flashes above Kiron's head, shining in sun's brilliant light. It clangs as it strikes the rocky surface. Calisto's war knife. Startled, afraid for his friend, Kiron scrambles left and right. Then he stops, petrified. Calisto is no more. What's left of his mighty body is a bloody stain of minced meat and bone fragments sizzling under a gigantic glowing rock.

Halea starts shrieking, a never-ending, monotonous, continuous wail

The ominous thunder of the approaching doom swallows up her screams.

From the top of the mountain a gray wave of pure malice is rolling downhill, its innards sparkling with fire and purple lightning.

Davit hears himself shriek, the giant amorphous black monster still suffocating him from all sides, instantaneously replacing the bright sunlight. Then the stone monument crashes right onto his forehead, extinguishing all his senses.

"Peter, spasitelju, I know what I'm saying, bre! It has "Atlantis" chiselled in the ancient Atlantean script all over its face. The word is identical to what's prcat secreted on the tablet in our basement! We're currently working on translating the long text on its rear surface."

Peter Schweinfurter, Curator of the Atlantida Museum, feels like repeating his previous sentence ("are you certain, tabarnaque"). For a whole year, without any luck whatsoever, multiple teams comprising the best Newlandean researchers searched for the chamber Dave briefly glimpsed during the Optimus Cave eruption. His colleague belongs to a small, carefully chosen group of personnel who know all Atlantida's secrets, therefore empowered to reach such conclusions. Yet, if Atlantida's Senior Researcher Samson Krombacher is right, and this foreign exchange student really discovered an ancient Atlantis artefact, it happened at a wrong location, one not previously searched (or even considered to be searched; so far nobody supplied a rational explanation why anyone was digging there at all). Either that location represents the entrance to another way in, a new gate opening the path into the room Dave glimpsed, or the famous CIC of MANATO (and Peter's great friend) simply miscalculated where he stood when lava collapsed that treasure room's wall.

Thinking more of it, walking through the flowing magma in those dark cave tunnels, protected by his personal MANATO shield (itself a miracle of Newlands science of exceptional magnitude), fighting off poisoning by various toxic gasses, and saving lives left and right (a feat the full reality of which Peter still couldn't completely grasp, but couldn't stop marvelling at, either), how could Dave be expected to precisely remember his exact whereabouts?

Especially since it was his first time in the Optimus Cave.

"Do you have a photo?"

"Orcae ita, indeed I do."

Samson Krombacher toys with his Blackberry.

"On its way, boss."

Ping!

Peter Schweinfurter reaches for his own Blackberry, on purpose sitting at the other side of his worktable (to lessen distraction and temptation). Ah, yes. There it is. The slate-colored, heavy looking, large slab of stone, as reported, mounted on a slightly wider pedestal. An inscription, which originally may have been colored white or light grey, carved into its surface.

"Atlantis".

Beautiful.

Powerful.

For a moment he feels like crying, a heavy weight on his chest. What other treasures may be hidden in that cave, waiting for rediscovery? What other treasures may have been forever destroyed in that underground eruption?

Samson is prcat right. "Atlantis", no doubt about it. Letter perfect. Identical to what's already in Atlantida. No doubt at all.

All right. No reason to further contest that point. Accept what your putz eyes know is real. Tutto finito, mister. Now.... what else should be on the agenda?

"How's the kid?"

Senior Researcher Samson Krombacher scratches his head, the videophone conversation faithfully transferring the sound his fingers produced passing over his millimetre long scalp bristles. Despite his somewhat Teutonic name, Krombacher is a dark-skinned black man with an oblong face, very dark rounded eyes, their yellowish sclera crisscrossed with visible capillaries, his wiry hair cropped almost to stubble. Short, well-kept moustache and beard are completing the picture: - "He's in Old City's University Hospital."

"I didn't ask where he is, Marka mu, but how he is!" – barks the Curator with a sharp and unpleasant edge to his voice.

"Peter, boss, you didn't let me finish. He's well. He regained consciousness. The wound on his forehead is healing. He has a mild concussion, which has to be expected. He broke his left arm. A pretty gahba bad fracture as that tablet is ochen bolshoy heavy. With its pedestal, it weighs more than hundred eighty kilograms, tabarnaque. Our doctors are optimistic; he'll fully recover though it will take some sakra time for

that arm to mend. It's unlikely that he'll be able to participate in further excavations during his remaining time here, Marka mu."

"Sorry my friend. I ochen balshoy apologize for my bad temper. You're not to blame for any of my problems. That stone is heavy, indeed, you're orcae ita right. Sharmoota haygana, the largest inscribed artefact we ever found, I believe?"

"By far. The largest by far, bre."

"And the kid suffered a lot, though I'm happy he'll recover. I suppose he's covered by our irrumatror health insurance?"

"Fully covered. I already checked. After all, I'm his supervisor. I'm responsible for his health. I feel that I failed him, tabarnaque."

"You didn't. Such merde accidents in the field can't be prevented. They just happen."

"Thanks boss, I ochen balshoy needed you to say that."

(For a moment, Samson appears undecided, as if uncertain whether to continue.)

"Go on, my friend. So far you did damned well."

"Listen, Peter. This isn't connected to archeology. And, if we're keeping to the rulebook, not really our concern. Putz not strictly so. Not Atlantida's concern. More something for our prc authorities, maybe the social services, maybe the police. The kid has a relative on Newlands...."

From his left pocket, Senior Researcher Samson Krombacher produces a paper.

"His name is Giorgi Okri-ash-vili."

"Another Georgian?"

"No, Marka mu. He's Newlandean. Born in New Belgrade, parents deceased, no other family here, some mrdat distant relatives in Georgia, one of them being our Davit. His parents were the irrumatror original immigrants. He lives and works in putz Norton. I gather that he's Davit's distant cousin, actually.... rather a very distant one. In hospital, I briefly bespoke him. I believe there's much more to their story than just being relatives. A sort of a special romantic human angle."

"A romantic human angle, Marka mu? Like in what, svih mu svetaca?"

"They are lovers."

"Ah, lovers!" – Peter chuckles; that's definitely a romantic human angle, coveted by our auditorium and thus the TV National – "Is the relative openly bragging?"

“Nyet. But it’s easy to read between his words. To me, he’s like an open book, Marka mu.”

“Hmmmm.” – let’s think this thoroughly through, and carefully analyze, consider all those hidden angles; I’m a scientist, after all, that’s what I should always do – “Am I right in assuming that the far-off Republic of Georgia isn’t an ideal place for a homosexual, especially an injured one, not to mention a gay couple?”

“I believe that you’re absolutely right, my Mo. Consider also that once their story hits our TV screens, it won’t stay secret and may cause a scandal back home in Georgia.”

Frown.

“Not may. Will sakra cause a scandal. Poor kid’s parents, they are in for a shock, but at this point it’s unavoidable.”

For a moment Peter pouts as well, thinking of what now needs to be done, charting his next moves.

“Samson, majke ti, I want all possible and impossible courtesy extended to them. All consideration. Them as in putz both of them, the couple. And make it as public as possible, Marka mu. That kid did well. He did us a great favor. A major discovery, one which won’t be easily forgotten. Calisse de merde, he will be famous, he has become a part of our history. He is already prc famous but doesn’t yet know it.

(chuckles from both)

TV National will certainly want to run his story, including the personal angle.”

“Exactly why I mentioned it. The reporters were already in the hospital. They are like bloodhounds when they sniff out a good story. Majke ti, it won’t take long to uncover the whole affair.”

Peter scratches his moustache, doing some hard and fast calculating.

This great archeological discovery won’t remain hidden like the previous important ones, hoarded in the basement of his museum. He already talked to the President. The Government of Newlands wants it public and revealed, not just to our nation, but to the whole wide world, possibly transforming this find into a new major tourist attraction. The newest transmutation in the tourist brand of Newlands, Marka mu, nothing less than that! Atlantis risen from the deep, and here’s our proof! TV National already covered kid’s cave rescue and dramatic transfer by an ambulance helicopter; they also showed the removal of the artifact itself, though it was shrouded in thick aluminium foil preventing any glimpses

of its shape and inscriptions. Once this story hits the screens, Atlantida may for a while eclipse even the resolution of this year's national football championship and FC Paloma's seemingly unstoppable triumphal march towards another title.

Sigh.

That's life.

(On two accounts: Peter's forced public exposure and the fact that FC Paloma isn't exactly his first choice for the next Champion of Newlands.)

I will be in the center of attention. There will be many interviews to give, many speeches to deliver.

That's my duty.

A disquieting thought: mindful of his secret duty within the five, Peter usually avoids such exposure.

But that's my prcat duty.

I'll have to talk to my five, too. There might be important security angles which I'm missing.

Problems, problems.

Decisions, decisions.

And one needs to be taken right this moment.

"Even better, Samson; listen, you're free, I'm taking this problem off your hands. Concentrate on that darned stone. Do all those analyses we mentioned, everything by the book, Marka mu. We need to shine in the eyes of the world, not to mention Newlands. I'll personally go to the hospital and talk to kid's doctors, his partner, and our authorities. Maybe, dormi mecum, even the President. Again. That kid did us a favor. A great favor. Let's sakra see how much this country can in return do for him."

# EFFICIENCY

Full of sadness, I'm watching a line of dejected humanity shuffling past. Bent heads, dropped shoulders, feet dragging over the hot tarmac.

And the handcuffs.

The unwanted economic migrants.

I didn't count how many already passed. Ten, fifteen?

I count.

Two – four – six.

A large group with children.... well, five in all. Eleven.

Thirteen, fourteen, sixteen.

Another group. Twenty-one.

"Watching the prisoners?"

I thought that I was alone, but Taske must have stealthily approached and is now standing next to me, his moustache drooping in disapproval (of migrants or me watching them?).

"You mean the migrants?"

"Prisoners, bre."

I sigh. I expected my friend's tough attitude. In my new homeland it's a generalized sentiment.

"Yes, my friend. What a pitiful sight they are."

Taske pouts his lips but doesn't answer.

"No empathy for them?"

"Empathy? For those criminals?"

"Taske, they just wanted a better life for their children and, I guess, themselves too."

"Madre de Dios, mister, listen to what you're saying! We're the best country in the world. Imagine if everyone on Earth, some tabarnaque seven billion of them, decided that they want a better life and just came over? They would suffocate us! In no time we would have hordes of the homeless like your countrymen are plagued with, racial strife also like your countrymen are tabarnaque plagued with, and the religious suicide bombers destroying shopping malls. How would that please you, majke ti?"

Now I sigh.

Stripping it to the bare bones, Taske is right, and I know it. This is a small archipelago with limited livable space; its peculiar culture can't admit people unprepared to live by its rules and contribute to the whole. Still, I do have lots of empathy for those wretched people.

"Sucatum tauri, you don't just raise your anchor, move somewhere else, and expect a better life! You bust your ass and create that better life where you already live! Our ancestors made this archipelago into the paradise on Earth. When they came here, it was just bare rocks and nothing else."

Taske's moustache is fearsome, bristling with inner anger.

Yet, I smile, then chuckle.

Taske just admitted that his ancestors came here from somewhere else. Once you dig sufficiently deep into the past, everyone in the world, wherever they nowadays live, came from somewhere else.

"And they are criminals, damn it. They broke so many laws...."

"Our laws."

"Of course, orcae ita, our laws! Why would we sakra care whether they broke other countries' laws? Or their own country's tabarnaque laws?" – Taske is filled with indignation; then he sees me ready to reply – "Stop.... Don't.... They broke those, too. The laws of the countries they came from, and the countries they travelled through, then those so-called international laws, the United Nations' laws...."

"Taske, what do you know about the United Nations' laws?"

"I.... Who sakra cares? What DO YOU know about the United Nations' laws?"

To say the truth, not much, Taske's got a point there. Maybe we should change the subject.

"I heard that we sunk their boat?"

"Yes, per the long-time standing MANATO orders."

"But couldn't we have somehow...."

"Used that old wreck? Marka mu, hardly."

I shift from foot to foot, at the same time turning to keep observing the moving line of prisoners. Migrants.

Whatever.

It's becoming hot out here.

Ceti II's middays tend to be the hottest ones.

"Taske, you said those are standing MANATO orders. Long-time standing orders. Do you remember when they were issued?"

"Way before my time, boss. Mook kebba, I believe.... let me think.... towards the end of the seventies."

"Thirty-five years ago?"

"Marka mu, give or take."

The prisoners are nearing two MANATO Dornier Do328 transport jets. The nearer plane is in the standard patchy blue camouflage. The one further away is the first I ever saw in the three-tone gray, the new pattern I approved (on Sam's prompting) after a bomb destroyed one of these perky, sturdy, and eminently useful smallish airplanes we imported from Germany.

"What was the reason for such an order?"

Taske snorts: - "Make a guess, my friend."

"Punishment for ship's owners through the loss of property, prevention of additional trips?"

"Indeed, calisse de merde, orcae ita indeed. Newlands law enforcement can't reach those pirates, smugglers, organizers who profit around the world from moving desperate people. Destruction of their property is the least thing we can do."

"Well, I'd like to see those people-smugglers punished too. And their operations shut down."

"Won't ever happen, boss. And you know it. Marka mu."

I do.

But I promise myself to give it my best try.

I turn away from the sad vista and slowly walk towards airport's sparsely furbished, spartan terminal (yet still recognizable as such: a glass and concrete building). Military people are almost the exclusive users of this airport. No need to pamper any of us with costly comfort.

"The jump of Nikola's efficiency in managing Swift – 1's business is mrdat incredible."

Taske's words startle me into almost stumbling in mid-stride.

Since Thom's spirit (aura, soul, essence) transferred into Nikola, a remarkable change came over my husband. He stopped sleeping, thus doubling his productive time. (To say the least; some efficiency coefficients and physical training data are way more than two hundred percent up!) Fearing a calamity and Nikola's impending breakdown, I discussed at length both with Nikola and Thom. They assured me Nikola does rest and sleep, managing more rest and longer sleeping hours than ever in his life, in the order of upwards of ten hours daily. When Nikola sleeps, Thom completely takes over his body, including all its physical and intellectual activities. Their real-life resemblance in speech patterns, mannerisms, emotional responses, vocabularies, and choices, which existed since their childhood years, helps camouflage the fact that two independent auras now share Nikola's functioning. I never managed to determine what Swift – 1's soldiers, unaware of the survival of Thom's aura, make of this sudden change in behavior of their new commanding officer.

At first, I couldn't believe such an alternating sleep arrangement was possible. On my request, Irena Panj ran all medical tests she could think of, imagine, even invent from scratch. Her first report was surprising. Additional reports, two and four weeks after the soul-sharing transfer, were astonishing. Not only has she failed to dig out any problems, but Nikola's body was somehow benefiting, in mysterious ways; frankly stated, never in his life was Nikola healthier.

If two men were ever meant to coexist in this way, Nikola and Thom are them.

Then the proverbial other shoe dropped....

Though I may look thoroughly alert, I'm only half-heartedly listening to Dr Panj's words. I'm concentrating on her appearance. Of late Irena always appears exhausted. And so do many of her closest colleagues, male and female, whom I'm so regularly encountering and interacting with (mostly in my capacity as their CIC but occasionally privately too, smirk, smirk). Are they overworked? (Am I overworking them?) After she finally delivers her explanation of what this newest "most secret" encounter in MARC's vaults is all about, I must remember to ask if she needs more staff. Irena and her scientists are brilliant, Nobel-prize-class and above, but I don't want them dropping out from burnout. Her team is easily worth many a new fighter, or even a newly constructed aircraft

carrier. If MARC needs to divert more funds from building those assets to engage additional brilliant-minded Newlandean scientists, so be it. Though, such decisions are never my own to make. MANATO's finances are among GHQ's privileges, to be collectively decided on. However, my wishes tend to hold sway if I put a bit of effort in promoting them.

That's a fact.

Which reminds me.... recently Fran explained the superior educational outcomes for the Newlandean children, as compared to their peers in the rest of the world. On average, our kids learn faster and better. Our scientists overachieve compared to world's top tier, albeit they yet have to win an international award acknowledging their success.

Why is that? In fact, this question is double-pronged: why are the Newlanders, especially our children, better in all branches of learning and science; and why aren't our scientists ever competing for those international accolades? Except for the top-secret boffin stuff relating to MANATO, our civilian and military space program, NIN, and a couple more core government activities, Fran was adamant that all other research is openly published in media available to everyone in the world. Yet, somehow, all those world's scientists read those Newlandean papers and smile, nod, and scratch their heads in wonder (at least I presume so), and that's that. Nobody seems to follow up on our research.

As for the learning prowess of our children, Fran did mention a number of hypotheses: the general lack of religious influences on scientific thinking, richly equipped schools with an emphasis on physical development of body and scientific development of mind (he gave me a Latin quote: mens sana in corpore sano – a healthy mind in a healthy body; I liked it so much that I decided to learn those words and incorporate them into my vocabulary), great social status and recognition our scientists in general enjoy, and Labyrinthium.

Labyrinthium, I asked?

Labyrinthium, answered Fran. Apparently, there exists a theory that the presence on Newlands of its weird, unique radiation stimulates minds, especially of young children.

Interesting.

In that case, I'm an exception. I don't feel that I became brighter since I arrived on Newlands. In fact, I suspect....

"There!"

Irena's shout of triumph cuts through my daydreaming.

We're deep in MARC's guts. I didn't count floors or ask for data, but this might be the deepest underground facility I ever visited on Newlands. Except for the Newlandean mines, of course.

"Sacre blue, there!" – repeats Irena.

I stare through the thick greenish glass into a brilliantly lit chamber partially recessed half a floor below the level I'm currently standing on. There's a metal table in its midst. More of a frame than a table. A frame with multiple supports and appendages. Industrial robots surround that frame, their arms busily moving up and down, rotating, screwing, placing, cutting, then repeating the whole process, accomplishing some totally mysterious tasks. There are four individuals inside the chamber, mostly standing at a distance from the frame, holding tablets or operating desktops. As they are dressed in bluish paper-thin scaphanders with darkened visors which make their forms amorphous, I can't guess their gender, not to mention try to identify them. They each carry a prominent plastic card attached to their left breast (probably their CREDIT but it's too far to be certain. The chamber itself is almost perfectly round; shelves and other means of storage cover most of its walls exclusive of the continuous glass ring of windows on top, stretching to the ceiling.

However, none of this seems important. Just marginal impressions to be swiftly noted and almost immediately forgotten.

For there's a form occupying that frame / bed.

An astonishing sight.

A Terminator.

A Robocop.

Or neither of them.

Similar but different.

Slightly larger than an average man (at first sight I'd judge it seven to eight feet tall), it's powerful arms and legs are obviously artificial, consisting of metallic parts, hydraulic pumps and pipes, electronic wires, printed boards, chips, semiconductors, whatever.... All on display as a transparent material envelops those mechanical parts.

"Marka mu, Dave, a blend of titanium alloys and KGZ. I mean that transparent shielding" – states Irena with confidence. She obviously followed my glance and correctly interpreted what I was inspecting.

Her words are a source of wonder. I had no idea anything like this was possible, in the plans, and certainly not in the works. (I'm their Commander – in – Chief, how come I was kept in the dark?) However, none

of that's important, her comment swept away by the incredible wonder I'm feeling. The upper torso, neck and head of the.... machine, device, robot.... the android being constructed may be of one metal or the other (it appears metallic to me), shielded by the same transparent material forming a glassy surface, but they have an unmistakably humanoid appearance. Each muscle and tendon, and all its organs (mouth, nose, ears, even the nipples) are in place.

And there's also the outline of a metallic moustache above its upper lip.

Thom.

"Dave, no matter how much Nikola is benefiting from their union, there are subtle signs hinting at Thom's gradual decline; we thought that Thom's spirit deserves a permanent home of its own."

I can't seem to properly hear her words.

I can't seem to turn my face towards her, to see her speak her words.

Everything seems to be slowing down.

All my being is fixating on one thing only: that metallic form, passive and motionless on its support frame.

A bit later (they say that twenty minutes passed), I'm sitting in Irena's office, staring at numerous screens. Some hold blueprints, some hold drawings, and two are cameras showing the android assembly room (that's how Irena calls it) from different angles.

There's a smile on Irena's face: - "Nature the great, you almost blanked out."

"I didn't!"

"You ochen balshoy did."

"Don't.... (tell anyone, you stupid cow!)"

"Tell anyone? Calisse de merde, why would I? I'm not implying any cowardice on your part. Verdammt, it was shock, at that an utterly unexpected one. Pic cocuk, something you couldn't even imagine seeing. You were faced with a situation you were completely unprepared for, utterly impossible in view of your whole life experience. Your mind took a couple of minutes to adjust. That's all."

I blink.

My mind encountered an impossible situation and bolted? For a couple of minutes? How cowardly of it.... me.

(A thought out of the blue, out of context: my mind behaved like a blue screen on a PC. "Your computer ran into a bit of trouble; we're collecting information and will restart it for you...." Is that what she's saying?)

I feel my face redden: - "Did I fall down?"

My hand reaches for a bottle of Coke. It's a green labeled Newlands Coke Life sweetened with Stevia instead of sugar. Not my favorite beverage, but I feel intense thirst. For a moment, I wonder; my hand automatically reached for it; my mind was aware of its exact location on the table beside my chair. Yet I can't consciously remember it being put there. What's wrong with me?

"Nyet, General, you didn't fall down. Your honor remains intact. Your rational mind went into fugue, but all your autonomous body functions were preserved, bre. You were just standing there, not talking, not moving."

"How did I get up here?"

(Irena's office is on one of the top floors. You need to travel by a couple of elevators and do a serious amount of walking to reach here.)

She shrugs, forming another apologetic smile: - "Well, I summoned two of my helpers and we guided you here. Step after the prcat step. It took a while to get you to the elevator...."

She smirks, which makes me angrier; at myself for being such a weakling and at her for summoning help.

"Svih mu svetaca, it later became easier."

Two helpers.

Which helpers?

What will those two helpers think of their CIC?

"They better not...."

"Yap about their experience? If they did, you're worried that your authority as our CIC might somehow suffer?"

Her words hurt.

Why do they hurt so much?

Because she's right; that's what I was thinking.

It's all pure vanity, I realize.

I need to work on abolishing such vanity. Put it to rest next to my vanquished jealousy.

I need to own up to my weaknesses the same way I enjoy my strengths. A real person possesses both strengths and weaknesses. Yin and young.

Yet.

Yet!

The Commander – in – Chief can't show any weaknesses.

No way.

"No worries, Dave. Dr Li Huei and Dr Aldevant Bradley helped me get you here. They are quite aware of both sides of your personality: the almost almighty superhuman, and the fragile human being. They know in minute detail how you tick, better than you do, better than anyone else."

Sigh.

Yes, indeed.

Those scientists know me very well, better than I know myself.

Enough!

Enough!

Stop thinking of yourself and your reputation!

Think of Thom (and Thom's.... android)!

"So, that's your full plan?"

"Yes. My plan. OUR plan. No matter how good a fit Nikola and Thom are, the prcat bottom line is that it's Nikola's body they are sharing. Eventually Thom will lose his individuality, then his identity, or maybe completely fade away. We hoped, then decided once our hopes turned into practical planning, to provide him with a superior body equipped with a positronic brain capable of housing his essence as we learnt to define it through our observations of Thom sharing your body and mind."

Such an elegant idea!

Mindboggling!

Who thought of it first? Whose spark was the initial one which kindled the fire? Did any of them dream of it? Dare I ask? Maybe it's better not to do it immediately.

Yet, so many questions, so many doubts.

What about....

"What about....?"

"Oh, Dave, I know. I know. So many questions, dixi. Exempli gratia, how will the android function in real-life circumstances? How will Thom adjust to his new android body? How will Nikola and the other Swift – 1 soldiers adjust to a robotic leader? Flocci non facio, how will MANATO adjust to having an android officer in its ranks? Strategically and legally? How will Newlands adjust to having an android soldier? Halleluiah chance, which citizen's rights can an android have in our society? And much more, beshoor so much more...."

"Yes, those questions flashed through my mind, but also...."

"How to multitax transfer Thom's spirit from Nikola to the android?"

I sigh.

My glance floats over the screens.

The relentless work on building the android.

The incredible object they are working on. Not in my wildest dreams did I expect to see anything like it, especially not today.

The amazing blueprints, hinting at the superhuman powers my husband will possess.

A future for my husband.

Apart from the humanity, completely apart, and completely alone. The first of its / his kind.

Yet an exciting future. A superhuman future.

Definitely an exciting and long-lasting future (Irena hinted that, barring unforeseen scientific problems, Thom's android body could be maintained indefinitely).

Yet....

That future would take Thom away from us, the Lionhearts. It's highly questionable he would be allowed onto the Main Islands. But more than that, no biological, sexual relationship would ever be possible again.

Remember, you idiot! Thom is already dead, his body destroyed, rendered into a handful of ash. Already no further sexual relationship with him is possible at all. If that simultaneously exhilarating and terrifying contraption is the only way to guaranty his continued presence on Earth, so be it!

And I know the answer to the question which Irena voiced in my name. The DFQL aliens below our feet. They keep moving Thom around: from his moribund body into mine, then from me into Nikola. Only they can transfer Thom's essence into its new receptacle.

"No, Irena. I already know the answer to that question. Both you and I know the answer."

"Woodla halum."

Silence.

"The aliens below our feet. Only they can accomplish such miracles."

"Svih mu svetaca, you're ochen balshoy right."

"What I wanted to ask, or comment on, is that there may be a new, different future for Thom in that android body, but he'll forever be

separated from the rest of us, the Lionhearts, his family, in every aspect of our marriage."

Irena transfixes me with her glance, then her eyes widen in surprise: - "Yakamishii, you mean sex!"

I nod.

Paradoxically, when Thom shared my mind, we shared each sexual experiences like never before. I'm starting to miss that unnatural proximity.

"Va te tripoter, when we designed the android, it never crossed our mind to enable it to participate in such biological functions...."

"I presume that it doesn't eat, breathe, digest, urinate, defecate, sweat...."

"Nyet. It doesn't do any of those."

I chuckle, somehow relieved: - "Then why the hell have to ejaculate?"

Irena shakes her head, herself timidly smiling: - "Once in the android's body, Thom's life will take a course completely diverging from human normal."

She's serious.

Something is on my mind, but I'm hesitating to bring it up. Instead, I manage to remember what I previously promised myself to ask: - "Irena, before you showed me your newest project, I was concerned that you and your staff all seem terribly tired. Exhausted even. Not just today, but for the last few weeks, months maybe. After what I just witnessed, I guess that the reason for that exhaustion is your effort to design and assemble that android. Is that so?"

Irena's eyes narrow: - "On one hand, MARC has for awhile operated with reduced staff. Any increase in financing dedicated to acquisition of qualified scientists and researchers is always welcome, tabarnaque.

(Bluntly and shamelessly put: if I get her more money, she might employ more staff. Those words tally with what I already decided needs to be done. Therefore, I pensively nod, in empathy with her plight.)

However, bringing to fruition the construction of Thom's replacement android is what physically exhausted my top scientists, myself included. This indeed was a tabarnaque unprecedented effort, unequaled in MARC's history."

She's lying! Or, at least, she's not telling the whole truth (and nothing but the truth). Something about her posture, shifting her glance, fleeting

tremors in her speech.... it all conveys a single message. I'm not getting the full information.

(Why? What else is she hiding from her Commander – in – Chief?)

"Thank you, Irena. I hear you. I give you CIC's solemn promise that MARC will be supported to the max.

(Now I decide to mention what troubled me before.)

Your android is probably unprecedented and unparalleled in human, not just MARC's history. Yet, I can't order Thom to simply switch again and become more a machine than a person. I'll ask him to do it of his own free will. I will also ask my family for their opinion. No matter how brilliant your achievement, this decision won't be a speedy one to reach."

# DFQL TORPEDO

A small torpedo-shaped object.

Bluish grey.

A single red character on its bow.

A Chinese character.

The same one I've seen before.

It's silent, brooding, immobile, lodged between a large rock and some reddish corals.

Vaguely threatening, but impossible to spot unless you're, like me, poking around the coral head in your diving gear.

A DFQL torpedo?

The fourth, never discovered torpedo?

Or a new torpedo? (Fifth, sixth, seventh.... who the hell knows how many there may be?)

"Gahba, yes, sir. We call it "the breathing rocket engine"." – says the diminutive moustached Urt Rossi, the Head of Newlands Space Program Study, his face lit with sincerity – "But their introduction will necessarily retard our program by about two years."

Nemanja won't like that. He wished to become our space-travel President.

Which is irrelevant, after all.

"But see here, General...." – butts in the huge, athletic, baldheaded (and likely moustached, of course) Milenko Petrović, Chief Engineer of MASP – "We may lose two years now, but over the next decade...."

My great buddy Dr Lenko Zdravkov, from MANATO's Weapons Design, now cuts in, his seniority making the other two give him precedence: - "More like the period up to the 2030."

Milenko: - "Right, until the mrdat 2030.... we would accelerate our prc program by more than four years, mostly through heavier payloads transported into orbit."

Like Urt, Milenko appears amazingly sincere, almost childishly so. Like a five-year old boy who believes that he just pronounced the greatest truth in the universe and now expects a pat on his head and some praise (or a cookie or two).

"I still don't understand, at least not fully, the advantage over the engines we already use. I do see your enthusiasm, so there must be some gain, but enlighten me further, please."

Urt: - "Well, with all SSTO systems...."

SSTO, SSTO.... It rings a bell. I was, after all, at least for a while, the head of MASP – MANATO's Space Program. Why can't I remember such details?

Zdravko, believing that he correctly deciphered my expression: - "Single-stage-to-orbit vehicles, boss."

Milenko: - "Yes, most of our rockets are SSTO. Sharmoota haygana, some of them are reusable."

Urt: - "At least partially, Marka mu."

Milenko: - "Exactly, ochen balshoy. The current Japanese and Russian rocket engines which we use aren't."

Zdravko: - "But our air breathing rockets will be."

Milenko: - "And with them we can make almost eighty percent of the whole vehicle return...."

Zdravko: - "And land."

Milenko: - "Da, and land, ready to be reused."

Urt: - "Therefore, orcae its, trice the current rocket power and no need to carry oxygen...."

Milenko, spreading hands: - ".... as propellent...."

Urt, seamlessly continuing: - ".... but instead sucking it in directly from the air...."

Zdravko: - "And the water vapor."

Milenko: - "Indeed. That will boost the power of their Labyrinthium engine...."

I raise my hand. All three of them are well-meaning and excited about their news. But they are also too fast for me. Too.... scientific. They aren't managing to pass their info across (or I'm too dumb to understand). It's not just their new rocket engine; I need to breathe, too. I need to recapitulate: - "All right. Stop. Timeout!"

I make the customary basketball hand signal for a timeout and vigorously display it in front of their faces.

"Do not interrupt me, please. Let me rephrase and recapitulate. In my own words. Let's see whether I've understood your technical jargon."

I take a breath.

"You want to replace our current tried and tested and exceedingly reliable Japanese and Russian rocket engines...."

Urt: - "Vastly improved by our engineers."

I nod – "Yes, vastly improved, indeed. So, you want to replace them with a never tried home design breathing air instead of simply burning propellent. If successful, it should have trice the power of our current rockets and would be reusable."

Lenko opens his mouth.

"I guess I forgot to mention that with no propellent we'll gain much more payload."

Milenko and Urt are beaming at me. Lenko again opens his mouth to speak.

"And the rocket's Labyrinthium engine will also be boosted."

Now Lenko nods, shakes his head in slow motion, and speaks before I can again stop him: - "More or less right, CIC, bre. Because of the fact that any vehicle traveling into space must eventually run out of atmosphere, hence of air to "breathe", this breathing phenomenon influences only the initial stages of flight. The same with the mentioned boosting of the Labyrinthium engine; once in stratosphere, not to mention the outer space, Marka mu, there won't be any water vapor left for boosting. Which means that we can't discard all propellent, nor all water, just part of it. A mrdat good part of it. Still, all those gains would increase the payload at least four to five **times**!

(After thoroughly stressing the last word, he makes a dramatic pause.)

Don't forget, being more reusable than ever, the frequency of venturing into the orbit will also be higher. It's a simple calculation...."

I chuckle.

"And someone just dreamt of it?"

(As I recently did?)

Suddenly the mood changes. Milenko and Urt glance at each other, then at me.

Urt: - "General, sir.... my Mo.... how did you prcat guess?"

My mouth loudly shuts.

DFQL!

DFQL again!

Through dreams of our scientists, they gave us this precious design for a superior rocket engine.

Why?

Is it a gift or a trap?

It certainly worked with Thom.

How to be sure?

"Well, Urt, it was just a sarcastic question, I guess. Are you implying that someone really dreamt this engine up?"

Laughter.

Milenko: - "Well, that's the story, hiljadu mu svetaca, if you're inclined to believe it. Two engineers suffered nightmares the same night. Next morning, they both had tabarnaque visions of new engine design in their heads."

Milenko glances at me with apprehension, as if trying to gauge how much I believe his statement: - "Sir, that's what they say. How can anyone prove it, majke ti?"

He saw something in my face.

It wasn't incredulity.

It was my shock at discovery of more DFQL meddling.

"When did all that happen?"

Lenko: - "I'd say a beshoor year and a half or two years ago. That's when we started working on the feasibility of their ideas."

The others nod in agreement.

So, at the time when they definitely, undoubtedly acted as our (worst) enemies, and repeatedly tried to kill me, DFQL aliens also gave us the gift of this superior design.

How do you solve that riddle?

By changing the subject of conversation before someone glimpses the true reason of my consternation.

"Lenko, by the way, why is your Blackberry constantly touching that....

(I'm searching for the correct word, searching for the correct word, searching for the correct word....)

.... funny armband on your left arm?"

I've several times noticed my friend lift his cellphone, briefly touch the armband, then deposit it back into his pocket.

For the briefest moment Lenko appears startled, his right hand impulsively jerking away, taking with it his Blackberry. Then he smiles: - "Ah, CIC, you haven't yet seen our prototype electricity producing polymer sweatband?"

"Electricity producing sweatband?"

Lenko: - "Electricity producing polymer sweatband, yes."

A bit annoyed with the numerous corrections, I repeat my words: - "Electricity producing sweatband? Is that even possible? What's it producing electricity from? Thin air?"

Lenko: - "Hardly, boss. Ii kagen ni shiro, its polymer component harvests the temperature difference between my skin and the surrounding air to generate a tiny amount of electricity. You know that our newest Blackberries can be cordlessly charged?"

"I do."

"Well, theoretically I can endlessly keep recharging my Blackberry using just my body temperature, grace of this polymer sweatband."

My eyebrows arch up.

"Lenko, that's a colossal idea!"

Milenko: - "Think of soldiers in the field who could maintain their smaller electronic equipment functioning during a battle with just their body temperature. Hijo de mil putas, it would be a grand advantage over any enemy."

"I agree! I just wonder how news of this invention never made it to my desk."

"We're just trying it out, General." – answers Lenko – "There are only a few polymer sweatbands in existence. To be truthful, I wasn't even charging my Blackberry. I was using my cell to measure the amount of electricity accumulated."

Lenko gropes at his sweatband and stretches it enough to encompass at least another arm.

"The material is flexible, it can be made to contain a layer of KGZ, and it doesn't need to remain just a sweatband. In the future, it could be the interior layer of our uniforms."

"Lenko, that's such a grand idea, I...."

My Blackberry starts ringing.

It's a shrill melody, revealing the identity of my caller.

Miki.

Calling from his MANATO cellphone.

"Yes, Miki?"

"Dave, emergency. We need you here ASAP. Yesterday if gahba possible."

"Miki, I'm in Old City."

"I know. I already sent Rob in an Osprey to fetch you."

"What's the problem?"

"Malik kahell, when you arrive."

"Can you hint at the problem?"

Miki's face appears very calm and composed: - "When you arrive, boss."

"That serious?"

A nod.

For a moment I try for once to think in a logical way: - "Concerning geology?"

The best I could think of at the spur of the moment, without mentioning DFQL in front of our engineers.

"Finally, some prcat appropriate thinking! Da, yes, ochen balshoy bre."

DFQL!

The aliens below our feet, hence my mention of geology.

What now?

What did they, what ARE they doing **now**?

Wait.

One more thing to ascertain.

"But not extremely urgent?"

If it were extremely urgent there would be an immediate need for decisions. Miki didn't ask for any immediate decisions.

Well, not yet. Not yet.

Some frustration shows on Miki's face: - "Frankly, tabarnaque, I've no idea!"

I frown, puzzled: - "No idea?"

Nod.

"Do we need Andy?"

I congratulate myself on thinking of him. Andy is our strongest telepath.

"I don't think so, Marka mu."

Therefore, not a paranormal problem.

At least probably not.

Hopefully not.

"All right. I'll be back as soon as Rob picks me up. Over and out."

While disconnecting, Miki bumps his chest.

"Guys, you sold me on all your ideas. Sweatbands collecting electricity and the breathing rockets and everything else we touched on. I will champion your ideas during the GHQ voting. Please do send over nicely presented, full plans with realistic timetables and all other details you can think of, especially elaborate on those gains, so that this old General doesn't risk appearing the dumbest of CICs."

Peter: - "You'll dive in nude, sir?"

Today's Peter is Sub-Lieutenant Peter Schneider, a naval diver standing next to me.

Miki: - "Pete, don't you know what an exhibitionist our Mo CIC is? He's more out than in his uniform, flocci non facio."

"Miki!" – I shout in mock alarm.

Newlands Airforce General Miodrag Raonić, my great buddy Miki, is also standing next to me.

"Don't listen to this clown, Sub-Lieutenant. The truth is, I only recently started diving and my family hooked me on nude diving."

Peter Schneider is slightly taller than me, with a powerful, proportionally formed body stuffed into black neoprene, and shortly cropped pepper and salt moustache and goatee below his lively dark eyes. By any standards, not just the Newlandean ones, an extremely military-like appearance, I might add. His rank is imprinted on his diving suit (glued, embroidered, sewed, stamped, whatever) on the left side of chest, as well as where his shoulders would harbor epaulets if he were in a uniform.

"We're not diving deep, Marka mu, nor will it be long. You won't be uncomfortable naked, sir."

"You're sakra encouraging him." – opines Miki.

"Orcae ita, only twelve meters deep, CIC." – ascertains Lieutenant Leta Margolin, also standing in my proximity.

"Exactly 12.5 meters, sir." – adds Lieutenant Jovana Glavan, likewise standing nearby.

These four soldiers are encircling me on the main deck of NLNAU103 tender *Main*, a large grey cargo vessel belonging to our Navy. I was cautioned that this ship got acquired from Germany, therefore its name should be pronounced as the name of the German river Main, after which it was christened, and not the English word "main". Since we landed, I was meticulously careful to do so (not to appear an imbecile CIC).

*Main* is almost exactly hundred meters long, with around three thousand five hundred tons of displacement, a high ocean-traveling prow, and a helicopter pad on its bow. A huge derrick in its midst is currently providing some shade from the scorching tropical sun. It was built twenty years ago and sold to Newlands in 2005 (the rumor is to cut our trade surplus a bit; it's doubtful that MANATO was in dire need of another tender). It's considered our most modern and up-to-date tender.

Naval Lieutenant Leta Margolin, *Main's* commanding officer, must have been utterly shocked with her newest orders. *Main* just returned from a trip to Germany, bringing more Leopard tanks and all kinds of support equipment, ammunition, and parts. It was supposed to leisurely depart the Atlantis harbor (Leopards are modified in the vast Titan works there) for Nordporte and a few days of R&R for its crew (and a quick trip home for some, if they happened to live nearby). Instead, the GHQ (I should say Miki), ordered it to remain at anchor and wait for the arrival of a group of high-ranked officers. I gather that no one told Leta which high-ranked officers were to visit.

Rob landed our Osprey on *Main's* helipad (to me it appeared decidedly too small, but I was assured that it was all safe, tried and tested). And here we were, Miki and I (we picked Miki on GHQs helipad in New Belgrade), two of the most important officers of MANATO's GHQ, all clad in our ebony splendor, in an (almost) unannounced visit to an unprepared ship.

Leta is medium tall, probably slightly taller than my Fanta, and rather strongly built while retaining all her feminine curves. She's a brownish blonde (what they occasionally call bronde), her hair a waterfall surrounding her head, freely falling onto her shoulders. She's wearing an everyday work uniform with her proper rank on display, but the cap on her head, though of correct shape and shade, sports the logo of one of our cargo shipping companies. (Where did that come from? There might be an interesting story behind that logo. I need to remember to ask. Later.)

A wave of hair partially obscures her left eye, giving her a somewhat piratical appearance.

Lieutenant Jovana Glavan is Leta's second in command. I checked, she's thirty-eight, but looks like eighteen! Huge round teacher's eyeglasses, breast-long golden blonde hair arranged in braid-lookalike strings, and a teenager's silhouette make her appear decidedly too young for her rank. Her dirty construction worker's fatigues were explained by the fact she was overseeing debarkation of the final items of ship's cargo.

"Sub-Lieutenant, thank you for rechecking my equipment."

Peter Schneider just finished tightening all straps, and controlling functionality of my equipment, especially my tanks. This was the third time he went through that routine. Probably nervous about diving with his Commander – in – Chief.

I look around.

*Main* is anchored near the eastern outskirts of Delta Shallows, about fifty kilometers southeast of the town of Luka and its mammoth cargo port. Whenever I glance towards the southwest, our gigantic volcanoes are clearly visible on the horizon. In the same direction but nearer to the ship, it's all white water as ocean's waves break over the spreading shallows. In all other directions the sky is blue, the sun is shining brightly, and the ocean appears choppy. I'm grateful for the offshore breeze that I can feel on my skin.

I smile.

Peter: - "Sir, we need to go down that ladder (he points his index finger) to the platform tied to the ship. Khange khodah, there I'll help you put your fins on; it's impossible to climb down with them on your feet. We already lowered our fins down and there are other crewmembers waiting to help us into the water. Hiljadu mu ajkula, I'll climb down right before you. I have experience negotiating tabarnaque constantly moving ladder like this one. Marka mu, today the waves aren't too large, but this ship won't quit moving to suit our needs. Please allow me to partially shield you by my body in case you accidentally slip."

Miki, grinning like the proverbial Cheshire cat: - "Now Dave, be a good boy and obey. This gahba soldier knows what he's doing."

I sigh.

Overprotection.

Again and always.

These soldiers need to feel that I'm safe and that they've done everything possible to make me so.

None of them has ever met me before.

To them, I'm the living legend.

They don't know how tough I am.

Or....

Am I really that tough?

Well, even if I'm not, there's my Labyrinthium shield which I can conjure out of thin air.

Or am I really able to conjure my shield out of thin air?

A strange thought.

How do I conjure my Labyrinthium shield in the first place? I never experimented, never tried to find a definite answer. Suddenly, a thought flashes through my mind. I'm naked. What am I going to conjure my Labyrinthium shield out of? My tank, goggles, and the diving vest? Is that possible at all? How can I be certain?

A group of sailors assembled nearby, standing at a respectful distance. Their unexpected chance to meet their Commander – in – Chief (in nude). I promise myself that after my dive I must spend some time with *Main's* crew. Am I uncomfortable naked in front of them, do I suffer any loss of dignity and authority? Am I uncomfortable being nude in the proximity of my two young female officers? Of course not. This is Newlands and the naked body is utterly normal, especially in MANATO.

"All right, Sub-Lieutenant. To put your mind at ease, we'll do exactly as you plan."

"Orcae ita, sir! Let's go down...."

I feel utterly serene, amazingly calm.

Sun's rays penetrate the blueness surrounding me in oblique strings of light. I hear the gurgling of water in my equipment and the swishing of waves as they collide with the shallows. The air bubbles form around me and slowly ascend.

How quiet it is.

How quiet I am.

And I shouldn't be.

Because I know what I'm searching for.

A new DFQL torpedo.

During the short flight between New Belgrade and Atlantis Miki keyed me in, after first asking if I've reached a decision on transferring Thom to his new android body (he's one of those in the knowing, a very few in all).

This newest DFQL torpedo was accidentally discovered by a civilian construction vessel. Newlands is currently laying underwater energy cables to connect all islands into a super-grid and provide an alternate source of electricity in case of colossal failure of individual islands' power systems (quite possible in an archipelago where earthquakes and volcanic eruptions occur daily). The vessel which discovered the torpedo wasn't surprised by it, nor by the Chinese character on its bow. After all, it's public knowledge that MANATO operates numerous warships obtained from China. Their immediate conclusion was that they stumbled on a lost piece of military ordnance and that MANATO should be immediately notified. Also, because of the danger of live explosive, all construction work in this vicinity has been temporarily suspended.

(Of course, no such danger existed as DFQL torpedoes aren't weapons. That is, if this one proves identical to the others we encountered.)

One question remains glaringly unanswered. Is this the fourth torpedo, never found during the "Sudden Cloudburst"? The one we were certain must be out there, somewhere, but could never detect? That time there was a torpedo approaching our archipelago from every side of the compass. The northern, western, and southern torpedoes were accounted for (two captured, one destroyed). What happened to the eastern one? Undetected, it could have serenely passed by Ceti III, our easternmost island, to lodge itself onto the shallows off the eastern cost of our Main Islands.

Or.... a disturbing notion.... is this a new DFQL torpedo? Or the fifth, sixth, seventh from their previous attempt? How many DFQL submersibles are there in our waters?

Peter waves his hand, firmly indicating direction to swim in.

He appears annoyed, even somewhat angry.

I check my watch. Ten minutes! I've already wasted ten minutes of our air frolicking under the surface, enjoying the pure joy of diving in these pristine waters. How much time is the Commander – in – Chief of MANATO allowed to waste while frolicking during a dive?

Finally, I collect my wits and follow Sub-Lieutenant Schneider's lead. We're closing on a wall of rock, obviously of volcanic origin. That wall is unmistakably the edge of magma's advance in an eruption which probably happened a long time ago. In front of it are luscious coral heads, growing in three or four parallel rows, sunshine revealing their colors, creating a magnificent opportunity for the underwater photography.

Another fleeting thought. I believe that it takes much more time for coral to create such bountiful growth than elapsed since Newlands Archipelago arose from the deep. As far as I know, coral doesn't grow a hundred feet below the surface, not to mention ten thousand. When did this coral manage to accumulate that much growth, then? Was this part of our ocean bottom somehow close to the surface much longer than our scientists suspect?

I'll have to ask Dr. Pardagh. Or someone else....

If I remember.

The very next moment, my breath is swept away.

In the narrow space between corals and the rocky wall, a long bluish-grey object is lodged.

The DFQL torpedo, exactly as I remember it.

I'm closing from its front.

The single red character on its bow is clearly visible.

A Chinese character.

The same one; I've seen it before.

It's silent, brooding, immobile, vaguely threatening, but impossible to see unless you're, like me, poking around those coral heads in your diving gear. From the surface it would be utterly invisible. Lodged deeply between the volcanic rock and the living rock produced by the tiny corals, it would be undetectable by any of the usual electronic means.

Darn!

Fifteen minutes later, I'm satisfied that nothing is to be gained by further wasting time poking around that torpedo. I was informed that *Main* has sufficient equipment and personnel to lift it off the bottom and transport it to Nordporte. As before, we'll isolate the torpedo in a research lab and try to do our best to understand its functioning.

Peter is already slowly rising towards the surface. It's not far to go, so we in advance decided not to do any decompression stops, especially since the mixture in our tanks is supposed to ward off bends.

I do the final slow pass following the length of torpedo from its propeller towards its pointed nose. Near its head, it happens. An overwhelming flash of pure telepathic thought, shattering all my preconceptions of what is and isn't possible.

And nothing in my life will ever be the same again.

An empty cargo hall in Nordporte near our fleet's main anchorage. A handful of people huddled together, not for warmth, but for comfort (for it's another beautiful, warm, winter day in this tropical archipelago, with temperatures surpassing thirty degrees Centigrade). Andy, Alan, Kieron, Fran, Miki, I. And Mietje, next to us, in her chair.

All our heads are turned upwards.

Under a support shaped like a half-circle, hanging from the ceiling, uncannily resembling inverted monorail track, two DFQL torpedoes are suspended. The first, one of the two which we captured during the "Sudden Cloudburst", here and there missing a few parts, partially (so they couldn't fit back into the whole) or completely destroyed during our research into its functioning, and the new intact one I last encountered in its underwater hiding place between rock and coral. They are facing each other.

Kieron: - "Marka mu, no wonder our scientists and technicians could never fathom the function of these contraptions."

Andy: - >Telepathic torpedoes. Tabarnaque, who would believe that possible?<

Andy is right. What so shattered my preconceptions while inspecting it in the ocean is that an inanimate object can be telepathic. I always associated telepathy with highly developed intelligence: humans, dolphins.... and aliens, of course, though we've no proof of that yet (but it appears almost certain).

But torpedoes?

Fran: - "When your alarm reached us, I thought you were exaggerating, bre. Yet, torpedoes with telepathic abilities.... this is of cosmic significance, isn't it?"

Andy: - "Ochen balshoy right!"

Kieron: - "Didn't we capture two enemy submersibles during the "Sudden Cloudburst"?"

I wince: - "Kieron, while testing them we almost completely demolished one. Not enough remains to be mounted here. What's more, we tested how it stands a Labyrinthium beam...."

Fran: - "It prcat doesn't."

"As Fran says, it prcat doesn't, but our Labyrinthium beam managed to destroy the area harboring its telepathic mechanism."

Kieron: - "Yatsume, I didn't know. A big faux pas, I believe."

Fran: - "Da, indeed."

Miki: - "We weren't exceedingly kind towards those contraptions, but now I don't think they were ever meant to endanger us. They, as all four of them taken together, calisse de merde. And by us, I mean the mrdat Newlands and our putz MANATO."

By now we reached consensus that this torpedo is the missing fourth from the original group encountered, not a new attempt at.... (whatever). That's a rare consensus reached. Almost every other point is still hotly debated.

"I agree, my friend. I believe that these torpedoes aren't elaborate devices. Not each of them taken alone. However, taken together, those four torpedoes form one special, unforeseeable, incredibly elaborate device. They were meant to...."

Mietje: - >They talk!<

>Yes they do, Princess, but not to us.<

Fran, not aware of our telepathic exchange: - "Communicate with the aliens below our feet!"

Commotion in our tight circle.

Fran: - "We always took it for granted that those torpedoes were of military significance and were, well.... some kind of intelligence gathering device. Majke ti, they didn't carry any explosives worth mentioning, therefore obviously weren't meant to be offensive weapons. Logically...."

Miki: - "Strategically bre."

Fran nods: - "And certainly strategically, if you want to spy on MANATO, this fourth submersible....

(Fran points with his right hand at the newly acquired offending instrument)

.... should have been positioned eastward or southeastward of Ceti III. Which is where we searched, Marka mu."

"Instead, it was positioned eastward of the Main Islands, deep inside our archipelago."

Alan, encircling the air with his hands: - "Calisse de merde, they bracketed just the Main Islands and almost completely omitted all MANATO installations."

More commotion.

Kieron: - "Marka mu, nobody yet fully explained to me construction of that specific mechanism which supports telepathy, which you constantly mention."

"Kieron, we ourselves weren't much certain until Mietje put two and two together...."

Alan, smiling at his adopted daughter: - "In fact, many twos and twos. Two plus two plus prcat two.... ending in a five-digit number! There were sakra too many twos and twos to put together. But she did it, like a putz supercomputer, integrating everything into a perfect theory."

>I love you my princess!< - I hear him talking to Mietje, making her smile.

"Mietje doesn't have preconceptions about functioning of specific weapons which we soldiers might harbour. She saw what we couldn't envisage possible."

Andy: - "Exactly."

Fran: - "Tabarnaque, the mechanism was present in the first two devices, too. During our initial research it was classified as....

(Fran checks his tablet)

.... interior supporting bracket.

(more checking of his tablet)

No apparent function.

(his statement elicits a lot of surprised gasps from all around him)

Composition, silicate rock."

Kieron: - "Aha!"

"Aha indeed, my friend."

A while ago, Kieron and Dr Marc Landau of the Volcano Watch theorized that the original bodies of aliens bellow our feet must be of animate rock (though their avatars, walking among us as DFQL Taoist priests, are very much carbon-based and, in many ways, identical to any other human).

"There's this V-shaped contraption, like two wires made of stone, connected to each other, projecting sideways and ahead of the torpedo. The free ends of those rock wires penetrate torpedo's outer shell and project a millimetre or two outside. The telepathic...."

I stop.

I was about to say, "telepathic thought". Is "thought" the right expression? Can a torpedo "think" at all?

Fran: - "Impulse, tabarnaque."

"Right, Fran, that's the word I was searching for. The impulse is projected along the wire and out. As I swam by it, it hit me full force like a ton of bricks."

Andy: - "Those not sensitive to telepathy would have felt nothing, bre. Our experiments proved that without any doubt. Not that you can understand the message even if you receive it."

"Right. It's overwhelmingly strong, but incomprehensible."

Miki: - "After Mietje's calculations, we believe that this beshoor impulse of yours is meant to connect with the two closest torpedoes...."

Andy: - "To form an incredibly precise diamond shape of pure telepathic thought."

Kieron: - "In order to....?"

Andy, scratching the back of his head after lifting his officer's cap: - "That one is tricky, my Mo, but Mietje believes that the diamond inverts itself and focuses its telepathic message downwards."

Fran, firmly pointing both his index fingers downwards: - "Towards Earth's center. Towards the aliens below our feet, wherever they are."

"By destroying and capturing three of their torpedoes we certainly thwarted DFQL's plans."

Miki: - We ochen balshoy did!"

"But should we have done it?"

Much more consternation than before. Some murmurs, no direct answers. Just a bit of background humming.

Finally, Andy decides to voice his surprise: - "What, Marka mu?"

Miki: - "But they are our enemies...."

"Miki, are they? Are they really our enemies?"

Sudden silence.

I have stated something that many still refuse to openly acknowledge yet are probably silently thinking, too. Is DFQL our enemy at all, or a strange friend whose actions we simply fail to fully understand (because, as Fran pointed out the other day, they follow a different, alien form of logic)?

Silence.

My idea is still too revolutionary; unwittingly, I've dampened the spirit of my chosen group.

Kieron looks upwards and breaks the uncomfortable silence: - "Something tells me that this specific arrangement of torpedoes isn't accidental."

"Kieron, you're right. We are here to try an experiment."

Miki: - "Experiment? Mrdat dangerous one? Do we need protection? Should I summon a Swift unit?"

Fran: - "No, Miki. What we're about to try is to move one of these torpedoes until it's at the exact ninety-degree angle to the other one. Va te tripoter, what we're going to try is to perfectly align the telepathic beams of these two torpedoes...."

Andy: - "To create one side of the diamond DFQL wished to construct, my Mo."

Fran: - "Orcae ita, exactly."

Kieron: - "Where's the mentioned experiment in that? What are we trying to prove?"

"Maybe that the mechanism actually works. We've no idea what will happen when those beams align." - Miki stirs, so I'm forced to rush onwards – "Miki, I doubt that a Swift team can protect from any danger which may manifest, especially since it's bound to be telepathic. I doubt that those among us who aren't telepaths will feel a thing."

Fran: - "Mietje, Andy, Alan, Dave.... Our top telepaths. If something needs guarding against, whom better than these four?"

A sudden strange thought: yes, and in similar circumstances we lost Thom Brdar. Better not say this aloud.

More silence.

And some lessening of tension.

Uneasy smiles.

"All right then. Let's do it."

Kieron: - "How do we move those torpedoes?"

Alan: - "Only one torpedo. The older one is fixed, it's too yatsume damaged to be dragged along the ceiling. Yakamishii, we'll move the new one."

Fran: - "And it will all be done by our computers, controlled by Mietje."

>You may proceed, princess.<

>Yes, mister moustache.<

For a moment, nothing happens. Then the screen on Mietje's chair starts flashing numerous windows, too fast for me to attempt deciphering what she's doing.

A loud metallic click sounds. Then the rumble of machinery starts, and hidden chains begin pulling the new torpedo along its rail. Closer and closer it approaches the other torpedo. Can't be long now and....

What?

What do I expect to happen when torpedoes get correctly aligned?

Fran: - "Just a few seconds to go, can't be long now...."

His voice is cut off by a dazzling purple flash. A laser-like beam of light projects from the side of each torpedo. Halfway between torpedoes they clash and connect in midair, then rapidly expand into an iridescent ball bathing the whole room in a kaleidoscope of moving colors!

The whole occurrence is silent, yet my hearing is stimulated by the lowest and simultaneously highest-pitched sounds I ever heard in my life. But that imagined sound is of secondary importance, just a note on the margin. Because our minds are instantaneously filled with a telepathic presence, alive yet dead, quiet yet loudly calling in a completely incomprehensible way.

We are utterly paralyzed, unable to move, our feet glued to the floor. Those of us sensitive to telepathy, as well as those who aren't telepaths.

But not Mietje.

Her mind isn't paralyzed.

Her screens flash from the rapid interaction with the suspension mechanism's control systems.

Our ceiling-mounted machinery (obviously not affected either) rumbles back into life....

"If DFQL succeeded in completing the diamond of its submersibles, they would have been placed at a distance of...." – Fran's forehead puckers with intense calculation – ".... something like five hundred kilometers from each other, tabarnaque. I'm certain their connecting effect would have been much weaker."

"You're right, hub. I believe likewise. The whole system must have been designed not to attract our attention."

"Exactly, calisse de merde, or their tactics don't make any sense at all."

"And we still agree that they tried to design a telepathic communication device which could penetrate the rocky mass of our massive Volcano Massif and reach to the aliens bellow our feet living under them?"

"Nothing else makes sense, mon General."

"Why?"

"Why putz why?"

"Well, those DFQL priests are the avatars of the aliens below our feet. It stands to reason that they already communicate with each other at will. Why need this new communicating device, especially something that large?"

Fran remains silent.

He doesn't know.

Neither do I.

Again, as Fran pointed out, the strange alien logic baffles us.

"Mietje showed me her projections of the completed system. She believes that with all four torpedoes connected, the telepathic...."

I stop, again searching for the right word.

"Beam, Marka mu? Wave? Pulse?"

"Fran, that's it. Pulse. The perfect word, thank you."

"I saw it too, bre. I mean, Mietje's extrapolation. She predicted that it would have curved downwards following the logarithmic scale. Once it got concentrated in a single point, it would have been a powerful method of communication, easily able to transfix our whole planet."

"Entirely telepathic though."

"I see what you're hinting at. We did uncover DFQL invading our internet and intranet, shapeshifting, employing hyper advanced technology we can't fully comprehend, performing some astonishing feats of spying, and manipulating people with perfect precision, there including their and our own. Yet, Marka mu, we never experienced direct telepathy from any recognized DFQL agent."

"Until now."

"Yes, and no, da and ne, ochen balshoy. We have now experienced telepathic activity from their machinery. What if...."

What if.

Even Fran balks at saying his thought aloud (but he already shared it with me). What if DFQL people aren't telepaths themselves, but require telepathic machinery to do their telepathy for them?

I sigh, a very heavy gut-wrenching sigh, which remains soundless in this noisy Kamov Ka-62 of the Newlands Coastguard taking us back to the GHQ: - “They might need telepathic machines to do their telepathy for them?”

Fran nods.

“What a grand thought. It would make their level of control of the physical matter even more advanced than we thought.”

“Indeed. Which means that they are even more powerful enemies than we thought, dormi mecum.”

I pause.

“Are they, after all, our enemies?”

“Did you mrdat forget Nova Britanija or the Seapeak Island?”

No, I didn’t. How could I forget those direct and completely unprovoked attempts on my life? I didn’t forget DFQL’s leader Zhang Sanfeng saying that I better be dead, either. Still, I wonder. Whenever we dig deep, really deep, really really deep.... DFQL seems to become more of a (strange) friend than an enemy.

I need to distance myself from these obsessive thoughts of DFQL.

I can’t spend my whole life thinking of those pesky aliens under our feet, can I?

I’m thinking hard of a different subject but Fran’s faster: - “Do we all agree that Thom should attempt transfer into the android body with DFQL’s help?”

We.

We the Lionhearts.

And that’s been a sore point, shattering our family’s cohesion. Deep down I believe that some of my husbands would prefer Thom to remain part of Nikola’s being even if that means skipping his chance at regaining an independent life. Frankly, to some degree, we’re all afraid of the obstacles facing integration of an android into our military and our society. That’s what all of us are openly admitting. Deep down, there’s more. An android husband. A machine. That’s frightening enough of its own.

“No. To my knowledge, almost nobody made up their minds yet.”

Fran sighs but offers no comment. This is all so painful, not least to me. Today was full of astonishing surprises. I don’t want to dwell on Thom’s future right now. Better find a safe subject to discuss: - “Fran, listen. A question.”

My husband enthusiastically nods, his curiosity aroused (probably himself wanting to change the subject of our chat), allowing me to continue with my thought.

"I recently found out that Newlands is the only operator of Kamov Ka-62 helicopters in the world! That came as such a surprise since they do seem to be giving us stellar performance. I mean, they are really good, great even. Why aren't the other countries buying them from those pesky Ruskies? How come?"

Fran chuckles, the sound of his mirth drowned by the noise of mighty helices thundering above our heads. He probably expected another cloak and dagger question. To him, this one must appear like child's play: - "Well, you're right hub, tabarnaque. The proper Russian military model is Kamov Ka-60. They decided to develop the Ka-62....

(his arms flail around pointing at the helicopter we're in)

.... as a civilian model.

But it proved beshoor unreliable, so they built only a few, mostly as experimental platforms. As far as I mrdat know, for their own purposes, they are still trying to develop their chopper further.

Their central problem is the turboshaft for its Saturn RD-600V engines.

I don't think they solved it yet, bre.

One of those experimental Ka-62s got shown on Newlands. Our engineers liked the promise of that civilian Ka-62 a lot. Beshoor lot! From the beginning, they envisaged it as a military helicopter of our own, Marka mu. And they asked our merde civilian government to allow us to develop an alternate turboshaft. It got approved. Seconded by people's approval in an Electocratic vote. Seemingly in no time, bre, we had a magnificent turboshaft and a new turbosupercharger for those Saturns, our brand-new components way superior to the original Russian products.

(A flash: did someone dream about those?)

The Ruskies tried out our new designs and were immensely impressed. We overpay them, I mrdat believe, but they are happily assembling and producing numerous Ka-62s for us, all but the turboshaft and the supercharger, and shipping them over here packed in crates. Those buggers are later assembled in Titan Aerospace, where our homemade parts get installed. Titan also installs all their weapons. We mostly use the same weapons systems which the Russians have on their Ka-60, so they are prcat happy to sell us those, too. And, in return, we get a

perfect, hugely versatile, half-domestic helicopter, which can tabarnaque magnificently fulfil our needs. Before you ask, we have no plans to export it to any other putz country."

Interesting.

Yet!

What about.... - "Didn't we then give those people a free and superior technological solution for their problem? Couldn't the Russians copy our solution and use it on their own models?"

"You'd ochen balshoy think so, but the answer is a resounding no. I was told that no industrial power on Earth can duplicate those components. Only we can produce them, Marka mu."

My ears perk up, the hair raises all over my body.

Wait, wait!

What did my hubby just say?

Nobody on Earth but us?

Was Fran's choice of words accidental of providential?

I cough to clear my throat and to gain time to think of an answer. I need that time because a dozen competing sentences are suddenly all crowding my mouth, waiting to be spitted out!

"As in.... (I pronounce very slowly, not allowing the rotor's noise to drown my words).... no one on Earth but us, but maybe the aliens below our feet as well?"

Fran almost jumps to his feet but is steadfastly held in his seat by his safety belt: - "I never, sakra never.... I mentioned Earth as a figure of speech.... But that observation of yours, so logical...."

"You wouldn't happen to know which of our engineers worked on those technical solutions?"

Fran shakes his head.

"Maybe it's a moot point, maybe they can't remember where the inspiration came from...."

"So much is happening right now and with the Thom problem...."

I sigh, very deeply, very painfully.

The decision about Thom's future is such a burden for all Lionhearts that we almost stopped caring for our peripheral agenda, including discovering which method DFQL uses to pass those fleeting messages to us which, seemingly, always lead to scientific and industrial improvements representing a net gain for Newlands.

Another thought strikes me.

A powerful thought.

Am I crazy to think of that?

Just now?

But still....

"Fran, is it possible to turn around this chopper and land on Paloma Silkwood or, at worst, the Coastguard International Airport in Camp David?"

Fran appears utterly perplexed, not able to follow my thread of thinking: - "Why hub, Marka mu? You want to go back to Nake?"

"No. What I meant is that I can't remember any pressing need for me to immediately return to the GHQ. How about you? Any immediate assignments?"

Fran chuckles, somewhat bitterly. Which immediately gives me my answer.

"Sorry, Fran, probably many?"

"Indeed, orcae ita. But I can delay all of them and Miki should by now be back in his office; he can take care of those I can't postpone. What do you have in mind?"

"Fran, I suddenly wish to pay a visit to Paloma's 88 Paragon Street."

Near the summit of the hilly Paragon Street in South Paloma, meandering up the very trendy and seriously affluent Holton Hill neighborhood, with an appropriately fortunate street number of eighty-eight, an unusual, albeit cozy property is on display. A low, black, worked-iron lattice fence separates that building and its garden from its neighbours, more decorative than protective, as it's easily scalable. Fenced in is a flat, grass-covered yard, stretching out from all sides of a centrally positioned low bungalow with whitewashed brick walls.

Bungalow's entire roof is covered by bamboo-green Spanish terracotta tiles mounted on a complex, undeniably Chinese, dougong Tang-dynasty-type bracketing system, indirectly connecting thinner gabled supporting beams to the larger, primary ones. Under the roofline, stone figurines of pomegranates and bats bask in the strong winter sunshine the especially important Daoist fortune symbols (I checked, it's currently twenty-eight degrees Celsius, quite an average winter day in Paloma).

Displayed by the main bungalow entrance, three large anthropomorphic figures of Fu Lu Shou stars also glisten in the sun. A

plaque positioned above them is adorned with three Chinese characters and an English inscription: “the three stars are present”.

(I always wondered why they translated only into English, and not Serbo-Croatian as well? Maybe because Paloma has more Anglos than Slavs?)

Between the lowest bungalow wall and the fence is a dugout garden bristling with rich plant growth, complete with brick walls, a sky well, and round Chinese doors carved out of ornamented wood. Some unusual but very oriental plant smells are wafting over from that direction.

Property’s gate is a pillared portal of carved stone, a “que” of the Eastern Han Dynasty variety, with a shiny brass inscription bellow its green-tiled mountain-type multi-inclined roof. This portal displays four large Chinese symbols. To any average Newlandean, they might be meaningless, but by now that observation may be obsolete as they were here for a full year. Their much less prominent translation, engraved in Latin alphabet, makes certain that the owners of this magnificent property can be recognized.

DFQL.

I’m standing by that gate.

By my side is a tall, magnificently moustached (unarmed) police officer, representing part of the security detachment assigned to DFQL’s archipelago headquarters. Constable Slavko Kondratiev is dressed in dark blue pants with thick golden stripes, and an azure-blue long-sleeved shirt with huge Newlands Police shields displayed on his shoulders. (How can he stand this warm sunshine in long sleeves? There are no sweat stains under his armpits, after all.) He’s stary eyed, protectively hovering by my side. I bet he never expected to be surprised today at his post by his very own Commander – in – Chief.

Fran is standing by our MANATO carpool Nissan Xterra, parked five parking spots down the street. We planned it that way. In need he can speedily cover that distance. But there will be no need for such actions, I’m certain.

A man is walking down the path leading from the main entrance. His hairless, round oriental face, with a marked half-smile (but not quite Chinese, not quite Chinese, these are aliens, after all!) is adorned with heavy eye folds and wide, flat nose. Below short eyebrows are darkly pigmented irises, covered and protected by dark sunglasses. I don’t know

why and how, but I feel an overwhelming intelligence oozing out of those eyes.

He's wearing a white Wudang Daoist Sanfeng school open-sleeved uniform, with black silken edges, combined with a black Wudang Daoist priest cap of Huyuan Jin type and handmade full leather Shifu tai chi black-and-silver shoes.

I turn towards my overzealous constable. Surprised or not, he executed his duties well. Let's make certain that I properly recognize his service. Maybe I should address him cordially in a personal way?

"Excellent job, Slavko. Later, you need to let me know your badge number so I can send a commendation. However, please join Komodor Lionheart now. My conversation with the DFQL representative may be confidential."

Without any objections, Constable Slavko Kondratiev salutes by bumping his chest and resolutely walks towards Fran, not looking back.

I turn to confront the DFQL priest.

(Is this Zhang Sanfeng? If he doesn't activate the characteristic iconic hologram, there's no way of telling. To human eyes, all eight Taoist acolytes appear identical!)

He's now just a few steps away, calm and serene, yet his walk conveying a sense of urgency.

Suddenly he stops, outside of the hand-shaking range.

Then he gives me a half-bow.

An athletic one, his body bending in half as if with no spine at all.

While I'm still trying to mimic his movements (the awkward half-bow), he starts speaking: - "General David A-H Anderson – Lionheart, sir. What a pleasure! What can I do for you, General?"

Hmmmmm.

Glib.

My turn to be glib, but my tongue seems frozen in my mouth, blocking the release of sound.

What do I say now?

All the wise words I planned to spill seem to have evaporated into thin air.

You wanted to be here, idiot; now say something!

"Sir...."

The Taoist priest smiles encouragingly but remains silent.

"Sir, I doubt that DFQL failed to notice that MANATO obtained four of your.... eh, submersibles.

(I sigh because there's no way to sweeten my next statement.)

I suppose that you do know that two got destroyed."

"Knowledge that is not replenished diminishes every day. Making a thousand decisions, even the wise will make a mistake."

"Huh?"

(What did he mean when he said that?)

"Not wanting to complicate, you uttered an untruth. You obtained three submersibles and destroyed one. Later, while trying to discover their secrets, you destroyed another one. Recently, you found the fourth submersible."

Hairsplitting.

Yet, astonishing.

DFQL is aware of the exact destinies of their torpedoes.

So much for all our pussyfooting and secrecy.

"I apologize for my mistake.... didn't want to waste too much time on unimportant facts."

"The beginning of wisdom is to call things by their right names."

"I...." – what now? What did he want to say? That I need to be more precise in my statements?

"No wisdom to silence, General. Not until just before dawn do people sleep best; not until people get old do they become wise."

What now? Is he saying that I'm not old enough to be wise or that I'm wise, therefore too old?

The (maybe) Chinese-looking avatar suddenly smiles: - "My dear General, I do believe that you wish to pass on a message to us?"

I sigh, for I feel under so much scrutiny by this one (alien) person like never since my training days as a grunt in the US Army. Suddenly, my tongue starts wobbling: - "Yes, sir. We finished our assessment of your devices. We believe that they pose no harm to Newlands broadly, and MANATO in particular. I won't apologize for destruction of one of your torpedoes in the ocean; it was off course and could have endangered our civilians and industrial facilities. However, I do apologize for destruction of the other torpedo; in our regime of research, that was probably inevitable. Still, two remain, more or less intact. We would like to give them back, return them to their rightful owners. Therefore, I wish to offer

your Council of Eight Immortals to reclaim them and use them as you see fit, whichever purpose they may serve."

(Yes, I recently remembered the term which Zhang Sanfeng, during our first encounter, used for his brotherhood of priests; all right, I just again lied, told another untruth; Raj recently made me listen to the original tape of my meeting with the mysterious Mister Sanfeng and there he mentioned the name of their council.)

There, I said it.

My impulsive idea from the chopper ride.

I haven't yet discussed this offer with anyone; not Fran, nor any other member of MANATO, nor the five, three, or any of our politicians, in government (Nemanja) or opposition (Li).

For a fleeting but unmistakable moment, unexpected surprise lights DFQL speaker's face, in its turn completely astonishing me. He also utters a flat "eeee", almost keening-like, weirdly sounding totally out of place in the glaring sunshine of this pleasant tropical day.

"General, that's a very generous offer and I freely admit being utterly surprised by it. As we say, great doubts deep wisdom. Deep doubts, deep wisdom. Small doubts, little wisdom."

Finishing his sentence, the Taoist priest makes a deep bow. A very deep bow indeed. For a moment, his body appears almost broken in half. Then he straightens.

What did he mean by that wisdom quote? That he has great and deep doubts of my offer?

Yet, I've seen the surprise on his face.

DFQL avatars are perfect copies of human beings. Similar to what was on last year's GHQ security footage, his surprise seemed genuine, but short-lasting, quickly brought under control. And he himself admitted being surprised so should I....

The priest rights himself and immediately starts speaking: - "I will discuss your offer with my compatriots and notify you as soon as we reach a decision. Now, it's my turn to follow some great ancient wisdom. Be not disturbed at being misunderstood; be disturbed rather at not being understanding."

Wait, is he talking about them, the DFQL, their darned Council of Eight Immortals? Or is that meant to be about us?

(Maybe Raj will later manage to solve that riddle.)

They shouldn't worry at being misunderstood (maybe that we thought them enemies?).

They should worry at not understanding us (me?) better.

Or is it us who should behave that way?

Didn't he just say that he, as he himself, needs to follow the ancient wisdom?

Damn!

Triple damn!

Why are all dealings with DFQL always so challenging?

Why did I order Fran to remain by our SUV?

My mouth again completely devoid of speech, I simply nod.

"General, I need to return to my duties." – saying this, the DFQL priest swiftly turns away.

"Sir, wait please! A question for your Council of Eight Immortals, if I may. Are your.... submersibles.... telepathic communication devices?"

He stops and slowly turns to face me: - "Intelligence is endowed, but wisdom is learned. Wisdom is attained by learning when to hold one's tongue. When you cease to strive to understand, then you will know without understanding."

"Chinky, I need to ask something."

Li and I are in Li and Rob's new home in Nake. In the back of the building one finds a beautiful porch which they turned into an open-air sleeping room. We're covered only by a thin pink sheet (who ever heard of pink bedding?). And by a lot of sweat.

"I never asked any of my family about this. I believe they have such strong opinions that it could cause a verbal fight."

"Aha, an extramarital question, tabarnaque?"

What Li and I were doing tonight was extramarital (though, in this land, quite socially acceptable), not my silly question. I missed having another guy with us.... Rob, Toša, one of my hubbies, someone else (anyone else, even a passerby, he-he-he); none are here in Nake tonight.

Worry about Thom's future and work-related pressures made me tired and depressed, and tonight Li had an insatiable, voracious appetite for sex (way above her everyday insatiable and voracious normal). Yet, I strived to do my best. I believe that I succeeded, at the cost of more tiredness, muscle ache all over my body, and a deeper depression.

I chuckle, playfully caressing her nipples: - “No, silly. What we were doing here is extramarital, though deemed normal in this strange land. Not my question. Listen: on the internet I often watch....”

Cutting my sentence in half, Li giggles: - “Porn?”

With my index finger I poke her under her ribs. She gives off a short scream, grabs one of the pillows lying in disarray all around, and hits my face with it. Then she pretends trying to suffocate me.

I let her.

Even if she was earnest, she wouldn’t have the required strength.

After a while she relents: - “What did you watch?”

I’m not about to let her off the hook so easily. First, my mouth searches for hers and I give her a long, quite passionate kiss (also for a fleeting moment chewing on her upper lip; she loves that so much and it was she who taught me that move!). Then I go on: - “I often watch those videos of kids and pets, sometimes just the babies, puppies, kittens. Those are precious. That’s my question. Should the Lionhearts now adopt a pet or two?”

Li sobers up and sits up: - “I wonder, Marka mu, where are you watching those video clips? No, I’m serious. I mean, which websites; ours or foreign? On the www or on our intranet?”

“I guess the www, the internet. The international internet. Maybe our intranet too. Why? Is there a difference?”

“Ochen balshoy, probably da. Don’t forget, calisse de merde, that the Newlandean pets have rights.”

“Pets have rights? Don’t forget? Silly statement. How can I forget something I didn’t know?”

Li laughs, hew clear laughter flowing like the chiming of bells in the warm wind: - “Occasionally I do forget that you weren’t born here.”

“So, what rights do they have?” – my turn to laugh, in advance, anticipating my own yet unspoken joke – “Are they allowed to vote?”

That does it.

Li’s laughter is so continuous and infectious that I’m forced to plant an eternally lasting kiss on her lips to silence her. Finally, to pin her down, my reinvigorated manhood forces itself inside her warm womb. Twenty minutes later, twice as sweaty as before and twice as tired, we’re ready to resume our chat.

“I hear that you returned those torpedoes to DFQL?”

"I did. I mean, I offered their return and they notified me they will be glad to take them off our hands. We haven't worked out all details yet."

"Marka mu, what brought such change of heart? Dealing with the enemy gives you a stronger erection?" – while talking, Li's fingering my thoroughly depleted manhood.

I stretch, change position, turn more serious, less playful.

"Since you brought up that theme....

(DFQL, not my erection)

I never had a chance to play for you the tape of our conversation. I would appreciate help in understanding some Chinese.... sayings, proverbs, I guess."

"You know very well that I'll be glad to help."

"Much appreciated. Li, I'm no longer certain that DFQL.... those darned aliens under our feet.... were ever our enemies."

"Have you forgotten all those assassination plots against you?"

"No, I didn't."

Becoming even more serious, I shift again.

"Even that...."

"Orcae ita, yes? Even that?"

"They once pronounced it's necessary for the good of Newlands and the humanity that I die. The good of Newlands and the humanity."

"A prcat lie."

"Possibly. But I believe that we simply don't understand their motivation or their logic. The more I know about them, the more I discover that they are responsible, mostly indirectly, for our greatest discoveries, all those major improvements we enjoy compared to the rest of the world, all those "miracles of Newlands". It's probably impossible to completely understand their way of thinking. Fran recently pointed out that our logic and truth-finding protocols, except for the inbuilt logic pertaining to the natural sciences such as maths or physics, are completely subjective, an artifact stemming from the level of development of our specific civilization, the historical facts, and the contemporary political requirements.

(I applaud myself for successfully repeating that sentence. I liked Fran's words so much that I made a conscious effort to remember them from start to finish.)

That if you're to retreat just a few centuries into the past, you wouldn't be able to fully understand the preeminent logic of those times because

it was based on different "truths". At least, he said something like that. Darn if I can repeat his whole argument.

(I smile, satisfied that I actually did repeat his whole argument; Li smiles back.)

Anyways.... back to our friendly deadly aliens below our feet. They want Newlands to succeed. For some obscure reason. Somehow, DFQL wants Newlands to succeed."

"Succeed in what, tabarnaque?"

My flabbergasted face is Li's answer.

"Triple damn!"

A long silence ensues. At one point, her breathing evens and I start thinking Li might have fallen asleep.

Suddenly, delivered in the most serious voice I've ever heard Li use: - "I hope you're right."

I sigh.

Another long pause.

"How did CCofGHQ take to your idea?"

"Oh, Raj was extremely supportive. He thinks that this is a capital opportunity to turn the tables on them, spy on DFQL, observe how they accomplish their moves, what they do with the torpedoes, and so on. We voted on my idea, of course, but only four of my officers were opposed. I must say, those with the least knowledge of DFQL and who they really are. Raj's enthusiasm for this operation carried everyone else along."

"You voted for, Marka mu?"

"Of course. It would be stupid to vote against my own idea."

I decided not to reveal my inner doubts. So far DFQL proved able to penetrate our AI systems almost at will, despite all recent security upgrades. It's almost certain that they will know about our intelligence gathering moves. They will let us see only what benefits themselves. Ah, it's difficult to contest your will against some aliens you don't completely understand.

But I don't want Li to worry about that aspect of our.... contest, struggle against DFQL.

I should be the one to worry. It's my responsibility.

Let's change this subject before I say too much and give myself away.

"So, which rights do they have?"

"Who, tabarnaque? DFQL? Your officers?"

"No, my sexy Chinky. Pets."

"Ah, we're back to pets! Sakra, well, their rights: the right to live, get fed, get sheltered, get medicated in need. Some conditional reproductive rights. They can't be abandoned except in dire need, and even then, it must be accomplished through specific nationwide organisations unless it happens during a yatsume natural cataclysm. Or war."

"Of course."

"Da, of course. For your own profit, you can't expose them to unwarranted danger, pain, or any suffering. That's why I said that what you see on the internet might differ from what's on our own intranet. Remember, here the online privacy doesn't exist. You make love to someone in public, you'll be highlighted in the social media before you get dressed, Marka mu. Properly identified. And everyone will applaud, bre, but that's not the point. Make a funny video in which your dog suffers so that you can increase your following, or profit if it's a sight with membership fees, and you'll get fined. Or worse. It's that simple, tabarnaque."

Ah, ok. I see what she means. We would need to be kind to our pets, observant of their needs. But Lionhearts are an all-military family. Our workload might create situations in which we won't be able to uphold our side of the bargain.

Li's right.

It's not as easy as grabbing a puppy or a kitten from somewhere. (Or a bird? How do babies relate to, say, talkative parrots?)

I will, after all, need to consult my family.

Indeed.

So.... who will want a cat, and who's a dog-lover?

Darn!

# ON THE PRECIPICE, AGAIN

On the edge of Ceti II Volcano's caldera.

Again.

Like a hugely powerful dèja vue, unfolding right in front of my eyes.

But that's where all similarity ends.

Last time it was just Nikola and me (and Thom inside my mind), hoping that our mission might succeed.

Today it's five of us (not counting Thom). We're all determined and fully concentrated to achieve another successful transition.

My state of mind is the crucial difference. What I plan to do, what must be done, I've previously already successfully.... performed, done, achieved. All I need to do is hurl my mind deep under the volcano and, at some point, the big black DFQL monster will appear and establish contact. Then it's up to it/them/DFQL aliens to accomplish the transfer. I won't interfere in what they do. Of course, I won't, as I've no idea how the whole thing is to be achieved.

Though I'm pretty certain they'll know what needs to be done.

Are they then permanently stationed here, under the Ceti II Volcano, ready to take on tasks we (or I) ask them to perform?

Certainly not.

We're convinced that their real abode is under the mighty Main Islands' volcanoes.

So, why do I then expect them to be here and wait in readiness for this contact?

Because I'm certain that they are aware of every move we make. At least, what's happening with Thom's aura and Thom's future android body.

Can these aliens under our feet read my mind? Is that how they gain their knowledge?

Yes, they're reading my mind like an open book, even when I'm not trying to be transparent, open to their mental invasion. (Besides reading my mind, they appear to be able to access all our data, no matter how hard we try to protect it.)

They seem to perfectly understand the problem at hand.

I'm convinced they're also aware of their role as the solution of that problem.

I'm absolutely certain they'll be here, ready, waiting.

That they ARE already here (somewhere in the deep below our feet), just waiting for my signal.

I don't want even to think what could happen if they aren't here or have decided to break off the miraculous connection existing between them and me.

Sigh.

By now we have tons of data on their avatars living among us in Paloma, yet we're nowhere nearer to understanding their functioning, rationale, and intentions. As for those silicon-based beings (made of the living, thinking, maybe telepathic rock!) in their boiling, violent, magmatic Earth mantle surroundings, who always manifest as that frightening brooding black entity, the Godjira of the volcanic world, we know far less and have no data to speak of.

Enemies or friends?

Friends.

Without any doubt.

Strange friends, with unfathomable motivations, not conforming to our definitions, alien.

Alien!

But still friends.

Right now, I've convinced myself they can be nothing but the best of friends. Or else my Thom is lost.

"Andy, place those two bags by the frame."

Andy rushes to obey. He's moving two MANATO-issue camouflaged tots filled with auxiliary equipment Dr Aldevant Bradley wished to have at hand in case something goes wrong.

In case something goes wrong.

At this moment of time, almost everything conceivable and unconceivable can go wrong. (I can't even start imagining everything that can go wrong.)

Frankly, we, and everyone else in the world, have zero experience in how to proceed.

Sigh.

Courage.

Everything will be all right!

It will.

I'm certain.

A squad of Andy's TPBs toiled for five days, encumbered with protective suites, to prepare this very spot for our use. They used their Labyrinthium beam weapons to remove rocks and even up the terrain, creating a level surface. The end-product of their toil is a strange volcanic amphitheatre ready for the drama about to unfold.

The same frame which held the android in MARC still safely embraces its humanoid form. One (of the only two we posses) Newlands Police Sikorsky S-64 Skycrane spider-like helicopter transported it with ease from MARC to the top of the volcano, suspended between its extremely long, widely spaced landing gear.

A solar generator was set in the first tear right above the frame, providing the crucial power for computers attached to the frame. In these cordless times, thick electric cords still snake between various pieces of equipment and interconnect the generator, computer desk, and frame.

Dr Aldevant Bradley is sitting by that computer desk.

Well, I know for a fact that the form shrouded in the protective suit with the darkened visor, uncomfortably sporting two air tanks on its back, is Dr Aldevant Bradley, not that anyone would be able to recognize him. Also, he's not really sitting, at least not with any degree of comfort. He's perched on the edge of an office chair. Of all the equipment dragged to volcano's summit, that office chair, mounted on five small wheels, seems the most out of place, the most ludicrous item. Its plastic parts squeak with every move, raising whiffs of reddish volcanic dust. Aldevant is

furiously typing, constantly protesting the inflexibility of his protective gloves.

"Gord, stand to my left, but higher up, on the third level.

(TPBs improvised amphitheatre has three levels.)

Your ability to manipulate emotions won't be of use today. Concentrate on the proceedings and help whomever needs assistance. You've already done a great job piloting and we'll need you again."

Master Sergeant-Pilot Gordon McKinnon of the $100^{th}$ Squadron flew our Police Skycrane all alone. Normally MANATO frowns on single-pilot operations but the distance involved is minuscule, and Gord is also a member of PsiMANATO and therefore informed about the DFQL aliens bellow our feet. I ordered Gord to park his Scycrane in a protected ravine a bit below the summit and completely out of view. Even if there was a full-blown eruption of Ceti II Volcano, it would be well sheltered where it stands. After completing his flying, parking his chopper, and changing into protective clothing, Gord climbed back to the summit. Once this operation is successfully concluded, he'll fly the frame back to MARC.

Simple.

Once this operation is successfully concluded.

No doubt can be permitted.

We will succeed.

DFQL will succeed.

It will all go as planned.

"I want it done. As soon as beshoor possible. No time to waste." – Pronounces Nikola using Thom's timbre of voice. The whole Lionheart family is by now accustomed to interpreting which personality is controlling Nikola's body by carefully listening to the characteristic tone of voice and the idiosyncratic difference. Not that Nicola and Thom, being so close throughout their lives, acquired many of those - "Of course, it's a risk. And it may end badly, Marka mu. For all I sakra know, it may be bound to end badly. Yet, what's the choice? I'm already dead and..."

Sam: - "You're not dead, pal, tabarnaque. Not for me!"

Thom overrides the murmur or agreement: - "Whose sakra plaque is in Pesak, then? Whose ochen balshoy ashes are inside that plaque?"

Nobody answers. The truth of his statement is self-evident.

"In Nikola's body I'm not fading as fast as I was in Dave's, tabarnaque....

(In Nikola's voice): - At least we don't sakra feel it.

(Back to Thom's pattern of speech): - Da. We don't feel it, not yet, but I'm still fading. Dr Panj showed us those objective MARC tests. Halleluiah chance, only one percent since I transferred into Nikola, and it's not an even curve.

(Nikola's voice): - Hiljadu mu mučica, those curves go up and down.

(Thom's voice): - But what's the future? To wait until I fade too much to be able to control that robot? Nyet, I say. Transfer me ochen balshoy right now and I'll wrangle that machine up and make you all proud of your putz husband!"

I was in MARC for a demonstration how their android performed. Controlled from computer consoles, connected by long, snaking cables to various equipment, it walked, jumped (without any running start, a world record in long jump in its first attempt), mimicked firing a weapon, even lifted heavy equipment. All it did was amazing, yet completely inhuman, completely mindless. That android was still only a machine obeying remotely delivered human commands. No one could guess how it would perform if a human mind was directing it through its positronic brain. And no one could think of a test which would effectively demonstrate that situation.

Ultimately, we were asking Thom to spend the rest of his life trapped inside an untested machine. How could any of us suggest that with any certainty of success? On the other hand, inaction would mean, without any doubt, the final and irrevocable death of Thom. But not immediately! He would have a year or two, and who knows what our scientists could accomplish in that time. How to balance such risks?

(Thom's voice): - "I prcat perfectly know that all six of you voted for postponement....

(Nikola's voice): - Being inside me, he could hardly miss our vote, tabarnaque.

(Thom's voice): - Of course not. But, orcae ita, I'm asking you to vote again. I'm asking you to let me try, even though none of you would give me an immediate green light. Try to transfer as soon as possible. Marka mu, A-S-A-P, in a day or two if possible....

(Nikola's voice): - As far as I understand the process, as soon as MARC can haul all the necessary equipment to the top of their volcano....

(Thom's voice): - Da, yes, ochen balshoy, orcae ita, yes, yes, yes!"

My eyes switch to the person closest to me.

Nikola.

(Well, just another space suit with diving tanks on its back, but I know without any doubt that's my Nikola.)

By a strange coincidence, the sun suddenly momentarily escapes shadows caused by toxic vapors rising from the grotto. His visor becomes completely transparent. Our eyes lock. All I can sense is full determination and full confidence.

At the end, with heavy hearts, we voted, six to zero, to let Thom try. Actually, that's wrong. Five of us gave him our blessing. By then Nikola was swept by Thom's enthusiasm and the urgency of the moment and converted into an avid supporter of Thom's position, so his yes was really meant from his heart.

Somehow, without any evidence I could point at, any explanation to what I was feeling (and why), I felt that someone.... SOMETHING outside our family was urging us all, pushing us all, to approve the attempt.

Strange and completely irrational. Probably just my fear of venturing into a situation completely unknown to humanity.

>You both ready?<

>Indeed, hub. Can't wait!< - answers Thom's mental voice with supreme optimism.

"Putz indeed" – pronounces Nikola, his voice amplified by suite's loudspeakers.

I make a fist and shake it to show my own determination and expectation of success.

Success.

There must be a success.

Not any success.

THE success.

The full success.

Thom's life is at risk.

There can be no failure.

(What about a partial success? Which outcome would qualify as a glass half full? Or would be considered as a half-failure? No, I can't even think of such outcome. Everything other than full, total, hundred percent success is a failure.)

Nikola returns the gesture: - "Whenever you're ready, Marka mu. Let's make the wonder happen."

Yes.

Nikola's right.

Let's make the wonder happen.

I step one step forward, even closer to the dangerous edge. Fearlessly, Nikola immediately follows suit.

Despite volcano's deadly proximity, Raj's recording device is still perfectly working. Last check before the (mental) plunge: - "We're ready. Any last cautions?"

Raj answers almost immediately: - "Negative, tabarnaque, from the Cosmodrome. Our satellites show no increase of volcano's activity, and the weather remains perfect. You have green light to proceed.

(pause)

Good luck!"

My moustache stretches in a heartfelt smile. Thank you, my friend.

Fran answers with a bit of hesitation, as if he's checking something, partially turned away from his microphone: - "Green light from the GHQ as well. No indication of any increase in tectonic activity. Go for it, bre. Good luck, hubbies."

No increase in tectonic activity.

Presumably, when they (DFQL aliens) travel from our Main Islands to Cety II there's no increase of tectonic activity. Unlike when they had to rush off to Benghazi (to do what exactly?), causing all those earthquakes.

Or none of that is true.

Maybe our conclusion about their behavior is poppycock.

I've no inkling of their underground method of propulsion.

"All right, everyone. Hold your station. Be ready to react as planned. On my count of three.... Three.... Two.... One...."

>Nikola, Thom. Brace yourself. Here we go.<

I close my eyes and almost immediately sense my spirit effortlessly separate from my body.

For a moment, I cherish the unparalleled freedom of being bodyless, my aura spreading in all directions. I briefly touch Nikola's mind, both himself and Thom tight with ebullient anticipation, exuding full readiness.

Next, I "float" over the volcano. Heat, stench, toxic gases.... I don't feel any of those. I'm certain they are there, all around me, surrounding me, penetrating my spirit, filling the space my spirit takes. Yet, they can't touch me, they can't hurt me.

What can't be felt, doesn't exist.

Therefore, I ignore it all.

Now for the big dive.

I "jump" downwards.

I hurl myself into the grotto.

I send my mind in the downwards direction.

I accelerate downwards, towards the boiling lava lake eternally spilling over volcano's southern lip.

I dive downwards.

I dive.

Probably none of these expressions can fully describe what I'm doing and how it feels. No downwards exists for an aura free of its body. There's no gravitational pull like in a normal jump. There's.... nothing. Just my will shaping my path.

I splash into the magma lake.

I don't splash at all.

There's no splash.

My aura doesn't in any way interact with the physical world surrounding it.

I seamlessly transit from floating through the air to floating inside the liquified stone.

Here, it must be scorching hot.

But I don't feel that heat.

I know it's there; it must be there.

I will myself to continue downwards: deeper, deeper, deeper.

Then, earlier than expected....

Fear!

Horror!

The black DFQL monster is already here, so close to the grotto, so close to the surface, smothering me from all directions, completely surrounding me!

I'm trapped!

I can't avoid touch, there's no space to distance myself, I can't....

Unexpected, unlooked for, surprising calm.

Peace.

And determination.

For a moment I feel the presence of an infinite intellect with strong purpose.

(Yes, shouts my subconscious. Yes. They were ready. They were prepared. They are already here. They know what needs to be done.)

Then, as my soul plunges ever further into the hot hell, it's all gone; the black monster is somewhere above me, between my aura and the people standing on the crater's lip. Somehow, I passed right through it.

The realization firms up, bolstering my spirit: it knows what must be done / they know what must be done. (I always feel the presence of a single black monster, the terrifying volcanic Godjira, but my mind is aware that it's eight aliens somehow bunched together.)

Whatever.

I circle around, avoiding the course which would carry me through the black monster again. I need to be up there, to support Nikola and Thom (if any support is needed).

I try to reach out.

I try to determine whether Thom and Nikola are now separated, or still together in one body.

Its difficult.

I fail.

I can't tell.

I need to be up there, to see for myself.

I float up, up, through crater's side.

Sunshine again.

I glide up the slope.

Up, over the rugged terrain.

Up, through the lava timelessly flowing towards the ocean.

Up through the toxic vapors which would dissolve unprotected human flesh.

There they are.

Five human shapes (including my body, rigidly upright).

And an android in a frame.

And lots of equipment.

There's a busy anthill not far from the park chess table Fran and I are occupying. There are thousands of tiny black ants busying themselves over their tiny, a couple of inches tall, volcano-shaped mound with three distinct openings, all continuously moving up and down, in and out, chaotically proceeding in all directions at the same time.

Thousands? Probably not. How can you count ants?

Hundreds probably.

But they are numerous.

And undeniably alive, busy with their ant shenanigans, whatever those are. Indifferent to the broader picture, unconcerned with where they live and what's happening around them.

Yet they are undeniably alive.

My Thom is undeniably dead.

Where's the justice in this world?

I'm losing this chess game.

Yes, I do play chess. But Fran is a better player. Occasionally I manage to surprise him with a novel approach, but not today.

I learned to play chess during my time as an US Army officer in Afghanistan, of all the places. Despite the incomparable poverty, the sets were readily available in many settlements we visited (probably as one of those reactions to the oppression of the Taliban time in power when chess was forbidden). And chess proved an easy-to-build bridge between us, the liberators (invaders), and the local population (male; you wouldn't see their women anywhere, not in those faraway villages heavily indoctrinated with Islam, as they were kept locked inside their homes). After I married Fran (and all the other Lionhearts), I discovered his passion for chess. After easily loosing the initial dozen games, I got convinced of his superiority. That spurned me into learning more about the game, in my precious spare time. I concentrated on the knowhow necessary to conduct correct openings, providing solid tactical footing for the reminder of the game.

For once, it happened to be an easy day in the GHQ. Therefore, during our lunch break, Fran and I decided to visit New Belgrade's vast River Park, a specific location in its heart near the Lower River Beach, hugging the shore of the playful New Belgrade River (Fran just explained that its original name was Nova Sava River, but that turned to be problematic for the community's early English-speaking inhabitants to adopt, hence the speedy change to its present name). Throughout that particular breezy and well shaded area, overlooking the swift but shallow river, were placed numerous tables dedicated to chess. A nearby hut is equipped with the necessary sets of white and black pieces and even chess clocks for lease (for an astoundingly small fee). Other nearby huts sell food and refreshments.

That setting proved to be a moment of bliss Fran and I shared whenever possible. Today, it's also a bit of relaxation from work and relief

of sadness while waging the thousand-years-old war of white versus the black.

Perfect.

Today, being white (determined by a schedule residing in Fran's tablet), I aimed at playing the ageless Spanish game, trying to drive Fran into its variant known as the Steinitz defense, whose weaknesses I (presume that I) know how to exploit. Somehow Fran beat me to it. After half a dozen moves, our game suddenly started resembling the famed Sicilian defense, its complicated Najdorf variation which I never mastered. For my fifteenth move Fran allowed me additional time to think by completely stopping our clock (we also needed to discuss some MANATO trade secrets).

While talking shop, I carefully appraised the board. What the hell? How did Fran conjure this game to morph into the Caro-Kann defense, its sublime Panov-Botvinnik attack form?

(Everyone, and I predominantly there mean Fran, knows that I'm lousy at Caro-Kann.)

That's when it dawned on me that I'll lose. And that brought thoughts of Thom, my poor Thom. Notwithstanding being white, I decided to retreat and build an impenetrable fortress, MANATO-style, around my king.

I needn't always aspire to win.

Nor is it written in stone that I must lose.

Let's this time aim at a draw.

A dozen (or two) moves later, Fran suddenly dangled a bait. He exposed his queen. And the whole side of his board where his queen resided.

On purpose or by mistake?

I tried to calculate five or six moves ahead. There was a glimpse of light glowing at the proverbial end of the tunnel.

A chance for victory, no less!

For once, Fran did make a big mistake. If I advance forward with my pawns, supported by my rocks and a bishop, I could force the surrender of his queen or, even better, a promotion of a pawn or two!

And victory!

I pounced.

For a couple of moves it all went fine, my plan obviously working. I forced unanswered surrender of a pawn, and all my assets were inexorably advancing.

Then Fran struck back.

It was all a trap.

A well-designed trap.

My long queenside castling suddenly felt enormously exposed. As I helplessly analyzed (by now I was reduced to the role of spectator, all my moves forced), the weakened defenses around my king speedily crumbled.

With each successful move of the black pieces, I thought less of chess and my worsening situation. I thought more of Thom. Of his death. Of my king's impending (figurative) death.

Then I spotted the ants.

A long time ago, Nikola and Fanta educated me about the abundance of insect life on Newlands. Many were purposefully imported, such as the bees and silkworms, while numerous species unintendedly arrived with people, their pets, and their cargo. Some suffered in their new abode and perished; the others gained a foothold and flourished. Ants, such as these, must have been stowaways because nobody particularly wanted them here.

Yet, they live and multiply.

And my Thom is dead.

>I'm here! I'm here!< - bellows Thom's mind, unmistakeably from the direction of the android shining with illusionary red flame as it mirrors the nearby volcanic tumult.

"I'm here! I'm here!" – bellows the voice of the android.

The transfer is accomplished!

So fast!

I can't believe it!

It's done, it's done, it's done!

We have succeeded!

We have won!

Thom now has a future!

Then I notice Nicola crouching, his left knee on the ground, as if trying to maintain his balance.

He appears shrunken, feeble, endangered, debilitated (I've never seen him so week), as if the loss of Thom's aura greatly weakened him.

(For a moment, a loud "why?" flashes through my mind. When Thom got transferred from me to Nikola, the feat supposedly performed by the same entity, that DFQL alien monster, I felt no ill effects, factually nothing at all.)

"Nikola, what's wrong?" – I scream trying to be overheard through the noise, for the moment completely forgetting my telepathic abilities.

"Gord, stand by that frame in case it unbalances during the prcat turning!" – shouts Dr Bradley to our pilot, making him instantaneously start running – "I'm sakra turning the frame!"

Up to now the frame was positioned horizontally on its mighty supports, the android facing upwards. To release its constrains, the frame must be swung into a vertical position. This is all part of a carefully (albeit hastily) rehearsed plan.

"I'm OK, don't worry. Marka mu, a momentary weakness...." – answers Nikola with more bravado than his croaking voice reveals.

I regain my body.

I can do a lot in my "spiritual" form, but Thom's android may need help which only my physical self can provide.

(What if I'm to jump into the android for a moment? See how Thom's doing? No, that's a bad idea. He had zero time to get accustomed to his new home; if I jump in, I might entirely dislodge him and push him out. Never!)

Dr Bradley: - "Andy, the couplings!"

Andy obeys, rushing to detach the massive couplings. This would allow the frame to slide down on its hydraulic pistons. The android will be able to simply step out of it onto solid ground.

"Cut me loose, cut me loose!" – bellows the android, its clear bullhorn voice with ease overpowering the noise.

Thom has instantaneous, perfect speech control!

That's amazing!

Android's positronic brain and its interface with Thom's mind must be working!

> Cut me loose, cut me loose!< - telepathically shouts Thom's mind.

Another fleeting question. Did we intend Thom's android to be telepathic? I don't believe so. I can't remember anyone mentioning telepathy. Ever! Yet, Thom now obviously is. Is that the repercussion of sharing my mind? Did my ability somehow rub off on him? Will he now be able to do other feats I can accomplish? Alternately, did he acquire his

newly found telepathy while being twice transferred about by the DFQL aliens?

I straighten out, breaking the rigidity my body assumed while my mind was away. My hands move. My arms move, too. I turn. (I'm forced to turn; if I'm to take but a step forward, I might slip over the edge and burn to cinders in the lava.)

"Aldevant, where do you want me?"

"Stay a bit away, Marka mu. You're our reserve in case everything else fails."

Reserve?

Everything else fails?

In the moment of this grand triumph Aldevant can only think of failure?

Dr Bradley: - "Thom, move your right leg."

Thom's android: - "I'm trying...."

Android's right knee flexes forward, then back. Its foot is still tightly strapped in the cradle.

Dr Bradley: - "Now the left leg, nature the great."

Thom's android: - "I-i-i-i-i-i-i-i...."

Hesitation in speech?

Interference in the interface between Thom's mind and his new positronic brain?

Just a glitch?

Or the first sign of trouble?

(A feeling of foreboding sweeps through my thoughts. I brush it aside.)

Despite his sudden speech impediment, Thom's left knee perfectly imitates what the right one did but a moment ago.

Dr Bradley: - "Perfect. Andy, the foot straps please."

Thom's android: - "No.... monster...."

What's Thom shouting about? Monster? Which monster? The monster in the volcano? The alien telepathic Godjira? Or is he trying to indicate something else wrong?

Andy works fast and android's left foot is in no time free. Then he gets stuck releasing the right strap: - "Gord!"

Master Sergeant-Pilot Gordon McKinnon joins him. They work for thirty seconds, and android's right foot is freed with a clang.

Thom's android resembles the painting of the Vitruvian Man. Its hands are still tied by strapping which secured them during the helicopter transport.

Dr Bradley: - "The hands, please."

Nikola joins Andy and Gord. Andy takes the left hand's strap while Nikola and Gord attack the right.

Thom's android roars above them: - "Free.... meew.... oo.... nster!"

Suddenly, Nikola succeeds. Android's left hand is free.

And everything happens with blinding speed; in no more than five seconds all hell breaks lose!

"Check."

Fran's castle is threatening my king. I take a deep breath and study my position.

Waterloo.

Perl Harbor.

Kursk.

Hiroshima.

My position is hopeless. I can't see how to squirm out of trouble. I must play a move.... something, though. But what? Think! Finally, I temporarily interpose one of the rare pawns I still own between Fran's castle and my king.

Fran's fingers hover over the board. It appears he intends to move his other castle, then he aims for a bishop. At the end, his hand lands on his remaining knight. Well before he moves his piece, his intention dawns on me; with ease, I can predict his next move. Damn, that's a bad one; I haven't seen that one coming!

(I could have blocked it. Two moves ago, it would have been so simple. Stupid of me.)

"Check."

This time it's not just a simple check. That knight has also put my last castle in jeopardy. By default, my move is forced; I must move my king. I'll slide it next to my castle. That castle is a goner, yes, but at least I'll have the satisfaction of dispatching Fran's awful knight.

As I'm moving my king, accomplishing the double goal of getting out of check and ascertaining demise of Fran's piece, I notice a fleeting smile rustling Fran's moustache.

Oh-oh! That always means trouble! (For me, of course.)

That's Fran's victory smile.

"You didn't notice, Marka mu?"

"Notice what?"

"The checkmate."

My heart stops for a moment, skips a beat: - "Checkmate? No way. Show me!"

Fran grabs his other castle and lifts it into the air: - "Way. Checkmate."

His castle lands on the other side of the board.

I blink.

Checkmate.

Can I move my king out of trouble?

No. Nowhere to go.

Can I interpose some other piece to shield my king?

Maybe, maybe, what about....

Nope, nope, nope. Goddamn! No, can't interpose anything.

Suddenly, I'm furious.

My Thom is dead. Those ants are alive. And Fran checkmated me.

What an awful day this is.

I kick my king flying to Fran's side, en route knocking a couple of pieces completely off the board.

My husband is watching impassively: - "Not accustomed to loosing?"

I sure am! At least, by now I should be. You always win.

I bite down my spiteful reply. I concentrate on a wiser repost, regaining a bit of my customary perkiness: - "MANATO never loses."

"True."

Silence.

Quiet.

We should be getting up, collecting the pieces, packing them, returning them (and our clock) to the hut (and returning to work).

Yet, we both sit there, both quiet, pensive, silent.

The silence is too painful to bear.

"Fran, how could have we miscalculated so badly?"

With the power of Thor's hammer, android's left arm flies in a semicircle (accompanied by the thunder of crushed air) and smashes into that part of frame still strapped to its right hand. With the utter astonishment, I notice Nikola being thrown a dozen feet into the air, landing among rocks precariously positioned near the caldera's edge.

A heavy thud accompanies his fall.

Is he all right?

Is he hurt?

No time to find out!

The impact of android's indestructible hand shatters the stainless-steel frame into milliard pieces like a wineglass thrown against a wall! A deadly rain of metal pellets strikes Andy and Gord. Unlike poor Nikola, neither of them is directly impacted by android's arm. Yet, they are tossed about like dolls, impotently landing on their backs.

The monster we freed jumps forward, graciously landing in volcanic dust with a mighty thump, in perfect balance and with perfect control.

Thom's android voice is curiously out of synch with its movements: - "I.... can't.... help! Help me!"

For a moment, Dr Aldevant Bradley seems fascinated.... horrified with developments, petrifying him into frozen inaction. His surprise doesn't last long, though. With speed and coordination, he swings towards his keyboard and starts furiously typing.

Cords are still connecting insertion sockets on android's head to his console! Realization hits me: he should be able to control it from there!

Not if the android has a say!

I watch with utter amazement as the machine rushes, with huge, perfectly coordinated strides, covering the distance in a blink of an eye, looking exactly like a Marvel's robot out of a comic book.

"I.... control.... not...." – bellows its voice.

In the back of my brain, a flash of understanding. Thom has no control over that darned thing. Yet, it acts with amazing coordination and a deadly purpose (and no hesitation whatsoever), displaying all the might of its bionic body we built for it.

But who's then in control?

Who's controlling the android?

Or, horror above all horrors, is it controlling itself?

(What have we accomplished? Does it possess a mind of its own? Is it self-aware, like in those darned Terminator movies?)

Up goes the right arm of the semi-crouching android. In a perfectly executed karate strike, its hand rips through Aldevant's keyboard, halving it, then demolishes the table into woodchips, finally swinging into the computer console. I never witnessed destruction of a computer from the

inside out, pieces of the motherboard, chips, wires, plastic, and other components flying out in unpredictable trajectories.

Horrified, I notice Aldevant's body curled in a ball by android's right foot (in perfect position for a kick right into the grotto!).

"Control.... out.... of.... way...." – the machine bellows as it straightens up and rips out the cords connecting its head to the shattered console.

Then it looks my way, its glistening artificial eyes firmly fixating mine. Thom may not control that android, but someone (something) certainly does. During a horrible moment of enhanced realization, I can sense a will of steel emanating from that fixating glance.

Which horror am I facing?

How can I win without endangering Thom?

Telepathy! Intangibility!

I must try!

In a rush I detach my aura from my body (I can see or feel it slumping to the ground behind me) and leap forward towards the android....

CRASH!

My aura slams into an impassable albeit invisible wall and is repulsed to the side!

Horror!

Fear!

The black monster is here, all around me!

Not in my immediate vicinity, but utterly filling volcano's grotto, right behind me!

(Unlooked for, my mind supplies an answer: DFQL aliens would be there, wouldn't they, after all? They've just accomplished transfer of Thom's soul from Nikola into that misbehaving robot. Where else would they be?)

"Flee.... run....!"

Is that a plea for my body to get out of android's way?

If so, I can't even start complying!

I'm disembodied!

I need to get back to my body, sprawling forlorn a dozen yards away.

The android starts running, not towards my (invisible) aura, but straight towards my body.

Huge, powerful strides, it will be there before I can reach it, my body will be destroyed, I'll forever be a bodyless spirit (so much like Thom, my poor Thom suffering in that berserk monster)....

In the millisecond during the near miss as Thom's android speeds by my aura, I telepathically scan its thoughts and sense its strength of determination and terrible purpose. Suddenly, its intentions are all too clear.

"Noooooooooooooo...." – bellows the android, while launching itself high into the air, over my prone body (not touching it at all). A monstrous, impossible jump for a human, but easy for this mighty machine. It performs a gracious somersault (just above my head). And its flight continues, on an ever-steepening parabolic course, right into the crater!

>Nooooooooooooo....< - my aura mentally shouts with all its might.

No! I send my mind streaking forward.

No! I know what it's doing!

No! I must stop it.

The android flies.

My aura streaks ever forward, as fast as I can project myself.

Just before the android would splash into the boiling lava, it appears to me as if the hellish magma parts all around it to receive it.

I plunge into the inhospitable maelstrom.

And the black DFQL horror is, once again, all around me, repulsing my attempt at rescue.

Forced to retreat, I find myself back above the molten lake.

Where to go?

What to try?

I'm Thom's last hope!

Strong as it is, the android can't survive more than a few seconds in that molten cauldron.

What to do?

What can I do?

I'm paralyzed with indecisiveness (stupidity).

The time slows into a crawl.

The last hope fails.

There's no hope left.

Thom, whatever was left of his mind, has by now assuredly perished.

Pain.

A crushing tightening grabs my aura, strangulating me.

Despair.

All my hopes are in ruins.

The uncontrollable sobbing shakes my soul.

I retreat towards my body.
All is lost!
All is lost!

"Why the hell do I need to sign your report and turn this hapless Army Lieutenant Slav Norton to our civilian police? Please, Nikola, repeat it all again."

I'm in my new office in MANATO's GHQ building in New Belgrade. Two weeks have passed since Thom's (second and final) death, the android's suicidal jump into a living volcano. Very few of my local colleagues knew of android's existence, not to mention what occurred on top of the volcano. For most of those daily surrounding me, Thom died last autumn in Benghazi, a pain dulled by the passage of time. Not two weeks ago on Ceti II.

Outwardly, I'm trying to behave as someone who finished with his mourning. Deep inside the pain is very acute. Outwardly, I never show my bad mood. In front of Nikola, I can be as cranky and inattentive as I want. He shares my grief. He'll forgive my bad temper.

A few moments ago, Nikola presented me with a file which, whether he liked it or not, he was duty-bound to compile. The Newlands Police asked MANATO to arrest one Army Lieutenant Slav Norton, based on Ceti III, for a crime committed two weeks ago in Crabtown. Our Military Police tried to execute the arrest. Unexpectedly, Lieutenant Slav Norton didn't comply with their lawful orders and became combative. After overpowering his arresting officers (no one seriously hurt), he escaped into the rugged, inhospitable terrain surrounding the tall peaks of Ceti III's volcanoes. GHQ then ordered Swift One, on Ceti III for an exercise, to accompany Military Police in their search for the aberrant Lieutenant and bring him to justice, with Nikola named the commanding officer of the combined operation. Nikola's team was quick to locate Army Lieutenant Norton and arrest him without any further trouble. Now it all hinged on me for the appropriate legal procedure to be enacted.

"Dave, this Army Lieutenant Norton is putz accused of raping an underage girl in Crabtown."

Not good. On Newlands that's a serious offence, I'm perfectly aware of that.

"How can we be certain that he really raped her?"

At the top of Nikola's report is a picture of the Army Lieutenant Slav Norton. A sexy bugger! Pictured in uniform but without any headgear, clasping an automatic rifle, he's confidently flashing an ice melting smile under his dark horseshoe moustache (exactly the same stache as his CIC, therefore me, proudly displays). Another copycat soldier, imitating the General in command of MANATO, in love with his CIC without being able to understand the force compelling him to feel that way.

Ah! Too bad. Maybe I would have enjoyed getting to know this young stallion.

As Nikola fires his tablet to help him answer my question, I briefly look at Lieutenant Norton's stats. Twenty-seven. Over two meters tall - (a rapid calculation on my desktop) – six foot seven; a tall guy! And strong. Hundred ten kilos, more than two hundred forty pounds. Strong enough to easily overpower a girl. But also, quite a striking stallion, someone who might have led an underage girl to willingly commit an indiscretion with him.

"Nature above, let me read his warrant to you."

"Yes, please."

"Ta – ta – ta, this is unimportant.... here, prcat here. Listen: Lieutenant Slav Norton cornered BF, from Crabtown, age thirteen, in his father's stable."

"Thirteen! Not good for him."

"Definitely not good. Yet, exempli gratia, when I was gahba thirteen, I was regularly practicing sex with both genders of similar ages."

I frown. Nikola is obliquely pointing at the age difference. He's twice older than her! That won't help our Lieutenant either.

"Listen some more: he ripped off her clothes, forced her to perform oral sex, then bound her and penetrated both her vagina and her rectum. Oh la vache, she was a virgin, so her hymen was intact; he took her virginity."

"I doubt it says that in the warrant."

"It does, I'm reading only what's written, Marka mu."

"I doubt it says: "oh la vache"."

Nikola frowns, makes a sour, disapproving smile, and continues: - "A bad and inappropriate attempt to lighten the atmosphere, Marka mu, if I'm allowed to say so. Let's move on, my Mo. What's worse is this part: while penetrating BF's rectum, Lieutenant Norton caused considerable injuries of soft tissues which required a surgical intervention to correct."

"Not good."

"Orcae ita, not good at all."

"Did he say why he ran away?"

"He didn't run away. He sakra fought and overpowered two Constables sent to arrest him. Here, my Mo, let me check...."

Nikola searches for something on his tablet.

"Constable Pablo Petkovski and Military Police Sergeant Max Zvezdanić...."

While he speaks, I type their names into my MANATO file explorer. I easily locate photos of the two military policemen. Big guys. Strong. (Moustache and moustache, but that's to be expected.) Also, I assume, very well trained. Not easy to overpower. Certainly not.

"During the struggle, Constable Pablo Petkovski earned a broken nose. Military Police Sergeant Max Zvezdanić fared worse. His left shoulder got dislocated."

My left eyebrow lifts in surprise: - "Did they manage to return the favor?"

"Malik kahell, apparently not. When we arrested him, Lieutenant Norton didn't sport any physical injuries."

Strong guy. Good fighter too. I'm always sorry to lose such cadre. On the other hand, his desperation may have temporarily increased his physical powers.

"He was desperate."

"That's how I read it too, Marka mu. Which, to me, is an acknowledgment of his guilt. Unfortunately, tabarnaque, but there it is."

"His guilt. Back to my original question. Are we certain that he's guilty?"

Why am I so obstinate today? Why am I fighting so hard for this junior officer who probably committed a crime?

I don't know. Maybe because I lost Thom and I don't want to lose anyone else.

"Dave, you never gave me a chance to read the whole warrant." – Nikola puts his tablet down – "I don't need that putz tablet to tell you this: BF had on her a NoNe medallion on a golden necklace. He tore it from her neck. Is cuma liom sa diabhal, she had the same medallion on a bracelet on her left arm. She even had the "no means no" Superman-style N letter on her underwear, ten centimeters across! You can't miss that one, can you? He ripped those undies off her."

"Impossible not to see, I agree."

A year ago, Alisa and Fanta explained the social agenda around the participation of teenage children in sex. Yes, in our society sex is welcome, a sign of maturity and adulthood, and young people are usually eager to start experiencing it as early as they feel ready. But Newlands was likewise one of the first countries in the world to adopt the slogan "no means no". Incidentally, in Serbo-Croatian that slogan can translates as "ne znači ne". This parsimony created two hybrid acronyms: the more complicated but effective NM/ZN, and the catchy NoNe. Early on, the Newlanders realized that sex isn't for everyone and Electocracy made it into our laws, not just social habits. Religion, cultural habits of foreign origin, unorthodox personal sexual preferences, they all tend to exclude some young people from experimenting with sex. Likewise, albeit encountered rarely, some structures on Newlands still value virginity, predominantly of girls, as a sought attribute for marriage. Those who don't desire to engage in sex are deemed to have full right not to. It's considered a fundamental freedom. But the onus is on them to make their wish to be excluded obvious, clear, and unmistakable. Thus, the use of NoNe and NM/ZN medallions, incorporated into rings, bracelets, necklaces, belts, watch straps, and embroidered on all types of clothing. Under any circumstance sex is a tricky proposition. Often there are misunderstandings about consent and content, whether spoken, indicated, implied, or assumed. The use of NoNe and NM/ZN symbols abolished this uncertainty. No, after all, means no.

"Inta shaz, right. But it gets worse for our Lieutenant."

"How so?"

"BF has a ten-by-ten-centimeter NM/ZM temporary tattoo on her posterior cheek. Sorry, my words were too technical, legalistic. On her butt. Right now it's fresh, she got it tattooed three months ago, but would have fully disappeared in two to three years. It's impossible to penetrate her anus without continuously staring at that tattoo."

"Oh my god."

"Da, da, I see you evoke your gods again." – Nikola chuckles, but in a sour way; since Thom's death the culturally unwelcome word "god" often creeps into my vocabulary – "Newlands Police concluded that Lieutenant Norton manifests as an aggressive pedophile who must be brought to justice and dealt with."

"Nikola, how does it go from here? Is the family of that girl suing? Or does the public prosecutor do that? Concerning our civilian justice system, my knowledge is very thin."

"In this case her family decided not to pursue any private justice and is concentrating on her recovery. Which, I'm told, is going to be slow and tricky. It's the public prosecutor who will bring this case in front of our civilian courts."

"So, is he guilty? Did he do what he's accused of doing?"

"Dodjavola, how can I say? I presume that our Police knows what they are doing. If you use that criterium, he's as guilty as mrdat proverbial hell. Maybe Andy and Alan still have friends in there who can, on short notice, further enlighten you, if you need more info to reach your decision. Ask them, tabarnaque. As for me, his actions speak louder than words. Why did he fight the Military Police? Why did he escape into the mountains if he isn't guilty?"

Yes, why?

Obvious admittance of guilt.

Or is it?

Did he flee because he felt trapped, with no chance for real justice?

Difficult to say.

"So, if I sign, what happens next?"

"Sacré bleu, he's flown to the mainland, under the Military Police escort, and handed over to the Newlands Police. We wash our hands of him, Marka mu."

"What happens to him if he's convicted?"

"Well, tough to say. It might be a stint in jail, or a stint in some kind of social rehab. If he really is a pedo, he'll have to be sexually restricted in the future. MANATO may dismiss him, though that's not mandated. Look at your Kieron. Majke ti, this guy might still rise to be one of our top officers...."

I sigh. At least, this man's future still exists, but it will be a difficult path to travel.

"Nikola, I'll sign. But I want to see this young man before he's sent back to the Main Islands."

"Right hub." – Nikola picks his tablet and scrolls up and down trying to locate whatever he's searching for – "Mo, as I thought, you'll have to rush. His Percival flight is in less than two hours."

I sign the professed document.

Somehow, whenever I get to the civilian Cety III Victory airport, it's a scorcher of a day. Today is no exception and even my KGZ uniform has problems keeping me cool. I'm standing next to a Percival Antonov An-148, one of those perky Russian high-wing regional jets I really like. What I definitely don't like about them are their goddamn noisy jets, and today these two are going to make me deaf.

Right in front of me stands Army Lieutenant Slav Norton, in his full parade uniform, his hands handcuffed behind his back, his face a study of dejection.

He's framed by two meanest police officers I've ever seen. I mean, Andy always appeared imposing in his police uniform (and twice as imposing as the Army-uniformed leader of TPB), but these guys would make the milk curdle! I was already introduced to them. Constable Stavros Filikaki is a bearded athlete. His uniform fails to hide the bulging muscles which, head to toe, completely cover his body. Police Inspector Donald Macintyre towers over Lieutenant Norton, not at all an easy thing. His maroon horseshoe mustache bristles with animosity (to the hapless Army Lieutenant, not me; when I got introduced, my name elicited a heavenly smile). On top of everything, his left foot is shackled to Lieutenant Norton's right one. Both police officers sport an array of guns, knives, and Teasers which I can't remember ever seeing so prominently displayed on any mainland policemen. These guys won't take any chances with our combative Army Lieutenant.

Still, my appearance and approach made both brighten up and smile with the utter pleasure of unexpectedly seeing their Commander – in – Chief, eliciting powerful chest thumps from both (somewhat less enthusiastically aped by Slav Norton).

What I had to tell them sobered them up and had an unsettling effect.

Inspector Macintyre: - "Sir, pardon me for sakra saying so, but your request...."

"Order."

Inspector Macintyre bumps his chest once again before speaking: - "Sir, your order, yes. It will completely screw up our procedure, making it far less safe for the other passengers."

"I do understand, though it won't change my mind. However, let's first recapitulate your procedure."

Constable Filikaki turns towards the Inspector as if asking for a permission to speak, but his superior is faster: - "Nature the great, we

were about to enter the plane and occupy its last row which the airline graciously put on our disposal. One of us would be sitting next to the prisoner in an aisle seat. The other would be seated across the aisle. When we're all settled, Marka mu, the remaining passengers would board. Once in Luka, we would be the last to deplane, after regular commuters and crew. Lieutenant Slav Norton would be transferred in a police vehicle to Corintian, the seat of court with jurisdiction in his case."

"Well planned, Inspector. Yet, I'll suggest a change to your plan. This isn't a trivial, frivolous whim of your Commander – in – Chief. I need to briefly confer with Lieutenant Norton. In private. What he's about to tell me may very well determine the course of his trial in the civilian courts, as well as his military court marshal which will follow. I don't have to remind you that he's also accused of attacking our Military Policemen. Inevitably, all of that will also determine Lieutenant's future in MANATO.

I also doubt that you have failed to notice that I came well armed. (I'm carrying a Titan LPP001 personal laser pistol, borrowed from Swift – 1.) I already had the chance to use it on a would-be assassin...."

Constable Filikaki: - "I remember, CIC, in Nova Britanija, tabarnaque."

"Exactly. If he misbehaves, I won't hesitate to use it on Lieutenant Norton.

My suggestion is that you let your prisoner into my care, for about fifteen minutes. Unfortunately, it means that the boarding will already start by the time I turn him back to your capable hands. I already informed the airline that they can start boarding at will.

(A gasp of surprise from both policemen; my statement also informed them that they have no option but to follow my orders.)

When everyone has boarded, you'll take the prisoner into the last row, but they will open the tail door for your boarding. I will be there to help you out. The three of us will have no problems safely handling the Lieutenant.

Now.

One more detail.

When you let him go, please remain here....

(I smile)

....shadowing under the wing, I presume. I would do the same, today is a scorcher.

Lieutenant Norton and I will walk onto the open tarmac (I indicate the direction), say fifty yar.... meters away and confer. You're heavily

armed, so have your weapons ready. If Lieutenant Norton bolts, you have my permission to kill him.

Additionally....

(I hand the inspector their written orders)

Here are my orders in a printed form. Even if there's a gigantic kerfuffle, you won't bear any responsibility for it. After all, you can't disobey a direct order from your Commander – in – Chief, can you?

Now, Inspector, please unshackle your prisoner."

For a moment Inspector Macintyre hesitates, then bumps his chest. Then he bends over and crouches by Lieutenant's foot.

(I notice that he never bothered to check his printed orders; my soldiers, even if they are civilian policemen, trust me.)

"Constable Filikaki, please free Norton's hands."

Constable Filikaki: - "But, CIC, you'll be in mrdat danger!"

I shake my head: - "No way, Constable. Lieutenant Norton here now has only two remaining choices: he can accept my advice and do my bidding, or he can die."

I notice a heavy frown on Lieutenant's face.

"All right, Lieutenant. You're now free of your restraints.

(I point to the open tarmac and unfettered glare of the powerful tropical sun)

Let's walk together out there."

"Any ideas why I wanted to talk to you?"

A timid headshake is my only answer.

"I want the truth. To all my closest associates, your actions are in themselves a colossal indictment, a veritable proof of your guilt. Yet, I want to remain openminded; I suspect there's more to your story."

"I.... General...."

"Yes, you?"

Nothing.

"Slav, I'll make a deal with you. I'm going to let you talk and explain, as much as you need to. Then I'll check the truth of your story."

"I...."

"Wait, wait! Accept this first: I'm able to check the truthfulness of every word you utter, hundred percent! Hundred percent!

(my index finger points at him)

You better believe this, or you're lost, and should immediately run and get killed.

(a gasp)

On the other hand, if I'm satisfied that you're telling the truth, no matter what it may be, even if you tell me that you're a pedophile who simple couldn't control himself...."

"I'm not a mrdat pedo...."

"Even if you are, I'll do my best to secure your MANATO future. That's my promise as your Commander – in – Chief!"

I let my statement sink in.

"Now, soldier, start talking."

Slav hesitates, massaging his wrists. Though temporarily free of restraints, Lieutenant Norton appears more dejected than ever: - "Throughout this ordeal, I miscalculated my every move, calisse de merde. Marka mu, I should have killed myself by the volcanoes. It would have been better for all involved. I was too weak, too ashamed of my weakness. Maybe the best thing for me is to run and end it all."

"Lieutenant, far from that I oppose a suicide if you feel that your life isn't worth living. That's your inalienable right. My goal is to make your life worth living. Here's your chance to help me do that. And maybe ease your way out of your troubles. I'm not suggesting that no punishments are warranted: you erred, sonny, now be a big manly man, as you certainly appear as one, and face the music. Take it, accept it, be stoic through your punishment, live a better life afterwards. Does that hold any appeal to you?"

A huge sigh. This huge, burly, manly man appears ready to cry.

"No, CIC. It doesn't. I've never been a patient guy. Tabarnaque, I'll still try your way. Hopefully, if things go very hard, there may be a further opportunity for suicide."

I'm flabbergasted, but for some undefined reason I'm still not ready to lose this soldier: - "All right. If that's what motivates you, here's another ironclad promise. If you decide to terminate your life, contact me. I'll make it possible to fulfil your wish. OK?"

"Ochen balshoy, sir."

"Right. Now tell me the full story."

"CIC, I never raped Fifi."

Fifi? Some dog? Is he aware of what his crime is? Not raping a dog but raping a girl....

Wait....

Wait a moment.

I remember that Nikola designated the rape victim as FB. F, F. Thus Fifi? He calls the girl he predated on by a dog's name? How sick can that be?

"Fifi?"

"Oh, General, I know it sounds silly, even impossible. Her putz family are Ashkenazi Jews, very orthodox. Originally from Ukraine, I believe. Fifi is a Hebrew name meaning a diminutive of Josephine. It means "god raises", or something yakamishii silly like that."

Oh, a girl truly named Fifi!

Almost good enough to laugh if the situation isn't so serious.

"Even their family name, Baratz, is an acronymic surname derived from the Hebrew patronymic phrase "Ben Rabi Tsvi"."

Luckily, Raj is spying on this conversation. I presume that Lieutenant Norton is still speaking English. Raj will translate for me. Later.

"Orcae ita sorry, sir. I see that I lost you. Their family name translates as "son of rabbi Tsvi"."

Son of rabbi Tsvi? The whole family can't be sons of rabbi Tsvi. What about the daughters of rabbi Tsvi?

Belay that. You know nothing of Hebrew names.

So, FB.

Fifi Baratz.

Sounds like this young man is telling truth.

So far, at least.

I barely stifle a giggle.

Be serious! Laugh aloud and you might cause this soldier to lose his life!

"So, you say that you never raped Fifi? What about her thorn underwear, all those NoNe pendants, tattoos, and all?"

Slav scowls: - "They made her wear those. They made her get the tattoo, tied her hands and legs while it was getting done. They hurt and punish her, Marka mu. She didn't want any of those."

Lieutenant notices my confusion and doubt: - "None of it is about Fifi and me. It's about our families. Our families are feuding since they met upon immigrating to Newlands."

"Is that so?" – a stupid interruption, but better than chuckling.

Norton nods: - "My family's name was originally Blau. We stem from Germany, survivors of the goddamn Holocaust. But my family are secular Jews. Calisse de merde, we always clashed with Baratzes over their religion, what else."

I nod. Finally, the ghost of a story is taking shape.

"They believe that they got me now. That they finally won, an ultimate win. I'm a single child, and with my future ruined, my family is done for."

Interesting.

And so horribly spiteful.

How do Germans call it? Schadenfreude. That's it.

Such far-reaching revenge plans.

For me, Newlands has been a wonderland. So much better than the rest of the world, much more just, truthful, open, honest, correct, transparent, logical, intelligent, educated. Yet, as in case of Thom Brdar, I'm always jolted to discover that misery exists on these paradise islands as certainly and inevitably as everywhere else in the world. It is, after all a common human affliction and Newlanders are humans (except for the aliens below our feet). A family feud being carried over half a century or more! (Well, probably; to calculate its length I'd have to learn when each family immigrated to Newlands.)

"Lieutenant, that's a good start. Keep on the good work. If you manage to satisfy me, your family won't be done for, especially since you're obviously fond of the opposite gender."

"I'm straight as an arrow, CIC. I accept bisexuality, homosexuality, transgender people, the putz hermaphrodites, those shifty gender nonbinary people.... and everyone else. Nature the great, you should be able to bang whomever you wish. I accept, but I don't understand. It's disgusting. How can they do it?"

Oh-oh. Faux pas, my friend. Yet, you admitted being impatient. That you certainly are.

"You're aware of my family, the Lionhearts?"

"Yes...." – suddenly, Slav's expression changes to one of horror – "Oh, sir, I didn't mean any disrespect to you and your...."

"Nonsense, Lieutenant. I asked you for the truth, at least as you see it. I appreciate your frankness. Go on, you're doing well. Back to the intercourse which is inevitably going to condemn you in front of our courts."

"Yes, da, svakako; certainly." – he's becoming talkative. As forewarned (Raj cautioned me about it), I notice the expected confession effect; once his armor cracked, he now wants to put it all in the open; he earns to be heard and understood – "General, Fifi and I have been in love for more than a year."

"You're an adult, she's but a child. That's not legal."

"It isn't. I knew it from the start. Yet, I didn't let it stop me and now it's too late."

I nod.

"She's very precocious. She has the body of a beautiful young woman, all curvy. Thirteen? No way, majke ti. If you're to see her, you'd never think her less than sixteen. At mrdat least."

"The age of consent."

"Orcae ita. We would meet when no one watched. Not often, but occasionally, yes."

"You had sex before this presumed rape episode?"

"No. No sex. We would gently kiss. Watch the clouds, whisper in tall grass. Talk about the future. Once or twice, we went to the beach. She wanted us to go to nude beaches, but I wasn't certain I could gahba stand the temptation, bre. She wanted me to let her experience oral sex, great nature above and beyond, but if that happened, I'm certain that I wouldn't be able to stop. So, I refused that as well."

"So often together. Are you neighbors, then?"

"Our families are. Each owns a farm near Crabtown. It's twenty minutes walk between the two, over pleasant rural terrain. Since I moved away from Crabtown, after becoming a soldier, we saw much less of each other."

"Wait, I'm confused. She's just thirteen, no? You said that you have been in love for a year. Yet you now hint at years of friendship?"

"General, it may sound strange, but I know her since she was five. We were strangely drawn to each other since the first time we met. Odd, but true. We always had to hide, from both families. My putz parents wouldn't like the idea of me dating that girl, either."

"Go on."

"We planned."

"You planned?"

"Yes. We planned to wait until her thirteenth birthday, but she wouldn't wait any further. Carpe diem, my Fif wanted me to get her rid of her virginity."

"Get her rid of her virginity?"

"Yes, General. When they are both sixteen, her family plans to force her into a marriage with a son of another Orthodox Jewish family. An arranged religious marriage. Already agreed and a contract signed by both sets of parents. She doesn't want to hear of it, but in their world, no one is asking her, she has no bloody say. Nor choice, my Mo. Her virginity was one of the signed obligations her family was cautioned to deliver. We figured that no virginity would mean no marriage."

Now I sigh. This is becoming tough and complicated. Fran, Miki, Marino, Sam.... everyone I know hereabout.... would state that it's always complicated when religions get involved. Luckily, Raj is recording, in case we need to iron out details.

"Why the anal sex, then?"

(After all, that's what got her into the hospital.)

"It was all part of our plan. Start with the vaginal sex, rip her hymen, then go on with anal sex. We didn't want to risk a pregnancy, and I knew I couldn't guarantee not to cum. Also, the tearing of hymen isn't always painless."

"And the pendants, embroideries, tattoos?"

"She was forced to wear those. On purpose she came in those NM/ZN undies she prcat hates the most. So that I can rip them up and she can throw them away. The deal was to rip them before...."

"Mating."

"Yup, da. Before fucking her."

Oh-oh. Here comes the prohibited "fuck" word. The certain sign of his turmoil.

Slav turns towards me, sincerity in his eyes: - "General, I love her. She's beautiful and intelligent and perfect. I want to marry her. We are forced to wait three more years, but...."

"Now it's all in the limbo."

"Figlio di puttana, it is."

"Why did you run away to Ceti III?"

Flat negation: - "I didn't."

"You didn't?"

"Hiljadu mu problema, I didn't. We had sex. It was exhilarating. It was perfect. We were both radiant, happy. She went home flapping her wings, walking two meters off the ground."

He looks at me, notices my seriousness.

"I mean, she went home happy, after climaxing a few times. And so did I, majke ti."

"Yet, you hurt her."

"I did. I do like it rough, sir. Dum spiro spero, for her sake I tried to mellow up, but...."

"She's inexperienced."

"That she is. And, during sex, I'm a...."

He falls silent, forcing me to finish his sentence: - "A stallion."

"General, that I am. Such is my reputation. It's well merited, tabarnaque, if I may say so myself."

I sigh. All those coincidences and secrets. Bad luck, at that. Poor girl. Poor guy. Happy at first, both of them, then shattered by the later outcome.

I need just a few more details: - "How then come the hospital and your indictment?"

"Next day I returned to my unit on Ceti III. Inta shaz, I didn't run; I traveled the same way I always do, by train and by plane. That's when she phoned that she's bleeding from her anus and it's painful. I wanted her to immediately go to hospital, but she refused. She said it would be alright. Then it mrdat wasn't alright. She went to hospital a day later."

"And?"

"By then, she was weak and scared, she had her parents with her. Oh la vache, from the beginning they insisted it was rape. When police checked her rape kit, some of my DNA was still in her anus. Then they got a warrant, searched my father's farm, and found her ripped undies."

"Why didn't she tell her story to the police?"

"She never had a chance. Police had to deal with her parents, putz through and through. With her, they talked only in their presence. Hueles a mierda, there was no opportunity to go behind her parents' back."

"How can you know that?"

"Fifi has a second cellphone her family doesn't know about. It's in my name and I pay her bill. I made it certain that it's identical to her official phone, I mean the same bloody Blackberry, so any chance disclosures, even when they happen, and they did indeed, go unnoticed, bre. Even

her brothers don't know about that phone. We regularly chat when no one is around."

I stop.

This story, weird and painful, proved very enticing and an eyeopener. It made me forget how warm it is and how strong this sun's rays.

(Thom, my Thom, it didn't make me forget you, but you did get momentarily pushed out of my immediate thoughts.)

It's hot.

Why tarry here until I get a sunstroke?

Let's finish this.

I turn towards the Army Lieutenant.

"All right, Slav. You told a convincing story. I want to believe you. But I need to make sure it's the truth."

I close the Lieutenant.

"What I'm about to do, you must never reveal to anyone. Under the pain of an instantaneous court marshal and life imprisonment without any recourse."

Slav Norton frowns (maybe with some foreboding), but then nods in agreement, completely unaware of what's to follow.

>Slav, open your mind to me.<

Army Lieutenant Slav Norton falls to the tarmac like a sac of potatoes.

I watch the AN-148 lift off into the brilliant tropical sky. Seeing Lieutenant Norton collapse, the two policemen ran to help, thinking that I've somehow killed their prisoner. It wasn't too difficult to get him conscious and standing up. Telepathically, I cautioned him to remain absolutely obedient of all orders and procedures. Also, I asked him to prepare a statement for the court, factually detailing the events as he sees them, revealing everything, including Fifi's secret phone number (though it would anyways now be easy for police to find that out, acting on the info I'll provide); everything but the fact of my telepathy. To maximally cooperate with the police, its investigators, even the prosecution. My cursory inspection of his thoughts exposed no inconsistencies in his story except for expected minor embellishments (which I gladly conveyed to my embattled soldier). I will use my behind-the-scenes influence to make the court aware of Fifi and Slav's predicament. However, he DID break our law; she IS a minor and he was aware of it. A punishment of some kind may be in order. But she's used against her will by her family, almost

like a slave for a religious purpose, and on Newlands that's also a heinous crime. She should be protected by our state. Once he serves his sentence, whatever it may be and whichever form it might take, he'll have to face the military court marshal. Nobody beats our military policemen and leaves unpunished. But, after all that, I need him in PsiMANATO. He'll be a valuable addition to our ranks. Hopefully, when she turns sixteen, Fifi will still want to marry him. There may be lots of grandchildren in the future of the Norton family.

# BY THE POOL

"I will certainly try; what do I have to lose, bre?" – pronounces Toša answering my question.

It's more than two months since Thom's final loss, his final departure. On the surface, my life is back to normal, especially since most of our friends and colleagues don't even know about MARC's android attempt. Strangely, my wives and husbands seem to be able to accept the separation from Thom with much less bitterness than I. In general, being Newlandean, they accept the inevitability of death. In a way, and certainly not by his actions, Thom tried to cheat his heroic death and almost succeeded. He was valiant and brave. That's all one can hope for faced with the inevitable destruction we all must suffer.

I'm much more torn about what happened, believing we all share the blame. Curiously, I don't blame DFQL. It's probably MARC's fault. My researchers were driven to try something truly colossal, outside of humankind's experience. Somewhere they made a mistake, probably in the construction of android's brain. Seen that way, Thom is a casualty of scientific progress. Inside, I feel like my pain will never diminish, but it's now compartmentalized, isolated, and buried deep in my heart and soul.

Like all other Lionhearts, I resolved to go on living to my utmost best. That's what Thom would want us all to do. That's the honest way to celebrate the astounding life of our departed husband. Hence yesterday's orgy with Li, Rob, and a couple of their guests.

And tonight's pool party.

Toša is sitting in a long chair by my pool in Rad (our pool; family Lionheart's pool).

Relaxed.

Naked (of course).

Despite our occasional sexual escapades with Li Lian, and even some one-to-one lovemaking, it took time for Toša to start behaving in a relaxed way naked in front of others we don't habitually have sex with.

"You may try, but you'll lose, majke ti." – confidently answers our President Nemanja Petrović, sipping his daiquiri, also comfortably naked and quite relaxed. Nemanja never had any problems appearing relaxed when naked in front of others.

All three of us are using the comfortable long chairs strewn around the pool. I made Toša try my newest invention, a cocktail based on imported Brazilian coffee, also containing some domestic rum, milk, and minced leaves of the (likewise imported) succulent Moroccan mint (and some whiskey; rather heavy on whiskey, indeed). Alisa considers it to be a variation on Spanish coffee. Toša loved it. It also made his tongue imprudently waggle.

"Orcae ita Tošo, you will lose." – chirps Li Lian. While the three of us are letting the sun bake us into cinder, Li and Rob are sitting by the nearby table, under its large sunshade, sipping some chilled champagne. Well, bubbly. I think a Spanish one this time. I know that the Spaniards may not use the word "champagne" because inside the European Union that's considered cultural misappropriation. But we can. Newlands doesn't give a damn about such misappropriations, they are unimportant. For some reason, the world lets us do as we wish; as for us, we're certainly not going to dictate to the world by which rules to live.

Eh, what a stupid digression.

For a while, Rob was somewhat restrained around all those top-league politicians his marriage with Li exposed him to, but that's now gone. His huge smile reveals how much he enjoys this conversation. Li and Rob are likely naked, of course, why even bother to specify.

"Li, you're now on his side? You should gahba support us, those who are in opposition, like you. Traitor!"

Li laughs: - "Tošo, Tošo. By now you should know. Dum spire spero, no one will take Nemanja's second mandate from him. Not even you."

Nemanja raises his daiquiri in salute to Li's forecast.

Toša: - "You think so, bre?"

Nemanja: - “Tošo, Li’s right. I will win. But, dormi mecum, you’ll be hard to beat, I bet. Because you’re like good wine, getting better as you age. Still, I’ll win.”

At this moment, Toša and Li don’t seam to be paying much attention either to Nemanja’s salute, nor the rest of us merrily giggling. I catch quite serious exchange of glances between the two of them.

Li, carefully pronouncing her verdict in a deep and seductive voice: - “Nemanja has been an ochen balshoy exceptional President. That’s clear, and our Electocrats are perfectly aware. Providing no unexpected calamities befall Newlands, he’s putz sure to be re-elected.”

Now Nemanja stands up and bows to Li: - “Thank you, ochen balshoy thank you. Didn’t expect such a statement from the most prominent leader of the opposition.”

Li shallowly returns the bow to acknowledge Nemanja’s praise, then clinks glasses with Rob.

“Tošo, look here bre.” – calls Nemanja turning towards NAP’s leader, forcing Toša to look his way – “Let me tell you something. Let me....

(he raises a finger as Toša attempts to speak)

Later.

Let me tell you this.

In November 2015, you will lose, yes. You must lose, Marka mu. It’s preordained.

(chuckling, smirking, laughter all around)

But in November 2020 you will win. Without any doubt, bre. After me, you will be our next President. Nature the great, that’s preordained, too.”

Li: - “Hear, hear!”

Toša seems utterly flabbergasted, rising from his seat: - “That’s an.... incredible complement, coming from a sitting President. I’m at loss of words....”

He shuts up, shakes his head, sits down fast, and grabs a couple of dumplings.

We all laugh.

This whole exchange started when I asked about the process, the legal procedures involved in the presidential election planned for November 2015 (the winner being scheduled to take power in January of 2016). Maybe not an exactly appropriate topic for nude pool time, but I needed to get some insight into our top politics (and stop thinking of Thom).

As today's host, I also needed to provide some food and refreshments. Refreshments were easy. By our pool we have a well stocked bar bristling with famous drinks, and a fridge filled with cold non-alcoholic beverages (and a bottle here and there of white wine and champagne). That bar is also my creative workplace where I concoct my cocktails.

Food was a bit more difficult. The best Lionheart cooks didn't recently visit, so our fridge is mostly depleted. Li's suggestion solved my problem. I ordered an assortment of dumplings and other fine finger foods from a nearby restaurant called "China Dish". To be truthful, its full name is "China Dish Three". It's a chain of three such restaurants strewn across New Belgrade. China Dish One, Two, and Three. The closest to Rad is number three.

That food proved to be a blessing, but also a considerable problem in self-restraint. I described it as fine food. It's more. It's delicious. So far, I singlehandedly polished off more than a third. I must make sure that others eat as well.

"Li, how come you're not eating? This food was your idea and it's incredibly good."

Nemanja: - "Right, nature the great. Must remember those guys when I need to host."

Li: - "I do eat. In moderation, bre. I'm kuchisabishii."

Rob, with a somewhat incredulous face: - "You're what?"

Aha, my dear Chinese lady. Kuchisabishii, is it? Well, this time you didn't throw me off with those oriental wisdoms.

"You're not hungry but you're eating because your mouth is lonely?"

Rob: - "Eh, tabarnaque?"

Li smiles: - "Mister wise General, aren't you now, Marka mu? Where did you hear that?"

I smile back: - "First, for Rob's sake, am I right?"

Li: - "You are."

"Akiko threw that same word at me a couple of days ago. I was so impressed with the possibility of its use that I wrote it down.

(Momentarily my hand reaches towards the location of my uniform's pocket, before remembering that I'm naked.)

So, this time, you didn't trick me."

Time for another victorious dumpling.

Yum!

As Li nods a compliment to me, Nemanja and Toša speak simultaneously.

"Did you say kucishabibishi now? I need to write that down too, might come in handy."

"How's our human radar doing?"

I pause.

Deliberately.

I'm never certain how to treat such questions from Toša. Officially, he isn't a member of any of our secret cabals. He's not supposed to possess such knowledge. Yet, he's aware of DFQL and of PsiMANATO. We fought together against the Ruskies on the Seapeak Island, therefore he's aware of (some of) my powers. How far can I discuss with him our incredibly gifted ex-Japanese human radar?

"Kuchisabishii, father. Ku-chi-sa-bishii....

(Li stirs; I must have murdered the pronunciation.)

Kuchisabishii.

Of course, being naked and by my pool, you can't write it down. Instead, I'll text you."

I take my Blackberry and ceremoniously type an SMS to our President. It all provides a bit of extra time before I must answer Toša.

"Here, sent. You can learn the correct elocution at your convenience. Or ask Li for guidance. Tošo, as for your inquiry, she's doing great. I saw her the other day, testing some equipment. She was beating our Cophots with her range of detection. Quite unbelievable."

General murmur of astonishment.

I figuratively kick myself under the table. Why did I need to mention the Cophots?

Before I can divert our chat to a more appropriate topic, Toša sizes the opportunity I provided: - "Our Cophots.... Dave.... Are they as good as we tout them to be?"

Ah well; a good question and one I can easily answer without revealing any top-secret stuff. Rob is, however, faster: - "Prc, Tošo, they are. A single Cophot can face a fleet of enemy warships and win hands down."

Sigh. More than I planned to offer, but well said.

"To be truthful, especially with the additional KGZ protection we're now putting on their outer skins, just one of them could face the assembled navies of the whole world and still win."

Toša whistles in surprise: - “Even against their nuclear weapons? I mean, couldn’t the enemy target a Cophot with a hydrogen bomb and eliminate its crew, Marka mu?”

Rob is ready to retort but our eyes briefly cross and I manage to convey the message to leave such explanations to me. To be additionally certain I ad a telepathic >leave it<.

Rob subtly nods.

“You’re right. They themselves don’t produce a Labyrinthium shield. Theoretically, you could try to target them with nuclear weapons.”

“But. You didn’t say but, bre, yet I can hear it hanging at the end of your sentence.”

“All right. But.” – I smile – “Remember, they are meant to fight only within our archipelago. Which means that they would be protected by our Labyrinthium Shield. Still, to allay your fears: even if targeted by a hydrogen bomb, it would need to explode very close, preferably inside a Cophot, to eliminate its crew. Yet....”

“Aha, a gahba yet is now in play!” – happily chortles Toša.

“What I wanted to say was that even if you somehow managed to eliminate the whole crew, all Cophots are fully automated and would continue the battle using our SpAiSu and UnS control systems. They can be virtually controlled from another ship. Or from the shore. No crew required on board.”

SpAiSu is our amazing Space-Air-Surface control system based on our military satellites, command center airplanes, drones, equipment mounted on ships, and stationary terrestrial radio stations, with multiple layers of redundancy which guarantee invulnerability. UnS is its undersea extension, supported by the Labyrinthium Shield buoys and the exclusive bottom transmitters. Taking into account the size of our archipelago, it’s by far the most advanced military command and control system in the world.

By far.

What’s everyday normal for us is pure science fiction for everyone else.

Toša jumps to his feet, assumes what I presume is a pose necessary to execute some martial art moves, then performs a fast karate thrust towards Nemanja’s jugular: - “Spai-su!”

“Indeed.” – answers Nemanja, remaining calm.

The rest of us chuckle at Toša’s antics.

Suddenly, a young exuberant voice sounds from the clump of trees and bushes separating our pool from yard's main entrance: - "Honey, I'm home!"

And into the brilliant sunlight steps my friend Pavel Varina. He's wearing a silver-and-blue trainer and dark-colored sneakers. There's an azure ballcap on his head. His cap, trainer, and sneakers are all embossed with FC Paloma's emblem, which even I by now recognize.

"Oooops, sharmoota haygana! You're not alone...."

Pavel is talking to me, of course, as if accusing me of not upholding our deal. I did invite him to visit. My invitation was for this evening. Not during the lunchtime. (Though I did make the mistake of telling him that I'll be home all day.)

I jump to my feet.

"Pavel, not a problem at all, come in, come in. You know all these guys."

"Da, of course." – Pavel's head swivels left and right – "The foxy Toša Popović sharing a pool party with the President and the lady (a mock bow towards Li) ex-President? Some kind of secret convention of Newlandean politicians?"

Pavel decided not to mention Rob, whom I wasn't certain how well he knows. (Can he recognize him at all?) As expected, he didn't blink an eye at our collective nudity (after all, I'm pretty certain that he planned to be naked here with me too). But, to answer his question, better not mention anything secret in front of our currently brightest football star. Let's entirely change the subject: - "How come you came over so early? Shouldn't you be getting ready for your game?"

FC Paloma is scheduled to play our local team, FC Rad, on Rad's stadium, located less than a kilometer away (twenty minutes of breezy walk, unfortunately mostly uphill), at two o'clock this afternoon (14:00 hours). I expected Pavel after that game, therefore after 16:00. It's almost noon now, just a few minutes shy, of that I'm certain. When I spotted Pavel, I immediately checked my Blackberry.

Pavel's moustache spreads in a somewhat sad half-smile: - "I should, shouldn't I? But I'm not."

"Nature the great, your injury again?" – immediately buts in Toša who obviously understood the implications of Pavel's cryptic remark much better than I did.

"Yes.... no."

Toša: - “Da, ne, da-da ne-ne, which one is it?”

Nemanja, speaking at the same time: - “Tošo, did I just hear a gahba hint of malice in your voice?”

Rob, speaking for the first time: - “I believe Toša is hoping that, if Pavel gets injured once more, his Union might stand a better chance to catch Paloma and win the crown.”

Toša: - “How did you guess?”

“You’re injured?” – I wince at the amount of concern I openly displayed. My feelings for the wiry footballer better remain my own. Not that anyone present here doubts what kind of mutual interest connects us, especially now that the mourning for Thom is finally over for both of us. (Albeit for the different dates of death, as Pavel is unaware of the volcano episode.)

“No. I mean, that’s why it’s yes and no, bre. I got slightly injured. My wrist this time.”

In the most stereotypical of all stereotypical gay moves, Pavel flexes back and forth his bandaged right wrist.

“A stupid prcat training injury, while warming up. Still, our coach won’t let me play. Wants me ready and in tip-top shape for our trip to Germany in two days.”

“Ah, then, maybe our Rad stands a chance to win some points?”

Though I lightly pronounced my piece of wisdom, I’m not joking. FC Rad desperately needs those points. Even I know that, though I’m not exceptionally fond of our local club (remember, my chosen horse is FC Tom Garrowitz, this year in a desperate battle not to be relegated into an even lower tier of competition than the already low one they currently compete in). Things are looking bleak for FC Rad, our local team. This season they may get relegated to the lower division unless they dig in and start winning. It’s the exact reverse for Pavel’s FC Paloma. They are leading the standings; seven points clear of its closest rivals (Union and Old City). And Pavel so far had a universally acclaimed brilliant season. However, many are of the opinion that this season’s FC Paloma is a one-man show, that one man being my friend. Therefore, no Pavel, no team.

“Not a chance, tabarnaque. They are as good as minced meat. Even without me Berto and my buddies will see to it.”

Li: - “What’s your forecast?”

Pavel: - “Three nil for us.”

With all my weight I'm pinning Pavel to our bed. He's face-down below me, moaning with pleasure. And not just with my weight. I'm literally pinning him in another way. He's transfixed by my raging manhood like a butterfly belonging to a wall collection, held in place by a sharp pin. I wasn't so horny since....

Well, since Thom left my body.

(Ah, Thom, my twice lost Thom.)

Yes. That's right.

Since then.

And I haven't yet used on Pavel my newfound technique of flooding my sex partner's pleasure receptors, nowadays such an unbeatable trump card in bed. Today, my dear boy, you'll get it all!

I promise.

You'll get it all.

Pavel groans as I perform a sudden very deep sideways thrust, the deepest so far.

"That's the number one...."

I pull out, then rush back with more force, accompanied by a shriek of delight.

"That's the number two...."

I pull back, take a deep breath, tense my whole body....

And forcefully plunge!

"That's the third! Three nil, mister wise guy! What a stupid prediction that was!"

In the middle of Pavel's contorted extasy, I penetrate his mind and cause his brain to flood with endorphins. His response is a prolonged shout, the contractions of his whole body, and a never-ending orgasm (he's spraying all over me and my bed; I had no idea he could produce that much sperm).

His mouth seeks my hand and the very next moment he bites with all the force his jaws can deliver!

Pain!

Major pain!

God, that hurts!

Occasionally I do outwit myself. When I next time decide to flood Pavel's receptors, I better keep my hands far away from his mouth....

I try not to scream, but the pain causes a maelstrom of disappointment; it totally spoils my pending orgasm which I was so close to.

Pavel's teeth are still clasped over my hand and fingers, unintelligible and unrecognizable sounds emanating from his throat.

Don't pull your hand back!

(My whole body, all my muscles scream: pull back!)

Don't pull back. He's like a Pitbull. If you tug, you'll cause more damage.

My unbitten right hand reaches up and traces Pavel's moustache, coiled around the fingers of my left hand.

No reaction, no relaxation of his bite.

What now?

Pain....

Hey, I don't need to take this!

I have powers!

I have extraordinary powers.

I concentrate and penetrate Pavel's enraptured mind.

I make him let go.

His bite relaxes.

I free my hand.

"Never.... never.... never...." – says Pavel, trembling in my embrace.

The pain in my fingers is subsiding. Finally, I can chuckle at my lovemaking technique, those three powerful thrusts to honor Pavel's wrong three nil prediction. In real life, his absence proved crucial; his Paloma lost two to one.

I shift my body (to better protect my injured hand), cradling my friend.

"You never did anything even remotely....

Majke ti, how did you do that? How did you do that?"

"I guess you liked it."

"It was incredible. I putz never experienced such a release. Yet...."

Silence.

I wait.

His breathing is still fast, excited. I can feel his pulse; it's racing.

I can't wait anymore: - "Yet?"

"Yet, Marka mu, we gahba didn't do anything we didn't do before. I always do the same with you, bre. So how? How?"

I embrace him tighter, kissing his neck.

"It's my secret. But it felt good, didn't it?"

"Yes, orcae ita, yes!"

"You want more of it?"

"Oh, ochen balshoy yes, why ask....

Promise me that you'll always....

That you'll always....

Promise me!"

Suddenly, Pavel looks sideways, gasps, and grabs my left hand.

"What happened to your mrdat hand? You're bleeding from your left hand!"

Darn!

"What happened to your mrdat hand?" – immediately after saluting asks the bewildered Cyber-captain Yoshi Soga.

I wave my hand, all covered in a light bandage, as if that movement may ascertain its health: - "Nothing, disregard, a stupid home accident."

"Good to know, tabarnaque."

"Good to know what?"

"That our CIC has those home accidents too, Marka mu." – smiles Yosh. Is there a smirk hidden in that smile? Did the MANATO grapevine already manage to report on the real origin of my injury? This morning I had a variation of this exchange with numerous officers here in Nordporte – "I'm certainly notorious for having those."

Alright.

"Yosh, what was so important to rush me here to the BK Base (my usual abbreviation for "Braća Karan") and refuse to ever hint what it's all about, even over our securely scrambled lines?"

Yosh shifts his weight and winces, displaying how uncomfortable this subject is.

"Boss, I prc can't contain them, calisse de merde!"

"Which them?"

"DFQL." – he turns towards the screen where a graph is displayed. (Or do they call such things charts? I'm a bit confused.) I believe this one is a histogram. (Or is that a bar chart? Damn the maths, I was never good in maths. Fran would certainly know; I'll have to ask him. Later.)

"Do you notice the change of color?"

"Indeed, Cyber-captain. Those bars quickly went from short and yellow to exceptionally long red. A study of dick sizes?"

Maybe a lame attempt at humor, but I dislike when Yosh is so self-doubting as he clearly today is. I'd like to see him smile and relax. Well,

I achieved a fleeting relaxation of his worried face. For maybe a tenth of a second.

Yosh, in a dejected flat voice: - "These are the numbers of DFQL penetrations into our systems."

Well, that's immediately sobering.

A thousand questions crowd my mind. Which should be asked first?

I blink.

"And their number was short and yellow for how long before this chart?"

(No time to discuss the proper name for the statistical method used; hopefully, I won't make an ass of myself.)

"Actually, dormi mecum, it was short and yellow, as you put it, since they settled in Paloma. A very predictable, constant number of penetrations, most of which we blocked. Dum spiro spero (aha, I recently checked that one, it means "while I breath I hope"), we never managed to discover how they latch themselves onto our intranet. No address is ever logged, no identifier for their computer...."

"There should be one."

"There prcat should be one as both NIN and the WWW are made to function that way. I always hope that one day we'll discover which magical trick of cybernetics they use to conjure their sakra wizardry. It would be so very handy to us when we're trying to penetrate...."

For a moment Yosh drones on but I've stopped listening. I have a fleeting, albeit majestic vision. Of a young, handicapped girl. Yosh is heavily embroiled with PsiMANATO's workings. Did he ever check how Mietje logs in when her mind .... (aura, soul, essence) roams the intranet or our internet? The ether void? Is she also there magically, like the DFQL? Is telepathy the answer to his puzzle? May this be the proof that the aliens below our feet are telepathic? (Immediately I remember that it may equally be proof that they have more telepathic machines than just torpedoes; some telepathic computers, maybe?)

"Sorry, Yosh, you lost me there."

Yosh stops, for a moment glares at me (how dare you be inattentive to what I'm saying?), relaxes a bit: - "I was saying, majke ti, their incursions have risen to the tenth exponent, and we're no longer managing to protect any of the databases they're penetrating. I've half of my staff scrambling to track and block, Yulia hasn't slept for a week....

(uh-huh, that would mean since the last time we had sex)

.... and I'm on amphetamines...."

I'm flabbergasted and concerned: - "You're on amphetamines?"

Yosh senses disapproval in my voice: - "No. Yes. You meant sakra amphetamines as drugs."

I nod.

"I can't use those. You need to go to a registered place and use them under control of their medical staff. I meant the gahba MANATO stimulants. Those are nonaddictive and approved for soldiers' use during war...."

All right. Much better.

Still, Yosh is using our wartime medication. In peace. Which means that he believes this to be of extreme importance. Which question to ask next?

"What are they penetrating?"

"That's what bothers me the most! All the stuff relating to our geology and geophysics. Not just MANATO! Volcano Watch, civilian authorities, universities, local data libraries too. Eruption predictions, daily crater data, everything relating to the composition of soil on our volcanoes, positions of the ore deposits, vehicle parks.... They trashed through TPB's files...."

"TPB files?" – not good!

"Ochen balshoy, but you'd think that they would look at weaponry, strategy, training.... Nada! They seemed to concentrate on capabilities of their vehicles, especially on their performance on volcanic slopes."

What the hell?

Yet, one word shines through like a beacon.

Volcanoes – volcanoes – volcanoes.

"They are concentrating on our knowledge relating to volcanoes." – I state very flatly.

"Orcae ita."

Silence.

Since their first trip to Mount Root, we were aware that DFQL is obsessed with our volcanoes. If their torpedoes would have worked properly, they would have bracketed the Main Islands' volcanoes in a diamond of pure telepathy.

Those volcanoes are their targets.

Yes.

But why?

If the real aliens live under the volcanoes, then wouldn't they already know all they are trying to poach from us? Or are their evaluating the level of our knowledge?

"And we can't stop them, Marka mu. They are everywhere. If they sense our countermeasures, they temporarily withdraw, then approach from another direction. It's bloody uncanny, it is!"

I chuckle at his discomfort. DFQL's acts are mysterious and puzzling, but are they threatening?

Not really.

Not really.

"Is there any permanent damage?"

"Well, loss of top secrecy of some of our documents is certainly huge permanent damage."

"No, I mean, is there irreparable permanent damage to our data systems? To our hardware, such as databanks, computers, Gaillon? Or our software?"

Yosh seems puzzled by my line of inquiry: - "No, tabarnaque. No damage at all."

"Yosh, do your best. I know what you're capable of, and that's indeed a lot."

For a moment, I hesitate.

Then I firm up my decision: - "Observe them, record what they do, but stop fighting, opposing them; do not try to interfere. Just analyze all they do."

"Sakra what?"

"Yosh, I have a theory. I'm working on it. Fran and Raj are helping.

(They aren't, not yet. But now they will; especially Raj, who's listening as always, or recording and listening later.)

Trust me."

Yosh's eyebrows rise in surprise, his forehead turning into a sea of creases.

"Do not antagonize, just observe."

"But...."

"Let them do whatever they wish to do. I'll send you your orders in writing; that way it's my responsibility, my throat to be cut if I miscalculated. Not yours. You're just following my orders, no? And send me back regular reports what they are doing. Say.... twice daily."

"But that's the other shoe to drop...." – Yosh rushes on – "We have putz evidence that they penetrated all our scrambling. Not some, all, tabarnaque! No safe way to send you a report!"

Ah well. DFQL, prove me right please, turn out to be friends, not the omnipotent enemies we can't in the end win against.

"Disregard their ability. Behave as if you're not aware what they are capable of."

Yosh's eyebrows rise even higher, his eyes round with surprise.

"That will be in my written orders too. None of this will be permitted to in any way tarnish your reputation. It's my decision."

Reluctantly, Josh smiles.

"You have your orders, soldier. I'll send them in writing. This is my decision, and it will be my responsibility if there's an evil outcome. Mine only.

Now, my friend, obey!"

"What happened to your mrdat hand?"

"Nothing, disregard, a stupid home accident."

If the situation isn't so serious, I would chuckle at the strong dèja vue sensation my often-repeated evasive answer elicits in my mind. I'm in MARC, urgently summoned by Dr Irena Panj. Immediately after the android catastrophe I avoided MARC and Irena. But today I no longer give her the cold shoulder. The reason for her summons is unusual and unprecedented. It's about Dr Lenko Zdravkov, MANATO's Chief of Weapons Design. He's suffering from an unspecified, but very serious medical problem.

"Don't worry about my hand, it will mend soon. Why did Irena summon me? What's wrong?"

(I skip saying "what's wrong with you". Lenko is such a fantastically dominant character, both physically and mentally, that it's impossible even to think he might have a serious medical problem. No, no, no. It must be something else. How about an unforeseen problem with a weapon under development with medical implications? Yes, that must be it.)

Usually eloquent Lenko balks at answering, producing only indecipherable gurgling. His eyes travel from my face to the corner of this strangely organized room. In many ways it resembles a corridor, one with a ninety-degree corner in its middle. There must exist a medical reason for such floor plan, though out of hand I can't think of any (almost

certainly some equipment behind that corner which requires shielding from). As I entered, I could check only half of the room, while the other half remained hidden behind the corner.

Then Dr Irena Panj suddenly appears striding around that same damned corner: - "I heard you enter, sir."

My ears perk up. Irena uses such militarily correct language only in the presence of important persons unaware of our close friendship. Lenko isn't such a person and he's quite aware of the cordiality between Irena and me. (Former cordiality. I hope it will soon recover. Irena isn't to blame for the android disaster.) Who else is there around that darned corner?

A man dressed in the white lab coat turns the corner behind Irena.

"General, I would like to introduce Dr Slaven Panajotović from the Upperland Mines Hospital situated in Uppland Village."

Tall, upright bearing, short black hair, seven-day moustache and beard of the same hue with no gray hairs in evidence, a prominent nose, eyes hidden under accentuated bone ridges covered in considerable eyebrows. Almost a boxer's face. A shirt as white as his lab coat. A white-and-blue obliquely striped tie. Black leather shoes. Young, self-confident, probably extremely well educated (and endowed with a god-complex, no doubt; even the Newlandean doctors suffer from that worldwide affliction of the medical profession).

I stretch my hand for a strong but cordial handshake.

"Slaven, this is General David Anderson – Lionheart, our Commander – in – Chief."

"Sir, Marka mu, it's such a pleasure to meet you.... though, of course, I would have recognized you even without Dr Panj's introduction."

Sewn to his white coat, or embroidered in that location (I'm not certain and am not about to ask), is the colorful six-pointed red cross logo of the Newlands Health System. Below it is the acronym UMH.

Upperland Mines Hospital?

Almost certainly.

Not almost.

Certainly.

I'm well aware that NHS uses those three-letter acronyms to designate most of its hospitals (the rare ones have acronyms consisting of four or more letters).

While I'm contemplating those unimportant details, the other part of my mind is bursting with questions.

Why is this obviously civilian doctor here?

What is his specialty?

What is the significance of the Upperland Mines Hospital he works for?

(I mean, that must be the smallest out-of-the-way hospital on Newlands! I better not dare think, or say, “backwards”.)

What kind of authority does such a civilian have in MARC, what’s his position here?

What’s his security clearance level?

What IS his security clearance level; does he have one at all?

We have so much top-secret stuff here!

Why didn’t they consult me about bringing him to MARC?

Irena swiftly cuts through my musings: - “CIC, before you ask, Dr Panajotović is here on my authority, and he urgently made this trip this very morning. Marka mu, I had no time to consult with the GHQ.”

The aha moment.

All right, I now better understand the ploy.

I extract some satisfaction from her words.

Then the lightning from the blue sky: - “Dr Panajotović is the preeminent specialist in the etiology of Labyrinthium caused malign tumors.”

Labyrinthium?

Of course, his hospital is the closest to our Labyrinthium mine!

Malign tumors?

Lenko!

“Lenko?” – I turn towards our best weapons researcher.... and my friend.

As Lenko shrugs without commenting, Dr Panajotović answers my question: - “Anaplastic Thyroid Cancer.”

Irena: - “The worst of the worst, tabarnaque.”

Dr Panajotović: - “Sucatum tauri, in the normal circumstances three to six months of life.”

Irena: - “But we’ll pull him through, we have a mrdat plan.”

Build another android? Stop being sarcastic, your friend’s life is in danger!

Dr Panajotović: - “Sir, we do, indeed. Yet, Marka mu, you will have to do without Dr Zdravkov for the next six months. At least.”

Six months without Lenko?

No way!

That's a calamity!

He controls so many weapons projects and....

But he'll survive, stupid.

You can't count on him for the best part of this year, but he'll survive and get back eager to accomplish even more.

Wheels turn in my brain.

Somehow, from somewhere, a thought materializes: - "KGZ?"

While nodding Dr Panajotović smiles: - "Dormi mecum, sir, that's very perceptive of you."

Irena, with a special spark in her eyes: - "Of all Newlanders, Lenko has the highest exposure to KGZ, much higher than anyone. And prcat years of it. We always thought it to be completely harmless, but that's now in doubt."

An understatement if I ever heard one! If KGZ can be dangerous after prolonged exposure, we will have to rethink our usage of it! That will force a huge change of all our safety protocols. (Not to mention how costly it might be; all that KGZ shielding we're putting on our planes, tanks, and submarines!)

Not good, not good at all.

In two steps I cover distance to Lenko and land my right hand on his shoulder: - "GHQ will approve whatever needs to be done. Whatever the cost. Lenko, never doubt that."

Again, he doesn't directly answer, but I believe there's gratitude etched on his face.

Irena: - "We definitely will, Marka mu. Localized surgery, some chemo but not much, some radiation therapy, but the main effort will be using the mRNA autovaccines, bre."

Whatever that means.

"But, CIC, Slavko is here for an additional job as well."

"Yes?"

What would that be?

"Well, to check you. After Zdravko you're the Newlandean with the second highest exposure to KGZ. Sir, would you be so kind to strip...."

"What happened to your putz hand.... sir?"

"Nothing, disregard, a stupid home accident."

The words of vivid concern arrived from Midshipman Janosh Zlin, a thoroughly unexpected source of openly aired worry. To be truthful, in all

my encounters with DolTeam's members Midshipman Zlin barely uttered a word; now this almost intimacy. I do understand. My soldiers like (love) me and are concerned with a display of even such a minor injury as a lightly bandaged hand. They can't help loving me and worrying; it's my weird superpower at play, after all. But here's also an unexpected chance to establish a closer rapport with DolTeam's burly, silent, workaholic member.

"Janosh, how did your morning dive go? I was informed that you and our dolphins rehearsed some very-deep-dive cooperation techniques."

"Mo CIC, how did you learn that? I returned barely fifteen minutes ago, tabarnaque, and didn't yet have time to report to my commanding officers!"

Somebody who can't lie told me, Janosh. Agama. You may never understand how much our dolphins can convey with their telepathic image transfers. Though, of course, my first sentence (thought) was just a figure of speech, thus not factual. Agama can't talk so she didn't de facto tell me. None of them can. She just thought it....

"Unimportant. Am I right?"

"You sure are, sacré bleu!"

I nod, then I concentrate on the whole picture Agama transmitted. All right; I just realized that I received more information than I at first thought. Let's astonish Midshipman Zlin a bit more: - "Let me guess. Your deepest dive was with Dolgam and Tilan?"

A gaping hole opens under Zlin's moustache, as his jaw drops in utter disbelief. Then his mouth snaps shut: - "How, sir, how.... How?"

"Telepathy, Janosh."

"Boss, did you sacra read my mind?"

I didn't. I can't, not really. I could go in there and glimpse thoughts, judge feelings, detect lies, but not really read a mind like an open book.

"What do you think?"

"You did, Marka mu, you did! That's how you know everything!"

I smile and Midshipman Zlin surprises me even more by grabbing my shoulders with both arms: - "CIC, you're gahba unbelievable!"

Then he laughs, a clear sound I never heard uttered from his lips. I stand my ground reveling in that sudden corporeal contact, reticent to scare Zlin away. Yet, suddenly, he stiffens and moves back a step. With my peripheral vision I can see two uniformed individuals approaching. They close fast; at three meters away they both stop, come to full attention,

and salute by thumping their chests (perfectly executed, their bodies militarily stiff, but I also notice smiles on their faces – if they had obeyed all MANATO rules, their expressions should have been blank, neutral). For no real reason, since we already exchanged all required formalities, Midshipman Zlin likely comes to sharp attention and bumps his chest too.

"At ease, Lieutenant Commander Fish and Lieutenant Plamen. Janosh, you too."

"Yes CIC!" – echoes from the multiple throats.

"Matt, how come you're here? And in uniform? I expected you to be in Germany."

"Sir, I'm in-between two sacra surgeries. Was visiting to see if Miki needs help."

My face turns towards the strongly built blue-eyed officer with salt-and-pepper hair and similarly hued stubble on his chin, but also a perfectly maroon mustache of considerable size. (Interesting genetics? Or dye? Not my concern.)

"Do you?"

Miki chuckles: - "Not really, sir. But Matt's concern and dedication are certainly appreciated, tabarnaque."

"How is proceeding your unit's integration into PsiMANATO, Lieutenant?"

"Tough but exciting, sir. An unprecedented change of our mandate. Yet, great nature around, CIC, just that fact.... learning that we're living with those aliens...."

Well, that must have certainly come as a shock, I bet.

"Figlio di puttana, I'm also surprised that we're keeping a defensive stance. I'm wondering whether any offensive action was ever undertaken against them?"

That's a very valid question. Actually, a very perceptive idea. Miki Plamen appears a capable leader. In the future I need to pay more attention to him (and his ideas).

"Great question, Lieutenant. A very astute observation. And the answer is.... no. We're not certain those aliens are really our enemies and...."

Matt Fish: - "Not our enemies? After those beshoor attempts to eliminate you?"

I raise my index finger: - "Matt, it's all uncertain, and daily becoming more uncertain. There are indications that those attempts were a colossal

misunderstanding. Remember, those are aliens we're dealing with, and they logic might be very far removed from our own."

Lieutenant Miki Plamen: - "Our logic isn't their logic, Marka mu?"

I nod, a sour smile on my lips, then pronounce in my best Spock voice: - "That's eminently logical, Lieutenant Commander."

Polite chuckling from all sides; after all, the average Newlandeans love their Star Trek.

Matt Fish: - "So, sir, what brings you to our small base?"

"Well, I had two chores. I wanted to inspect the work on your new quarters, and I needed to speak with our dolphins."

Janosh Zlin, in a dreamy voice: - "Beshoor speak with our dolphins...."

Of course, you can't really speak with the dolphins. Mietje and the Cybercommand have developed sequences of telepathic images which can be interpreted as templates for asking questions. When trying to use them, you need to buff them up with your own mental pictures describing the core of your question.

It's not easy.

But it's exhilarating.

I felt the need to find out something no one yet dared ask: have our dolphins ever encountered the DFQL aliens living below our feet (and below their flippers)? If they did, what was their impression? Did they also sense the gigantic shadowy terror pushing out its dark protuberances?

It took some time. Three hours of nude swimming with dolphins. As always, they were fascinated by me, continuously crowding me, competing for positions closest to my body. Logically, as they swim much faster than I do, those spots were transitional. A particular dolphin would manage to win the best one, then almost immediately speed past and another would in turn temporarily occupy that spot. A continuous dance with lots of splashing.

Yet, the strange truth finally emerged.

Yes.

And yes.

MANATO's dolphins were aware of the aliens bellow our feet (and flippers). Somehow, I got an impression that they thought of them as ancestors; maybe the same way Oriental cultures imagine the presence of spirits of their forebears. And yes, their images were dark and large, though maybe not as monstrous as the human minds interpreted those pesky friendly deadly aliens.

"Nobody actually speaks with the dolphins, Janosh. It's an exchange of telepathic images."

Matt Fish: - "Dr. Isaak Garrowitz told me you shared a meal with him."

I chuckle to blunt the sharp edge his words exposed. Unexpected jealousy. Matt's jealous that I spent time with DolTeam's veterinarian and not him. Or them. The commanding officers: - "All true. I chanced on him in the dolphin's pens, and he fulfilled an old promise to tell me a couple of stories about our quintessential hero, Tom Garrowitz."

(Best that one Matt, if you know how!)

Matt: - "Those stories about Tom Garrowitz must be very important to you sir, tabarnaque."

He uttered his words without a hint of sarcasm, as a pure statement; at that a profoundly observant one.

"Matt, you're right. For many in MANATO Tom Garrowitz is a flesh-and-blood person whom they knew well....

(I notice them all getting ready to interrupt me)

.... of course, you guys are too young to have known him, but we have Methuselahs around here....

(smiles and chuckles)

.... who trained, lived, and crucially, fought side-by-side with Tom Garrowitz and Mack McKolins. Their memories, even if distorted by the passage of time, are what I'm after. And they are priceless."

"CIC, what happened to your mrdat hand?" – asks bewildered Robi Prosinac, pointing at my bandage.

"Nothing, disregard, a stupid home accident." – that so often repeated lie now slips from my lips with practiced ease – "You're flying today, Robi?"

I'm still on Ceti II, having spent my whole morning with the DolTeam. I do now need to get back to the Main Islands. New Belgrade, precisely.

"Ochen balshoy, CIC. Master Sergeant-Pilot Misha Zec is my co-pilot, though he outranks me and has tabarnaque many more hours on Ospreys." – answers my buddy, Pilot Robert Prosinac, pointing towards the silver and blue Newlands Police tiltrotor behind him. It's emitting some unusual whining from its two wingtip-mounted, skywards pointing engines, slowly turning the gigantic horizontally-spinning helices, forcing us to keep away and confer on the hot, sunbathed tarmac – "As you can

see, Sergeant-Pilot Zec and our guest are already inside, bre, preparing for our departure. Youngster Edwards is to accompany us."

Alex Edwards!

Rob's scheme to train him to become 100$^{th}$ Squadron's first "home grown" pilot must be in full swing!

"How's he doing?"

"One day he'll be an ochen balshoy great pilot.... sir. Tabarnaque, he has a great positional awareness, always certain where the machine is in the air. Never seen anything like that, and I've seen a lot...." – Robi's words trail into silence as he probably decided that he presumed too much in telling me his judgements.

"Robi, firstly, your first sentence should have been "one day he'll be an ochen balshoy great pilot, Dave". (As usual, I manage to murder the pronunciation of the Russian affirmation.) Secondly, I always prefer to hear my soldier's sincere thoughts and observations, no matter how opinionated or subjective they might appear. Never hesitate to tell exactly what you think. Never say what you think I might want to hear, bud.

(to his utter delight, I place my hand on his shoulder)

By the way, you're now comfortable piloting these Ospreys?"

"I'm comfy flying any plane, CIC."

His answer opens him to the use of Toša's often used countering: - "But? You didn't say but, yet it's there, hanging at the end of your sentence."

(Robi laughs and, in return, places his hand on my shoulder)

"But.... they are slow and loud, Dave."

"Yes, I remember. You like our fighters. Fast and loud! Enough of dillydallying, let's get out of this sunshine."

The reason I needed to rush home was a conference of the five, in our tighter, all-Newlander formation, without the German Bundeskanzlerin, but including Li, as our discussions concern the DFQL aliens under our feet.

"What happened to your mrdat hand, mister?" – asks Li, frowning at my bandage.

"He certainly didn't have that bandage yesterday, tabarnaque." – pipes in the President.

"Nothing, disregard, a stupid home accident."

I give myself an imaginary slap even before I catch the astonished jump of her eyebrows. Of course, Li was continuously in Rad; yesterday

afternoon, and evening, and during the night, and was still at home when I left. She isn't aware of any accidents severe enough to require bandaging my hand.

"Liar, liar, pants on fire." – pronounces Li in a low, even voice, then fixes me with a long hard glance.

For a moment, I struggle. What happens during my lovemaking shouldn't ever be five's business. Yet, this fellowship is about trust and truth.

"All right, all right. My guest got a little frisky, and I got careless, that's all."

Now Li chuckles, accompanied by the President. Kieron appears smug as if he understands the whole plot (no way, how could he?). Francis laughs, as if he heard a good joke. Probably my tone of voice set off his merriment. Fran isn't with us, he's in command of MANATO until 7PM (19:00). That's when Miki will take over, Andy accompanying him as part of his training to gain more experience in handling the reigns of our powerful organisation. Which is why we had to rush this meeting. Andy must soon leave. Andy and Peter are the only members of the five who appear not to have a clue of what's going on.

"Nature the great, do you think we're missing something?" – Peter asks his companion in ignorance.

"Enough. We have no time for private jokes." – especially not when they are about Commander – in – Chief's sexual mishaps – "We must conclude this meeting in twenty minutes to let Andy go to his command class."

Nods, murmur, agreements.

They all know, WE all know we're talking about some deadly serious stuff.

"I'm pleased to report full success."

President: - "You do? Your dolphins know about DFQL?"

"Yes, indeed. They are your dolphins too, mister President!"

Li: - "Concur!"

"And, similar to us, they envisage a dark, ominous presence in the depths."

Andy: - "What about that omnipresent appendage, threateningly stretching towards us?"

Us being mostly me since I seem to be the only one getting to regularly interact.... communicate.... (get terrorized....) with/by that colossal dark

presence. Alisa certainly didn't feel anything remotely similar. What Thom Brdar felt will always remain a mystery. Akiko's mind interpreted the DFQL aliens as a gigantic sea dragon.

Tough.

I shake my head: - "No, Andy. Their pictures are clear. No appendages."

Francis: - "How could they convey it in such detail, bre?"

"They transmit telepathic images; I have to interpret what they transmit. One thing is certain, it doesn't look like any picture a human brain would transmit. The perspective is all...."

Andy: - "Putz screwed up. Nature above, their eyes are on the sides of their head. They do not have binocular vision characteristic of all land-dwelling top predators, including the apes, thus the mrdat hominids as well. Us."

I smile. In a flash Andy's explanation dispelled my confusion about the angles of their eyes. Now everything is in place. Why didn't I ask someone before? Stupid of me and stupid me (as if I've never seen a dolphin!). I was always thinking that the confusion was in my brain, that I couldn't properly interpret their telepathic messages.

"But could you determine the timescale? Does it coincide with our gahba conjectures of Atlantis' sinking?" – asks Peter Schweinfurter, the Curator of the Atlantida Museum.

The President cuts in with accustomed authority: - "Wait a moment. Calisse de merde, timescale? Marka mu, do our dolphins now understand our time units? Days, months, years.... Are they now able to count? Sucatum tauri, how can they understand maths and our time units?"

"They do and they don't."

Francis: - "Which one is it, my friend?"

Li: - "They count but don't understand our time units? Nyet, gahba, it would be the opposite...."

I shake my head: - "Well, I'm myself a bit confused. If Mietje or Yoshi were here, they would explain better. Our dolphins understand day and night, that I'm certain of. They do NOT understand seconds, minutes, hours. I was told those don't relate to anything happening in the ocean or in DolTeam's base."

Andy: - "They do understand tide and ebb, morning and evening, and they note the cyclic weather patterns, which take much longer...."

Li: - "Months, Marka mu."

Andy: - “Orcae ita. Months. Great nature beyond, they do note the positions of Sun and Moon, their tabarnaque angles.”

“Well, to shorten the story, Yosh and Mietje, or is it Yoshi’s people and Mietje, working with Andy and Inspector Wykes....

(Andy nods in agreement)

.... developed a series of mental images, call them mental measuring tools, which one could envisage....”

President: - “Which YOU can envisage, son, bre!”

Well, you’re right, father. You couldn’t. Nor could Li. Or Peter. Or Francis. Or Kieron, today so mysteriously silent.

“Actually, Andy’s much better than me.”

Andy starts rebelling as if my praise somehow wasn’t merited.

“Don’t listen to him. He’s by far our best dolphin communicator. But today it was my stint to chat with them, so I did.”

Kieron, suddenly waking up from his deepfreeze: - “I carefully listened to your words. I also noticed how you avoided answering Peter’s sakra question. Majke ti, you appear troubled by something you didn’t share.”

Sudden silence falls onto our intranet circle. Kieron managed to penetrate my musings deeper than anyone else. Once again, we’re meeting online, not in person. I’m in the GHQ, so’s Andy, but in a different office. Francis is at home. Li’s still in Rad but will afterwards return to Nake. Kieron is in his New Belgrade apartment. Peter is in Old City. President is in the Newlands Congress, not far from here. We can chat about the top secrets of Newlands without physically meeting, totally certain that our connection is secure and impenetrable; the wonder of encrypted intranet which NIN and Cybercommand bestowed on us. No secret service in this world can penetrate our codes; certainly, none of the cybercriminals can.

Well, let’s not fool ourselves; we’re not that secure, after all. I’m pretty certain that DFQL is cruising the width of our NIN at will. Yet.... (the horrible thought).... is that really as bad as it sounds? Or is it maybe bringing unexpected benefits? Are they, after all, our enemies, or our friends? How to answer that dilemma?

I sigh and fix my eyes on Kieron’s image.

“Kieron, you’re right. I’m confused about the timescale. Maybe the mental measuring parameters Yoshi and Mietje developed, and I tried to implement, didn’t work as well as we hoped.”

Kieron: - “Da?”

"Most of the answers indicated that the dolphins' contacts with the DFQL aliens happened fifteen to twenty thousand years ago."

Peter: - "Prc twenty thousand years ago!"

Kieron: - "Our calculations indicate that DFQL then wasn't present on Earth, Marka mu."

"I know, I know! Seven thousand years, give or take. But...."

President: - "Could your tools be that imprecise, tabarnaque?"

Andy: - "Ochen balshoy possible. We created them from scratch; they are probably not yet sufficiently calibrated. It's going to be years before we're certain about our putz calculations."

Francis: - "Dave, I'm not Kieron, but I think that you're mrdat still hiding a detail or two. No?"

My lips compress.

Andy: - "Maybe you should tell us, even if you're not certain."

Li: - "What are you not certain about, dear General?"

"Li.... all of you present.... whether we can somehow reconcile our calculated seven thousand years with dolphins' fifteen thousand is only one facet of the problem. There's more. At the end of my visit Radarion told me.... well, telepathically projected his images.... that DFQL was present on Earth, at least in the ocean, at least a million years ago!

19:15.

7:15PM.

GHQ

In my sturdy but completely uninspiring bed in my new office. "New office" is a colossal overstatement. We discovered this barely used storage room while contemplating reshaping all above-street GHQ floors to stretch the useful life of this venerable, old building until our delayed spanking new Ceti III GHQ is built. It's on the second floor, more or less in the center of the building (therefore not on GHQ's protected underground levels able to withstand direct nuclear hits). It has no windows. It's T shaped, as if constructed of five cubes, each three meters by three meters by three meters. The artifacts stored inside were quickly moved to another storage. Then we redesigned the room and connected it to my military empire using every communication system imaginable. With that high ceiling, the interior space was sufficient for me to assign one of those three-by-three-by-three cubes to Rob and his 100$^{th}$ Squadron, so we're again working from the same office. The opposing

cubicle became my office, the middle cube forming the entrance area. Sequestered behind a partition, the two cubes forming T's tail became an auxiliary bedroom with a small bathroom for me, my family, and anyone else who happens to be in command.

Fran and I, helped by Alisa and Fanta, worked with elan to make it a presentable and functional bedroom, but we also decided to use only our spare furniture, trucked over from Rad and Nake, without incurring additional expenses.

My bed is only queen sized and old (but still firm). Compared to the much larger beds in most of our homes, it appears tiny. Especially with two muscular guys performing sexual gymnastics. Ten minutes ago, Fran arrived after turning the overnight command of MANATO into Miki and Andy's able hands.

"What happened to your putz hand?"

Enough of my customary lies!

"Last night I was careless, and Pavel got too frisky."

"Pavel got too frisky, aha?"

Fran arrived ravenous for sex and wasted no time in getting naked. Then I let him do something I rarely do; I relinquished all control. I transformed into (what they told me is called) "a bottom sub" and let Fran push, poke, restrain me in some uncomfortable positions, and show me his power at every step of the way. And, to my utter surprise, I enjoyed every powerless moment. Now spent, we're somewhat embraced (despite strong air conditioning it's too warm here for a more intimate stance).

"You still intend to get up at four and join Miki for Andy's additional tutoring?"

"Certainly, Fran. That's why I stayed here."

"Do you want me to prcat help?"

"No, hub. No reason why. You can sleep an additional hour, wake up, use the gym, get a breakfast, and take over your shift at seven, ready for another day in paradise."

Fran nods without speaking.

There's a long lull in conversation and our breathing evens out.

"Fran.... are you still awake?"

"Marka mu, da."

"Fran.... a million years. How's that possible?"

Fran was in command during our meeting of five, but Raj fed him the essential details.

"Dave, I was thinking, tabarnaque. Why are we sakra assuming that when DFQL arrived seven thousand years ago...."

"Or fifteen, as our dolphins think!"

"Orcae ita, or fifteen, as it appears our dolphins seem to remember...."

"Yes?"

"Why are we bre assuming it was the first time those silicone aliens visited Earth?"

I'm stunned!

What a colossal thought!

Of course, those aliens might have been coming and going throughout our planet's history, observing its development. If Radarion thinks they were here a million years ago, some of them might have really been here a million years ago! Not necessarily the same creatures, as nobody yet postulated that they possess longevity surpassing that of Earth's lifeforms. But others of the same species, why not?

"Fran, that's a colossal thought! I'm amazed no one ever voiced that idea! Notwithstanding the fact that wasn't what I wished to ask."

"It wasn't?"

I place a light kiss on his cheek.

"No. Fran, what I wished to ask.... our dolphins.... how can they remember something from a million years ago? That sounds utterly impossible."

Fran suddenly sits up, as if I prodded him with a Taser: - "Da and ne, my beloved CIC."

"You're teasing again, mister Second – in – Command! Which one is it?"

"Flocci non facio, as far as we know, our dolphins, or prc whales, or any other putz species of mammals, or any animals.... or even plants, Marka mu.... have no mediums for recording history remotely like we humans do. Nor would our own means of recording last us a million years in any case, bre."

Self-evident. I nod: - "Go on."

"Therefore, any such claim of remembering events from a million years ago must be wrong, ochen balshoy right?"

"Right."

"Wrong."

"Wrong?"

"Wrong, nature the great."

"How?"

Fran absentmindedly scratches his chest: - "The more our scientists penetrate into DNA's secrets, the more obvious becomes that it also carries memories; the so-called genetic memories, svih mu svetaca."

"Genetic...."

".... memories. Those which make birds, for uncounted millions of years, undertake their gigantic migrations; as do butterflies, sharks, wildebeest, locusts. Memories which allow eagles to know exactly how to make a nest without having to learn it, or crows to throw a nut under a moving object to get it opened, svih mu svetaca."

"Fran.... I.... lost you. Eagles and crows. What's your point?"

"Figlio di puttana, those genetic memories are transmitted to the next generation, then to the next generation, and so on, nature the great."

"For a million years?"

"Ochen balshoy, without any doubt."

I sigh. This didn't go the way I planned, but I learned a lot: - "Fran, what I intended to ask at the beginning of our conversation was whether, for dolphins, a million years is at all possible? I mean, in the evolutionary sense.... did they even exist a million years ago?"

For a moment Fran pouts, thinking: - "I do remember an illustration which I saw during my studies. Dolphins, in their present form, and the sakra first humans, coexisted some five million years ago. Orcae ita, some of the contemporary whale species are more than thirty million years old. Therefore, my CIC, yes, da-da-da. They existed a million years ago and probably didn't differ much, Marka mu."

Headache.

How do we prove those aliens visited Earth a million years ago?

"Fran, how do we prove DFQL aliens visited Earth a million years ago?"

"Is your prc hand improving?" – asks Andy with some concern in his voice.

I flex my fingers to show that everything is fine: - "See, no worries at all. Stop being so damned concerned."

"I don't know. Your prcat Pavel is sweet, but while having sex I never bit anyone's palm! And made it bleed. That's.... that's perverse, Marka mu."

I chuckle (as if anyone on Newlands truly understands the definition of perverse; here everyone is a bit perverse – or not just a bit!): - "Andy, it

wasn't his fault. Not at all. We had sex and I decided to give him an extra strong dose of telepathically induced endorphins."

I open my palms wide, in the universal gesture of helplessness.

"And he bit you in extasy?"

"He spasmed so much, his whole body did, that his mouth locked over my fingers. Like a Pitbull! I didn't expect such reaction. Couldn't free my hand!"

Andy's forehead puckers, indicating that he's thinking hard, correlating: - "You relaxed him with your mind?"

"Yes, how did you guess?"

Andy shrugs: - "The only way out, tabarnaque. You must be more careful when you do that to people...."

"Maybe. It's not like you're careful at all. You do it without even thinking."

"My point exactly, Marka mu. You convinced me that I'm doing this, but I never...."

"You must have suspected."

"Ne, I didn...."

"You must have."

Andy's face reddens.

"Huh, caught you. You knew."

Silence.

"You might not have understood the mechanism, but you were aware that you're different. Better than the others."

A sigh: - "Orcae ita. I was aware that I'm getting superior results. Everybody was so gahba ecstatic after experiencing sex with me, even when I felt that it was mediocre or even bad."

I'm about to retort but I let it pass. Andy's lovemaking is indeed special, and he exerts special influence on everyone who ends in bed with him. He should have been aware what's happening, more than he's admitting. However, fundamentally, that's not my concern.

"Andy, how's your rib?"

Demise of Thom's android brought Andy the gift of a broken rib.

"Sakra perfect. As good as new."

"That's good.

(Oh, Thom, my poor Thom.)

So, what news?"

"Amazing news, indeed. The tabarnaque microchip experiment was a full success."

I perk up. Great news, indeed.

Andy, Alan, Mietje, and various members of Cybercommand are working on a microchip which would be able to read someone's thoughts and allow them to interact with a keyboard. In a way, once this process is perfected, whomever gets this implant will have a fraction of Mietje's skills which allow her to directly interact not only with computers, but also with all webs out there, such as the www and our NIN, and all databases and cloud storages.

"Ochen balshoy, you should see Gonzo."

"Who's Gonzo now?"

"Gonzo is a macaque, in Cybercommand."

"Macaque.... that's a...."

(My brain momentarily stops; what the hell is a macaque?)

"Putz monkey."

"Hell, monkey! I knew it!"

Andy seems happy with my glitch: - "Well, he has the implanted chip."

"Where?"

"In his sakra brain, of course. Remember, that chip measures brain currents. To read one's thoughts, it has to be close to the brain."

"Our scientists now know how to read monkey thoughts?"

"Evidently, boss. You should see him play video games. Ochen balshoy hands free! I could never match his scores, Marka mu."

Now I must purse my own lips and my brow creases with a sudden idea: - "Andy, don't tell me...."

>Yes, we'll be able to read their thoughts too.<

Andy has plucked my thought from my mind before I was able to form it into words. I had a sudden revelation. Our Cybercommand is gunning for direct communication with our telepathic dolphins! (Besides, Andy is right; why waste time on spoken words when we have a telepathic link?)

>How? What's the whole system going to look like?<

>Two-way communication through a computer interface, tabarnaque. All humans and dolphins involved must have the implanted chip. One of our supercomputers will be providing the necessary computational power, bre. It will be possible to record such communication, even print it out."

Another thought crowds my mind.

>You're mrdat right; we can't make them submit to brain surgery. They are sentient, intelligent beings. They have their rights, bre. We asked for volunteers.<

>Are there any?<

>If I understood correctly, they had some kind of powwow, some form of democratic decision.<

I blink.

Our dolphins practice Electocracy.

Interesting. Is that a coincidence or DFQL influence?

>Whom did they pick?<

>Radarion.<

I blink again.

Wise decision.

A younger non-alpha male, not indispensable for reproduction.

Radarion.

My chatty buddy.

Now I sigh.

>Dave, believe me, our veterinarian surgeons are good. There won't be any danger, calisse de merde; I guarantee.<

>You shouldn't offer guarantees for things not under your control, but our vets are indeed good, that I'm certain of. When?<

>Within the next three months. Radarion will have to go through intense training in computer communication. What's more, the pod will be helping, tabarnaque. They will all learn together."

I sigh again. It will be a gigantic step forward, one we all hoped for. But there's also some risk involved.

>Well, I'll be looking forward to the first direct communication.<

Andy sems to hesitate: - >Dave, there's more, my Mo. Much more.<

Much more? - >Like?<

>Dormi mecum, forget about dolphins for a moment. Concentrate on this: all prc MANATO soldiers who receive a microchip implant may one day be able to operate their tools, vehicles, and weapons solely by the power of their thoughts, hands free! Sam flying an Aurelia just with the power of his mind, Salvador firing the gun of his tank just by thinking of it, Fran firing a torpedo....<

# GRAND FINALE

Mount Palamar is trembling, shaking, and throbbing, below leaden skies streaked with orange and red fireballs, arching high and disappearing downslope.

It feels like I may any moment lose my footing.

It feels like a low intensity earthquake, but an endless one.

Not the environment anyone would choose, not to mention enjoy being in.

Not a situation anyone would rush into; yet I've rushed into this one of my own free will.

(Maybe my own free will, maybe not; who can tell?)

Shake. Shake.

Tremor. Tremor.

Fear.

Yet, the permanently disorienting shaking under my feet isn't the worst of the sensual input. The worst is the all-permeating sound.

A low vibration. One of those with a frequency range which panics human beings and animals into stampedes.

Low.

Low.

Very low.

Ominous.

Dark.

Penetrating.

Tortured.

And torturing.

At the same time tortured and torturing.

As if the bones of the mountain itself are breaking, crushed by some unimaginable force.

I mustn't panic!

This chain of events started when I received a powerful telepathic message in the middle of an important strategy session, consecrated to coordinating plans for subtly thwarting the American (and any other country's) spying drones.

>General, be ASAP on the northwestern slope of Mount Palamar, on the plateau in front of the Volcano watch observation building, about three hundred meters below caldera's edge. Alone, please. When you approach that spot, I'll provide further guidance. This is a "now or never" opportunity, so don't fail us, please.<

I never received a sharper, more crystal-clear telepathic message, immediately aware of its arrival from a profound distance.

Not distance.

Rather, a profound depth. Deep, deep, deep below my feet. And no such telepathic message ever petrified me more.

"Dave, bre!" - shouted Miki in alarm, after I froze for a whole minute and stood motionless, my mouth opened and drooling, my eyes unfocused, staring into (the deep).... nothingness.

I was forced to blink.

That voice!

(That voice which is still echoing in my mind....)

I blink again.

No doubt. No doubt at all. I heard Thom Brdar's voice. In my mind, I heard dead Thom Brdar's telepathic voice.

Impossible.

Unbelievable.

Yet true.

I blink again.

"General?" - from Salvador Kuul.

"Dave?" - from Henri Deladin.

Worrisome expressions on Sam and Rob's faces. Someone presses a button. Fran, in command while we yapped, enters running, the door slamming behind him.

Then the ground starts to shake.

"Red alert for all MANATO units." - I calmly state.

They jump to comply, but I have more to ad: - "And someone please tell me how to get to the Volcano watch observation building on Mount Palamar.... alone!"

It took time.

It took time to explain about the message.

(First to ascertain that I didn't go cuckoo on them, then explain the source of my information.)

It took time to explain about my destination.

(Always keeping in mind that not all my officers are informed about DFQL's alien origin.)

Then it took thrice that much time to decline all offers (pleas, logical arguments, imperious orders, begging, calls to reason) to accompany me (or to take a whole Swift team with me).

I'll be going alone, as requested.

Why?

Because....

Strange as it may sound, I trust Thom Brdar. I fully trust Thom Brdar. He died protecting me. Well.... everyone thought him dead, me included. But we thought Thom dead, too (oh, Thom, my twice dead Thom). Which doesn't diminish his level of sacrifice a bit. Now he's demanding my presence and I intended to fulfill his wish (order).

Thom Brdar.

He.

Or is it now an it, as in he/she/it/they, an all-powerful alien, posing and masquerading as Thom Brdar?

The usual trick of DFQL aliens? Shapeshifting, their everyday ploy....

For I haven't for a second doubted that all this must be connected to them, a DFQL show.

Why the earthquake?

Why the eruption?

Maybe.... maybe (oh god, or nature around us, let me be wrong about this).... maybe the real DFQL aliens are moving towards Mount Palamar's summit.

The idea made hair rise on my arms, but not with the usual force of a premonition. Rather with the force of a stunning vision. Soon, I

will be standing on that crater's lip. Alone. Am I today to meet some unimaginable alien beings made of molten stone?

(shudder)

There were other pleas, logical arguments, imperious orders, begging, calls to reason, which I didn't dismiss and disregard. Right now, Andy is flying in from Ceti II, to be stationed in the GHQ. As close proximity to DFQL aliens as we dare expose him, having in mind that he's our most powerful telepath. He'll be my mental support whenever I need him. Sam and Robert will lift me to the crater using a Newlands police Osprey. Henry dug out a spare mountaineering oxygen tank and mask, with enough precious gas compressed into it to last two hours or more in an (many believe inevitable) emergency. I'll be landing near the summit of the 5777 meters tall crater with that one single accommodation to its low oxygen conditions.

It will be very tough.

Yet, at the end, Fran pulled me to the side, handed me a tiny portable toxic gas analyzer, and suggested to keep from using my oxygen supply if I can; instead, to treat it as a golden parachute in case of trouble.

How will I then breathe at that altitude? I'll be dead in ten minutes!

No. Fran believed that I must put trust in being(s) which issued that summons.

Trust DFQL?

Trust DFQL....

After they almost managed to kill me on multiple occasions?

Really?

Really.

Foolhardy?

Stupid?

No.

Wise.

Deep down, I agree with Fran.

Deep down, he needn't have wasted his breath convincing me.

Yet, if he's wrong, it will be my lungs and my body which will suffer; not his.

And they're now suffering.

But I'm far from dying or being dead.

It's a miracle.

(Don't ask how it works; I don't feel anything special. I doubt it's a miracle concocted by me. It must be produced by someone.... or something.)

Still, I'm grasping for breath. In fifteen minutes, I ascended from the ocean level to more than three and a half miles up; not good for your health!

My heart is drumming in my head. My eyes are watering.

It's cold!

I'm standing ankle-deep in snow!

(Exactly where Rob and Sam left me, removing their Osprey to a safe distance; so far, I didn't make a single step in any direction.)

How am I going to find strength to start making those inevitable steps?

It's cold.

It's cold.

Yet, it's warm, too.

Waves of warmth are exploding from the grotto, in quick windy impulses (stinky with sulphur, but my belt-mounted toxic gas analyzer isn't sounding any serious alarms, just occasional initial warnings).

While I was still in the GHQ, it became apparent that Mount Palamar was enjoying one of its periodic eruptions, by the usual scale of volcanic activity a mere burp. Nothing sensational so far. No reason to evacuate anyone. Yet, here, in the epicentre of this event, lava is now slowly, lazily, but inexorably (and unstoppably) flowing over crater's lip, in its path violently melting the accumulated snow and ice, producing huge plumes of white steam. To me it appears as if this eruption is quickening.

Though, it still looks nothing like last year's Mount Root eruption. No explosions. No fiery missiles, or very few, far between. No rivers of lava hurling themselves towards unprotected towns lying at the feet of this volcanic massif. Just lava overflowing the caldera's edge in circular waves, dropping onto volcano's shoulders, and mostly remaining there.

Like....

Like water in a tub overflowing its edge as a large object slowly surfaces in tub's middle.

In the middle of volcano's fiery lake.

I believe that I know what (who) is surfacing in the middle of this volcano's fiery lake.

Our friendly DFQL aliens.

It must be.

It must be.

Nothing else makes sense.

Andy's mental voice. Urgent but reassuring, disquieted but patient: - >Marka mu, anything worthwhile to report?<

>Nothing so far, Andy. Lava is overflowing caldera's ridge like.... well.... water, if something is surfacing in the middle of the tub.< - I smugly repeat my analogy. Anyways, Andy is powerful enough to telepathically reach into my mind and find out what my eyes are seeing, that is if he becomes convinced that present situation requires such a drastic action.

>Please, keep us in the loop, bre.<

>Do not worry, Sharkticon. Do not worry.< - Despite gasping for air, I somehow tap into a reserve of mental strength to send him a telepathic caress full of erotic promise. I immediately feel relief on his side of our telepathic connection. Andy probably believes that I wouldn't be sending erotic caresses if my life is in real danger.

>My former teacher is a very powerful telepath.<

Shock.

I'm shocked, as I almost worked myself into believing that I'm alone.

Thom Brdar's voice is so clear and loud in my mind that I can't escape the impression that he's standing next to me. I quickly glance left and right, and over my shoulder, before realizing the utter futility of my actions.

>Thom.... how?

(Astonished pause.)

You're alive?

(More astonishment, but also an impression of an utterly wasted word; I held his dead body in my embrace, didn't I?)

How could you still be alive?<

Soft laughter.

>Am I now prcat alive, General?<

Very long pause.

I'm all ears. Thom used the Newlandean curse byword "prcat". Either that's really Thom Brdar addressing me with his mind, or DFQL learned much more of our vernacular than I expected. In all our encounters they never used a single Newlandean swear word.

Never – ever.

>In a strange way, I am. My body died, of course, of that you’re aware. Majke mu, my being, my mind, my aura, the essence of who was Thom Brdar, was absorbed into a much stronger and larger consciousnesses which needed my knowledge. I miss my corporeal form, but I’ve passed to another level of existence.<

>You’re now part of DFQL?<

The moment I uttered my question, something happens.

A rupture in my spirit.

A rupture in my way of thinking.

Instinctively, I understand how silly my question was.

DFQL may prove not to be the answer to this riddle!

Light is shining through the newly formed crack.

The light of.... understanding?

>DFQL? There’s no DFQL here, my General.<

Still, no DFQL? No DFQL at all?

How’s that possible?

No.

I can’t quite trust his simple statement.

Not just like that.

I can’t just surrender.

No DFQL?

Then who?

Who else?

Else....

Else!

(That’s the key!)

Is he hinting that our poor Earth has been invaded by more than one type of aliens? Maybe he’s in some way deluded?

>I feel your turmoil. I’ll explain, General. Multitax, I’ll explain everything, or as much as you give me time to. However, I suggest that you leave this spot ASAP. Marka mu, you definitely aren’t safe here. Please shelter, as requested, in the Volcano watch observation building.<

Despite my trust, I hate being pushed around like a marionette.

>If you haven’t yet noticed, Thom, I’m three and a half miles above the ocean. Here the oxygen is so rare that I can barely breathe. I won’t be moving anywhere very fast.<

A chuckle.

An Olympian chuckle, to be precise.

>You state such a thing, despite that prcat oxygen tank wisely provided by your colleagues?<

He knows everything!

My heart sinks.

>General, do not worry. You're having a bit of a physiological problem adapting to this new situation, this new reality. If I qualify it as unexpected, that will probably be a huge understatement, but I/we are providing a survivable atmosphere and conditions around you. Once you get inside that building, I/we will be able to create a perfect environment for you. Otherwise, without my/our intervention, you're as good as dead, multitax, oxygen tank or no oxygen tank.<

I'm as good as dead. My life depends on aliens providing a suitable atmosphere. How far can I trust this statement?

>I/we?<

This time there's no chuckle; instead, I taste a brief but profound sense of remorse.

>I was too callous with my words, Dave. Calisse de merde, I should have said that the Old Man will provide everything necessary for your comfort. Marka mu, my role is tiny, indeed. Advisory. And a that of a mouthpiece.<

Advisory role?

Mouthpiece?

Old Man?

>Old Man? Who's that?<

A moment of silent thoughtfulness.

>Old Man. My nickname for the entity I'm now part of. Though, assigning a connotation of gender to this star dweller is prcat funny. Old Man is always amused when I do that. His kind has no concept of gender such as our line of evolution developed for most of Earth's lifeforms.<

No males and females?

No.... sex?

No.... fucking?

Stop such thoughts!

Be serious!

Concentrate on the amazing revelations!

>Star dweller?< - We're finally getting somewhere. But still: no DFQL? Is he kidding me?

>No time to waste, General. All in its own time. If suicide isn't your goal, mrdat move, now!<

And another miracle happens.

My lungs quieten and stop gulping the air. The endless background drumming in my head subsides. My pulse stops racing. I relax.

I start moving.

Fast.

I try running.

Easy peasy!

Easy peasy lemon squeezy and it shouldn't be so!

How's this possible?

Behind me the volcano suddenly roars and the ground doubles its trembling.

In my turn, I double my pace.

A vast cloud of smoke envelopes mountain's tortured top.

As I reach for the unlocked door of the futuristic concrete building half buried inside a mound of petrified lava spewed out of this very same volcano a long time ago, deadly fireballs start landing all around.

Shake. Shake.

Tremor. Tremor.

Fear.

All this massive concrete around me, and building's foot-thick bluish glass windows, appear totally inadequate to protect from volcano's unleashed fury.

(A fleeting thought reminds me that this, after all, is Mount Palamar, our mightiest fiery mountain.)

Yet, the permanently disorienting shaking under my feet isn't the worst part of the sensual input. The worst is the all-permeating sound.

A low vibration. In a frequency range which panics humans and animals.

Ominous. Dark. Penetrating. Tortured.

As if the bones of the mountain are breaking, crushed by some unimaginable force.

There's also a feeling of utter failure. Failure of (human, our) reasoning. Failure of (human, our) logic. Failure of (human, our) fact gathering (intelligence, analysis process, computation skills). If we're

dealing with two independent groups of aliens, then everything we deducted and think we know may be wrong.

Who's friendly?

Who's the enemy?

Or, maybe, are they both our enemies?

(Is it too much to hope that they are all friends?)

Or, for goodness' sake, what if there are THREE different kinds of aliens mucking around? Or a whole bunch of them? A.... a Galaxy of aliens!

I mustn't panic!

>You won't panic, sir. I'll see to that. I guarantee. You're safe here, Marka mu. You're among friends.<

I can't fully trust him (not yet), but this declaration of friendship is welcome. Besides, he's reading me like an open book. A very uncomfortable situation.

>I am. Augmented by Old Man's mighty mind, my telepathic powers are now limitless.<

Unbelievable.

>Limitless by our.... or should I say your yutz human standards, of course.<

Another earthshaking chuckle.

>Old Man would never allow one of his best creations to be harmed. Never, tabarnaque.<

Here we are. My skin tingles and the hairs rise, this time with the force of a premonition. Each word Thom Brdar uttered is a factual, indisputable truth!

These aren't the DFQL aliens!

And this entity, with or without Thom Brdar, is (in some sense) my "maker", my creator!

>Your peculiar inborn truth-judging system serves you well, Dave.<

I must ask something. I can't let him retain full control of this situation.

>What's happening? Whom do you represent, then? Why this eruption?<

>Oh, that's putz easy to explain. We're leaving.<

Shock.

>Leaving?<

Is Newlands doomed, then?

Will their leaving sink us?

Again?

>Ochen balshoy, da sir.<

Da to what? My spoken question? My mind's unspoken questions?

And, who's leaving?

>Who's we?<

A chuckle, manifesting like thunder in my mind. I suppose Zeus used to chuckle like that. Or Jupiter. Or Thor (Odin, whichever....)

>Our little colony. Old Man. Me. Thom's android iteration. We, bre.<

Genuine surprise on my part, mixed with sudden pain at the mention of my twice dead husband.

>Thom's android still exists?<

>Indeed, sir. Tabarnaque, the Old Man made it appear out of control and jump into the lava. We needed it. We prcat protected it during its descent into Earth's mantle, then welcomed it into our home. It's the last essential ingredient necessary to enable our enclave to leave this planet.<

I don't doubt a word, but I'm receiving shock after shock.

>We will have more time to talk, General. Well, a bit more time, to be precise. However, you've got a pai pai crisis on your hands. Your people observed the worsening of this eruption. They are putz genuinely worried about your welfare. I suggest that you contact.... (a moment of searching my thoughts; I can't resist; I can't even get myself to try to resist).... Sam and Rob....

(a partial withdrawal from my mind as if his search took Thom further away)

And Andy.<

He's right, of course. My husbands and all my officers must by now be terribly worried; Andy most of all, I bet.

If I get in touch with him, they will all be informed.

Right.

Despite feeling ridiculous about my intent, I turn partially away, as if to shield from the possibility of Thom Brdar somehow peeking over my shoulder.

>Andy?<

>Dave! Are you safe, tabarnaque?<

(tons of worry in his mental voice)

>All safe and in communication (no need to announce with whom). No need for any action on GHQ's part. Stand down red alert for MANATO. Repeat: stand down red alert. Keep observing the eruption. In need,

protect our capital or any other threatened place of habitation. Repeat, do not wait for my orders. Protect New Belgrade or any other settlement. Will keep you informed.<

>Yes, CIC. Stand down red alert; protect New Belgrade in need.<

Formal and professional. I've successfully conveyed to my friend and lover that I'm currently not private in our telepathic exchange. But I know Fran. He will keep MANATO on yellow alert, I'm certain.

Chuckle.

Another Olympian chuckle.

>No, sir, you're not private, for sure, tabarnaque. Besides, your Andy is powerful enough, spasitelju, to read from your mind what's happening here.<

I'm again genuinely surprised.

>You're aware of the extent of Andy's powers?<

>Constable Andrew Lighthouse is another Old Man's genuine success.<

Obviously.

(Tiny consolation. He didn't mention Andy's new temporary rank. Brdar may not know all. Can I somehow keep secret that tiny grain of knowledge? As a tiny personal triumph over these mighty alien minds? Let's try.)

I sigh and try to publicly flash my next thought across my mind: still, Andy and I, we're just small fries in someone's larger chess game.

>No, you're not, Marka mu. And yes, you are. Difficult to explain.<

>Why?<

>Because of its timescale, my friend. This chess game lasted, as much as I could prc ascertain, more than half a billion years. Even that was difficult to calculate, malik kahell.<

Half a billion years?

How?

Why?

>Why?<

(Not again! Even to myself I sound like a broken record. Yet, that's the pertinent question right now and my mind voiced it before I could force myself to consciously think of a more precisely formed alternative.)

>Because the Old Man measures time in the units of galactic phases. Multitax, it took me a lot of effort to reconcile his system of measurement

with the length of Earth's revolution around our sun, which is what we base our time calculations on.<

Galactic phases? Way above my level of astronomical knowledge. Did I ever hear any similar description of time calculus?

>Therefore, a mighty figure that you might be, and certainly are, you are a very recent arrival to this game. Very recent. If this game took one day of ours, your arrival would happen in the last hundred millionth of a second. Yet, this chess game, as you called it, ends today.<

>Today?<

>Ochen balshoy. In about five minutes.<

>Five minutes?<

>Da, my friend. Your surprise was anticipated and expected. However, majke mu, I must somehow bring our conversation back to its main track. Otherwise, I won't be able to explain much in the putz remaining time.<

Petulantly, I can't stop asking irrelevant questions.

>Am I going to meet your Old Man?<

Laughter which seems to shake the mountain.

>Hardly, sir. Hueles a mierda, a corporeal human being can't meet my Old Man and survive. He's a being, and an intellect, and an alien intelligence, solely based on plasma. Tabarnaque, a being of plasma, a natural denizen of stars, or, in this case, Earth's mantle.<

I may require one of my scientists to completely translate Thom's thoughts (and unfortunately, Raj's communication device can't record these mental exchanges). Yet, a breathtaking vision is slowly taking shape.

>You said a space traveller made of plasma? A denizen of stars or the molten parts of planets?<

>Yes, orcae ita, right on the ball! Old Man is all that and much more.<

Suddenly, Thom's presence gets completely withdrawn.

For a moment, I panic. Did I make a wrong step, ask a wrong question? Is something going wrong?

The intensity of eruption outside my shelter doubles.

Then Thom returns.

>Everything is ready, General! Alea iacta est! Watch that window!<

"Watch that window" is meaningless in the absence of someone pointing the direction of observation, especially since I'm surrounded by four windows. And I'm still alone here, no one's pointing to the right spot. Yet, I'm immediately certain which window is in question; I approach

and through the thick polarized glass peer downwards into the raging volcano.

Some changes happened while I wasn't paying attention.

The lava pouring over crater's edge is no more. While I talked with Thom, the lava must have receded (or gotten fully expelled).

All blown away?

In front of me a sharply downward inclined slope, ominously glittering and shining with lava red, stretches for about two hundred yards. Then the ground sinks in a cascade of ledges and steps towards the distant lake of boiling stone. The whole slope is covered with glowing puddles. That lake's molten stone surface is a maelstrom of activity, its bursting bubbles launching fiery projectiles high into the air, though very few now seem to be on trajectories leaving the crater.

Ground shakes continuously, smaller and larger stones constantly being dislodged from the slope, bouncing and rolling to fall into the cauldron.

Then the bubbles intensify into a geyser of hot lava, a Bellagio-like red fountain, scorching-hot and deadly.

Still, breathtaking.

Still, magnificent.

Suddenly, I became certain that IT is coming.

IT?

A huge, dark, shadowy, amorphous monster, maybe?

The dark monster....

Godjira....

Old Man....

A second, another second, and....

And the top of a magnificent sphere of incandescent lava pushes upwards from the lake, its diameter growing with every second, until the whole lake is consumed.

Then dread and utter despair return.

A slap on my face, but not physical, not pertaining to the material world of reality around me.

My mind screams: danger, danger, danger!

The huge black amorphous monster materializes in my consciousness and stretches a tentacle towards me. The feeling of horror is multiplied by the force of repeated experience. I've experienced all this before.

>Something this way comes.< - echoes Thom Brdar's voice, precisely repeating my thought from the moment of his death.

Yet, I don't fly.

I've no urge to escape.

I surrender.

I stand still.

I await.

Then I hear it, as I knew I'd be hearing it.

Sound. Thought. Word. Words.

Deep. Deeper than the bottom of the ocean.

Thick. Thicker than the mightiest tree.

Opaque. Black on black on black.

Sound.

Vibration.

*I..... Ja..... Io..... Ich..... Ma..... Khnhom..... Mi..... Ngar..... Naneun..... Je..... Fi..... Tôi..... Eu..... Yo..... Ik..... Me..... Saya..... Jag..... Aku..... Khony..... Jeg..... Watashi..... 'O wau..... Moi..... Ek..... Unë..... 'Ana..... Yīshì..... Yes..... Aš..... Én..... Men..... Maim..... Ikh..... Nāṉ..... Ego..... Mé..... Eu..... Jas..... Ya..... Man..... Mimi..... Bi..... Ahau..... Mise..... Jaz..... Mama..... Ben..... Hum..... Egó..... Mna..... Phm.....*

>Old Man is saying hi, General.<

With this casual comment, the frightening bubble bursts. I feel no more fear or revulsion, astonishment or extasy. I accept. I understand. This IS the being which dwelled under our volcanoes and over eons shaped this archipelago's destiny. And more. Of this whole world. My defences drop, and I open my mind to this strange plasmatic intelligence.

>Hello, Old Man!<

A feeling of merriment floods my mind.

Old Man is acknowledging our fleeting contact.

I try to project my mind, like I do with so many people. I touch....

Not a dark brooding monster.

Not a terrifying Godjira.

Something archaic; terribly old; wise beyond human understanding; benign, but treating the humanity as we do ants, not paying much attention to us at all.

And hot, unimaginably hot.

I withdraw.

>Watch!< - advises Thom's mind.

The tortured air is throbbing and screaming as if ripped by innumerable whips.

In front of my unbelieving eyes, the object is still rising from the crater. Slowly, majestically.... unstoppable now. It's starting to resemble an uneven prolate elongated spheroid, made of.... something very solid and very dark.... with no reflection of light, no crystalline glitter; covered in liquid, mobile lava, cascading back over its surface to drop into crater's lake of magma, now rapidly shrinking. The object is now almost as wide as the crater itself. Then, the spheroid's stubby knobby projections start scratching caldera's walls, a battering ram of destruction much harder than the stone forming this volcano's spine.

Again, and again, the stone is shattered and pulverised, but I can't hear any sound above the already omnipresent all-pervading din.

>Marka mu, pure neutronium, General.<

Neutronium? That can't be! I know a bit about this fabled mythical substance.

>Thom, I can't believe you, sorry. Is neutronium even possible?<

>Ochen balshoy, sir. It derives from the heart of an exploding nova. Old Man's interstellar vehicle was crafted and shaped in the final moments of a star's death rattle, during his prcat previous home's convulsive dying moments, a billion years ago.<

A star! An exploding star! A star which has gone nova or supernova! Old Man once lived on, or inside, a star, before coming to Earth!

(Well, what better home for a being made of plasma than a star?)

Thom is rumbling on, this time disregarding my logical deductions.

>You know, Old Man never intended to hijack my mind and thus involuntarily subject my body to an untimely death. It was a coincidence, a mistake. That event by the lake.... It was trying to contact you, sir. After many long millennia, Old Man thought there now again existed one extraordinary person he could contact. Sakra pure truth. Unintentionally, I interfered. Gahba, even tried blocking it, defending you. And I got absorbed, bre.<

We were right. I was the intended target!

>Not a target, sir. An attempt at communication, nothing more. Sakra, Old Man calculated that our Newlandean civilization was sufficiently developed to deliver the final ingredient for his escape from the confines of Earth. Dodjavola, he simply decided to ask you to deliver it.<

>The final ingredient?<

>Da, General.<

As he speaks, an illuminated niche, perched on spheroid's side, rises from lake's molten rock. Encapsulated in the purple radiance, untouched by lava, a humanoid form frantically toils there, seemingly controlling levers of pure light, utterly ignoring my scrutiny.

I'm too far for details to be readily visible, yet I've no doubt who that form must be.

Thom's android body!

(Still carrying the essence, mind, spirit of my beloved husband!)

>Yes. Your Thom's android. The final ingredient.<

Pain fills my heart such as I never knew could exist. I'm about to lose my beloved Thom again! For a third, unlooked for, unexpected time, as no one of us (humans) was aware that the android survived its plunge into lava! Killed in Benghazi, resurrected by our brightest scientists while his mind sheltered in Nikola and me, only to suicide by jumping into Ceti II volcano's grotto....

Here, intact, living, functioning....

(and not paying any attention to me)

And about to embark on a journey which will take him away forever, to whatever unbridgeable spatial gap this plasma being has in its mind!

>General, we don't have much time. Khange khodah, I need to explain as much as possible. Our spaceship will very soon start accelerating. As soon as it's free of magma. It's fully shielded, no one on Newlands will be able to detect it. Neither will the rest of this world, Marka mu. To everyone, this will be just another eruption of a Newlands volcano, a small one at that; nothing exceptional in any way.

A more mundane consideration: as we rise through Earth's atmosphere I'll remain in contact, but our link will fade as we reach Earth's stratosphere.<

Such a short time to learn as much as possible!

>What about you, Thom? What's your destiny going to be?<

More chuckles.

As we are finishing this exchange, the bottom of the rugged spaceship suddenly rises from the lake of sticky boiling stone with a huge plopping sound reverberating through my concrete shelter, displaying a brilliant beam of purple light.

Labyrinthium? It has to be! It has to be!

(The million-dollar thought, coming from afar as if somehow implanted into my mind by someone else.... Labyrinthium belongs to this untouchable being! Somehow, for some reason, this powerful alien shared its Labyrinthium with us!)

Accompanied by a second mighty gurgling sound, the lava lake collapses into itself, its level suddenly lowered by a hundred feet or more. Dark smoke still billows, hiding from view most of the upper part of the gargantuan space vehicle.

No more magma is spilling over diminished lake's rim.

For all practical purposes, this eruption is over.

Mount Palamar emits a palpable sigh, then seems to settle under my feet.

Apparently soundlessly, Old Man's ship speeds upwards.

>I will remain an independent part of the whole. Non omnis moriar, General. My body is already dead, but my aura will survive. At least another couple of billions of our years. Then, when the next period of reproduction arrives, I'll be fused with Old Man's mind to be dispersed into his offspring. His end will be my end, too, Marka mu. That's his sakra promise.<

A lifespan of a couple of billion years! Longer than Homo sapiens existed on this planet if the story of evolution is to be trusted. (Longer than life existed on this planet.) Much longer than our species will exist in the future, if the scientists know what they're talking about.

>Yes, my friend. What a putz strange fate. I, one of the most odious Newlands criminals of all time, will practically live forever.<

>What about my Thom?<

The moment of truth arrives.

>I don't know. I really don't know. Please believe me. Oh la vache, when I asked Old Man, he glavom i bradom refused to give me an answer. He hinted at a surprise ending for Thom. That's all I know.<

I can't anymore see the spaceship.

Only the billowing smoke remains.

And my tenuous mental contact with Thom Brdar's aura.

So, a surprise ending for Thom. Good or bad? And surprise for whom?

>Dave, our communication will soon be cut.<

Thom Brdar's voice now sounds muted and distant.

>In the future, if I'm able to, I'll contact you. That's a mrdat promise. One more thing. Just to avoid surprise when you decide to leave. They are waiting for you in front of the building. Dixi.<

And Thom Brdar is gone.

An emptiness remains in my consciousness, which he thoroughly filled, even dominated, until a moment ago.

(sigh)

So.

I blink.

I feel a tear drop from my right eye.

This is the end.

Thom Brdar's end.

And my Thom's end.

The end.

Then....

Who's waiting for me outside? Brdar stipulated that "they are waiting for me in front of the building".

Who are they?

Then a sudden thought: Andy, Sam, Rob and the rest of the GHQ! How long was I out of touch? Are they waiting for me in front of this shelter with as many MANATO soldiers they could mobilize on short notice?

I look out of the closest window.

Nothing.

No one is outside of the building.

Next window.

Still no one.

Next.

Wait!

With my peripheral vision I catch a movement!

Shock – utter surprise – a whiff of fear for my safety.

There's one person out there.

An almost seven feet tall, long-limbed figure.

Undeniably Chinese.

Undeniably a man.

Long white flowing robes. Not really white, more the color of raw cotton or ivory. Except, it's all silk; some of it almost transparent. With

broad gold-colored hand-patterned edges. Held tightly by a hand-braided beige belt with intricate dark brown patterns.

Dark leather boots, brown or black.

A face from the Chinese past, or from a historical movie.

Long flowing white beard. Long flowing white hair creating a halo around his head, at the same time forming an ordered tight bun and side braids in place of sideburns. Dark eyes under fierce white eyebrows. Eye folds; less eye exposure.

Yellowish-brown skin.

Ancient skin. Ancient face. Very ancient.

And a long sword in a scabbard.

Zhang Sanfeng, of the darned DFQL.

My nemesis or maybe not my nemesis. Everything is now so uncertain.

I haven't finished pondering the significance of appearance of this DFQL elder NOW and HERE, when my mind bolts for the comfort of contact with Andy or any other telepath who can offer me support (and the military reinforcements that contact should bring): - >Andy....<

Shock!

My telepathic message bounces, as if I'm locked inside an impenetrable ball, and keeps bouncing as an echo, slowly diminishing.

>Alan! Sam! Rob!<

Bounce – bounce – bounce.

Then silence.

>Do not worry, General Lionheart. You are quite safe and among friends. Your safety and life aren't threatened in any way. Your security isn't compromised. This time, however, we isolated this venue so that our conversation can be private. You won't be able to contact your subordinates until our chat is finished.<

In my mind, I hear every word.

I wish to trust every word.

Yet do I have the right to trust a DFQL envoy?

Any DFQL envoy?

Particularly this envoy?

>Yes, General. You can fully trust me. You can fully trust us. We were never your enemies. We were never the enemies of Newlands. Please, feel free to come out of your shelter. We are able and will remain able to maintain the local transmutation of atmospheric conditions, created by the solar alien, as long as needed.<

Then the realization hits me! Telepathy! For the first time (to my knowledge) Zhang Sanfeng, or any other member of DFQL, is using telepathy to address one of us / me. Here's the proof we, MANATO, searched for. DFQL aliens are telepaths. Besides, a more mundane sub-thought (do sub-thoughts exist?). The solar alien he mentioned.... who's that now?

>Solar alien? You mean the Old Man?<

>We're not aware of that designation, General Lionheart. Our designation “solar alien” refers to that being which just left your planet in its spaceship. Our more intimate designation for this species of alien beings is “Ball”.<

Old Man. Solar alien. Ball.

All singulars.

Or are they?

Can Ball be a collective name for a whole species?

Well, maybe.

Still singulars. Maybe because DFQL isn't aware of Thom Brdar's aura within the Old Man? Or my Thom's android? It behooves me to be careful not to reveal my information.

So....

Decision time!

I take a deep breath and resolutely step towards the door of this Volcano watch compound.

So be it.

Once again, I need to attempt conversation with the enemy.... Or not enemy?

I exit onto the high plateau still wrapped in the toxic, billowing smoke.

Same as the last time, standing side by side, Zhang Sanfeng dwarfs me. However, this time, after bowing slightly to each other, we embark on a slow walk around crater's rim, like two friends who meet after many years spent apart with lots to tell each other. Zhang Sanfeng is careful to pick a path avoiding the cooling pools of the recently spilled lava. I'm content to follow his lead.

“General, we must first resolve one dilemma. Should we for our forthcoming communication use our voices or telepathy?” - asks Zhang in his normal (I almost got myself to think “natural”; though it's by no way natural, inborn for him) voice, which I remember so well - “If we use

our voices, your peculiar secret recording device will be able to operate, which won't be possible if we embark on a fully telepathic exchange."

"You're aware of Raj's satellite communication system?"

"At first we weren't expecting such sophistication stemming from the mind of just one single human. Therefore, last time we had a long chat, you surprised us. I guess, you're perfectly aware of that; you thwarted our intentions.

(He chuckles; I chuckle too; two good friends, indeed.)

Afterwards, we learned better. I believe that by now you better understand us, too. And we understand all of you, Newlands and MANATO, and you personally, General, much better. Our penetration into your secrets can be minimal or all-encompassing. I believe you're aware of that. On the other hand, this conversation may be your window into ours. Sir, my point is that there might be lots disclosed during our chat which your scientists may like to dissect at their leisure at a later date."

"You wish to present us with this scientific knowledge.... (why?).... no strings attached?"

"Yes, General Lionheart. The paradigm has changed. That...."

(he points his finger upwards, as if indicating the spaceship which recently departed this location)

That changed everything. To our astonishment, the mission Ball assigned to Newlands got successfully fulfilled. And we were wrong. You were the major actor in that success. However, that being said, our mission here is of necessity now over, too.

(He must have read the confusion in my mind as he rushes to go on. So few words, but so many layers in them; they generate so many questions! Right now, the upmost of them being that he didn't qualify his mission as successful, unlike "the success of Newlandean mission which Ball assigned to us", whatever he might be referring to.)

See, sir, when we finish our conversation, my people will also leave this planet. No further communication will be possible in the immediate and even foreseeable future, spanning thousands of your years."

"You're leaving.... too?"

"Oh, certainly! Earth's peculiar life forms, which mostly inhabit the interactive zone between your atmosphere, water, and land, were never of major interest to us, General. Your kind of life is too different from ours to embrace a meaningful lasting communication and interaction."

"You and I, we seem to have no problems communicating."

(and interacting)

"True, sir. But only because my people went out of their way to render possible this form of communication. You wouldn't want to, nor could physically, meet us in our natural form."

More beings made of plasma?

"Mr. Sanfeng, are your people also plasmatic beings?"

A soft human chuckle. At the same time Zhang's holographic image blurs at its edges, then steadies.

"No, hardly. As your scientists already guessed, our life form is based on the element you know as silicon."

Bingo! Some of our thinkers' deductions are proving true, after all!

However, I still have a pebble in my shoe with a painful itch. There are thousands of questions I know I should and must ask. But this one always floats to the top: - "You claimed that you were never enemies of Newlands. Yet, you mercilessly spied on MANATO, and the Newlandean institutions in general, and their secrets whenever you got a chance. You say that I'm completely safe in your presence. Yet, numerous times, DFQL tried to dispose of me."

Zhang turns towards me, sincerity splashed over his face.

"To explain every facet of our actions, the underlying logic and the imperatives, would take too much time, General. As for those attempts on your life....

(A shrug? Did I detect a brief, thoroughly human display of regret?)

Suffice it to state that we believed to have accumulated enough knowledge of star dweller's plans to consider you an unplanned aberration. A dangerous one. That's why we felt that your Newlands, your USA, and the humanity itself, would be better off with you dead. We were wrong. We were thoroughly wrong. Today proved us wrong. I apologize for our mistake."

A simple and short statement; yet, releasing me from the greatest burden in my life, the constant worry over my safety. It should make me happy. At least, relieved. Instead, I feel growth of an uncontrollable anger. They thought they understood Old Man's plans. Therefore, they decided to eliminate me. How cozy!

(Here I am being angry that they misunderstood the Old Man's plans when five minutes ago I didn't even know there were two species of aliens involved!)

"You aren't right, General. You put yourself into the center of our actions. And MANATO. And the humanity. Wrong. None of those considerations were of paramount importance. Everything we did, and we do, and will do.... well, it's to ensure the success of our own prime directive, which always was and still remains to establish a direct communication with this Ball and, ultimately, all Balls, their whole species. We fear the unknown, too. We fear making mistakes. We fear the repetition of history, so to say. We were afraid of the possibility that Newlands could be punished, sunk, if you, as its leader, undertook wrong moves. As it appears to have happened before. Better you dead and Newlands safe. A safe and stable Newlands was the crucial ingredient for success of our mission."

Yes! Another deduction of ours proven correct. DFQL was steering events in such way to allow it to freely operate in our archipelago!

"Then, why threaten Newlands? So repeatedly, so often?"

"On many occasions our logical moves were taken as threatening by MANATO when they were nothing of the kind. For example, our submersibles. As you now perfectly know, those submersibles had nothing to do with Newlands, my dear General. We believed that they were positioned out of your reach and would be invisible to MANATO. Not to mention that they were harmless, as you too well know. Not often, but obviously occasionally, we underestimated the strength of your military prowess. Constructed to function through telepathy, those so called "torpedoes" were an attempt to build a sophisticated communication system to reach your solar alien. They were a huge failure, a huge disappointment; however, I must state that our efforts to produce useful devices through actions of our human agents and their allies often proved unsuccessful. Too many compromises."

A treasure-trove of knowledge in just that one statement! Yet, I also collected another pebble in my shoe to increase the itch as my insight into DFQL's modus operandi increases.

Besides, dare I really believe his words? After all those penetrations of MANATO GHQ and our Cybercommand?

"Ah, those, General....

(chuckle)

They were never about MANATO. They were always about the star alien. Unknowingly to your people, MANATO, as well as some other Newlandean scientific outfits, occasionally recorded star alien's

underground and aboveground activities. We needed those records to better shape our strategy."

"You're reading my mind?"

"I could. I easily could. But am not. I only read your anger with us, sir. It's strong enough to carry across the gap between our minds without an effort to penetrate your consciousness."

Ah, so....

"Then, what about my wife? Alisa? Why attack her?"

"Oh, that, General. Alisa's mishap was completely unintentional."

"Unintentional, hell? It almost wiped her out!"

"Unfortunately, yes. Completely unintentional, I repeat. Somehow her empathic ability...."

"You know about her empathy?"

"Yes, General. PsiMANATO recently spiked as our favorite topic of study. If you don't mind me pointing this, PsiMANATO is a direct result of Ball's interference with your species. Anyways, Alisa's empathy tripped a rearguard defense mechanism we employed whenever we browsed your military intranet. That mechanism was created to fend off your powerful telepaths.... and especially you, sir.... whenever one of you happened to stumble on our online presence. It was designed to make you forget the encounter, and nothing more. Just erase that encounter, no other memories. It got used, many times, with no ill effects. On you, too; you stumbled on our online operations numerous times. Yet, do you have any ill effects? I reiterate: it wasn't supposed to hurt anyone."

"What, but...."

"Your wife's plight surprised us, too. It was totally unexpected. We had no remedy to correct our mistake."

Pardon me?

"Yet, you somehow managed at the end."

"No, we didn't."

Pardon me again?

"You didn't, but...."

Zhang shakes his head in a very human motion of negation.

"You didn't, but maybe a weakness in your program.... trap.... whatever you seeded on our intranet...."

Another shake.

"No."

Saying so, Zhang again points his finger upwards, indicating the departed spaceship.

The space alien!

Oh, god, I owe my wife's.... our wife's recovery to the Old Man! Ball! And maybe, just maybe, Thom Brdar's influence!

So many angles, so many doubts, so many insights. A burning question now scorches my mind: - "Did you follow the communication between me and.... Ball, while its ship was departing?"

"No."

Surprise.

"I note your surprise. Another strong emotion.

(A purely human sigh; he can be perfectly human when he wishes. Pardon me; IT can be perfectly human when it wishes.)

No, we didn't follow your conversation. The solar alien subjected this whole summit to a mind repulsing field which was too strong to overcome and penetrate. At least, to our chagrin, we were too weak, and maybe too unskilled, to battle through. Maybe somebody else wouldn't have failed so abysmally. We also don't exactly understand whom it was meant to stop. Us, or the other humans."

I suddenly realize I arrived at a fork in our discussion.

"Mr. Sanfeng. Please, tell me the truth. And, as we tend to say where I originate from, the truth and nothing but the truth. Everything hinges on the truth, if you understand that saying. Did you ever penetrate my mind?"

Chuckle, chuckle, with lots of stifled merriment behind it. Maybe I expected a more serious approach to my question.

"Oh, many times, General. You were often our most reliable source of information."

God, or nature the great, as my people would say, what a failure! I, Commander – in – Chief, the biggest traitor of them all.

"And you still maintain that I'm under no threat from your people?"

"None whatsoever, General. Nor is your wonderful country and its armed forces, whom you so ably command, in any danger."

I sigh.

Too bad I'm not an empath, like my Alisa. I would know if he's telling the truth and nothing but the truth, or he's holding back. Or lying.

OK.

Right.

Full trust or not?

Full trust, or not?

Think!

And the decision is.... full trust. For what have I to lose?

(My life; who cares....)

Now for the riskiest step.

A big one. I wish I can consult someone endowed with logical thinking. Fran. Miki. The five. The three.

Or Andy. I wish Andy was here with me.

But he isn't.

And won't be.

Therefore, it's my sovereign decision; a very first time for the humanity, as far as I know. I'm about to invite a strange, maybe horrifying alien being into my mind.

No.

Yes.

Yes.

No more dillydallying. Let's do it.

"Mr. Sanfeng. If I willingly open my mind to you, can you detect, or read, or.... whatever, what happened during the takeoff of the alien vessel?"

"Certainly."

"Then.... tell me what to do."

Just a moment of hesitation on his part. As if he expected my offer.

"Just relax."

I do.

I drop all my defenses.

My eyes turn upwards, furiously blinking; then I close them and concentrate on the emptiness. On the void. On the endless cosmos.

I feel my mind fully open itself up, like occasionally it did for Alisa. Or Andy. Or Thom (oh, Thom, my Thom, lost to me for the third time).

I imagine I can feel Zhang's light footsteps rummaging through my memories. Scurrying around. Testing, probing. Yet, his probing of my mind holds no resemblance to Old Man's august presence.

Then it's all quiet again. I surmise that the alien has withdrawn.

"Interesting."

(pause)

"Yet, your recent experience does fill some gaps in our knowledge."

"There were gaps in your knowledge?"

More chuckles.

"Probably many."

For a moment we walk in silence.

"Mr. Sanfeng. How does your species relate to Ball's kind?"

"We don't."

I'm genuinely astonished: - "You don't? But then why...."

Why were you here at the same time as this other alien?

"It's a long story, General. If you want to hear it in its entirety, it will take some time. Which, if you wish so, I can certainly afford to provide. On the other hand, my story could also provide you, your politicians, and your scientists, some deep insights into the functioning of our universe."

"I'd like to hear it, sir."

No pause, just a tiny nod.

"Ball's kind may very well be the oldest sentient lifeform in our universe.

(I won't insist on repeating how genuinely astonished I am.)

Some of my people's deepest and mightiest thinkers believe that the first generation of the solar aliens got born during the initial micro-bits of time after the explosion of matter the humans refer to as the Big Bang."

"Big Bang was real?"

"Indeed, sir. Earth's scientists got some of their mathematics and physics wrong, and have not yet determined all facts and factors; and, indeed, you don't yet recognize the full sum of natural laws which govern such extraordinary events. However, in general, your scientists are on the ball with their contemplations and calculations. As our name for that alien species indicates, these solar aliens are star dwellers. They live inside a star from the moment they enter their new home until the moment of that star's death."

"Nova or supernova."

"Exactly. Only the future novas and supernovas are populated by this species. They inhibit only those categories of stars which will turn nova or supernova. That moment is very special in a solar alien's life, of critical importance, as it's also the moment when the parent organism fashions crude but almost indestructible spaceships for its offspring, then splinters by fission into three or four new star dwellers.... To be sincere, we're far from certain of the number of offspring. It may be just two. It may be hundreds.

(Feeling my renewed astonishment, he pauses to let his info sink in.)

But there exists reasons why we believe it's three or four.

Anyways, the final collapse and explosion of its home star gives offspring's neutronium ships the initial impetus to depart towards new, not yet inhabited suns. New Balls are born inheriting the full knowledge transferred from their parent and retain its achieved level of intelligence. That way, with each new generation, their kind attains a new pinnacle of mastery. Do you understand now, General, why my compatriots so desperately want to establish contact with those solar aliens? If we could exchange information with them, a grain of their knowledge would be enough, we would have teachers who have witnessed the whole history of our universe!"

Awesome thought! Yet, I have another more mundane question on my mind: - "How many Balls per star?"

"Only one. We never discovered a star with more than one."

"What happens if a Ball finds itself in a star already inhibited by another Ball?"

(A war of Balls?)

"We don't know, General. Yet, take my word for it, it never happens. Nowhere in the universe."

"Then, how do they know where to go, whether a star is already inhibited by a Ball?"

"We don't yet know."

Frank and sincere.

"Though, we do have what you refer to as an educated guess."

"You do?"

"Yes. And, sir, you must be aware of that answer. The base for our educated guess."

"I do?" I blink.

And the answer is obvious: - "Telepathy?"

"Telepathy."

I inhale with my full lungs.

"And our solar alien was destined to colonize this part of the galaxy?"

"Exactly, General. We believe that it made a mistake in navigation and impacted Earth."

"When did it arrive, then? Seven to fifteen thousand years ago?" - I remember the timescale Doctors Kieron Pardagh and Marc Landau elaborated.

Chuckle.

“Oh, no, General. Earth’s solar alien arrived here more than half a billion of your years ago.”

Did he just mention half a billion?

As in half a billion?

Half a BILLION years ago!

“Wait! You said.... half a billion? Or did I misunderstand you? We’re not taking five hundred thousand years; we’re talking five hundred.... million years?”

I can’t believe it! I can’t! I can’t!

Yet.

Yet.

Yet!

Think!

Thom Brdar did mention a chess game lasting half a billion years. I clearly remember that. Yet, somehow, I never connected all dots. Obviously, his Old Man had to be on Earth for half a billion years to play a half a billion years long chess game.

“I feel your confusion, sir. Yes, we’re talking about half a billion years. Your mind informs me that your scientists marked that period as the time when foundations of Newlands archipelago broke off from one of Earth’s first cratons.”

Now I remember Marc mentioning something like that.

“We strongly believe that the cataclysmic event your scientists mention resulted from the collision between solar alien’s neutronium vehicle and Earth.”

“Half a billion years ago.... is that (think in the mode of evolution, forget the religious stories of creation).... is that before life crawled from the primordial ocean onto dry land?”

(My “group of three” scientists would be proud of me!)

“Yes, sir. Based on the accumulated human knowledge, we do believe so.”

>Then, did Ball have something to do with the evolution of Earth’s species?<

(I’m not talking anymore. Too astonished, I’m letting my mind ask its own questions.)

“Probably.”

Colossal!

"To produce a species which could develop civilization adequate to Old Man's needs?"

"Yes."

"Which could eventually help your Ball-alien escape the confines of this planet?"

"Certainly."

Marc and Kieron were right! They (it was an IT, actually) needed help to go home!

Another smug afterthought: Steven Spielberg was right, too!

"Escape where?"

"Your sun, General."

Our Sun!

Sol!

So close!

Somehow, I surmised that the alien who just left is taking a trip halfway across the galaxy. Or maybe even further. Somewhere far, far away.

A pang of pain pierces my heart. Maybe some dull ache as well. The omnipotent alien isn't moving very far, after all. Just into our Sun. Just eight minutes away at the speed of light! (I'm sure of that fact, I heard it before, from a reliable source. Alisa.) The last living remains of my husband are with him, and they will now forever be out of my reach. Eight minutes away as the light travels. So close but so far.

"How can you be certain of that?"

"We are certain, General. I didn't lie to you. We don't know how the species which we designate as "Ball" detects those uninhabited stars, or each other, though we surmise there must exist a communication network connecting all of them, probably telepathically. If it does, it's a very slow but an almost eternal form of communication. However, between the stars, we can detect faint markers of their spaceships' passages. Between various stars. Or, more precisely, between a dead, exploded star and a young star. There are none leading into your Sun except for that one which abruptly stops somewhere around Earth's orbit."

"But that happened half a billion years ago!"

"Exactly. We developed a method of measuring drifts of those faint markers over almost limitless time. That ability was essential in determining which star dweller entity to try to establish contact with."

"Hence, Earth."

"Yes. It's definitely easier to try to contact a being living inside a planet than one living inside a star."

Suddenly, my mind tacks outside the beaten track, as a novel lane of exploration forms in my thoughts: - "Pardon me for asking, but.... how many species of intelligent beings has your civilization discovered among the stars?"

For no reason I could point at, I felt that my question was an uncomfortable one.

"Three, General."

"Only three?"

"Yes. Balls. And the two Earth intelligences. That's all."

TWO Earth intelligences? Two! The cetaceans! That's whom he's counting in as the second Earth's intelligence! Like MANATO's dolphins!

"Correct, General."

Fancy that! For all their technological and mental superiority, DFQL aliens got to meet as many alien forms as humanity so far did.

Well, at least some of us did meet those two alien lifeforms.

Stop kidding yourself.

There's only one person on this planet who knows of the existence of those two alien lifeforms.

Me, moi, glavom i bradom, as Thom Brdar would say.

But that will change when I get to share my knowledge.

"We were convinced that you tampered with our dolphins. You, the DFQL."

"I see that in your mind, General. That's wrong."

"Ball cultivated our cetaceans? Like he cultivated the humans?"

"Yes, but a long time ago. A very long time ago. We believe that he switched to humans as the main executors of his plans and ideas as far as fifty thousand years ago."

Nature above, beyond, and wherever! Boosted by Thom's Old Man, the dolphins have been sapient much longer than us, the people.

"This will surprise you, sir. Searching your geological records, we believe that we discovered proofs that Ball in the same way interacted with some of your ancient dinosaur species. Human scientists have so far failed to notice those clues."

"Dinosaurs!"

Shocking.

A Newlands populated by intelligent T-rexes.

I blink.

Later.

Too much to think about right now.

Back to the questions about Zheng's species: - "You traveled far and wide, though?"

"Oh, certainly, General Lionheart. Our spaceships, many of them fully automatic, without crew, and some with crew, traveled far and wide, as you called it, covering about a fifth of this galaxy. We started researching the enormity you named Cosmos before humans developed their intelligence. There's plenty of varied life among the stars, many lifeforms which would completely astound and baffle you. You, the humankind. But not that much intelligent life. Intelligence is fleeting and rare. We discovered traces of some extinguished ones, hints about the potential existence of others. Some disappeared billions of years ago. Some were almost our contemporaries. Those rare intelligent species come, reach their apex, and depart; they rarely coincide together at the same time. It's amazing how few artifacts survive visible to the next civilization which comes along. Time levels everything.

(he fully turns towards me, then smiles in the friendliest possible way)

In the realm of space exploration, my good General, my kind has a great advantage over humankind."

Zhang's hologram flickers again, then steadies.

I notice a brisk increase in cold wind. Dark smoke shrouding volcano's top, previously rising in an impenetrable thick column right into the stratosphere, is now being shredded. Here and there I can spot blue sky.

And clouds.

Real water vapor clouds. Newlands will soon be drenched in another ubiquitous tropical evening shower.

"Yes, sir, which one?"

"Our advantage is our longevity, General. In your measurement of time, I'm around forty thousand years old, of which seven and a half were spent here on this planet. Yet, I'm pretty much in my prime; I lived through about two thirds of my life cycle. I expect to live another twenty to twenty-five thousand, though most of my remaining life may be spent on the planet which you designate as Mercury."

Astounding!

So much new information!

I'm talking with a being which will live a lifespan six to seven thousand times longer than mine, if I'm lucky not to succumb to dangers of my job and manage to reach some respectful deep old age!

"General, I feel your astonishment. I will explain, one item at the time. However, with weather conditions changing, it's becoming difficult for my colleagues to maintain this focally localized high air pressure, and therefore high oxygen concentration. If we're to return to your shelter, we'll be easily able to maintain that high concentration inside the building, allowing us to continue our cozy chat."

I stop.

"Though I see a hologram in front of me, your people work through engineered human life forms hidden underneath. Correct?"

"Yes, sir. Your scientists were correct about that. Those bionic avatars.... engineered human life forms, as you call them, have higher tolerances than the average human beings and are multiple times more physically capable. We can operate in the rarefied air longer than the average humans. We can withstand your fierce adverse weather better than a real human can. But not substantially longer, I'm afraid."

Easy choice, then.

"Let's return to the Volcano watch observation building."

"Agreed."

For our return trip, we now embark on a slightly brusquer tempo.

"You mentioned seven and a half thousand years on Earth. If so, are your people responsible for the rise of Atlantis?"

"Ah, General, I see that you keep returning to your scientists' timeline. To be sure it's not exactly perfect, but it's adequate. For the time being, until it becomes the property of your vast instituted academia, you should certainly go on using it. However, the answer to your question is no. We had nothing to do with the archipelago of Atlantis and we weren't responsible for its rise to the surface of the ocean. Nor for its ultimate demise. We landed in Mongolia."

"Mongolia? Why Mongolia?"

"I'll explain later. General, my colleagues need to bunch up a bit to be able to maintain the pressure of breathable oxygen and neutralize this strengthening wind. Will you find it threatening if they approach and encircle us?"

A moment to think about it; yet, of course, they already surround me, therefore my situation won't change much: - "No problem. Bring them closer."

A vaguely Chinese-looking head rises over terrain to my left. Then another one to my right; then another. Soon, all seven of them are in the circle of my vision. All wearing the indistinguishable grayish sweatpants, earth-colored tees, and black, sturdy walking shoes.

The seven DFQL monks I've seen before.

"Mr. Sanfeng, much as I'm becoming fond of your cinematographic hologram, if I ask you to change into your proper form, will you maybe become the eight Taoist monk from DFQL's Paloma mission?"

A human chuckle briefly fills the space between us, then Zhang Sanfeng transforms. Metamorphosis is almost instantaneous, therefore appears quite unnatural. Now all eight Taoist priests stand by my side, all identical to each other.

I nod with sincere appreciation. He smiles back. Then grows serious again.

"To understand our part in this tale, you need to understand solar alien's timeline. We're pretty certain that we successfully identified which supernova was Ball's birthplace, its point of origin. From there, Ball already traveled more than half a billion of your Earth years, all the time maturing through accumulation of its species' knowledge, before it approached your solar system."

"How far is his origin?"

Chuckle.

"Sir, maybe we should let Newlands develop its own method of tracking Balls. However, let me assure you that it's in one of the far galactic clusters."

Another chuckle and a soft intake of air. Very Chinese, indeed, or so I think.

"Let me tell you one thing, though. The cruising speed of Ball's spacecraft is around one third the speed of light. We know this for certain. We observed a couple in flight, though not in this galaxy. I believe this info will be a good starting point for your scientists."

Well, I hope so. At present, as far as I'm concerned, it doesn't correlate much.

"So, once again. We tracked its path. We're pretty certain that Ball ships are on ballistic courses...."

What?

Today I saw an engine at its bottom!

I'm certain that I clearly saw the exhaust of a gigantic Labyrinthium engine!

"Yes, General. I saw that picture in your mind. To escape Earth, Ball had to modify its ship."

Of course, idiot!

"Still, let's return once again to the original series of events. Once near to your Sun, Ball changed course, oriented its ship for a fast, direct plunge."

"How do you, in space, change course of a ship without its own source of power, travelling on a ballistic trajectory?"

"Logically, sir, you can't. Except with the help of...."

I nod.

Always the same answer.

>Telepathy.<

"Yes. Telepathy. But not anywhere. Such a change is possible only inside a strong magnetic field, close to a star. So, Ball aimed for your sun. Instead, certainly a vast surprise, his chunk of neutronium squarely hit your Earth."

"You always say Ball did this, Ball did that. Couldn't its ship's computers...."

"No, General. You've seen the ship. It's rather crude. No computers on board. No need for those, in fact. Ball itself is a supercomputer par excellence."

Right.

"When it hit, it must have generated a fairly significant, albeit localized catastrophe. Alien's spaceship crushed the edge of an existing craton, then plunged underneath into the molten mantle of your planet. When the tumult subsided, the foundations of your archipelago have been created.

On the other hand, trying to determine where and when the space alien landed, we studied many other meteorite and comet impacts on this planet's surface, mostly prompted by research of Earth's own scientists. The initial moment of impact, when the spatial body almost instantaneously vaporizes, is usually characterized by a huge explosion, more massive than any weapon humanity so far devised, causing the largest and most lasting damage."

"Depending on meteor's size and composition, of course."

(I feel proud that I could think of that detail)

"Indeed, sir. But I was talking about those spatial bodies with comparable size or mass to solar alien's vessel. In case of its neutronium vessel, despite the hit, no explosion occurred."

"Shouldn't it have exploded on contact? Isn't neutronium supposed to be a potent explosive?"

Chuckle.

"Potentially, yes. Some of your scientists named it "the doomsday explosive", I believe. Under certain conditions, it can certainly be dangerous. When needed, my civilization uses it as a powerful tool. But Ball fully controlled the shape of its spaceship; thus, it didn't explode. Self-evident, since you watched it lift off, quite intact, just a few moments ago."

Silence.

Uncomfortable silence?

I believe I felt something, a subtle change.

For the last part of his sentence, his tone of voice was wrong.

"Quite intact or.... not quite intact?" - something prompted me to ask that question, though I couldn't fathom the reason why I might think the alien's ship flawed in any particular way.

Another chuckle and Zhang's first deeply personal glance; one of respect and admiration: - "Indeed, General, you detected a discrepancy in my thoughts. We believe that it suffered some damage on impact. Maybe it was only slightly damaged. Even in the absence of damage, the momentum of its flight, provided by the initial explosion of the supernova was now spent. The ship would require a new, physical, drive, the Labyrinthium engine you noticed, and a physical presence controlling it, to guide Ball's ship into your Sun."

"Thom's android! That's what it was doing during the liftoff! It was piloting Ball's ship!

(And for all I know, the android is still piloting it. Or did it already crash into our Sol?)

That's why Thom Brdar referred to it as the final ingredient."

"True, sir. True." - Zhang simply nods as additional affirmation, then continues - "Ball, itself, is completely incapable of physically manipulating any mechanisms, except by telepathy. We don't know the limitations of Ball's telepathic abilities in executing control over a Labyrinthium powerplant."

God, another colossal truth!

"Back to the history, General. The timeline for much of those half a billion years of solar alien's captivity on Earth completely lacks any traces or proofs. It's only what we surmise, therefore it's pure speculation, an exercise in logic. Yet, some steps must have been undertaken in logical order. Ball must have first ascertained and diagnosed damage to its ship, then formed a plan how to finish its journey into your Sol, its permanent home, one it will live in until the end of its lifetime and the arrival of its reproductive impulse of procreation by fission. If the communication network between various Balls exists, as we speculate that it does, based on telepathy, others of its kind may have been helping with ideas and advice."

Zhang's framework now appears obvious to me, so I triumphantly interrupt his story: - "To accelerate evolution of species on Earth until a sapient intelligence can develop the kind of civilization able to produce a sturdy, artificial physical form necessary to pilot its ship into the Sun?"

What a plan! And what a timeline for its execution. Half a billion years!

"Right, general. Remember, some five to six billion years of life remain to your Sun. After all, it's a relatively young star. Therefore, our solar alien sacrificed only a tenth of its potential lifetime to secure its future and the future of its species through its final act of procreation by fission."

I shake my head, examining that peculiar calculation: - "Reasonable."

"So; to execute its plan, Ball embarked on studying, then subtly controlling Earth's biological processes."

"How?"

"Telepathy; maybe some form of telekinesis. Chemical interaction."

"Chemical interaction? How?"

"Ball's telepathy is different from the human concept of telepathy. It allows meddling into physical and chemical processes. From a distance. By the power of its mind. That's how Ball moved various materials through Earth's mantle. And influenced the evolution of life forms. Slowly, patiently, doggedly, indefatigably."

Colossal! Unbelievable! Fantastic!

I smile.

I nod.

"Near its home, probably over a considerable length of time, it accumulated numerous raw materials potentially necessary for realization

of its plans. Needless to say, General, there's evidence that natural events such as meteor strikes, earthquakes, ice ages, and cataclysmal volcanic eruptions, repeatedly wiped-out star alien's evolutionary endeavors. Ball was forced to restart again and again."

"Your alien must possess an infinite patience!"

"It's your alien too, General. General David Anderson – Lionheart's alien. It took direct action to create you as you are. It's the real parent of all your superhuman abilities."

I shiver.

I'm aware that Zhang's statement is completely true.

I accept those facts.

Yet, to have a godlike alien as THE source, or the spring (or call it parent like Zhang Sanfeng did.... or the god who made me, as many Earth religions would understand it), of my most cherished (and most hated) abilities....

Stupefying!

Click.

New idea; new question.

"So, why Mongolia?"

I could now see Volcano watch observation building at the sheltered point of track's next curve, hiding behind a large outcropping of ancient volcanic rock. In five minutes, we'll be inside.

"Mongolia....

I'm coming to that.

General, my civilization became aware of these solar aliens about a hundred thousand Earth-years ago, therefore much before I emerged from my neonatal cradle.

(A dozen questions concerning the reproduction of DFQL aliens spring into my mind; immaterial, of no pressing importance; no time for such curiosity right now.)

It took a generation of our scientists to develop reliable methods of tracking solar alien's movements. Then, just a short time before my birth, of course by our scale of measurement, we learned of Earth and its solar alien. You see, General, my species reproduces and produces offspring for specialized purposes only. In my case, from the time I became a conscious, self-aware being, I knew that I will one day become a space traveler bound for the mystical planet named Earth."

Astronaut from birth!

Also, did he just imply that his species calls our planet "the Earth", too?

No, that's stupid....

"You certainly don't call it Earth in your own language?"

My tongue was again faster than my mind! I hope he doesn't think me silly!

"We don't use a language, sir. Therefore, we don't call it at all.

(A joke? Or a deft use of the English vernacular?)

It has a mental designation which I can't repeat to you, as your human form isn't equipped, nor adapt, to communicate the way our species of origin does."

Did he just imply that DFQL aliens communicate by telepathy? Or not? I must persist on discovering more.

"And the proper name for your species? I can't go on calling you "the DFQL aliens" forever, can I?"

"The same answer, sir. The way we "call" ourselves is unrepeatable, and can't be translated, as it's not formed in any language as such. We don't use mechanical oscillations for communication, such as is the base of your speech. Nor do we keep written records as you do. And yes, please feel free to apply to our species and civilization any convenient designation you might think of, such as "the DFQL aliens"."

We reach the shelter, and I open its door.

"Interesting architecture." - announces the DFQL elder, studying its interior.

"So, back to Mongolia...."

"Ah, Mongolia. All right. It was our firm belief, anticipating Ball's influence on the intelligent species, that the area on Earth with the most developed cultures and the strongest civilization would prove to be where our solar alien is hiding. We became elated on arrival to your planet, as we could immediately detect Ball's presence within its spheres. We also verified that Earth's teaming with lifeforms, some of them intelligent. One water-bound intelligence was receding, though. A failed star alien's experiment? Maybe. On the other hand, the land-bound intelligence was obviously blossoming! This confirmed all our information and speculation we amassed from afar. However, none of that revealed Ball's location. Even more, we had yet to glimpse the framework of Ball's masterplan. That we had to deduct, discover. Studying from the orbit, there wasn't any doubt. Seven thousand Earth years ago, the most developed civilizations

of indigenous land-based intelligent species, the humans, were on your Asian continent, grouped relatively close to each other."

"In China and India, I guess?"

"Indeed, General. Not just in these two locations, but the two you mention were prominent candidates. Though, mind you, neither China nor India at that time were in any way united. Both presented as clusters of focal civilizations. They were flanked by other great civilizations of the epoch. From the initial planning moments of our mission, we firmly decided to produce artificial beings in the image of whatever Earth's indigenous intelligent species we might discover, as the best way of ensuring freedom of action of our agents within the indigenous societies. Thus, we arrived with full necessary equipment. Ah, I caught your fleeting thought, sir. How did we know there was intelligent life on Earth, or life at all, in the first place? An automated scout ship preceded our mission to Earth. It revealed high probability of intelligent species on land, completely missing the water-bound culture. That's how we were informed. But that was more than ten thousand years before our arrival."

"A logical move."

"It took us almost five hundred years, but our efforts were crowned by manufacturing our eight engineered androids. The eight of us you see here. From your mind I can see that in your opinion they only vaguely resemble the contemporary Chinese. However, I assure you, seven thousand years ago, they would perfectly blend with the inhabitants of Mongolian dessert, and the nearby Chinese cultures."

"You had your holographic technology as a backup, I assume."

"Assuredly so. Our characters could take any human form and shape. In your atmosphere our holograms function somewhat imperfectly; you yourself witnessed this. Though, over time, we engineered some improvements in their performance. However, during more than six thousand years of their interaction with humans, we never had a major incident because of that deficiency."

"When did you discover that your estimates were wrong?"

"Soon after landing, sir. I'll explain that. However, I want first to emphasize how big a gamble our landing was."

"Gamble?"

"Yes. Our ship landed in today's Mongolia, in the Gobi Desert, in a desolate corner. It's still hidden there, way below the strata of rock that

participates in your biosphere, therefore by its presence not polluting and endangering any earthly lifeforms. By all practical standards, it's inert."

"Close to Earth's molten mantle?"

"Yes."

"Our scientists postulated a theory that your silicon-based lifeforms might prefer mantle's warmth over our oxygen-rich atmosphere."

"Essentially, they are right. Though, we couldn't have survived inside mantle's molten magma under all that enormous pressure. That's Ball's natural abode, not ours. There, your scientists are wrong."

I nod my understanding.

"So, our gamble: look General; we who surround you, we're much more than some engineered human beings. We're also hollow vehicles which shelter intelligence and auras of the original crew, while our real bodies lie hidden underground in deep stasis. You're aware how much the telepathy is important to us. It might not come as a surprise that every moment of our existence we remain in telepathic contact with our former bodies and our ship itself, especially its information systems which parallel your computers."

That's.... astonishing, brilliant, quite handy indeed.

"However...."

Now it's my turn to smile: - "There always seems to be some however."

My remark is awarded with a return smile.

"Isn't it so? However, our Earth surface mission is a trade-off, General."

"How so?"

"We could download our auras into the engineered humans and put our natural bodies and our ship itself into stasis only once. Only once."

My eyebrows arch.

"Uploading back into our natural lifeforms and activating our ship will mean the inevitable death, cessation of existence, of all our manufactured earthly agents."

"Is that why you said that once you leave, there won't be any communication between us?"

"Yes. That, and the fact that we have so far failed in our main mission, which, I remind you, is to effect contact with the solar alien. All our energy must be channeled into achieving that goal and erasing our failures up to date."

Something stirs in my mind. It appears that some bruised egos and a specific concept of honor must be involved in his last statement: - "So that you can finally return home in triumph?"

Some sadness creeps into his voice: - "No, General. The eight of us will never return home, will never again be part of our civilization. It's difficult to explain without understanding our society and the ways of our civilization. Yet, it's as I stated. We were all born to be spacefarers. Whether successful or not, we will die as spacefarers, accomplishing our duty to our kind."

Outcasts for life, but still fully devoted to their kind.

Sad.

Curious.

I'll have to think more about their situation.

Later.

Let's switch the subject.

Let me think.

Blink. Blink.

"So, your Asian gamble didn't pay off?"

"No, it didn't. Relatively soon upon starting to mix with local cultures we encountered news....

(he chuckles)

By "news" I meant rumors, legends, stories, tales....

(more chuckling)

.... about the rise, both a figure of speech as well as literal, from beneath the ocean's waves, in a place far, far away from Asia, of a special seafarer archipelago. It was rumored to have been elevated from the oceanic depths by its powerful protector gods. Fables, myths, and legends enshrouded that faraway gods-protected population, living at the other side of the world. It all led to a startling conclusion. Ball wasn't guiding and improving any of the existing civilizations. It was literally producing both its chosen land and its inhabitants from scratch."

"You're saying that the original inhabitants of Atlantis were engineered, too?"

"No. Yes. In a way. Not directly, as Ball simply recombined the materials at hand. Small groups of neighborhood humans were carefully selected and brought.... enticed to undertake a move.... or guided there; it's hard to tell....

(I nod; of course, much of this is pure logical deduction, as there aren't any witnesses.)

One way or the other, they arrived in their new archipelago home to procreate and build a powerful empire."

"Did you visit Atlantis?" - suddenly I wish I was one of those DFQL aliens, walking among the temples of our old Atlantis, thousands of years ago.

"No, Dave. Remember, we're talking about the time six thousand years ago. Earth wasn't easily traveled then. Especially not its oceans. It took us more than your century to arrive to the western shore of the continent which you now designate as "Africa", over high mountain ranges and through impassable desserts. By then, the cataclysm already occurred, and the core of Atlantis' civilization was destroyed and now lay underwater. Some remnants still existed. We visited the apex of this very volcano exactly hundred sixty-two years after Atlantis sank. We saw the pitiful leftovers of the once powerful empire, its remaining people defenseless, raided by neighbors and sold into slavery in the rising empires of the Nile and Euphrates deltas. But Atlantis was, at one time, unimaginably grand, General."

"They had electricity."

"Yes, what you today label as the direct current. They even had an electrical weapon, somewhat like your Tasers of today. It was much bulkier, but very effective against the enemies which had no concept of electricity. Those primitive opponents took it for a weapon of the gods."

I smile. I've seen it in the tablet message. They WERE mighty, indeed.

"Much more important to us, the sinking of Atlantis had gigantic repercussions on our mission. We couldn't make contact with Ball. We couldn't even sense its presence! We calculated that Ball would now be forced to continue its efforts through an existing civilization. For the next thousand years we vacillated in the vast area between Egypt to the west, China to the east, and India to the south. We also investigated Japan, but it was a far cry from today's sophisticated society. Three of us spent almost five hundred of your years traveling to Mesoamerica, to check on civilizations rising under the shadows of Earth's tallest and most active volcanoes."

"You expected that proximity to volcanos would still be the main giveaway of Old Man's presence?"

"Yes. You might not realize it, but the geography of many ancient Earth civilizations encompassed at least one active volcano; often many more."

"Territory you mentioned.... including China.... hence DFQL?"

"No. DFQL came along much later, in the twentieth century, when we had to realign our strategy. Yet, for the longest of our time on Earth we did dwell in China. I'm not bragging, General, but I did know the real Zhang Sanfeng. For about three years I was even a disciple of his. I also shared meals with various Chinese Emperors. And some Mongolian ones, for a good measure. Always pretending to be a different person, of course!

(we both smile)

One of us was a pal of Alexander the Great. We lived alongside Cleopatra, Cesar, Mohammad, some famous and infamous Popes, the rulers of the Indian Mogul dynasty. Oh, I forgot Buddha. He was an interesting person indeed, albeit different from the later image he's accredit with."

I feel the rise of jealousy and envy; at the same time, I also feel pride. These almost omnipotent beings (well, less omnipotent than Ball, of course) had accumulated an immense understanding of the human civilization; yet, we of Newlands, for a long time successfully held them at bay.

"General, if lived through, the human history hugely differs from what you learn in your schools. I can't even start to name all inaccurate facts and ideas which today's humanity holds on historical persons and events. Yet, distortions and untruths have always been the way of humanity, the foundation of your history and civilization, especially its religious backbone."

"Unfortunately, my friend, you're right."

All my hair stands up on my arms. For the first time ever, I've called this alien being "my friend". Yet, I can't escape a feeling of.... brotherhood with these eternal astronauts.

"What will happen with DFQL when you leave?"

"In a diminished form, they will continue their political struggle. We had nothing to do with that part of their agenda. Of interest to us was only DFQL's Daoist foundation, which we exploited for our own goals."

Understandably so.

"What will happen with your engineered human selves when you leave?"

"Officially, we have already left, this morning, from Paloma's Marina, on a chartered yacht "*Bulbuder 2*". On a pleasure cruise to Bermuda. Our yacht will disappear along the planned route. No trace will ever be found of it."

Astonished with his disclosure, I raise my eyebrows.

"The owners have already been reimbursed tenfold times for their loss, though they don't yet know it. We saw to it that they don't retain any permanent memory of the whole endeavor. In the meantime, with the newest assumed identities, we will board a Newlands Airlines flight to Zhengzhou...."

"China."

"Yes. From there, we will proceed to our secret base in Mongolia."

I nod.

"Once our auras are successfully uploaded into our proper lifeforms, these eight bodies will be utterly destroyed, atomized."

"No.... Why?"

"Another very powerful human emotion, General, which I can feel even across the distance separating us. Can it be that you're now concerned about the fate of our engineered humans, though you would have done your best to destroy them until....

(a smile)

.... about an hour ago?"

"No.... Yes.... I mean, your avatars, though engineered, are still human, no matter what. And even your species can't predict the future; you yourself told me about your failures. Why not spare yourself the need for spending another five hundred years rebuilding your human bodies, just in case?"

"What do you have in mind, General?"

At the end, my ideas got fully accepted. Once the uploading of their auras is successfully accomplished, our friendly DFQL aliens will leave Earth. Before their spaceship leaves our atmosphere, a pod will be detached, containing their deactivated human (superhuman) bodies. Undetectable by any human technology, it will land by MARC's lake on Ceti II, then completely disintegrate.

The bodies will be collected.

By us.

By MANATO.

They will be kept in hibernation in MARC, forever if needed. DFQL aliens even permitted gentle, noninvasive experimentation on those bodies, so long as they retain full potential for a future revival, however unlikely that would be in view of their conviction that they can download their auras into these avatars only once.

I will make certain that we treat those bodies with utmost respect. And I will make certain that all CICs coming after me do the same.

It turned out than Zhang Sanfeng worried about much larger dangers than simply leaving their engineered human bodies behind, revealing to humans the underlying technology needed for their construction. When they manufactured them, they gave them all attributes of normal human beings, including full reproductive ability. I had to promise that MANATO won't embark on production of human / alien hybrids; not just promise but also offer to formulate a secret military law forbidding such activity, supported by top political structures of our state. Such hybrids have happened in the past, mostly unintentionally, but either swiftly died of biochemical imbalances or were taken care of before they could disrupt biological equilibrium of humanity (I was assured that such indiscretions were resolved by sterilization or castration, not elimination).

Zhang clarified his statement concerning the planet Mercury. When their ship leaves our Earth, its destination will be the sunward side of the innermost planet of our solar system. Mercury. Once there, they will be as close as possible to the solar alien inhibiting our Sun. As Mercury slowly rotates, taking almost two Earth months for one rotation around its axis, their ship will keep relocating to remain on planet's sunward side. The same shields which protected (and still protect) their vessel from Earth's prowling eyes and ears will keep protecting it on Mercury. Zhang had no alternate plans. He and his crew will stay on Mercury until communication with the solar alien gets established, or they perish.

Grudgingly, Zhang allowed that Newlands might one day build space vessels able to get to Mercury and reestablish contact with his people. However, he urged MANATO to instead concentrate on Mars and the other more distant astronomical bodies, which promise more chance of permanent human settlement than the hell-hot Mercury.

At the end, we shook hands like longtime friends. And then, like shadows in the night, the eight Taoist priests disappeared.

It was as if a balloon suddenly popped, and the reality shimmered and changed. Hundreds of MANATO soldiers and machines descended

on Mount Palamar's apex. I smiled at their approach, for I had a mighty tale to tell, backed by Raj's secret recordings!

Sam has just climaxed.

I searched for a wet hanky to clean our bodies.

Undisturbed by our playing, Alisa cuddled in our big Rad bed next to us, fast asleep, exhausted with her part in coordinating PsiMANATO's response to my apparent abduction and stranding on top of our tallest volcano a couple of days ago (and, tonight, some demanding sex with Sam and me).

I kissed my beloved husband, habitually chewing on his bristling moustache.

Then my cellphone rang.

Dedicated melody informed me that it was Dr Irena Panj.

(What now? With all aliens gone, what's the emergency? Something to do with the DFQL bodies which arrived yesterday?)

"Yes?" – I might have sounded more unpleasant than usual. This time Sam did achieve his climax faster than me (a rarity), and a raging erection was weighing down my mid-section, demanding some urgent release (indeed, Sam's left hand was diligently traveling up and down my shaft; after the initial discomfort, I've developed a strange sexual fetish: I now prefer being masturbated by his metallic hand).

"General Anderson – Lionheart, we have a red alert magnitude emergency in MARC! Please, can you fly over at once?"

Emotional words.

She sounds almost scared.

And, despite the cooling of our relations after the android disaster, that formal way of addressing me at the beginning.... Since when am I not Dave?

"What's happening?"

"Please, not over the phone.... you must see this for yourself, bre!"

Not even over the secure and encrypted MANATO Commander – in – Chief's cellphone line, now free of DFQL's prying?

"I...." – First, I need to cum, lady!

"Please, sir!"

Think!

Think!

"I'll wake up Rob and.... I'll be there ASAP.

(then an afterthought.... thinking is so difficult when all you want to do is ejaculate)

As I progress, keep informing me of any changes in your emergency (whatever it may be)."

"Yes, sir."

My cell goes dead.

Sam is glaring at me, his left hand still firmly holding my penis.

"Why do you prcat need to wake up Robert?"

"I.... because I need his.... 100th Squadron's service, of course." – I reply with some force, my heart sinking at the same time. Sam's a pilot, too; our best ever. And his rank guarantees that he can commandeer any flying machine as efficiently or more easily than Rob.

"What about me, mrdat silly CIC?"

How do I escape from this trap of my own doing?

I lower myself onto Sam's chest and give him a humongous kiss.

"I was wrong, dear hubster. You're right.

(Sam immediately brightens, as he so enjoys being proven right, especially if I'm simultaneously proven wrong.)

Can't think while you're holding my dick, silly. Stop squeezing my dick! No time for that!

(he chuckles and lets go of my pride)

YOU can secure for us some transportation. And fly me to Ceti II. On your feet, soldier; you have your orders!"

(pause)

Alisa stirs, studying the face of our bedroom clock: - "Mrdat three after midnight! What's wrong now?"

"Another emergency in MARC, my moon and stars; Irena couldn't talk over the phone, so it could be anything; it must be important, I guess. I'm afraid it could be something to do with the bodies. Sam's going to fly me there pronto.

(Pronto is Salvador Kuul's beloved byword; under his influence, I find myself using it more and more often.)

I'll keep you informed and let you know if it impinges your work."

I kiss my wife on her right cheek.

"Take care of our children.... (Zhengxiang is tonight sleeping over with our sons, in the next room, so that Li and Rob can have a night of uninterrupted sex.... pardon me, uninterrupted rest) and say hi to Fran and Fanta when they arrive in the morning."

“Marka mu, I will. You two, be careful. I distrust those weird MARC emergencies! And I’ll never understand what on prcat Earth possessed you to make that pact with DFQL!”

Still, it took time.

Sergeant-Pilot Hans Prust was the 100$^{th}$ Squadron standby flyer in Nordporte. Sam ordered him to commandeer the sole available Newlands Army NH Industries 90 heavy helicopter from the Braća Karan airbase (Nordporte’s mighty airfield). He was to meet us on the Luka airport. Though we had to drive there, we managed to beat him hands down (by about ten minutes). Upon his arrival I cordially greeted our copilot (short, thin, hummingbird quick, of intelligent eyes and the inevitable colossal 100$^{th}$ Squadron-type moustache). However, in my mind I resolved to inspect the amount of red tape a relatively junior pilot faces when ordered to commandeer a machine. I need to slice and trim all that bureaucracy into a faster procedure, if any way possible.

One day.

When I get some spare time.

(After I cum, heh.)

But I’ll firmly note it for future reference.

We were soon on our way, flying into a tropical night adorned with dramatic post-eruption low pressure front transiting between our main island group and Ceti II, with incessant lightning illuminating our darkened cockpit and occasional heavy rain drumming against helicopter’s windshield, drowning all possible conversation.

Sam piloted surefootedly and efficiently (as always), but the NH Industries 90 isn’t made to fly high over adverse weather like an airliner. By the time Sam landed in MARC’s very own courtyard (after I had to override orders of a way too cautious junior overnight Airforce ATC who, over the top worried for the safety of his Commander – in – Chief and his Exec, insisted that we land in the airbase on the other side of the island), I felt like a thoroughly shaken milkshake.

Nay.

I felt like a thoroughly shaken bottle of Coke, ready to explode!

Sergeant-Pilot Prust remained to guard our chopper, while Sam and I ran into compound (dodging some oversized raindrops), swearing at security procedures initiated by its automatic gates, introduced by my

very own orders (for which occasion I reminded myself how to use some of the juiciest American cussing).

"What's your red alert about? What's the emergency? Something to do with the bodies?" – I shouted at Dr Panj as soon as I spotted her. She was waiting for us in the main hallway. If she happened to be less of a scientist, my bellow would have blown her through a side door. Somehow, her scientific knowledge helped her keep her balance.

Even more ludicrously, though she tried to keep her face straight and impassive, I felt an inkling that she was stifling a broad smile.

What the hell?

Then it hit me: where's the flashing? Where's the audible blaring of klaxons?

Frowning at Sam, I glanced at the colored lights strategically placed along the wall.

Yellow for yellow alert.

Red for red alert.

All quiet!

None flashing!

No sound at all!

What the hell, on the second power?

No red alert?

Not even a yellow alert?

(I kicked myself for being so trustful and not distance-checking MARC's status; I'm the supreme boss around here, I could have easily done it from Rad.)

What game is Irena playing now?

"What the hell? What the hell to the max?"

Irena motions with both hands, as if warding off evil, at the same time turning and assuming a fast pace down the corridor. Sam and I had no chance but to try to catch up: - "Be patient, CIC. Give me a moment, bre. Marka mu, I have something extremely important to show you."

"Important? No red alert? How dare you.... (interrupt my sex when I'm just about to have an orgasm).... to.... to.... summon me...."

"Dave, when you see what I want you to see, you will be grateful."

Grateful? Enough to spare her the firing squad?

Suddenly Irena changes her tack and charges one of those fully paneled side doors. Despite my multiple visits to this compound, I never

bothered to ask (check) what's behind them. Seemingly, I'm about to find out. Right now.

"Calisse de merde, see for yourself, sir!"

She reaches for the knob, presses it, and the door opens.

A man, dressed in surgeon's fatigues and flipflops, steps out of the shadowy room.

Tall.

Broad, wide-shouldered.

Muscled.

Immaculate.

Domineering.

Beaming eyes.

Moustache.

Moustache!

Moustache!!!

"Thom!!!"

Maybe I grabbed him first; maybe he was faster; later, I couldn't remember. We jumped and hugged and kissed and giggled like school children, then a projectile struck me from behind, another body pressed into both of us, and Sam's metallic left arm undulated its way around both Thom and me.

For the next fifteen minutes the three of us shrieked and babbled and cried.

Maybe longer.

Amid our celebrations, I caught a glance of Irena's face.

She was crying, too.

And I thought of Ball.

# EPILOGUE

Abandoning the last remnants of Earth's atmosphere, Ball's neutronium ship slightly corrects its course, then surges towards the still distant Sol on a perpendicular trajectory destined to score a direct bullseye.

After leaving the planet, which was for such a long time its home, under the full Labyrinthium thrust and fully shielded so that no human device (on land below, in the air, or imbedded in the panoply of satellites above) had a hope in hell of detecting it, the spaceship swiftly accelerates to about one third lightspeed, its designated cruising speed, even before it passes the Moon.

At such speeds, the measly hundred fifty million kilometres separating this system's dominant local star, which the humans name Sun or Sol, and its third planet, known as Earth or Terra, more favorably compares to a comfortable suburban train ride than to real space travel.

Ball is in a hurry.

In the moment of its greatest triumph, the completion of implementation of its inhumanly long vintage plan going back half a billion years, this ageless and almost immortal star denizen detects a novel, thoroughly unexpected, and somewhat strange mind setup coursing through its core being.

Impatience.

(Emotional contamination from the absorbed human unit, impatience being the commonly occurring human affliction? Maybe. Governed by the profound natural laws ruling the whole universe, Balls do not possess emotions in the human sense of that word. Now, however, this Ball detects vestiges of many emotions churning through its mind: yearning, nostalgy, impatience; impatience above all.)

Home – home – home.

Its new home approaches with terrifying speed and a logarithmic-scale hike in the intensity of all kinds of radiation. A deadly shower for a human (or any other carbon-based lifeform), but a balmy bath to a Ball.

How beautiful.

How welcoming.

How pleasant.

Home.

The new home.

The one Ball waited for more than a billion years.

Suddenly manifesting in the background of Ball's mind, Thom Brdar softly chuckles: - >Impatient, are we, eh?<

Thom Brdar was definitely an accidental, unlooked-for acquisition, arriving way too late in the game to contribute to the master plan. Absorption of local intelligent minds was never envisaged as part of the final solution. Neither this Ball's plans, nor any modifications suggested by other Balls cooperating through their universe-wide telepathic network, opted for such an attempt, never recorded in the long history of their species.

Ball left many of his favorite human units back on the planet which, for half a billion years, served as its impromptu home. The one most beloved of all (if only Ball could feel love) was General David Anderson – Lionheart. That unit required the most time to take care of; incredibly and contrary to the plan which didn't forecast any further interaction with humans, now it's certain that there will be a place for this unit in Ball's future. Some, or more precisely a tiny amount of Ball's abilities, knowledge, and understanding were transferred into that unit, more than into any other human being ever. Still, that unit got it all wrong about Thom Brdar and his position within this strange interstellar symbiose. For, though completely and irrevocably immersed within Ball's being, Thom Brdar's aura remains completely autonomous.

Thom Brdar's acquisition (absorption) was a purely unpremeditated accident. In the last ten thousand years Ball developed, then perfected, its method of extending a fringe of its massive intellect towards a human unit (towards the consciousness of that particular human unit, mostly while the human in question is asleep, but occasionally when alert, too), to secure understanding of an idea, plan, plea, request.... Or order.

(Thinking this, Ball almost chuckles to itself, immediately realizing that chuckling and humor are also imports from the pesky but indispensable humans; then chuckles again at its own analysis of chuckling. The reason for all this chuckling? Invariably, all humans thus contacted perceived Ball as an enormous, dark, amorphous, or even lizard-like monster. That was obviously the way their peculiar indirect senses perceived Ball's reality, augmented by the strange social artifact referred to as "culture". None

of them managed to penetrate past that repulsive image to perceive the majesty of a star dweller consisting of pure plasma.)

On that fateful day, Ball judged the time ripe to attempt such communication with General Anderson – Lionheart. Instead, an unknown and up to then disregarded, overlooked, not-paid-attention-to unit named Thom Brdar stood there, both physically and mentally barring the way. Then it telepathically pounced.

(Ball generally boosted genetical transmission of telepathy genes among human units, mostly in its chosen archipelago, though some also strewn all over the Earth. Usually, it managed to keep close tabs on all humans who developed that skill, but Thom Brdar somehow slipped through a crack.)

Unit Thom Brdar had no idea what it was pouncing against. Ball's communication extension automatically defended (before Ball's intellect could analyze the situation and decide on the appropriate course of action), and on reflex absorbed Thom Brdar's aura. And left that unit's depleted material body to briefly linger, aura-less, brainless, mindless.

From the very first micro-bit of coexistence, maybe to atone for the unplanned mistake, Ball preserved Thom Brdar's aura intact and independent within its mode of thinking. Soon, positive sides of that decision manifested. The new aura possessed strange but intricate thinking patterns and judgment criteria, mostly childish in the eyes of the eternal star dweller and its peers, but still providing a separate, autonomous, and (in its own way) logical checkpoint, to judge all Ball's actions with, those still only planned and those already undertaken. In the endless time ahead, Brdar's will remain a welcome opposing point of view, when intricate matters of physics, astronomy, and philosophy, in their turn, get contemplated. Ball will keep Thom Brdar autonomous until the last moments of its own existence. Only when this nearly immortal spacefarer becomes ready to fission into its progeny will their two minds fully merge. Each progeny unit will inherit a part of what once was Thom Brdar. Will Thom Brdar manage to remain a separate entity inside those new Balls? Ball doesn't and couldn't know. And, by default, will never know.

A lifespan measured in billions of years (much longer than the probable lifespan of humanity itself) should be enough compensation for destruction of Thom Brdar's physical unit back on Earth.

Compensation.

Compensation isn't the fitting term.

Much more than compensation.

Award?

Sun's gravitational pull exponentially increases. Pulled by that massive gravity right into star's bosom, neutronium ship's speed increases, too.

The heat radiation surges, causing a rush of utter pleasure.

Telepathy.

The force which binds and connects the universe, spanning it from end to end.

Telepathy is much more than humans, or dolphins, understand it to be. To them, it's an extraordinary way of communication, and not much more.

In fact, it's everything, one of nature's fundamental forces, alongside gravity, electromagnetism, and weak and strong nuclear forces. In many respects, telepathy trumps all of those and is the most potent of all, under specific circumstances able to influence the other fundamental forces and operate at any scale of existence.

Telepathy is alchemy.

Ball was amused when the "group of three" scientists advising General David Anderson – Lionheart voiced the idea that mineral riches accumulated in Newlands archipelago got painstakingly, over long time, assembled from all over the planet, using "highways" burrowed through liquid magma. What would be the need for that? Using telepathy, Ball simply changed the atomic and molecular structure of materials at hand. Certainly, a decidedly slow process, occasionally taking extraordinary long time (but time is what a Ball rarely lacks). Production of metallic deposits was easy, as they mostly consist of one simple compound, obviously necessary for success of a civilization which needed to achieve the ability to construct almost indestructible androids. The easiest of all were pure deposits, such as diamonds, gold, platinum, platiniridium. The most difficult was oil, requiring production and mixing of various complex organic molecules. Ball's mind would telepathically scan other Earth's deposits, study their transformation and ripening into a useful source of energy, then emulate the process in convenient spots in its chosen archipelago. So, if Ball gave all that oil to his people/pawns (not all of it yet discovered, as Newlands is graced with double the amount of oil the rest of world possesses, though that reserve is probably redundant as the whole archipelago economy seems poised to leap into the carbon-neutral

one powered by Labyrinthium fission and renewable energy, for which all required raw materials have been accumulated too) why not coal as well? Another misconception of those Newlandean scientists. Coal, universally found all over the world, located on all its continents (and deep under the Arctic ice and under the bottoms of the oceans), wasn't depleted in the process of moving those other essential materials to the archipelago. It was simply never produced. From the dawn of human civilization, the time way before the industrial revolution, Ball perceived how a population explosion could combine with coal exploitation to form disastrous results for Earth's biosphere, changing the chemical composition of its atmosphere and hence the thermodynamic conditions on planet's surface, hampering development of the supercivilization needed to help Ball back into space. Oil demonstrably had the same potential, but the math was a bit different, its detrimental curves less pronounced. Ball's bet was that the needed level of civilization could be achieved before disastrous consequences of fossil fuel usage would be unleashed.

The next obvious question begs to be asked. What then of Earth's future, so long Ball's home? Well, the persistent fact, which those human-centric perspectives always seem to forget, is that the inorganic planet itself is in no way threatened by the global warming and other pollution calamities unleashed by humankind. Mankind doesn't (yet) possess powers to threaten a planet's existence. Neither does the Ball civilization! It's quite probable that Ball will still serenely monitor its previous home, from not that far away, peacefully circling its new solar abode, long after the humankind works itself into extinction, one way or another.

Telepathy is botany.

It was telepathy which made possible the outstanding, surprising growth of plant species transplanted from all over the world. In less than half a century the barren archipelago, just risen from ocean's depths with nothing alive on its rocks and sands but the fast dying (and as fast rotting) pellagric flora and fauna, turned into lush subtropical jungle with abundant presence of birds and aquatic fauna. Yes, the Newlandeans helped with incessant volunteering to spread soil and plants all over the archipelago, but Ball's telepathy made the flora grow at far faster pace than is natural; telepathy also summoned birds, fish, sea mammals, and even various useful insects. Once Ball understood the curious promise of winemaking, its telepathy enhanced Newlandean vineyards into some of world's best. Telepathy made corals grow at depths they are traditionally

unaccustomed to colonize. It also influenced various species of phyto and zooplankton to colonize archipelago's waters, providing the indispensable food source for the abundant ocean life.

Telepathy is microscopic research.

And, at that, much more powerful than the finest electron microscopy humanity has so far fashioned. From the earliest days of the simplest forms of cellular life, Ball studied the magnificent molecule of DNA in all its variations, one of the most conservative molecules ever developed, on which all carbon life was based, the true ruler of Earth's biosphere. Ball amassed the infinite knowledge of every atom, every element, every compound and structure forming the mighty DNA (and RNA) of all lifeforms on the planet, existing and extinct. It perfectly understood how specific genes related to expression of certain traits or abilities in humans, dolphins, social dinosaurs, and a dozen other species or groups of species it tried to work with in order to catalyze development of the supercivilization it envisioned.

Throughout the eons of striving, Ball made countless minuscule, but significant changes in DNAs of its chosen subjects.

Yes.

From that point of view, the humans living today in the Newlands archipelago, the Newlanders, no longer completely belong to the Homo sapiens species. They are more like an improved version of Homo sapiens; toying with the ancient Latin, Earth's scientists could.... and would probably classify them as "Homo sapiens melius (the improved Homo sapiens)", if they suspected that a change occurred (telepathy effectively prevents such suspicion). Healthier, with a marked absence of many debilitating and disabling genetic afflictions, boasting a changed function of leptin and other fat deposit regulating hormones, redefined functions of neurotransmitters such as dopamine, endorphin, and enkephalin, a slightly better conversion of oxygen, a slightly stronger structure of tendons and skeletal muscles, more efficient digestion, etc. etc. etc. (the list is almost endless). More inclined to logical thinking, less prone to be ruled by the collective mindlessness of their instincts and the unconscious, resistant to the religions and other groupthinks, partially resistant to mind-altering substances. Better coordinated, with some crucial anatomical ratios slightly improved to deliver enhanced function, considerably empowering the final assembly. With improved intelligence,

especially in the formatting years of their early childhood, able to achieve speedier maturity.

Next, those subtle changes in the human DNA needed to be retained and concentrated, not watered down by mixing the modified Newlandean DNA with that of all other populations of human beings, represented by archipelago's newest immigrants.

Humans in general, abroad as well as on Newlands, are just about to step up their research of microbiome's functions; their individualistic egotism and self-centred philosophy prevents them from understanding that they aren't independent individual beings, but complicated colonies of millions of different beings, mostly microscopic. Microbiome is responsible for the human development, smooth functioning of their minds, it controls their immunity and body shape, and much more. Microorganisms forming the Newlander microbiome are far superior to any other combination found elsewhere on Earth, and that didn't happen by chance but by Ball's design.

Those changes in microbiome now also needed to be preserved and strengthened.

So, how could all that be achieved, how could the DNA and microbiome changes be safeguarded?

Controlling the DNA and the composition of microbiome were the less important facets of the whole story.

Ball often played another, much more potent, trump card. Most of its desired effects were accomplished instilling specific genetic memories. Ball's telepathy easily integrated those genetic memories into the human genetic code.

Genetic memories, present at birth, existing without any sensory experience, incorporated into the genome of all species over long spans of time, are the backbone of processes which control behavior of most species on Earth. Yet, the human scientists have made but the tiniest steps into acknowledgment of their existence, not to mention understanding their underlaying biochemical matrix and mode of functioning.

Thus, Ball's telepathy evolved into intergenerational storytelling. With its mastery of DNA molecule, Ball learned how to share stories with its subjects through their genetic memory. That never worked with social dinosaurs but gave positive results with the cetaceans and primates, mainly the humans. Right into the genetic code of a subject, Ball could insert information about ideas, technological procedures, locations of

materials, methods to be used to achieve a certain goal, likes and dislikes, attraction, and fear.

It is always stated, usually in the form of an observed, immutable fact, that Newlands, itself starting as a hundred percent immigration society, in a couple of short generations became a country very severely restricting further immigration. The children of immigrants started voting against the new waves of immigration. This was explained as a peculiar form of selfishness, or lack of altruism; that the young Newlandeans didn't wish to share their parents' and their own brilliant achievements with anyone in the world who wasn't contributing. Much did those respected social scientists know!

Ball was responsible for the introduction of a two-step worldwide genetic memory into the human genome. Step one was to make Newlandeans leery of the outside world. They remain curious to learn, may occasionally desire to go out and explore, but nothing of the reminder of Earth holds much permanent attraction: cultures, ideas, religions, even people. Hence a gradually ever-toughening stance towards the immigrants.

Compared to the massive second step, that first prong was but a tiny challenge to Ball's telepathic ability. That second endeavor was making the whole humanity go generally blind towards the achievements and advances of Newlands, instilling a general benevolent liking towards Newlanders, and lenience towards their more controversial undertakings and transgressions of established world order. But the second step proved successful too, and all those things came to pass.

As a result, Newlandeans don't notice the world much.

As the additional larger result, the world doesn't mind too much what Newlands is doing.

Even in Ball's absence, these established effects will keep affecting humanity's behavior for centuries to come, finally slowly diluting and dissipating.

What did the genetic memories bring to Newlands?

These are just some examples:

They revealed the positions of most of its mineral riches, including where to find the Labyrinthium (the richest of its deposits is still hidden, but that information is already instilled into the Newlander genome; when the outside conditions turn appropriate, Newlandean researchers will "know" where to look).

Deep tilling process which revolutionised the food production in the archipelago.

Blueprints for machines, instruments, and weapons far outperforming anything else on Earth (the superior spaceships and space stations are about to become the reality, too; indeed, some superweapons have been provided as well, in case Newlands is every realistically threatened from the outside).

Access to unlimited energy.

Medical knowledge and procedures that others could only dream of.

Much deeper, almost instinctive understanding of functioning of the World Wide Web and the Newlands Intranet Network.

Even the industrial-scale procedures which will be necessary to arrest the global warming, rise of the greenhouse gasses, and the catastrophic temperature variations (if the world doesn't unite around the idea of limiting damage to its planet caused by the industrialization, and those industrial-scale efforts become necessary).

The smoking ban.

Openness to legal drug use.

The acceptance of sex as an important form of direct interaction and communication between all members of society.

And multiple less obvious effects.

There was never a reason to use just a single method of influencing, when combining two or more would achieve better results: yes, the ideas of deep tilling and the necessary equipment to achieve it were passed on to Newlandeans as genetical memories, but Ball's telepathy first changed the accumulated deposits of the useless ocean bottom silt into the richest, most fertile soil on the planet, creating a reserve which could last thousands of years. However, it won't have to, as the blueprints for complete transformation of Newlander food production into hydroponics-based plant nurture and creation of lab-grown cloned meet have already been installed into their genome, waiting for everyday life's appropriate triggers to emerge into the conscious thought and get transformed into the path-altering action.

What of the android Thom Lionheart unit? It's still here, an intricate forcefield protecting it from Sol's destructive radiation, fatefully navigating this ship on its course into the sun. Even before leaving the security of Mount Palamar volcano's subterranean chamber, Thom Lionheart's aura was successfully transferred to its newly cloned biological body,

developed in MARC under Ball's unconscious telepathic guidance. Thus, Ball had no alternative but to directly, telepathically, assume control of the metallic android suddenly bereft of its "soul".

An easy thing to do. After all, the long years of Ball's numerous knowledge transfers to biological units on Earth were all sublimated into that android's construction. Ball is intimately aware of every single intricacy of its design and performance.

Android's bio-metallic body won't survive this collective's immersion into the Sun. Nor will Ball's neutronium ship (which, unlike the instantly perishing android, will slowly dissolve over the next billion years or so). Both have fulfilled their purpose. It's time they cede place to new things.

Neutronium ships of the newly born spacefaring Balls are launched into space, on their predetermined and precalculated courses, in the final moment of the orgy of destruction of their birthing supernova. Their target stars are carefully chosen in advance, and their trajectories calculated well ahead of their launch.

Mistakes rarely occur.

When Ball's mistake did occur, it rendered its ship, itself produced without any active propulsion but the inertia gained in the final supernova explosion, lodged into Earth's mantle without any possibility of creating a supernova out of this tiny world to regain the energy needed to finish its journey to Ball's new home.

Over time, the joined minds of all Balls strewn across the vast universe (for telepathy almost instantaneously connects all of them), found an answer to this problem which never occurred in the memory of their species; therefore they had no experience with resolving it.

Labyrinthium was to be the solution.

Ball's ship will be able to move to its target star under the Labyrinthium propulsion!

Ball needed to fashion a Labyrinthium engine for its ship. Though most of the manufacture and control could be achieved telepathically, grace to ship's almost indestructible neutronium hull and its imperfect aerodynamic shape, there was need for a robotic device, an externally perched machine, to finetune spaceship's navigation on its trip from its cradle under Earth's surface into the waiting star. However, some facets of manufacturing of that robot appeared impossible for unaided telepathy to deliver. Help of an indigenous civilization, capable of assembling such a robot, became imperative.

(Labyrinthium propulsion was thus invented eons ago as a solution to Ball's precarious situation, not as an energy source which would give its chosen civilization an unbeatable advantage over its competitors.)

The Sun is getting ever closer.

Ball grows lively with the increase in radiation, its plasmatic metabolism increasing tenfold times.

Almost home!

Labyrinthium.

Humans have yet to understand what Labyrinthium really is.

If they ever manage to transgress their preconceptions.

Bluntly speaking, they might never fully understand what Labyrinthium is.

For Labyrinthium isn't a haphazard collection of strange elements and compounds. It's much more. It's the single material by-product, a spinoff of Ball's living processes. A metabolite. A leftover. Almost excreta. Very vaguely resembling the urine, feces, milk, sperm, sweat, vomit, honey, spit, silk, sap, slime or any other secretion or excretion of carbon-based Earth organisms. But it's much more than excreta. It's the means every Ball uses to change its home star to adapt it to the lifecycle of its species. It's the ultimate creator of the supernovas. Slowly diffused over uncounted billions of years into a star's volume, Labyrinthium will force a star with a different stellar destiny, predetermined by its starting mass, to go supernova. For the metallicity is the only other factor which can offset the mass-determined destiny of a star, and Labyrinthium is a superheavy concoction of metals.

What could be the need which birthed such a gigantic experiment in alchemy?

Simply stated, the length of a Ball's life.

The massive stars which the universe predetermined to become supernovas usually have much shorter lifespan than the less massive stars which normally end their lives as white dwarfs. By synthetizing and deploying Labyrinthium, Balls developed a method of availing themselves of the longer lifespan of those smaller stars, without relinquishing the spectacular supernova ending necessary to propel their offspring ships through the endless cosmic void.

Yet, as always, there's even more to Labyrinthium than that spectacular function.

For, defined by human standards, Labyrinthium is alive, aware, and with full telepathic ability! (No wonder no human outside of Newlands managed to synthetize Labyrinthium or any similar combination of chemical elements in a lab; it's not so simple to create a non-carbon life form.)

Even in its most diluted form, such as the original batch presented to the Newlandean ore prospectors, Labyrinthium is fully telepathic and sentient. What's more, even in its depleted form, as the protective material MANATO named "KGZ", Labyrinthium can still sense a telepath's distress, and act accordingly. Thus, his KGZ clothing protected General Anderson – Lionheart during the volcanic eruption in the Optimus cave, and during his car crash, by creating a strong personal shield, as his mind was aware of those threats. But it couldn't protect him when he rammed a branch into his forehead because he never spotted and recognized that danger.

The more concentrated Labyrinthium, such as the second batch recently presented to humans on Mount Root, is in the presence of a telepath able to do limited thinking and acting on its own. When the unit Sam Roberts – Lionheart stumbled on it, the concentrated Labyrinthium toned down its radiation to preserve that unit's life. Major-General (with flight endorsement) Sam Roberts – Lionheart led a charmed life; on two other occasions his body encountered Labyrinthium: when he crashed the "enemy" submersible, and when his Aurelia super-fighter exploded in midair. Recognizing a telepath, on both occasions Labyrinthium acted to preserve his life.

The fully concentrated Labyrinthium, still waiting in the murky underworld for its chance to meet a telepathic Newlandean, will, for that telepathic person or persons, be able to act as a liquid supercomputer.

Yet, Labyrinthium isn't a toy. Its chemical composition is absolutely inimical to carbon-based life such as the entirety of Earth's life. The consequence of frequent exposure is inevitable cessation of life. Even the exposure to the super-diluted form of Labyrinthium, such as the Labyrinthium shield at its lowest power setting, or the KGZ, will ultimately result in some detrimental effects on health of the exposed person.

Momentarily pausing the musings of its mighty mind, Ball chuckles again. For the consequence of the immutable truth of the incompatibility of Labyrinthium and carbon-based life forms is the newest addition to his master plan, the one requiring further contact with some of its favored

human units. Dave, Sam, Nikola, Thom have all been heavily exposed to Labyrinthium. Ball now had a different destiny in mind for those exceptional units. Maybe, just maybe, to make justice to the society it created, the whole Lionheart family should be treated in that manner.

>Assuredly so.< - ads Thom Brdar's aura.

Assuredly so.

As the neutronium ship zips through Sun's corona and into its deeper layers, the transition region and chromosphere, Ball briefly reflects on the three independent and temporarily unconnected civilizations of human units which finally empowered it to free itself of its prison. This recollection wasn't as difficult as a human would judge it, based on the span of time separating these attempts, as Ball retained perfect, undistorted memory of every single event which happened over its half a billion years of life on Earth and its more than a billion of personal life (as well as the accumulated knowledge of all preceding generations of Balls).

Senher.

Atlantis.

Newlands.

Senher.

Atlantis.

Newlands.

Senher, the very first attempt.

A great folly. It was too early (too early for humans, not too early for Ball). Though biologically competent, those human units weren't sufficiently intellectually and socially advanced. Developed from diverse groups of humans twelve thousand years ago, nurtured by Ball, and boosted by telepathy, a dispersed civilization emerged on Africa's western shores. It sputtered and struggled. In its own way, Ball was too impatient, enforcing learning at a greater pace than those human units could absorb. To make it palatable to the underdeveloped humans, all knowledge was camouflaged as magic, sending reverberations of extraordinary experiences deep into the future, persisting to this day. At the end, that whole region of Africa was devastated, as individual units, escaping all attempts at direct control, toyed with destructive forces beyond their understanding. Destruction and disruption were so widespread to postpone the natural development of human civilizations in that geographical area for thousands of years to follow.

Hindsight analysis easily concluded that guiding and controlling a human society from afar (the humans based on the continent while Ball comfortably dwelled under its submerged volcanoes) isn't practical.

Up to then, influencing from a distance was Ball's favored way of behaving, pioneered on various species of aquatic and terrestrial reptiles and dinosaurs; then again, much later, on the amorphous cetacean cultures. Millions of years of work on dinosaurs got erased through cosmic events Ball had no control of. Much later, those promising Cetacean civilizations kept progressing onwards, but in tiny increments and excruciatingly slowly even for such a long living being as Ball. And it appeared that no manufacturing capability would ever emerge among them. Ball lost its interest in a possible Cetacean civilization more than two hundred thousand years ago, though he kept supporting some family groups of enhanced dolphins.

In the last fifty thousand years or so, Ball became certain that the hominids, emerging as Earth's dominant intelligence, are to be the only possible answer to its civilization-building efforts.

After the inexorable march of time erased all echoes and memories of Senher, Ball was ready to try once again, an improved plan in its proverbial hand.

Time for the second attempt with humans as star performers.

This time, one with hands-on control.

From the ocean depths rose the magnificent archipelago of Atlantis, incessant work of its volcanoes (and Ball's accumulation of supplies of strategic elements and materials underneath them) swiftly pushing the tall peaks of its mountain summits right through the clouds.

Atlantis.

The majestic archipelago.

The magnificent culture.

From the melange of outcasts and involuntary seafarers rose an Ocean Empire trading and conquering at will all over the globe. The human empires which arose at later dates usually claimed that they were the largest ever witnessed by history; not true, as none compared to Atlantis which literally ruled the whole globe. Though tiny in numbers, thousands of years more advanced Atlanteans unceremoniously plundered from their contemporaries whatever they needed (or simply coveted): territories, food, raw materials, art, knowledge, immigrants, recruits, and slaves; slaves above everything else.... while only occasionally engaging in

what could be termed fair trade and even less often sharing and spreading their own knowledge. After all, the ignorance of the rest of humanity was the best protection for Ball's chosen ones. Through religion and genetic memories, this message was permanently etched into Atlanteans' minds.

With no peers in this world to restrict them, successful and by now rich, Atlanteans passionately believed in their uniqueness, entitlement, and their mighty destiny, charted by their all-powerful gods living under their archipelago's volcanoes, obeying every command reaching in various ways from that hot underworld.

They flourished.

Their Ocean Empire flourished.

Ball's plan also flourished.

Then the moment of truth arrived. Poor, poor Sixte Ber Idaal, the Emperor of the Ocean, a giant of enormous physical strength, undefeated throughout his life in any contest, physical or mental. Possibly the cleverest, brightest, most intelligent, and most powerful human unit that ever existed (though completely lacking in empathy and compassion, as those weren't character traits Ball aimed for). After a brief but successful fusion of minds, Sixte Ber Idaal fully accepted his god's (Ball's) final ideas and wishes, outlying what needed to be done to please his omnipotent deity. To his god he promised to attempt to fashion an artificial human unit the supreme being desired, assembled from metals, plastic, biological materials, and electricity.

The work on the final ingredient started.

However, one more thing needed to be done before Ball could attempt its escape. From its resting place, a sort of cradle, a bed of diamonds among the superheated rock under inhuman pressure, the exact place where it got wedged after crashing the Earth, its ship needed to be shifted into a new position underneath the grotto of the largest Atlantean volcano.

Unexpected and unlooked for, disaster struck.

After the passage of so much time, Ball's neutronium spaceship proved more solidly interconnected with Earth's crust than the calculations predicted. Great force and pressure were needed to pry it lose, which Ball delivered by compressing and controlling Earth mantle's magma flows. The harnessed force temporarily overpowered Ball's telepathic hold on its vessel. Its spaceship buckled in the molten flow, striking, then shattering, the very roots of Atlantis. The gigantic pressure burst the geological anchor of archipelago's foundation, the ancient craton's segment. As the

unimaginable, catastrophic earthquakes shook the tortured islands, all volcanoes of the ancient Atlantis simultaneously erupted. For a time, it appeared inevitable that the top-heavy archipelago must completely overturn and disappear into Earth's molten mantle, while its foundational craton slipped underneath the African tectonic plate.

Ball worked incessantly, doing damage control, saving and safeguarding the accumulated raw materials, correcting its vessel's movements, stabilizing its position. To prevent the overturning, in a controlled fashion it slowly lowered the archipelago into the ocean's depths.

By the time Ball could restart paying attention to its doomed great seafaring Empire, and its hyperintelligent and hyper-cruel Emperor of the Ocean, they were no more. The great settlements and ports of Atlantis have been destroyed by nature's wrath. Half of its landmass was irreversibly flooded, some of it already deep under the sea. Many human units perished. Some dispersed in all directions. Those lucky ones, in position to use the surviving ships of the once incomparably grand Atlantis fleet, escaped to the less affected nearby archipelagos to the north, northwest, and southwest, or the unaffected African mainland further away to the east. Some still clung to the fiery mountaintops, precariously balancing between the lava flows, toxic gases, and the ocean waves, eking a living from the last areas of fertile land and the unfriendly ocean, the light of their great civilization permanently extinguished.

There was no stopping Atlantis' plunge. Ball had to let the archipelago completely sink bellow the waves. Though saddened by the demise of its promising chosen culture, Ball now needed to stop dwelling on what might have been, reorient, and concentrate on the future, on the next attempt to fulfil its half-a-billion-years-old plan. Because there never was doubt about plan's ability to succeed, either in Ball's mind or throughout the Ball network. With its longevity, Ball could mount as many attempts as needed to achieve success.

It could fail as many times as it wished; it needed to succeed only once.

Atlantis finally reached the nadir of its sinking, the plunge into the deep finally arrested; for a long time, its position remained frozen.

Then the work on a great geological healing started.

Reshaping, repositioning, assembling supports.

For Ball, it was but a blink of an eye. It lasted thousands of Earth years.

And resulted in the birth of Newlands.

Educated by its mistakes in shaping the Atlantis civilization, Ball oriented the inhabitants of Newlands in a completely different direction. Democracy and logic replaced religion. Subtle influence replaced direct contact. And it all succeeded beyond any hope. Newlandean human units were destined to fulfill Ball's eternal plan in less than seventy Earth's revolutions around its Sun.

Remarkable.

>Treća sreća, as my mom used to say (third time lucky).< - comments Thom Brdar.

In a microsecond, Ball dissects Brdar's statement. The third time lucky proverb isn't mathematically correct, but it appears to be a widespread superstition among the humans. Too late to change any past outcomes, Brdar's statement still sheds new light on some historical events.

Interesting.

As always, Thom Brdar is an inexhaustible spring of novel viewpoints.

The Sun is now filling the whole view ahead of the neutronium ship. Nothing exists anymore but the Sun. Not long now. Just a few more micro-bits of time....

It's calm, at least for such an active star. No solar flares today. As if the Sun itself is welcoming and embracing its new inhabitant. A being which will reshape its destiny.

What of Newlands? How will it fare without Ball's guidance?

Ball spent one millionth part of a micro-bit pondering this rhetoric question, reaching an unequivocal answer.

Newlands will fare fine.

In the form of genetic memories, Ball has supplied it with ideas, knowledge, and directions that will keep Newlands well ahead of any other human culture for centuries to come, if Newlandeans remain true to their original mission and purpose. And then, there's the Labyrinthium. Ball's main metabolite, the side product of its living processes, itself a powerful energy source, fully sentient and telepathic. At first, like in case of Atlantis, Ball provided a diluted mixture to the Newlandean miners and scientists. In case of Newlands (unlike with Atlantis), its technology progressed enough that the more concentrated stuff got delivered too, with the fully undiluted Labyrinthium waiting hidden under the ocean's

floor. Even if Newlands exponentially increased its Labyrinthium usage, it would still last them at least fifty thousand of Earth years.

At least.

Probably thrice that long.

Will Ball ever influence his chosen human units again?

Not likely.

Not likely at all.

Lifetime spans of the two species are incomparably different, inequal. In a blink of an eye, all those Earth units which Ball knew will disappear.

After its hectic fiery birth in the heart of a dying star, Ball travelled across the universe to its new home more than half a billion years. Then lived another half a billion inside Earth. Now, for the first time in its life, it was to enjoy its promised home, immeasurably long ago predestined to belong to it. It will immediately start changing its new home as well. There should be enough of this star's lifetime left for all changes to be accomplished. Like a giddy Earthling about to enter the first independently owned place, Ball couldn't wait to start exploring its new home's limits and begin altering functions of its inner mechanisms.

What about the other alien beings, those silicone-based units which for the last five thousand Earth years (give or take) desperately attempted contact?

Well....

Ball didn't doubt they are aware where it's heading. Ball is certain that, to maintain their proximity, they will now also leave Earth and move closer to the Sun (maybe Venus, maybe Mercury, maybe simply to orbit the Sun). Ball is curious about the possibility of contacting those beings. They appear to be much longer lasting lifeforms than humans, their civilization much further developed. Maybe they will be interesting companions to spend the eternity with.

Maybe.

There will be lots of time to decide.

Despite their efforts to establish contact on Earth, Ball avoided direct communication because all its energy was centered on fulfillment of the grand plan, especially since it was obvious that they were sufficiently developed to be able to interfere with it, accidentally or willingly. But that grand plan has now succeeded.

Good.

>That's not the whole truth.< - opines Thom Brdar.

It isn't.

Deep down, Ball was leery of the capabilities of those silicon aliens and their intentions. And a bit sentimental of his handiwork, the human civilization created to set him free of his planetary jail. The genetic memories which will be triggered when it's time for Newlanders to discover the fully concentrated Labyrinthium allow two major breakthroughs for humankind (more precisely, the people of Newlands) to take place. The first breakthrough is the blueprints for ultra-fast spaceships powered by the concentrated Labyrinthium, attaining one third of the speed of light.

Thom Brdar doesn't seem willing to remain fully satisfied with that brief explanation: - >Incidentally, the top speed of those ultra-fast spaceships will be twice the best speed silicone aliens can attain, giving Newlands the upper hand in any spatial conflict.<

True. And those hyper-fast Newlandean spaceships will have another asset. A terrible weapon. A Labyrinthium planet-wrecker device able to destroy whole words. Just in case one of the civilizations Newlandeans may relatively soon contact turns out to be bellicose.

A superior spaceship and an unmatched weapon.... Whatever happens in time to come, Newlands has a bright future ahead.

>Here we go!< - enthuses Thom Brdar's consiouseness.

Ball's neutronium ship manages to hit Sun's photosphere at a perfect ninety-degree angle. Its penetration causes a plume of heated matter and plasma to rise, quite visible to Earth's astronomers, the only evidence of Ball's passage which humanity will ever record.

Then everything returns to everyday normal.

The Sun serenely continues to burn and shine, as strong as ever.

# DEDICATION OF THE ATLANTIS TABLET

My phone rang just as the judge whistled game's end. Accompanied with Fanta and Sam, we were spectators on the National Stadium in Old City to witness one of the final games of this year's Newlands Football Championship, FC Old City versus FC Paloma.

FC Paloma won two nil, with Pavel scoring both goals, one in each half. Pavel's Paloma was already promoted as the new Champions of Newlands for 2012/2013 season, their lead in points becoming uncatchable a couple of weeks ago. On the other hand, as a consolation, FC Old City won, for the first time in its history, the League Cup. Certainly, a far less prestigious trophy than the Championship, yet one of the three which can be yearly won in Newlandean football competitions. (The third trophy, the Newlands Cup, was a month ago won by FC Dark Star in a thrilling game on this same stadium.)

Eager to watch Pavel play and to celebrate Paloma's Championship, Fanta, Sam, and I arrived incognito, in civilian clothes. Much did that avail us! We were recognized and soon an official delegation appeared to greet us (consisting of both teams' functionaries and stadium managers). Soon we were whisked away to the glamorous box seats.

Leaving the stands, I stumbled on an idea; could our new hosts donate our tickets to some fans who would otherwise miss the chance to watch this game? At first, I was sorry I ever mentioned it; the officials seemed to trip heads over heals to make my idea come true. I felt that I've pushed them into lots of unnecessary additional effort (obviously, they would have rather spent time in our company, basking in the fame of being

spotted with the famed CIC of MANATO. Yet, just after the game began, they returned with a report. They announced my gift of seats on the local radio, and it took them exactly sixteen seconds for the first caller to respond and secure those tickets for his family.

Despite my initial discomfort, I felt inordinately pleased.

Most of our hosts were immediately disappointed when Sam and Fanta declared their love for FC Paloma. They applauded my neutrality, as I professed, as usual, that my heart belongs to the feeble FC Tom Garrowitz, competing in an inferior league (it really does, but I've chosen to support a weak team indeed).

Soon, the developments on the field made me pleased even more. From the beginning of the game Old City players pressed forward, intent on demonstrating that, albeit their opponents may be crowned champions, the team in red and green striped jerseys is the real king of the National Stadium. FC Paloma played a defensive game, most of their players stationed on their half of the field. (I remember glancing at the statistics near the end of the game; Old City had sixty five percent of ball possession. Not that it mattered at all.) Paloma had only one player up forward: Pavel. But that was enough. For all their ball possession, throughout the game Old City didn't manage to create a serious scoring chance. On the other hand, whenever Pavel received the ball, danger was imminent for FC Old City's net. Varina could have easily scored half a dozen times if the home team's goalkeeper wasn't hellbent to deny him such triumph. At the end, his two blistering shoots, both from distance of about fifteen meters, both straight under the bar, couldn't have been stopped by three goalkeepers acting together.

And the best of all, I never had to interfere!

Pavel did it all by himself.

As the game ended, accompanied by Fanta and Sam, very pleased with the outcome, I hoped to seek out Pavel and congratulate him on his brilliant play. That's when my phone rang, changing all plans.

I briefly scan my cellphone's screen and immediately press the answer button: - "Yes, Peter?"

Curator of the Atlantida Museum Peter Schweinfurter is using his secret Privilege of five number to call. No time for niceties; I'm immediately suspecting something is wrong. Maybe even very wrong.

"Hi Dave, where are you?"

Peter didn't seem very perturbed. Is anything wrong at all? Or did he just long to hear my voice (smile)?

"Why ask?"

"Marka mu, did you forget what you promised?"

I tend to promise multiple things, most of which I (unfortunately) tend to forget: - "Which of my many promises are you talking about?"

"Dave, Dave.... I can't prcat believe that you'd forget. I should have reminded you. The dedication of the Atlantis tablet, nature beyond and above."

A sudden light explodes in my brain, erasing the cobwebs of forgetfulness. Dedication of the Atlantis tablet! Nature the great, as my family would say! In the excitement about this opportunity to watch Pavel play on the National Stadium, I did completely forget!

Wait a moment. The dedication of the tablet is to happen in the Atlantida Museum, here in Old City. Not that far away from this stadium. Maybe it's not yet too late, maybe Peter is calling to remind me, worried that I haven't yet appeared. If I rush....

"Peter, by pure chance I'm in Old City, on another duty (liar, liar, pants on fire; and it's a stupid lie because they were giving away your seats on local radio!). Can I still make it?"

Peter audibly chuckles, mirth evident in his voice: - "Nyet, my friend. I must surmise that you forget the starting time of the ceremony as well. It was held at noon, tabarnaque."

Noon? Darn! It's almost five in the afternoon. That's actually an early ending for a typical Newlandean football match but in this case this game started earlier to be televised.

"Darn! Sorry my friend; I can't turn back time.

(Silence from the other side; despite his jovial chat, I feel a hint of a problem. Something is bothering Peter. How to find out?)

How did everything go?"

"Woodla halum, it was great. The Master of science Joshua Krüger, an anthropologist, and Professor of chemistry Dr Ofer Bar-Yosef, who both analyzed the tablet, gave entertaining revues of their work. We even got putz Davit...."

"Ah, the youngster who recovered the tablet! Dave – it."

Peter chuckles: - "I see that you can perfectly remember when a name resembles your own...."

"Without any doubt. But don't ask me to pronounce his family name."

"Jighauri."

"Whatever."

"Well, inta shaz, Davit should have been the star of the show. We did push him into reading a couple of sentences from a script he prepared."

"Shy?"

Another pause. Aha, there's the problem. Something about this kid Davit?

"Peter, is there a problem with our young hero?"

"Maybe, tabarnaque. I'm not a doctor."

"His arm isn't mending well?"

"Oh, no, nyet.... The arm is perfect."

I spread my hands in helpless wonder: - "So where does a doctor then come in?"

"Dave....

(Peter stops, coughs, then restarts.)

Dave, Marka mu, I think that our young Davit is at the verge of a mental breakdown."

Oh-oh. Not so good news.

"Should we get him to a psychiatrist?"

There are many quite qualified ones, among the civilians on our Main Islands and in MANATO's medical corps. I don't see how getting one of them to check the newest Newlandean hero could be a problem.

Surprisingly, Peter shakes his head: - "No, Dave. I don't think it's a problem concerning a psychiatrist. Marka mu, I spoke myself with the kid. He insists...."

Peter's sentence fades and falters.

"He insists what? You're not making much sense, my friend."

Suddenly Peter regains his voice, increased in pitch, becoming almost petulant and argumentative, as if he himself is fighting against every word he's uttering: - "Svih mu svetaca, Dave, Davit insists that he has a message for you! From the old Atlantis!"

Davit Jighauri and I are crossing the intersection of Atlantic Boulevard and Markov Put in Norton. Norton is a small town, very suburban (no tall buildings here), with Nordporte the only Newlandean settlement on the long, straight, and mostly desolate northern shore of Anan (the reason for this is that shore's unmitigated exposure to the ocean). This small town is generally never busy, but the intersection in question is very close to

another vastly more important one, between Highway 2 and Highway 102, those roads stretching south towards Old City, west to Nordporte, and east to Luka, thus connecting millions of inhabitants with the major industrial and military facilities of our land. Also, the intersection we're currently negotiating joins four of Norton's most important tourist spots, frequented mostly by visitors from Old City: the Andromeda and Sirius beaches, the Port of Norton, and the True Nord golf course.

It's later than I planed, just past 7PM (19:00). This late visit couldn't be helped. It took time to disentangle from the National Stadium, briefly confer with Peter in Atlantida, grab a MANATO carpool vehicle from the Old City airport, and drive north to Norton (after sending Sam and Fanta home to Rad by train). Some sunset colors are still present in the western part of the huge, unimpeded sky dome above us, playfully mixing with brilliant-yellow street illumination (the new LED bulbs becoming ubiquitous all over the archipelago); but the scintillating moon and stars already rule towards the east.

And it's hot.

Stifling hot.

Repressively hot.

Shielded by its big roof and the natural draught of the huge building, it never seemed that hot on the National Stadium. I'm still in my civvies, but I'm starting to wish I could dispose of some of my clothing.

The kid is walking next to me, all distraught and agitated.

The kid.

In my mind, and occasionally in conversation, I keep calling him "the kid". Which he definitely isn't. He's a young man, whose life took an unexpected turn. A turn that caused it to appear completely outside Davit's control.

Davit is of a much lighter frame than mine, maybe five foot five (I'm still not used to expressing someone's height in meters and centimeters). He's proportionally built but it's obvious that gym and sports were never very high on his agenda. Additionally, he seems to have lost weight during his recovery (somehow his skin appears to hang on his bones), maybe because of the stress he's experiencing. Stunningly, even for Newlands, he's dressed wholly in glowing pink (talk about a person recently out of the proverbial closet!). A glowing pink cap, with glowing pink shorts, a silky muscle shirt of a lighter but still pink hue, and even his sneakers are mostly pink (and black). There's some dark chest pelt visibly displaying

where his muscle shirt abundantly uncovers his skin, and so are his bushy armpits. The night-black moustache dominates his face under a prominent bulbous nose. Though trimmed with care, it's all crooked and bent, betraying his frustration and displeasure. His eyes are very dark but hidden behind a pair of overly large sunglasses with brownish tinted lenses. At this time of day, there's no need for such sunglasses. However, their presence seems to be a welcomed barrier behind which Davit's troubled soul feels secure.

"General, sir, are we going to the beach?"

I invited Davit to take a walk with me. To try to solve the challenge he poses, I need to be alone with him. For some reason my request frightened his cousin (and soon husband) Giorgi Okriashvili, who really looks like Davit's older twin (if that would be anyway possible). When Davit disappeared for a brief change of attire (upon my arrival he was wearing only his mundane swimming trunks), he started begging me, literally on his knees, not to hurt his lover. Some strange fear of the military authority? I've never encountered it on Newlands; that is, not until today. In Afghanistan, yes, of course, but here? A remnant of his Georgian-family upbringing, some bad experience his parents had before emigrating here, who can tell? To calm him down I had to promise on my Commander – in – Chief's honor that my intentions are only friendly and nothing but friendly.

"Yes Davit. As I indicated, that's my intention. We should have considerable privacy there, especially with the nightfall driving most of the beachgoers away."

Davit nods. There's a green light for pedestrians; therefore, we proceed to brusquely walk across the Atlantic Boulevard. This far east it's narrower and quieter than further west. Giorgi's small home is about fifty yards eastward from this intersection, on Boulevard's southern side.

"Your cousin is concerned about your welfare."

Davit nods again, then answers. His English is heavily accented, but correct (probably a Georgian accent, though I don't recognize it as such). Not only correct, perfect: - "Truth be told, General, I'm very concerned about my welfare."

I keep walking in silence, hoping that my posture conveys sincere support.

"The change of country...."

"Of course. I remember how it felt."

"You changed countries, too?"

"Yes. I'm American. Originally."

"Interesting."

We walk on in silence. There are homes on this northern side of the Atlantic Boulevard, but they are further between, separated by broad treks leading to the public beach.

Without much deliberation, we turn onto one of those treks.

"I can sense there's more that troubles you, Davit."

"I.... I came out of.... Did you hear that I'm gay?"

"Indeed, I did. Nothing to be ashamed of."

"You really think so?"

"Indeed. I'm married to four husbands and two wives. I'm certain you can do the sex arithmetic."

Davit perks up: - "Really? That's awesome!

(something is still puzzling him)

But, sir.... Am I permitted to ask? How can so many people get legally married?"

"You didn't yet hear about the Newlands marriage? Up to seven people can intermarry here, irrespective of their gender.... Davit, let's go to our right."

"Towards the golf course?"

Obviously, or away from the port.

Whichever you like.

I simply nod.

"So, seven can marry?"

"Yes."

I can hear a change in his voice. My information has resolved some doubt he had about his future life here. I carefully extend my mind towards his and caress his inner soul.

Satisfaction.

Pleasure.

Good. I'm right.

Unknowingly, or by pure chance, I solved some kind of a dilemma.

"Giorgi and I are getting married."

"Yes, I was told so."

"You were?"

"Yes. Peter Schweinfurter, the Curator of Atlantida Museum, is a very dear friend of mine."

"Ah, the Curator. He's your friend? Great. Yes, we're getting married as soon as I become a citizen of Newlands."

"Let's keep away from that large group over there."

"All right."

We slightly change our path.

"What else did the Curator tell you about me?"

"Davit, what he told me, just two hours ago, mind you, brought me here in a hurry."

Somehow my words seem to frighten or repulse him; he steps away and keeps a larger separation: - "You must think that I'm a lunatic."

"Davit, I'm not thinking anything. I don't have any preconceived ideas about you."

"You probably think I'm sick. That my mind is sick."

"I'm not a doctor."

"You're not a doctor. A psychiatrist, then?"

"Davit, I'm a soldier. I served all my life. I've no medical training.

(pause)

What-so-ever."

"But if you're not a psychiatrist, why would you come here?"

"Because you're not sick, ill, or crazy. You don't need medical help. Of any kind."

"I don't need medical help? How do you know? How CAN you know?"

That's a series of illogical questions, but they betray his inner turmoil.

"Maybe I do need help. Maybe I'm cuckoo."

I look around. Ah good, providentially a bench, surrounded by a patch of grass. No one anywhere near.

Perfect.

"There, Davit. Let's take that bench."

Davit obeys, though his shoulders appear more slumped than ever. He's completely distraught by the turn of events and what I so far disclosed. Peter was right. The burden he's carrying is overpowering. And I'm the only possible help. (Well, Andy, Alan, or Mietje could help Davit as well, or even better. But they aren't here. I'm alone here.)

It's so hot.

Hot, hot.

The forecast for this evening is ridiculous (upon arrival to Norton, as soon as I felt the heat, I checked my cellphone). Going into the night, the temperature of air is scheduled to rise by almost five degrees Centigrade.

This is caused by the advance of a warm and rather moist front which will tomorrow bring torrential rain to our Main Islands. This being the exposed shore, a very heavy swell is forecast too.

"Davit, do you mind if I take off my shirt?"

Before he can answer (though he eventually acknowledges by nodding), I pull my t-shirt over my head.

Davit waits a moment, then takes off his muscle shirt. Apparently, he needs to feel equal. Interesting.

Then a long silence ensues.

I again slowly extend my mind, careful to avoid betraying my presence. It's as I knew it would be. My paranormal attraction is at work again. Davit is physically drawn to me, experiencing a full sexual crush. Ah, well. Maybe I can use those feelings to better help him.

"Sir, I...."

I sigh.

Time to spring my trap.

"You're physically attracted to me."

Davit almost jumps, then recovers and sits down as distantly as possible: - "How? How can you know that?"

"Davit. Please, listen very carefully. I need to tell you something important."

Davit calms down and somehow seems to shrink into himself. His moustache droops further: - "Yes, General."

I spread my hands a bit, palms facing up, to further indicate no ill intent: - "Nothing serious. Not yet. The serious stuff comes later. When you went to change, back in your home....

(I deliberately designated Giorgi's humble house as Davit's home)

Your husband begged me not to hurt you in any way."

I laugh, loudly and merrily (and intentionally), to lighten the atmosphere and disperse any fear.

"I promised on my honor as the Commander – in – Chief of MANATO, the mighty Newlandean armed forces, that I mean you well. And, sincerely, I do."

Davit blinks: - "But, sir, why.... what can a General of MANATO do for me?"

My hand lands on his shoulder, eliciting an electrifying response of his whole body, shaking under my touch: - "That I don't yet know, mister. Not yet. Firstly, I need you to let me know the secret you carry. The one

you outlined to Peter. Then I'll know how to (help you)…. what I can do for you."

Disregarding my incoherent sentences, Davit interlaces fingers of both hands into a tight, nervous ball and sighs deeply and quite unhappily. At the same time, I can feel his whole body willingly push against my hand anchored on his shoulder, like a dog or a cat would do. Whether he's ready to openly acknowledge or not, he's reveling in my touch.

"It's…. like…. this voice…."

"Yes? What does it say?"

"I…. can't…."

"What do you hear, Davit?"

Intense shaking of his head: - "I don't know."

That sounds strange. Impossible even.

"Words?"

"No. Yes."

"Which one is it?"

Out of the blue, a scream: - "I don't know!"

Then much softer: - "I don't know. Maybe words. Or a written message, like reading from a paper. A message. For you. I know that it's for you. It….

(My heart skips a beat at the mention of IT!)

It says so. That's it."

Peter indicated it's from Atlantis. Davit must have told Peter so. However, he now skipped that detail. Not certain of what he feels / hears / experiences?

Interesting.

I withdraw my hand from Davit's shoulder and place both in front of me, clasped together, as in prayer or meditation. Then, for a moment, my forehead bends forward and touches my bunched fingers, briefly resting on them. It's clear what I need to do. I need to penetrate Davit's mind and uncover what's bothering him. Peter said that it's a message from Atlantis, for me. Davit just repeated that. For me! For me? How could anyone from Atlantis, thousands of years ago, hide in the Optimus Cave a telepathic message to be transferred to a lucky passerby and be delivered, in the present time, specifically to me?

Impossible.

Impossible?

Is Ball impossible?

Yes.

All our scientific knowledge ascertains that a plasma being isn't possible.

Are those pesky DFQL aliens impossible?

Yes.

We never encountered silicon-based life, though we theorized it may be possible.

Yet all that makes Ball and DFQL no less real.

Davit's message must be real, too.

Maybe something else we've never encountered?

"Davit."

How to begin?

"Yes, sir."

"When you made your great discovery, when you had your arm broken, when you decided to stay on Newlands, become one of us, marry your cousin.... When all that became reality, I bet that in front of you materialized a hugely different future than what you planned before arriving here."

"Oh, yes, you're right. As they say here, ochen balshoy right."

He smiles at successfully using one of our bywords.

"Right. Now, I want you to consider something completely different. What happens here in the next five minutes will cause you to experience a future which will be as distant from your imagined life on Newlands as that is from the future you dreamed about while still in Armenia."

Davit's eyes open in surprise: - "You mean Georgia?"

(Stupid CIC. Me, myself, and I.)

"Pardon me, Georgia."

"But I...."

"As much hassle as it must of necessity be, as unpredictable as it is, you like the future you imagined for your life on Newlands, by your husband's side, finishing your studies, maybe doing some further archeological exploration?"

"Yes, yes."

"Davit, listen, please.

I can promise one thing.

You will have all those things: home, diploma, work, husband, love, respect. Oh, pardon me once again; you will have all of those if you

two remain together, your health persists, and you suffer no accidents, something no one on Earth can guarantee.”

Another chuckle: - “Right. Life is unpredictable.”

“But here’s the proverbial other shoe to fall. Ready?”

“Uh-huh.”

“Here it comes. Brace for the landing!”

I feel Davit stiffen, despite a fleeting smile. Time to again place my hand on his naked shoulder. Reacting to my touch, he stiffens even more, but stands his ground.

“A part of your future will also be within MANATO.”

Surprise makes Davit rise from his perch: - “MANATO? The Newlands army? I mean, not army as army, but....”

“The Armed Forces of Newlands, yes.”

“But! But I’m not a....”

I nod: - “You’re not a soldier. True.”

“Then mrdat how? Why?”

Aha, when surprised you can curse well in the Newlandean vernacular, my dear friend. I smile: - “Davit, in the next minute or two I will reveal to you one of our core secrets: why this country is as powerful as it is, and why its armed forces don’t have a par in the world.”

“Wait.... don’t.... if you tell me, will you have to shoot me?”

Now I laugh with abandon, a clear, merry sound, dispersing the heavy gravity of our talk: - “I’m in shorts, mister. And sneakers. Where am I supposed to hide my gun?”

Davit keeps staring at me, totally perplexed.

“What do you think makes Newlands militarily unbeatable?”

“I never thought.... I guess, Labyrinthium?”

“You know about Labyrinthium?”

“It was part of our curriculum in Atlantida, in preparation for the excavations. Just in case....”

“Just in case one of you stumbles on it while digging.”

An affirmative nod.

>It’s more than Labyrinthium which makes us strong. Much more.<

Davit jumps, stifles a scream, falls into the beach sand in front of me.

He croaks, his voice unrecognizable: - “That’s....”

>Telepathy.<

Slowly, painfully, the young Georgian straightens, sits on his haunches, blinks, remains silent.

>To uncover what's bothering you, I intend to use my telepathic abilities. I will gently probe your mind. It will be completely painless. You won't be hurt in any conceivable way.<

Davit regains his voice: - "Are you certain? Did you ever do that? What do I need to do?"

>Nothing, my friend. Just let me in. And yes, I'm certain. And yes, I routinely do it. No one ever complained, I can assure you. My probing is and will be harmless. Do not fight me. I promise a fun experience.<

"How can I...."

>Trust me?<

"Trust you."

>Your call. Trust me. Or don't trust me. I can't force you to trust me. I won't even try. You can't turn trust on and off, just like that. But I'll prove that every word I uttered is true.<

A long silence.

"I trust you."

(Yes. Well. Suddenly you perceive that you not only trust me, but also desire me. And, paradoxically, you feel that you love me, despite having no idea where that came from, you poor man.)

>All right. Here we go.<

Once again, I gently extend my aura and touch the surface of Davit's mind. This time I go much deeper than before, not bothering to disguise my presence. The effect is immediate. I can feel Davit fantasizing, daydreaming.... let's check.... of course, of sex.... with me. Eh.

Looking around, looking around.

Searching, searching.

Where is it?

Where can it be?

Nothing out of order, nothing; what's then upsetting our Georgian boy?

What's then ups....

BLAAM

Everything happens suddenly and forcefully.

A presence. A dark presence (not THE monster, though).

A mighty mental voice.

(Ball? Can it be?)

A message.

For me!

THIS MESSAGE IS FOR GENERAL ANDERSON – LIONHEART, MANATO'S COMMANDER – IN – CHIEF.

And then it starts: a memory, a movie, a tale, a story, theater, opera. Slowly unfolding and playing out in front of my telepathic senses (whatever they may be) in all its majestic tragedy. The brief interaction between Kiron, Halea, and Calisto plays until its bitter and horrible end. Yet, I'm elated. I've witnessed (seen, felt) a moment of true story of Atlantis. Unhoped for, I've learned about its history, and economy, and geography. About its society, its religion, its conquests. About its enemies. About the knife which resides in the museum of Atlantida. About the artifacts we're slowly discovering in the Optimus Cave.

My hands surge forward and take hold of Davit's shoulders, drawing him closer. And there, on the beach, publicly, openly, I kiss him with utter abandon.

"Everyone, thank you for staying so late. I'm aware that all of you have various responsibilities waiting for your attention. But my friend Peter Schweinfurter here....

(my hand points towards my buddy)

.... insisted that I swing by for your full reports."

Besides Peter and I, there are three more men in this conference room on the upper floor of the Atlantida Museum. Master of science Joshua Krüger, the anthropologist, Doctor Nathaniel Causgrove, the oceanologist, and Doctor Ofer Bar-Yosef, the Professor of chemistry on the University of Old City.

Peter: - "General, here are my colleague's printed reports. Nature above and beyond, we could have easily emailed them...."

Master of science Joshua Krüger: - "Which we did, all three of us."

Peter: - "Of course, and by now they must be in your inbox, there with dozens of other...."

"Hundreds; thousands."

They all smile.

Peter: - "Well, Marka mu, apparently you receive more emails than I do!"

More smiling and some chuckling.

Peter: - "You're flying back tonight?"

"Yes. My MANATO carpool vehicle is on the parking lot."

Peter: - "Hummer?"

"Yes. I need to return it to the airport, and I have a ticket for one of the late-night flights to New Belgrade."

Peter: - "Then back to Rad via the metro, I see."

"Certainly."

Peter: - "We won't hold you too long, bre. I wanted you to meet our most trusted scientists, and to hear from them some of the salient points of their reports."

"Glad to be here."

With Ball's strange message received and memorized, my evening in Norton finished very fast. After showing my gratitude to Davit by publicly kissing him on the beach, I didn't tarry. We parted at his doorstep after exchanging information about various means of communication. I invited him to visit me in GHQ in two days. I was certain that there's only one possible future for our diminutive Georgian, in the ranks of PsiMANATO's support unit.

Hence enough time to pass by Atlantida on my return trip and make Peter happy.

Peter: - "Nate, please tell our CIC your most salient points."

Dr Nathaniel Causgrove: - "My pleasure, Marka mu. As an oceanologist, what piqued my interest was the question whether our tablet ever got exposed to ocean water."

Nate Causgrove has the looks of a typical teacher with undisciplined medium-length hair and a serious moustache, both of a very dark hue. He's a young guy who's intentionally trying to appear older than his age.

Master of science Joshua Krüger cuts in: - "Or, to ask bluntly, did it ever sink?"

I nod. An intriguing question: - "And? Did it?"

Dr Nathaniel Causgrove: - "As far as I can say that tablet was never exposed to seawater."

"Never, as in never at all?"

Dr Nathaniel Causgrove: - "Never at all, tabarnaque. Not for any prolonged time, to be exact. A wave or two could have temporarily got it wet, but that's not what we were trying to prove."

Peter: - "The science is clear. Throughout its history our tablet remained dry, exposed to air poor in oxygen."

Dr Nathaniel Causgrove: - "We employed various chemical analysis to prove that point, but our team's conclusion is irrefutable, based on solid scientific evidence. Intentionally or not, that part of the cave, where the

treasures of Atlantis were hidden, never got flooded. What's more, the lack of oxygen betrays no communication with the air in our atmosphere. Marka mu, that tablet remained fully isolated since deposited in the cave."

"Peter, pardon me if I'm too dumb to fully understand that point. I thought that for thousands of years, since Atlantis sank, Mount Palamar remained fully submerged under the surface of the Atlantic Ocean. By default, the Optimus Cave must have also been submerged."

Peter: - "Orcae Ita. Right. Parts of the Optimus Cave were, without any doubt, exposed to sea water. For thousands of years. There's solid evidence pointing in that direction, mainly concerning various chemical compounds, the shape and composition of cave's jewelry, and the remains of marine life. Yet, the part where the treasures are buried wasn't."

"Could you judge if that was intentional or pure chance?"

Master of science Joshua Krüger: - "General, as the anthropologist of our team, it was my task to try to determine if our tablet was intentionally preserved out of water's reach. What an exciting duty that was, tabarnaque!"

I turn towards the ginger-bearded scholar and smile at his enthusiasm: - "And, what was your conclusion?"

Master of science Joshua Krüger: - "The tablet itself can't answer that question. However, I tried to examine the structures within which it was entombed, and the construction of the room itself, what little is left of its walls and supports. There's no sakra doubt at all; both were designed to at least attempt to stop water from submerging the treasures, including the tablet."

Peter: - "Dave, that conclusion is much more important than you may think."

Master of science Joshua Krüger: - "General, those walls were solidly built, using layers of different materials. Such endeavours require time."

Peter: - "Dave, they had time to shift their treasures into the cave and try to protect them there. Nature the great, that leads to two separate conclusions. The catastrophe wasn't instantaneous. Maybe the mrdat initial earthquakes were, but enough of their population must have survived to make sheltering of the most important artifacts of their culture a viable and doable enterprise. But also, they were aware that the tabarnaque archipelago was sinking and that water will be the enemy to guard against. They knew, Marka mu!"

And I'm perfectly aware of that, too. I wish I could tell all of you the story of Kiron, Halea, and Calisto. And of the knife you so valiantly preserve in your museum. Especially you, Peter. You deserve to know. I will tell you.... eventually. I promise. But not right now, in front of these scientists. That would be too complicated, would involve too much lying. Maybe later tonight, if there's time to tarry a bit longer in Atlantida and speak in private.

But I'm also hugely excited by what those researchers uncovered. It will be possible to tell the story of the last stand of the culture of Atlantis without invoking the telepathic message Davit delivered.

Peter: - "Ofer, you've been too quiet so far. Ochen balshoy, tell us about your work. Dave should be informed."

Professor Doctor Ofer Bar-Yosef: - "Certainly, Peter."

He's an older gentleman of unmistakable Arabic or Jewish descent. Darker skin, husky voice, round face, the typical nose of a desert merchantman, black moustache (despite the short grey scalp hair and abundant grey chest pelt protruding above his shirt). I'll have to ask Raj or Fran about his ancestry; that is, if I don't forget. I do forget many of those instances when I promise myself to check. At the first impression, his name sounds both Arabic and Jewish to me.

I guess that's life.

My life.

Unaware of my musings, Professor Doctor Ofer Bar-Yosef continues his discourse: - "Since chemistry is my trade, I did help Josh and Nate with their investigations. However, my special area of expertise covers changes in structure of materials subjected to various tools and even weapons. Calisse de merde, I did occasionally help our police with such forensics."

Impressive. I'll have to ask Andy if he remembers this guy.

Or, even better, Alan. As a Police Inspector, he was much better connected than Andy in his lowly Highway Patrol role.

Professor Bar-Yosef continues: - "From the first moment I saw that tablet, I was suspicious of the way those glyphs were engraved into tough stone. My report holds all the scientific explanations and reasoning, bre. CIC, I won't bother you with that. Suffice to say that I'm almost hundred percent certain.... I believe that your people favor the sentence "beyond reasonable doubt".... that the inscription was carved by high-precision electrically powered tools, Marka mu."

Peter: - “Dave, that’s a putz independent proof for use of electricity in Atlantis....”

I nod. Your knife is another proof, Peter. It’s a blade which functions like a Taser, heh. That you’ll get to know as soon as possible. When I speak with you alone, hopefully later tonight. I have to speak with you as soon as possible. I must. Patience, my friend; you’re in for some amazing revelations!

“Doctor Ofer, I guess that you meant the Americans, when you stated that my people favor the sentence “beyond reasonable doubt”?”

“Ochen balshoy, sir.”

I nod: - “I am a proud American. Never doubt that. It’s common knowledge. But I’m prouder of being Newlander. Never doubt that either. And, right now, I’m proud of being a distant heir of the amazing Atlantean Empire!”

Andy and Mietje, in one telepathic voice: - >Incredible!<

Andy: - >And beautiful and frightening.<

>There you have it. A message from five thousand years ago, containing tantalizing but irrefutable hints at culture, society, geography, even history of Atlantis. And it also explains the knife we have in Atlantida and why it was found on Mount Palamar.<

Andy: - >It’s staggering, Marka mu. How can we authenticate it?<

Mietje: - >I transfer to computer.<

>We can never hope to authenticate it. We can only accept it as is or.... Princess, what did you just say?<

Mietje: - >I transfer to computer.<

I believe she means the Gaillon 3, which we’re currently consulting in Nordporte: - >Princess, how can you transfer a telepathic message left for me over the historical gap of five thousand years....<

Andy: - >Or more, bre.<

>Right! Or more.<

Mietje, affirmatively nodding: - >I transfer to computer.<

Long ago I stopped wondering how Mietje does what she does, and what her telepathy has to do with computers and internet. But, for the life of me, I can’t see how a telepathic message, located in my mind, can be transferred.... or transformed.... into a computer file (completely idiotically, a joker in my intellect tries to guess whether her file is going

to be in .mov or .mp4 or some other format): - >Mietje, my Princess, how is that even theoretically possible?<

Mietje, her nodding becoming a bit naughty and disapproving: - >I transfer to computer. Don't doubt Mister Moustache. It much more. Not telepathic message. It story.<

(One of the longest sentences I ever heard her use. I'm not in mood to dispute her English grammar. What she's hinting at is intriguing and, just maybe, a bit frightening, too.)

Andy: - >Mietje might be right, tabarnaque.<

>What are you two talking about?<

Andy: - >Listen, flocci non facio. This.... story, as Mietje calls it.... was first in the mind of that Georgian boy....<

>Andy, he's a young man. Young, yes, but very much a man. Soon you'll get to meet him.<

Andy: - >Orcae ita?<

>As you say, orcae ita. I'm enrolling him into PsiMANATO, as one of our helpers.<

Andy, after a considerable pause: - >Ball or the DFQL aliens?<

>My feeling is Ball, but who can tell? I'm pegging it on Thom Brdar, a parting gift to his people, a redemption from beyond the grave....<

Andy, returning to the topic of our newest member: - >Touched by Ball, immediately embraced by PsiMANATO, tabarnaque?<

>Yes.<

Andy pensively nods without disclosing whether he agrees with my logic: - >Back to what I wanted to say, my Mo. That story was at first in that YOUNG MAN's mind....

(I chuckle at his mental emphasis)

.... Then in yours....

(I nod)

But it's still letter or picture perfect, whatever.<

What now?

>What are you trying to say?<

Andy: - >Dodjavola, he receives it, apparently from a stone tablet, in a moment of mortal danger....<

>It wasn't so dangerous.<

Wasn't it? A strike on his head? A complicated fracture of his arm? None of that is naïve.

>OK, you're right. It was dangerous.<

Andy: - >Danke.

(He has stollen that from my Fran!)

So. What I want to say is how does it always get so faithfully transferred? Letter-perfect? From a tablet to a mind to another mind, Marka mu? It's not a simple telepathic message; it certainly isn't a memory as we define those. So what is it?<

Mietje: - >Story.<

Andy raises his index finger: - >She might be onto something. Your Atlantis memory has chapters, and appendixes, and explanations inscribed on its damned margins....<

>What the hell are you talking about?< - and as I'm saying that, a massive premonition wave strikes me. Head, body, arms, legs. My skin crawls with certainty.

Andy is right! Andy is right!

Unaware of my new premonition, Andy trundles on: - >Yakamishii, I can only compare it to a picture on the monitor. If you put your mouse over its thumbnail, you get info about its size, name, etc. Open its properties, and you get much more info.<

>What?< - I'm still baffled, though I'm now certain that he's onto something.

Andy: - >Kiron, Halea, and Calisto. I perfectly remember every word exchanged, how's that possible? It transferred picture perfect into my mind, too.<

Mietje: - >Picture perfect.<

I frown: - >Shouldn't you say letter-perfect?<

Andy shrugs and rushes on: - >There's more. When Kiron thinks about Calisto's history.... from boy slave to de facto ruler of the land.... I see it, bre, like a film playing in the background. That's what I meant with my computer analogy. If you linger on a thought, or a picture, or a piece of information, there are further pictures, films, data within it. More info. More of everything. You just need to make a tabarnaque mental effort to access that additional info.<

Mietje: - >Story.<

For a moment, despite my premonition, I can't accept what Andy and Mietje are implying. Not immediately. It goes against my whole personal logic; I know what a memory is, what a story is, and what a computer file is. Yet, at the same time, my mind searches for clues which support their stance.

I concentrate and try to look deeper.

Andy is right. My memory is crystal clear, every single detail perfectly preserved. I stop, converge, concentrate on the moment he mentioned, Kiron thinking about Calisto's amazing life. Yes! Yes! A whole new story opens. One after another, in a speedy rendition like fast-forwarding tape, Calisto's story plays itself out in front of my eyes.

Andy is right!

Mietje is right!

This is amazing!

Another thought occurs. Kiron and Halea are discussing the treasures hidden in the Optimus Cave. Would I be able to stop, or pause, at that very moment of their conversation? I try. Twice, nothing happens. The third time I get a list of all treasures secreted in the cave! The whole list! That's amazing in itself!

(Peter and his teams will exactly know what to search for!)

Mietje: - >Finished. Look at computer!<

Two weeks later, once again I ring the melodic doorbell of the timid home on 53 Atlantic Boulevard in Norton; Giorgi Okriashvili's bachelor house which is now Davit's home too. In the first couple of seconds pure silence follows the melodious chime. Then, when I almost decide to press the button again (I know you're home, I know you're home!), the muffled steps are heard. A tiny crack appears between the door and its frame, a face momentarily fills the void; then, with a woosh, the door flies open.

"CIC!"

The thoroughly surprised Davit is back in his swimming trunks with nothing else on his body and feet. From my previous visit, I clearly remember his Speedos with the imprinted map of Newlands. I also know where he got them as that's a proprietary product, targeting foreign tourists, exclusively sold in Paloma's Platon Mall and nowhere else in the archipelago (it's a unique and relatively small batch manufactured by Speedo, which up front prominently displays the famous Speedo logo combined with Platon Mall's cracked amphora). Therefore, Davit has already made it to Paloma. He's getting to know his new homeland. Good to know.

I thrust my hand forward, shake Davit's, then embrace him while tapping his naked back.

"CIC, General...."

"Dave."

Davit smiles: - "Well, Dave then. But it's so disrespectful of your rank and position...."

Copying Andy's mannerism, I raise my index finger: - "Dave. Remember Davit. Dave. I will always be Dave for you. When no one is around, and no formality is required."

Additional smiles, with his nice and even (though somewhat yellowish) teeth peaking under his dark mustache: - "Dave. I didn't expect you. Not at all. What brings you to Norton?"

Now it's my turn to laugh: - "You're the only reason I have to be in Norton. I'm here to see how you're doing."

"That's amazing, I didn't think you would be so concerned with welfare of a new lowly associate." – Davit suddenly strikes his forehead – "Silly me, you're standing like a beggar in front of my doorstep. Please enter, please enter."

Well, I'm finally past that doorstep.

"Pardon the mess, I didn't care where I threw stuff; I didn't expect a visitor."

"Where's your.... relative?"

(lover, fiancé)

"Giorgi is still at work. He will be done soon, though. He commutes to and from Old City, so he'll be home in an hour, maybe an hour and a half, depending on traffic."

"He drives to work?"

"Usually. There are transit connections if he doesn't want to drive. They work great. Today, he drove." – Davit grabs some of the clothes discarded on the floor and rushes around trying to generally tidy up – "What can I offer you? What would you drink? Would you like to try some Binekhi Estragon? It's chacha, the national drink of Georgia. I brought it from home."

I drove to Pesak. In view of my Western Uppland car accident (and the imposed fine), I nowadays never drink, even the smallest quantity, if later I must drive.

Still, I'm intrigued.

"What's chacha?"

"Brandy. It's made from grape pomace, and unripe or wild grapes."

Davit opens a cabinet and produces a curiously contorted bottle filled with yellow-tinged transparent liquid. Printed in Latin alphabet,

the words Binekhi Estragon are clearly legible. Above them is some kind of stylized drawing of two.... plants maybe? And the word "chacha" clearly rendered in the Cyrillic alphabet.

"Davit, how did you manage to import a bottle of brandy into Newlands?" – imports of any alcohol are completely forbidden. The sale of alcohol is an absolute monopoly of the state, though various state - private partnerships are the foundations of all stores selling liquor. On the other hand, all kinds imaginable of alcoholic drinks are available in those stores. I confess that I never looked for chacha; up till a few minutes ago I didn't even know it existed. Maybe it can be found on Newlands (if I decide that I like it, I'll try to find it to surprise my family and spice up my cocktail-making skills) – "Import of any alcohol is strictly forbidden."

"Yes, now I know. I didn't know when I landed. Naively, I told your customs officers...."

"You're a Newlander now. They are your customs officers as well, Davit."

"True, you're right. I told OUR customs officers about my bottle, and that my cousin is of Georgian descent but never tried our national drink. I wanted it to be a surprise. They almost broke my heart by telling me I can't import it and that it must be discarded. But then, probably seeing how crestfallen that news made me, they gave me an exception and let me bring the bottle in."

That happy memory causes him to smile.

"Normally, I don't drink and drive. But you have piqued my curiosity. I confess I've never tried chacha. So, I'll let you serve it. There's one condition, though. We drink together. OK?"

"Of course. I love chacha. It will be a pleasure to drink with you. We can make a toast."

"Do you have a very very tiny whiny small glass for me?"

"Sure."

Davit produces two small shooters and pours the opalescent liquid into both. Finger-deep. Sideways finger deep. That's really a small quantity, I tell myself. It shouldn't be a problem.

As per Davit's wish, we raise our glasses and join in drink. Conceding the right of choice to my newest recruit, I let him pick the toast: - "To Newlands!"

I shiver as sharp liquid speeds down my throat: - "That's wholesome indeed!"

He chuckles.

"I notice that half of your bottle is already gone."

"Yes. Giorgi really took to chacha. He daily drinks a bit. Well, maybe not daily, but often. Until today I never tried it. I mean, this bottle which I brought. It's all right, I brought it for him."

I relax in the armchair Davit put me in: - "Excellent drink, mister, but it's time for more serious topics. The first week in PsiMANATO is behind you. What are your impressions?"

"Oh, it's exhilarating. But shocking, too."

"You learned about the aliens who lived here until quite recently." – I'm not really asking, because I'm aware that's a fact. I tasked Andy with explaining about Ball and the DFQL aliens.

"Yes. Can you imagine that? Completely unbelievable, yet true. Even when I arrived here, I knew that Newlands is different. But not that different! And, General...."

"Dave."

"Dave. I now understand the message I was tasked with passing on to you."

"You retain the full knowledge of that message?"

"Actually, it's the other way around. Before, it was all fog, I couldn't understand its meaning. I mean, not just the meaning, but nothing really! I could feel it in my mind, but.... like.... just there's this object in my thoughts and I can only see its shadow, never the whole thing. It was a chorus of confused vocalisations, babble in the dark produced by so many voices that you couldn't isolate a single one, the stuff of nightmares. Once I learned about the aliens, suddenly...."

As his voice falters, I nod empathically to encourage him to express his experience.

"Everything suddenly fell into place. As if you're nearsighted and someone gives you glasses. Thus, it's not that I retain the knowledge; it's wrong to say that. I just gained it, I never had it. I can now see the whole message, every detail. I mean, in my mind. From start to end. Like a movie. It's all clear. I know the story. There's even more. Likewise, I now understand where I was digging and what's buried there."

Now I hesitate a moment trying to formulate the important question, while an offshoot of my mind concludes that this was meant to be, Davit was meant to understand the message once he got accepted into our ranks (Thom Brdar's doing, no doubt, no doubt at all; thank you, my....

friend): - "Davit.... when you think about that Atlantis message.... did you notice that inside the main message hide multiple.... for the lack of a better word, we call them "substories"?"

"Yes! Yes! Ki! Madloba! Thanks! I thought I was going mad, maybe suffering concussion from that strike, imagining things that weren't there, daydreaming. But now you imply that you can see them too...."

I'm not an expert in foreign languages, far from it; yet I think that Davit, in his excitement, slipped back into his mother tongue. I also perceive the need for further cautioning: - "Davit, of course I'm aware that you gave a solemn oath when we enlisted you into PsiMANATO. That oath was very specific about guarding PsiMANATO's secrets (I'm certain of that because it wasn't our standardized MANATO oath; Andy and I concocted it together and added all kinds of safeguards). Please, don't misunderstand what I want to say; I don't want you to feel threatened or unjustly scrutinized. I'm not speaking as your Commander – in – Chief but as your friend. Please, please. This is important. Your cousin, who I'm certain is a wonderful guy, and I've nothing against him, must never know about your engagement in PsiMANATO. Your "message from Atlantis" is still listed as "above-top-secret" and it will certainly remain so for the foreseeable future, maybe our whole lifetimes. While it must become the core lore of PsiMANATO, very few in MANATO itself know about it, and even less of those outside our armed forces."

Davit's eyes sparkle when I again declare myself a friend. He doesn't immediately answer. Instead, another glass of chacha gets poured for both of us. We make a new toast to Newlands, then dispose of the fiery liquid.

"Giorgi knows that I'm to split my workdays between Atlantida and MANATO. He is very proud of my miraculous success. He believes that MANATO has an interest in archeology and that's the reason for my employment. As instructed, I told him that my MANATO work may occasionally take me to its New Belgrade GHQ or, alternately, all over the MANATO part of the archipelago. I...."

Another silent encouragement.

"We talked about my oath. I bluntly told him that I'll probably never be able to openly discuss my work in MANATO, and that even the Museum of Atlantida has some secrets which must be protected by silence."

"That's true. Curator Schweinfurter showed you his basement?"

"He did."

(I know that he did; nowadays I get to decide who gets to see our sacred artefacts.)

"Right. You are now informed of those archeological findings that are still completely unknown. Not just to the outside, wider world, but to our own citizens as well."

"Exactly. But, to retrace my steps a bit: Giorgi understands that not sharing secrets is part of my work in the Museum and certainly part of military work. He fully accepts that."

"Good. I'm really glad to hear that. From the bottom of my heart. It's great news. Let's make a toast to the success of your marriage."

More chacha poured, more chacha tossed into our mouths.

"As I understand, PsiMANATO will benefit from your services two days per week and Atlantida three. You will have to manage your studies in-between. The reminder will be your days off, but no one can guarantee those will always fall on a weekend."

"I'm somewhat sad about that because Giorgi almost never works weekends. We hoped to spend those in his raft-house on Lake Old City."

"Nice. I haven't yet visited those parts of Old City, though it's on my list of things to do."

"You haven't?"

I shake my head and continue my sermon: - "You will get used to the occasional separations. At least, I hope you will. I don't want you to resign, I don't want to lose you. I believe that you're very special and that we haven't yet discovered all your capabilities."

(I don't want to lose Davit because insuring that he doesn't reveal to the wrong ears what he knows about MANATO, the aliens, and Atlantis, would be an everlasting nightmare. Also, I do believe there's a more profound reason for him being chosen to deliver the message than simply accidentally being in the right place at the right time. Ball and Thom Brdar don't operate by exploiting parsimonies. Everything they do is planned. Another consideration why I wish Davit to be successful is that I rushed his acceptance into our ranks by the force of my position as Commander – in – Chief, disregarding advice of my closest colleagues, friends, and family members who preferred a more cautious approach. I want to be proven right, too.)

"You mean that the aliens contacted me because of some special ability, not by pure chance?"

I acknowledge while downing another glass of chacha. I feel the comfortable warmth spreading from my belly into every corner of my body. I notice the slowing of my reflexes, the mellowing of my emotional response. I'm certain what that persisting tingling heralds; I'll have to make alternate arrangements to get home. Tonight, I won't personally be driving anywhere. Someone will have to do it for me.

"We will watch carefully, and your talent will soon manifest." – enough, let's change the topic – "I heard that you met my husbands."

"Thom and...."

"Nikola."

"Nikola! Yes! I did! Amazing soldiers! Amazing...."

"Men." – I'm certain that part of his amazement is sexual.

Davit blushes. He scratches his forehead.

"Yes. Pardon me, please. I can see why you married them." – then he adds in a whisper I have trouble overhearing – "I would, too."

I smile and that makes my Georgian youngster blush even more. I watch his hands as they manipulate the bottle and divide the remaining chacha between our glasses. Another toast, another quick toss. God help me, I'm drunk, but Davit is much further along. His moves are becoming uncoordinated, his pupils dilated.

"Dave, do you wish to know a secret?"

"Certainly, if you wish to share."

"I wish. The person I'd most like to marry...."

"After Giorgi, of course."

Huge smile: - "Yes, after Giorgi. You yourself told me so. Seven can marry. I wish that the third guy in our marriage was you."

Davit pronounces his wish in an even voice, with conviction, and with open love (though while terribly slurring those words).

Uh-oh. This time my charm worked overtime.

"Young man, I'm already fully married."

"I know. I never stood a chance. You got married before I arrived."

Well, no one ever said to me anything like that! (Wrong: Mary, President's wife, did.) This young man sports a huge ego, nurtured by successes he had of late (and by chacha, of course): - "One day, when we have much more time (when we're not drunk), I'll tell you the story of how I got married. I believe you'll then be able to understand that no one, especially me, had much free will in getting into that marriage."

Puzzled with my words, Davit blinks hard. I re-examine my sentence. Darn! I implied something I didn't mean to say: - "Davit, I'm not trying to say that my marriage isn't happy or successful. The Lionhearts are the best family that ever existed, blessed by unbeatable cohesion!"

For a considerable time, Davit remains quiet: - "On the beach. When you kissed me...."

"That was because you passed on to me one of the most important messages I ever received. Important for the whole of Newlands, not just me."

"Yes, I understand. Yet, it felt so great, so personal." – Davit stands up, unsteady on his feet, and shuffles to where I'm sitting – "Kiss me again. Please."

I blink.

I think about it. One second, two seconds, ten seconds.

Why not.

Why the hell not.

I can see the bulge distorting Davit's Speedos; I wouldn't mind seeing him out of those.

Slowly, I stand up and straighten.

Carefully, from both sides, my hands snake around his torso.

That's the last slow action I undertake. Suddenly, I unleash the strength of my muscles and embrace the youngster with all the power I can muster. My mouth is on his, my moustache brushing against his, my tongue forcefully probing under his lips. A long, humongous, utterly erotic kiss, a full body embrace making our ranging manhoods clash like lightsabers made of flesh, albeit still sheathed in clothing.

At the moment of our highest passion, there's a click as a key is pushed into the front door's lock. Davit and I barely have time to separate when Giorgi enters: - "Davit, tabarnaque, the covers are still on our patio lounge chairs. I texted you to gahba remove them, it's about to rain heavily.... General!"

I smile: - "Hello Giorgi."

Giorgi: - "Oh, General Lionheart, what an honor! Why are you here...."

I chortle: - "Again?"

Disarmed by my lightheartedness, Giorgi laughs as well, dropping onto the kitchen table two bags with unidentifiable contents: - "Yeah. Again, Marka mu. The second time in two weeks, majke ti, give or take a day or two." – he turns towards Davit, his head nodding towards the

bags – "I brought the prcat meat for tomorrow's barbeque with Stan and Budo."

"Giorgi, to tell you the truth, I'm checking how my newest recruit survived his first week with us."

(Liar, liar, pants on fire. I'm also checking how your husband looks when ready to drop his Speedos.)

My answer makes Giorgi laugh. Then his pupils narrow as he spots the obvious signs of Davit's arousal. They contract even more as he next espies the empty, overturned, and utterly abandoned bottle of chacha: - "I see that someone celebrated, tabarnaque."

"We did, you're right. I'm afraid I'm no longer in shape to drive home. I'll have to leave my car parked in front of your home and make some other arrangement."

"Ah, that Magna is then yours?"

I nod.

Obviously shaken by the fact that his future husband almost walked on him in another man's embrace (this is Newlands, Davit; nothing wrong with that!), Davit finally regains his voice and wrestles back from chacha a semblance of solid control of his tongue: - "Giorgi, I'll pack the meat. Later. Just leave it there. There's something I want to tell you now."

Giorgi, a bit of worry and suspicion creeping into his voice: - "Go ahead. Something serious, nature above and beyond?"

Davit: - "Yes. I'm serious. My love, didn't you tell me that we still need to find our best man?"

Giorgi: - "Orcae ita, indeed I did, I did tell you. We still do need to find our best man, bre. I hoped to ask Budo tomorrow, hence the barbeque. Unfortunately, I'm not certain he's willing...."

Davit: - "I have a different idea. Why not do it right now? We're both here. Isn't this a perfect chance? Why don't we, together, ask my Commander – in – Chief to be our best man?"

Sacré bleu, as Fran would say!

This kid has guts!

A light of pure bliss lights Giorgi's face. He steps towards Davit, gives him a peck on his right cheek, embraces him, and faces me: - "General Lionheart, my husband...."

Davit: - "Future husband."

Giorgi blinks, silently mouths an unidentifiable word, continues: - "Sir, Marka mu, my future husband and I would like to ask you to be our best man."

"When is your marriage?"

Giorgi: - "On Wednesday 26th of June, General."

All right, that's pretty far ahead; there's enough time left to arrange everything.

Davit, definitely unsteady on his feet, relying on Giorgi's embrace to remain standing, but becoming quite talkative: - "Here, in Norton. On the beach. A romantic wedding, Atlantis style."

For a moment, I remain silent.

Yet, once again: why not? Why the hell not?

Davit: - "Please, please!"

"I agree. Under one condition."

Giorgi: - "Which one?"

"That you stop calling me General Lionheart, Commander – in – Chief, or mention any other similar unemotional and grandiose titles. From now on, you will call me Dave. Both of you. Simply, Dave."

"Dave!" – almost shouts the pair. Giorgi laughs, Davit shrieks, they kiss.

Giorgi: - "Halleluiah chance, Davit is drunk, you say you're drunk too, you are both wasted. If I let this clown out of my embrace, he'll fall to the floor. You, Gen.... Dave, you don't bre appear in much better shape."

"Well, it's all that powerful chacha. I hinted at that, didn't I?"

Giorgi: - "You did; you ochen balshoy did. Dav, sit down, forget about meat. I'll sort it out when we finish. General...."

"Didn't we just agree how to address me? Should I call off being your kum?"

Giorgi: - "No, sorry, sorry, I'm an idiot. Dave. Listen, I wanted to ask, why make alternative arrangements? Is it important to get somewhere this very evening? Vai a morire ammazzato, if it is, I'll drive you there myself. My car is outside, though it's just a Titan – Ford Ka, not a Magna. Otherwise, why not stay overnight and depart in the morning, sober and refreshed?"

Davit: - "But Gio, we have only one bed...."

I immediately grasp that sharing his bed with me is Giorgi's main intention. A real Newlandean sex entrepreneur. I can appreciate that kind of initiative: - "I have no unavoidable tasks scheduled for tonight, so

you won't need to drive. I will have to inform GHQ and my family where I'm staying, but otherwise.... Giorgi, why not? I'll be honored to be your guest."

"Grand! Putz swell! Who would have dared hope.... Dav, love, can you keep Dave's company a bit longer? Majke ti, I desperately need a shower. It's so awfully muggy outside, I sweated all the way home."

While talking, Giorgi starts unbuttoning his shirt.

"Gio, before you start stripping, one more thing."

Gio continues unbuttoning, but slows down: - "Yes, Dave?"

"I already reserved a table in the "Master's Restaurant". I was told that's Norton's best, isn't it? I planned to have my dinner there to try its renown grand paella. After you get refreshed, I'll take you both there for dinner."

"Tabarnaque, perfect."

Gio lets his shirt drop to the floor, then unzips his office pants.

Nice body.

Good man.

Davit made a great choice.

Well, I've made my own choice for today. Since I already did, why not explore all the opportunities?

"Giorgi, I believe that Davit would benefit from a hot shower, too. And so would I. Definitely. Is there enough place for three in your shower?"

A wolfish grin lights up Giorgi's dark features, making his moustache dance in anticipation: - "Indeed there is. Indeed, there sakra is."

Despite my ever-growing gay experience, the indisputable fact remains: my butt is simply not flexible, wide, stretchable enough to fully enjoy accepting Rocco Stelle's oversized.... well, you know what (manhood, penis, cock, dick, call it what you want). Today, during our lovemaking, he insisted on being the dominant guy, the top; I willingly complied with everything he asked me to deliver (telling myself that it's just training for a more enjoyable future).

"Rocco, you're a pig."

My remark makes him laugh with mirth: - "I hope that you understand that, as far as sex goes, that's quite an ochen balshoy compliment."

"Is it now?"

"Assuredly so, Marka mu."

I relax and stretch on my GHQ bed: - "You pigged me up everywhere, you swine. Now I need a shower."

"Irrumatror, let's take it together and I'll pig you up some more."

I'm discovering that, though my posterior hurts, my mind isn't yet satisfied with the quantity of sex we enjoyed: - "I might take you at that offer, you boar. But let's wait for a moment. I've something else to show you before we get wet."

I get up from my bed having to beat off Rocco's numerous attempts to grab various parts of my body: - "Wait a moment, porker! I'm back in a sec."

(Suddenly, I feel pride in my vocabulary. I wasn't aware I had it in me to describe a pig in so many ways!)

I grab my MANATO Surface and jump back into the fray, in the process receiving a slap of Rocco's dick on my face: - "Oversexed porker!"

(That one describes him in a nutshell!)

All our military Surfaces are fast, and mine is super powerful, therefore faster than almost all the others out there. Yet, its speed is barely enough to keep me from being (once again) raped on the spot: - "Keep your hands off me, piggy!"

"That one is tabarnaque weak."

"Piglet, sow, shoat, piggie.... I've many more words for you and they all fit you in a nutshell, oversexed porn star."

"I'm not a porn star. I'm a movie star who also happens to do porn while making his movies."

"I bet that's what you tell those naïve movie producers and directors in the wide world yonder. And your even more naïve co-stars. I wouldn't film with you. I'd know in advance my butt would be sorry. Or my cunt, if I had one."

"Silly, your butt is your prcat cunt."

Finally, my Surface is ready. I tap two icons: - "Here, warthog. Watch this. For once, be serious, please. Concentrate your piggly brain. This is important."

I start playing for Rocco Mietje's computer rendition of the story of Kiron, Halea, and Calisto, which we, in the small (but ever widening) circle of those in knowing, nowadays refer to as "The Great Atlantis Saga".

At first, for a couple of minutes, he chuckles and giggles. Then, as the tragic situation unfolds, his demeanor changes: - "Is this for real?"

I press pause: - "It is, it absolutely is."

"But how? A movie from the old Atlantis? Where did you find it? How did it survive all that mrdat time?"

"Rocco, it's difficult to explain what it is and what it isn't. It's not a movie, nor is it a computer file. It's much more. Much, much more. My experts managed to render it into this mp4 file...."

"Putz mp4?"

"Yup. Don't laugh. Let me ask a thing. These three, Kiron, Halea, and Calisto, which language are they talking in?"

"Halleluiah chance, English, of course. Perfect, contemporary English."

Is he trying to tell me that the perfect, contemporary English negates the possibility of the movie being authentic?

"Wrong, oversexed porcine. For all we know, they are speaking in the Atlantean language, whatever it may have been. You're hearing it in English, but others hear it in their mother tongues too (Davit was getting it in Georgian, Nikola and Alisa in Serbo-Croatian, Fran in German, Josh and Akiko in Japanese, Li in Chinese....)."

"It has an inbuilt translator? The proverbial "universal translator" science fiction always assumes is around the corner?"

Our initial thought exactly, leading us in the wrong direction on a wild goose chase: - "No. It hasn't. I dare say that it's something never encountered by humankind, at least not during our recorded history."

"Dodjavola, svih mu svetaca!"

"This whole message, even when transformed into an mp4 file on our computers, is telepathic, in a somewhat unprecedented passive way."

Rocco shakes his head, still doubting my words: - "Passive telepathy, Marka mu, what's that now?"

"It's.... never mind, forget that for now. I'll explain once we finish. Now, just listen, ask your questions later. This message sort of.... somehow, we don't yet understand the whole process.... detects your mother tongue and delivers its whole narrative in that language, picking specific phrases and expressions right from your own mind."

(That's not my sentence, but Alan's. I couldn't articulate a complicated thought like that. But it's such a perfect description of how the Atlantis message operates that I stole it outright and now regularly use it. We started suspecting this facet of its capabilities when Andy commented that the Atlanteans cursed in pure Newlandean vernacular! Of course,

that was so for him and those like him. I never heard a single Newlandean curse word. Only the American ones.)

I press play again: - "Watch till the end, then we'll talk."

During reminder of the story, Rocco stays mostly calm, slowly loosing his customary smile, his face getting grimmer as the tragedy unfolds. The ending finds him crestfallen (except for his still raging erection; that's NOT going back into my butt, at least not before our shower; my sphincter needs a timeout).

"They all perished."

"Likely, though not certainly."

Rocco nods: - "Except for poor Calisto whom we saw die in front of our eyes."

"Yes."

"Putain de bordel de merde, how was that message made? An Atlantean used a video camera, survived the eruption, then hid the movie in the cave?"

"No, my friend. Listen very carefully to what I'm going to say." – I caution Rocco with my waggling finger – "No.... human.... being.... made that message."

For a minute or two the loudest of silences reigns supreme.

"No human....

Then how?

DFQL!"

Rocco was never told about Ball. Like every other member of PsiMANATO, he understands about the aliens below our feet. He still thinks that "DFQL" equals "aliens below our feet". He also knows that they have left, hopefully forever: - "Yes. A telepathic message from our previous roommates. I see it as a parting gift, a big "thank you" to our people. It solves all those unsolved puzzles, explains everything we ever wanted and needed to know about Atlantis...."

Rocco rebels at my words: - "Everything? Tabarnaque everything? Not even remotely so. It hints at things, a few things at most, but those are such yatsume tantalizing snippets that it's impossible to form a clear picture."

"Wrong."

"Wrong?"

"Wrong."

Rocco falls silent, watching me, waiting for an explanation.

"I'll explain. All right, let me rewind this story. I need to find a certain moment.... OK. OK. Here.

(I stop the player.)

Watch my cursor. Now, if I position it above Kiron's head as he's talking about the valley where they can grow crops...."

(As if by magic, a map of Atlantis appears, containing numerous details.)

"Scheisskopf!"

"That map is in English for you and me, but also in Japanese for Yosh, or Serbo-Croatian for Nikola."

"That's unbelievable."

"Now look here; this is what I was searching for. Here's Calisto's whole life compressed into twenty minutes."

We watch in silence, overwhelmed by the strange experience.

Then I fast forward to another spot.

"And here, we found a list, accompanied by a map, of all settlements on the island. Notice that their main town really was Atlantis, and it was located where today the Old City Lake stands.... sits.... flows.... whatever."

With his finger Rocco traces the shore of the vaguely familiar island silhouette: - "Nora, Varga, Lira, Kreminon. Such romantic names. Gahba unbelievable."

"That's just a few examples. There's more, much more. It's practically endless. There are multiple side stories, we call them "substories": about their religion, the structure of their society, their wars, their conquests, their libraries, their food, their families. We have the evidence of their industry and what they manufactured. We know which subjects they were teaching their children. We have blueprints for their ships and step-by-step directions for their assembly. And we learned how they constructed their buildings. To name just a few items."

"Dave, va te tripoter, that's sakra unbelievable."

I giggle, making our chat a bit less serious: - "No need to tripot myself, or however you say that in French. (The French curse which he used translates as "go jerk off".) You saw to it yourself. My balls are empty."

The pleasant memory makes Rocco smile.

"Roc, there's a reason I showed you this."

"Ochen balshoy da?"

"This is above-top-secret material, and it will remain classified that way. Yet, the President, the managerial team of Atlantida, the twelve...."

"And probably the five."

I sigh: - "You're NSS. But not one of its executives. Are you aware who forms the five?"

Rocco immediately nods. He's certain who our members are.

"Do you know about the three?"

"Orcae ita. Your scientific thinktank, to which you later added Fran."

Rocco knows everything, he's extremely well informed. All right, I need to adjust my message. Momentarily, I also feel a tug of guilt. He should learn about Ball, too. And about Thom Brdar, whom I still praise for this Atlantis message.

"Roc, I made you aware of this because we, all of those mentioned, would like to somehow introduce certain selected parts of this treasure trove to our population."

"What? That's.... Grand! What's your plan?"

"There's none yet."

"Mrdat none?"

"I thought you might have an idea how it can be done."

Roc stares at me for more than ten seconds: - "You're right, Marka mu. I know precisely how it should be done. This story is precious, my Mo."

Interesting. Did Rocco read my thoughts? I was trying to steer him in direction all my co-conspirators and advisors chose: what if the Newlandean cinematography, concentrated around New Belgrade's locally famed Newliwood, was to produce an action movie, or a series of movies, rated as sci-fi or epic adventure, based on the information contained in "The Atlantis Saga" but ostensibly presented as a projection and extrapolation of "small and unconnected details" discovered by our archeologists? A "Lord of the Rings" – type saga, the Atlantean way?

"This could become the best Newlandean movie ever. The story is pure. It has lots of potential.

(Rocco nods numerous times, mostly to himself)

Not putz could; it MUST become our grandest movie ever.

(more nodding, while he absentmindedly scratches his neck)

I want to play Calisto."

"No doubt about that, you'd be a great Calisto!"

"Verdammt, I'm not joking. I must play Calisto. But I want more."

"Yes?" – I'm not certain what Rocco is hinting at. He wants to play other characters as well?

"I always thought that I'm perfectly capable of becoming a great script writer, but nobody would give me a chance. I want to write the screenplay for this movie. Mo, can you give me that opportunity?"

I must do some fast thinking. That's not my decision to make. I'd say that it should be decision of the studio, the producer, the director (not that I know much about the film industry). Still, if I allow Rocco to write the screenplay, this file will remain safe from any accidental exposure as I won't have to let a Newliwood stranger have it. I could ask Rocco to write it here, in the GHQ, and he'd easily understand the reason for secrecy. That way this alien file would never have to leave the security of this building.

(That way we'll spend lots of time together and Fran will benefit as well, since Rocco and him do enjoy occasional epic romps.)

I examine my conclusions from all angles. I wish Fran and Raj were here to consult. But they aren't. It's going to be my decision. Again.

After all, I'm the CIC around here.

Finally remember that, stupid.

Decide, then.

"Right. Roc, I agree. But there will be conditions...."

For fifteen minutes we talk, deciding on numerous details and procedures. We also concoct a cover story, to explain Rocco's almost permanent presence in the GHQ. Parallel to writing his script, he's also going to try his hand at producing a movie, his very first such attempt. It will be a documentary about life of our cadets.

All good.

All this serious talk had a grave and unwanted repercussion: Rocco's erection is a goner: - "Khange khodah, I lost my appetite for sex. That shower fuck you planned will have to wait for the next opportunity. Instead, show me how those, whatchma you call 'em...."

"Substories?"

"Yes, the substories. Show me how they are invoked. I'll have to go through all of those, Marka mu. I might need to consult you which of those details I'm permitted to include."

"Yes, for those choices we'll also consult Peter Schweinfurter. He could select with more ease those which can plausibly be explained as discovered, or positively identified, by our archeologists."

"Hmmm. Two important consultants. My, my. Your prcat names will be prominent in the end credits of my movie."

"How are you going to call it?"

"I haven't thought yet. Maybe "The Great Tragedy"?"

"How about "The Great Atlantis Saga"?

# EPILOGUE TO ALL SIX PERCEPTIONS

***July 2018***

"Daddy, daddy!"

"Tata!"

The two boys flail their arms and jostle each other for a better position as they negotiate a tight turn around the half-open glass door leading to the pool area of our Nake home.

"Hippy stole my ball!" – complains Little Dave, at six and a half the older of the two. He's dark-haired like his father, I briefly muse. Likewise, obviously taller and stronger than Ralf, his half year younger brother. And far more talkative.

For the non-Newlanders, our Lionheart family is terribly complicated. It boasts two wives and double their number of husbands. And our eight sons. Two of them just entered my abode. Little Dave is Fanta and Sam's son. The skinny blond Ralf, Alisa and Sam's.

"She's our guest, Dave. Therefore, your guest too. Let her have it.

(Besides, it's not your ball. It equally belongs to all your brothers. I skip adding that wise advice containing some rather judgmental words, though we're all aware of Little Dave's tendency to appropriate everybody's possessions. I feel that we've chastised him too much; after all, he's only six and a half. It's just a phase.)

Son, she'll be leaving soon. You two can play when she's gone."

Hippy in question is Hippolyta, the seven-year-old daughter of Žana and my blood brother Bogdan. With her mother, she's visiting Nake.

Taller than either of these two Lionheart boys, and quite intelligent for a first-grade pupil, she's been manipulating our sons since her arrival. Not just today. For our children, Hippolyta is one of those insolvable enigmas. Whenever they meet, it's certain in advance who's going to profit the most from their time together. (Not just Dave and Ralf; all our sons fall victim to her charms. I fleetingly wonder whether the fact that all our children are male somehow strips them of defenses when their female peers are around. Will this later in their lives transfer into their sexual behavior? Will our sons be suckers for any passing girl?)

Chuckle, chuckle.

"What are you eating tata?" – asks Ralf as he comes to a halting stop in front of my work desk. For such a skinny boy, he's always hungry. In reality, I was only chuckling to myself, not eating. But there's food by my side. Ralf got that right.

All Lionheart sons are perfectly bilingual. We encourage them to use the term "father" only for their biological father. All their other legal fathers are to be called dad, daddy, or the Serbo-Croatian equivalents "otac" and "tata". Thus, for these two, I'm usually daddy or tata, though I never object when Sam's sons decide to call me father (and never correct them).

I place the mouse onto its pad and turn my laptop away so that my sons can't see what I'm doing. They are all a very inquisitive bunch and these two will certainly try to spy. Then I reach for a platter covered in cup-shaped popped wheat broghies filled with shrimps, cheese, mayo, and mushrooms (and some unrecognizable, green-leafed spices). This morning, after we agreed to host this episode of socializing, Fanta hurriedly conjured a few dozens of those quickly prepared tasty appetizers.

"Broghies, Ralf. With cheese and mushrooms. Fanta made them for us."

On purpose I skip mentioning shrimps since neither of these two is very fond of them.

"May I take one?"

I nod, extending the platter towards my blond boy. He grabs the closest broghy and scampers away.

"And me?"

"You too, my namesake."

Muttering a muted "thanks", Dave is fast to hurry after Ralf, biting his broghy while running. I watch as they negotiate the same route which

brought them inside. They appear clumsy but suffer no mishaps. They know what they're doing. For a moment, I study their perfectly tanned backs. As well as their perfectly tanned posteriors. For this is Nake. When in Nake, our boys are constantly naked, bronzing under our tropical sun.

And so am I.

Quite naked, just a MANATO ballcap on my head, and soft sneakers on my feet. Not that I'd waste one second worrying about my nudity (or my nudity in front of our children); by now, it's second nature.

A touch on my calf.

A gentle, careful, furry touch.

Pelt passing along my skin.

Then a soft meow.

TJ.

TJ is our four-year old tomcat. We got him from his mother's owner, Fanta's university colleague, who lives in Atlantis. His full name is "Tom and Jerry", a pun on the popular cartoon, which is still often shown on Newlands (since they don't care about the way black people are presented). He's an identical copy of Tom, as much as a living cat can be, including the white endpoint on his black tail. Yet, you can't really call a cat "Tom and Jerry", can you? That would utterly confuse him, wouldn't it? It was I who came up with "TJ", and everyone among my family and friends is aping me.

TJ got castrated when he was about a year old.

Sorry, buddy, no sex for you.

The soft meow gets repeated.

I bend and scratch the sharp ears.

"Are you hungry TJ? Want some shrimp?"

There are pieces of shrimp sticking out of the mass with which Fanta filled her broghies.

Purring like a tractor, TJ butts his head against my leg, then arches his back as his fur polishes my skin, giving me that amazing feeling of touch with another being different from us.

>Hungry, buddy?<

On multiple occasions I tried telepathy on TJ, as well as on Marx and Engels, our three-year old Rottweilers, today with Thom, Nikola, and Swift – 1 (whose living mascots they swiftly became). And I always fail. There's nothing there, not the tiniest spark of telepathic ability.

Ah well.

Not every animal is a Newlandean dolphin.

Enough of philosophy.

I dig out two pieces of shrimp, lick away the mayo mixed with various hot spices, then deposit them on the floor next to my chair.

TJ swiftly pounces and in a second devours the offering. He again glances up, as if trying to judge whether there would be more coming. Deciding that he pushed his luck as far as it'd go, he softly meows a goodbye and exists with his tail bending left and right, forming those amazing question marks.

I turn to my laptop and continue working. Today is the last Tuesday in July of 2018. A rare day off for me (Commander – in – Chiefs rarely get days off, indeed). There happens to be nothing important to accomplish, so I embarked on a task assigned to me (by myself) a while ago and never accomplished: to put in order all photos downloaded onto this laptop since my arrival to Newlands seven years ago (well, I arrived seven-and-a-half years ago, but I possess this laptop, Fran's gift, almost exactly seven; nowadays, despite considerable upgrades carried out by MANATO's cyber experts, it's an anachronism mostly catering to various personal needs while I use other, more modern hardware for military tasks).

The photos I'm looking for are found in many separate folders, haphazardly strewn here and there. I'm grouping them together by their content, assigning dates (if remembered), proper titles, and returning them to corresponding folders (or creating new ones). It's a never-ending task (I'm certain that today I won't manage to finish it), but also a very emotional one, bringing lots of melancholy.

Here we go.

One – two – three – four – five photos of us!

Family Lionheart in front of the Nake Casino metro station.

Very soon upon my arrival to this land and my becoming an officer of MANATO, I learned, probably from my wives and husbands (who can now remember such details?), that Paloma is heavily engaged in stretching its metro network, digging new tunnels under the city, and building overland extensions into neighbouring less densely populated areas. One of those extensions was to reach Nake.

Finally, it did. On the thirty-first of December 2016, the extension of Burgundy metro line from Stonehill to Nake Casino was opened for service. Because of our family emergency, it took us about a month

to gather in force, all together with our children, and inspect the new station. For our children it was a welcome happy event, to distract from....

No.

No.

Let's not think of sad events. Not today.

Two more boys run in. Mansy and Rok.

"Father!"

"Dad!"

"Where did Little and Ralfy find their broghies, Marka mu?"

Mansy. Mansur. Our son, Alisa's and mine. My son. My only biological son. At seven, he's the oldest of our bunch and by far the darkest. His hair is raven black, like his mother's. His skin tans like he's the child of at least one dark-skinned parent (not true, as both Alisa and I are rather fair skinned). Despite being our oldest, and all those predictions of MARC's scientists, he's the shortest of the bunch. (I know, I know, at his age it doesn't matter; he might still develop into a tall basketball or volleyball player, as predicted.) And my Mansy is eloquent.

He uses a wide variety of words plundered from adult speech. Fanta has officially pronounced him ready for entrance into the first grade, which will happen in slightly more than a month.

"They got them from me, love."

My hand stretches. I grab a broghy and deposit it into his open palm.

"One for me, too! Me, too, please!" – chants Rok. Rok is still fair-haired, though the pigment of his hair is steadily darkening. He's the sturdiest and strongest of our boys, steadfast and dependable. And quiet. Rok rarely speaks.

"One for you as well, love."

"Hvala, daddy!" – Rok purposefully departs, somehow avoiding the show of incoordination Dave and Ralf exuded while cornering our patio door.

Mansur remains, silent, quiet. Then he leans over and gives me a peck on my cheek, giggling (as always) when my massive moustache tickles him. Then, as suddenly as he arrived, he's gone, too.

I make an inventory of my broghies. Three left. I confess that my selfish intention was to eat all, enjoying one after another, in an ordered and timely fashion, to make my self-imposed chore a bit more pleasant (tasteful).

Alas!

I click on the next picture and open another window. Me and Obama, snapped in the American Embassy in New Belgrade during his initial 2011 visit.

Me and Obama. Man-to-man, we remain friends even after the end of his mandate. Last summer he (alone, without his family) visited Newlands and us, the Lionhearts, as a private citizen, enjoying relaxing time spent predominantly in New Belgrade and all over the various touristy destinations of Newlands, including the brand-new Garrowitz City.

But not Nake.

Nor the Lighthouse Island.

Obama and nudity, not a good mixture.

As Obama's minor advisor, to the end of his mandate I remained consistent and true to my understanding of his military and political problems. However, as professionals, President of the United States and Commander – in – Chief of MANATO, our relationship was an unpredictable rollercoaster, reaching its nadir during the drone collision crises, but occasionally hitting some satisfying heights.

The simple fact remains, the Americans never got to trusting us.

Sad.

I will always like that eloquent, eloquent, eloquent man. And his great family. And he, he'll always haplessly love me, never realizing which force compels him to do so.

(Smile. Rumor is he avoided bringing his daughters to Newlands because of our sexual openness. And the fact that they both express continuous admiration for Bogdan, our President's son, whom they met during MANATO's Washington mission in 2011 and afterwards kept in occasional contact on social media. Therefore, Obamas felt it prudent to keep them home, with Michelle as a chaperon. Another smile.)

Click.

Sent into its proper new folder.

Good work!

My cellphone rings.

I glance at the caller identification.

Sue.

Good; this should be interesting.

"Hi, Sue! Whatsup?"

"Yo, fucking big moustache!

(Upon arrival to Newlands, Sue took some time to get used to my hairy facial ornament. Then, after the renewal of our sexual relationship, thought it the sexiest thing in the world. Then again morphed into flipflopping between adoration and complete dislike, driving her husband crazy: grow it! Don't you dare growing it! I believe that right now she's in phase when the sight of it once again wets her vagina.)

I bet your dick is big, too, dirty minded soldier!"

I chuckle. Sue's dirty English never improved on Newlands. Also, it never fails to arouse me; she's right, my flagstaff is now quite obviously pointing upwards. Luckily, we're not on a videophone connection, so she won't be seeing it.

"What did you and Leo do so far?"

"Fuck!"

"Yes, that too, but that's expected.

(Expected, as the charm and sexual appeal of our apartment's adult sleeping room is quite irresistible. I bet they didn't sleep in our children's bedroom.)

What else?"

"Name what you want to know, dumbass."

"Well, do you like our flat?" – Sue and Leo are for the first time visiting our stateroom on *NLLS550 Freedom Ship*, the new floating city of Newlands, slowly cruising around our main island group. They arrived there yesterday. Today *Freedom Ship* is.... well, let me check its website.

Click, click. On my browser, it's among my favorites. Should be here....

Yes.

Click.

Position.

Map.

Click.

Ah, not far, about fifty miles north of Paloma.

"Oh, it's some incredible shit! The best apartment I've seen for a while, anywhere in the world!"

"Glad you like."

(Lionhearts spared no expense in furbishing our space onboard; nowadays its our closest friends who more often get to enjoy it than us – no spare time.)

"Restaurants?"

"Yesterday evening we went to that goddamn "Nirvana" which you all recommended. Tasty."

"Expensive?"

"Expensive like shit, but worth it."

(I'm not worried. Leo's earnings are huge, he can support her lavish lifestyle. Sue deserves it all.)

"And to "Pizza-pizza" this morning, too."

"Ah, but that's a direct opposite (a cheap fast-food pizza joint)!"

"True, but also tasty. As they say, tabarnaque!"

Quoting a Newlandean cuss word, Sue chuckles.

"Crap, I need to rush. Leo already left to the airport upstairs (Freedom Ship is a gigantic civilian aircraft carrier; its upper deck is an airport able to receive all kinds of commuter planes, while all its lower decks are a gigantic hotel or condo building). Leo booked a panoramic flight for us, which will include overflying Paloma. Even your damned Nake!"

Well, I'll wave if I hear a plane pass overhead, though Sue is unaware I'm today in Nake and won't be trying to spot me.

"Then speed on, luv. Have fun!"

"I plan to, sexy stallion. Until the next time we get to fuck...."

Click.

Right.

Sue.

Sue and Leo.

I saw their pics somewhere.

I diligently search some folders. Apparently, I have Sue and Leo's photos everywhere, not just somewhere. I group them all in one folder. Now let's change the name of this folder from an impersonal "new folder" to.... (fucking hot Sue, my old love).... no, no; to the respectable "Sue and Leo".

Done.

Movement on the other side of my workspace.

Žana Petrović, one of my blood brother's wives, escorting Costa Miller – Bertoni and Violeta Petrović. Violeta Petrović, better known as Vio, is daughter of Alina, Žana's wife, and their husband Bogdan (my blood brother and our President's son). She's also seven. Costa is the son of Rigoberto Bertoni – Berto and Jana Miller, his wife. One of his wives. They are both intermarried to my good friend Pavel Varina, one of the

feelings maybe for the first time ever. And for the reminder of morning, she stuck to Costa as much as she could.

Now I could hear Žana talking to Violeta: - "Vio, you shouldn't ask Costa to escort you to the toilet, bre. If you need help, one of us, the adults....

They sortied onto our patio and out of my earshot.

Too bad I didn't catch all that serious adult advice!

A smug smile spreads over my face.

Good girl. Who knows, maybe there will be much more of Costa in her future, especially once he starts "getting hard" and grows a moustache and beard like his father.

Enough of speculation.

Next picture.

Me and the President Trump. Now that's a memorable memento!

Even during his campaign, Trump only timidly mentioned Newlands, numbering us among those nations "exploiting and raping" America with unfair trade practices. Once or twice he also touched on our refusal to protect intellectual property (there including our own), especially the American patents, software, art, and industrial products, as well as our strange insistence on being friendly to everybody in the world.

But that was all. Once he achieved his goal and became the President of United States, we didn't figure in his foreign policy and strategy. Too small, I guess, and too unimportant, especially compared to the volume of American trade with China, the future of NAFTA and NATO, and his beloved plans for a Mexican border wall.

(How convenient for the American politicians to gloss over the might of MANATO, world's strongest armed force, more powerful than all the other armed forces of this planet put together, just because we happen to be geographically small and remote?)

Yet, Newlands wasn't and still isn't inimical to Trump. Not by a large margin. The events during Obama's term in office convinced our Electocrats that no American President can be fully trusted, even if he speaks nicely and smiles a lot. As Obama's Secretary of State, Hillary Clinton impressed the Newlanders even less. She happened to be unequivocally critical of our political practices, but mostly strayed away from our shores. In general, Newlandeans harbor a deep-rooted belief that every nation deserves its rulers. Guided by this belief, on the eve of

the American 2016 elections, twenty-two percent of polled Newlanders prophesised Trump's victory, opposed by only nineteen percent of Hillary's fans. The rest mostly answered that the personality of American President is unimportant (or that they couldn't care less who will become the next American President).

Trump took the office, progressing from one of his twitterized crisis into the next. Then, in May of 2017, Newlands started trending in his tweets. Though bilateral trade between the USA and Newlands doesn't figure as very important to either of us, its bottom line is obvious. America is importing ten times more goods from Newlands than it manages to sell here. Even if services are to be added to the simple trade, an area of economy in which Americans best us by a ratio of 1.5:1, American trade deficit with Newlands still amounts to nine times the value of American exports to our land.

From the United States, we mostly import consumer electronics (read computers, cellphones, and their ilk), software, airplanes, some cars, some private yachts and boats, and some military equipment (a significant amount of it, true). In return, we export prepared food and wine (lots of wine!), juices, fresh water, fruits, vegetables, beer, fish, meat; and a truly vast array of minerals, precious and semi-precious stones, rare earths, precious metals, steel, and aluminum. Just our exports of gold suffice to pay for all our imports from the States.

Suddenly, Trump's minions were circling our shores and collectively descending on New Belgrade. In no time, an official visit by the American President was in the works. And the day before he landed on Capitol International, he tweeted that Newlands better mend its ways, or face tariffs on various exports.

Our President Nemanja Petrović arranged for glamor and pomp suitable to sate Trump's endless vanity. To his vast surprise, Trump discovered that the Newlandean political practices don't differ much from his vision for America. Equaling his "America first" is the Newlandean resounding "Newlands only", practiced for the last fifty years or so. Echoing his distrust of multinational bodies and treaties is the fact that Newlands never belonged to the United Nations nor any other multinational body, neither did it ever sign a multilateral treaty. We don't accept any war refugees, a practice clearly dear and envied by the new American President. We heavily discriminate and screen the potential

immigrants, something Trump is keen to introduce into the American border practice.

When Trump brought up the total of Newlander exports to the States, he was confronted with evidence suggesting that the American importers battle with other countries to secure Newlandean products because of their high quality and low price. If the President wanted to curtail those imports, Newlands will effortlessly find whom to sell its goods to. We'd like to keep selling to America, but it can as easily be Iran, or Zimbabwe, or North Korea for that matter, as we don't partake in trade sanctions against any country in the world. This made Trump flinch; he was aware that he possessed no levers to control Newlandean foreign policy, as it isn't based on any international treaty. And when Trump finally raised the question of forcing Newlands to buy more from the USA, he was shocked by Nemanja's simple answer: "we don't buy trash".

Then he was passed into my tender care.

I challenged Trump to equal what Obama already did; ney, even best his predecessor's audacity. Obama shared with me a plunge to the bottom of the ocean, then a flight into the stratosphere with Sam. I asked Trump to accompany me on an afternoon journey of discovery of MANATO's abilities.

Just him and me.

Alone.

Despite (or maybe because of) the furious opposition of his cabinet members, advisors, and security personnel, he accepted.

Escorted by the newly acquired Newlands Police Mustangs, our first stop was Nordporte. To please him, I showed Trump some of the imported American flying machines we put to good use: a Newlands Government Air Transport (NGAT) Boeing C-17NL Globemaster, an Old City Cargo Lockheed C-130J-30 Hercules, a naval Lockheed F-35B fighter, an Airforce Grumman Gulfstream G550 early warning airborne radar, and a NGAT Sikorsky S-92A helicopter from our President's own flight. I even demonstrated plans for MANATO's next generation Lockheed Martin C-24NL Perseus transport plane, which the Californian company will exclusively produce for us over the next ten years.

Between inspections of those planes, we were driven in a small fleet of Hummers and Humvees, obviously purchased from America.

But that's where our ass-licking stopped. Next, I had Ron (Ron Sparks, the Colonel-Pilot of Newlands Airforce and our "Inspector of

fighters") perform some non-ballistic maneuvers in a Rudius, then demonstrate its beam weapon. This made Trump's jaw drop. Apparently, he didn't know Newlands had such advanced beam weaponry! Swift – 4, which happened to be on standby in Nordporte, presented their beam guns, even allowing the American President to himself melt a couple of improvised targets. In the main fleet's anchorage, NLCB05 *Yam*, our Cophot flagship, demonstrated its ability to dive. NLCB04 *Hell*, our experimental Superdestroyer, suddenly surfaced, and fired its tremendous main battery of beam weapons into the air, bringing down all twenty "attacking" drones in less than three seconds (those were the older model drones which we don't care for, but Trump needs not know that, no?). Raj demonstrated our Labyrinthium Shield's primary nuclear defense function, then flattened and sank an old tanker to emphasize how it can also be used against the enemy shipping (I tacitly explained that if we wished we could also easily flatten his White House, with him inside). The pilots of the 33rd Experimental Squadron "Hawk" flew in with a pair of Aurelias, in an incredibly spirited display of power and might, unequaled anywhere in the world, which couldn't leave anyone's blood cold.

Finally, without consulting the President, five, twelve, three, or anyone else, I made Alan Wykes, the Inspector of Newlands Police, now on permanent "detached duty" in the General Headquarters of MANATO, bespeak Trump in his crystal-clear black man's telepathic voice from across the airfield (all recently acquired intelligence ascertains that the western intelligence system is aware of telepathic components playing part in PsiMANATO; therefore, technically, I wasn't giving away any secrets).

"You see, dear Mister President. We already possess diving battleships, space-going fighter planes, telepathic soldiers, ultra powerful beam weapons, and a mighty shield to use against any nuclear attack. What more would MANATO need to import from America?"

For the reminder of his visit, enjoying a dinner with our politicians, Trump appeared quite subdued, civil, and friendly. Two hours into his return flight, he tweeted the introduction of 25% tariffs on Newlandean steel, aluminum, and silver.

If he expected a flurry of indignation and combative diplomatic reactions from our side, he was disappointed (hence his Twitter rants against Newlands soon died out, starved of fuel). His actions got a lukewarm, barely noticed response in our press, among our political parties,

and among our Electocrats. President Petrović publicly acknowledged the right of the Americans to change conditions of our bilateral trade. That is, after all, the main Newlander credo: trade should be arranged bilaterally, with each side responsible for laying out the foundations. But he pointed out our right to do the same and follow the American example. A calm discussion ensued in the Newlands Congress, followed by an Electocratic vote. Our people have spoken. Any damage which the American President inflicted on our export industry will be tabulated and calculated. Though all essential contracts with the Americans will remain in place, any increase in imports from the USA was now temporarily forbidden. The bulk of imports from the United States will be lessened by the calculated amount of damage to our industry, specifically targeting products of those states and groups which support Trump. This ban included all new weapons and car purchases. Goods which America stops importing will be first offered to the states inimical to the USA, such as Iran, Venezuela, or North Korea. If they don't take them, they will be offered to everyone else in the world. Initial math indicated that the American trade deficit with Newlands will rise, from nine times to eleven times the sum value of American exports.

And America itself will have to produce, or import from somewhere else, replacement goods of inferior quality.

As usually, though they probably made his voter base happy (and me, personally, sad), Trump's actions hurt one country only: the United States.

Three more pictures of Trump and me are dispatched to their proper folder. Then my attention switches to boys playing football on the grassy patch beyond our pool (obviously, after somehow regaining their ball). Our sons Vid, Athom, Vuk, and Stein. All six years old, all different. Besides Costa, with them is Sam Novotny, Pavel and Cleo's son, just a couple of months older, a fast friend of our children since they all learned to walk and talk.

There are three adults ostensibly watching our children at play, chatting in the shade of a palm tree. The edge of the pool is close, maybe too close for comfort. And that side of our pool is more than six feet deep (sorry, two meters; Newlands is metric, but I still occasionally forget myself). Yet, all our boys are already good swimmers, and so is Sam, the darling of our family. I'm not worried.

In the shade of our three palms are my wives Alisa and Fanta, and our friend, the ex-sex worker Eaton Magnificent.

Alisa and Fanta are crowding this newly promoted movie and TV star and successful wine seller (employed by Pavel), clear adoration in their sparkling eyes. Years ago, they both got to spend an exquisitely sensual (and as exquisitely expensive) session of lovemaking with Eaton. Since then, their bond is unbreakable. Now a married man (to the flame-haired Amanda Ross, our family doctor, and still the youngest Newlandean heart surgeon ever), Eaton occasionally highlights his full availability to my wives (now for free). It simply never happened (yet, but it certainly will). Amanda is, after all, such a good friend. Though she, of course, in the strictest of all Newlander traditions, (at least publicly) has no quarrels with Eaton having sex with other women, married or unmarried.

Over the last couple of years, mostly working in the office of the Ambassador of MANATO, first in New Belgrade then later on Ceti III when our GHQ finally moved to its new building, without changing her bubbly personality and erotic enthusiasm, Fanta gained some weight (lots of weight, maybe twenty or even thirty pounds; I never insist on learning the number), making her desirable curves even more desirable (at least in my opinion and my fun-filled sexual experience; some of my husbands beg to disagree), becoming a true rendition of the classic loving mother's form.

Perversely opposite, Alisa is nowadays leaner and meaner than ever. (I suspect that her replacement hormonal therapy may be on the stronger-than-needed side, though by a hair width.) About a year ago, to boost her sexual appeal (not that she lacked any), Alisa dyed her waist-long raven-black hair straw blonde. It was a stunning change, a breathtaking reversal, which made me ludicrously (and obviously) lust for the love of my life, my Moon and stars, whenever we happened to get together. Which isn't too often. Between duties to her eight sons, her job as the coordinator of our ever-growing prisoner employment program (nowadays fully mandated through a law approved by the Electocrats), and her central position in PsiMANATO, she's now a woman with a dearth of free time.

(In return, noticing and savouring the effect of her blond hair, she asked me to double the length of my stache. Moustache is Alisa's main sexual fetish. At first, I protested. Then I let it grow. As it grew, I could observe the same increase of erotic lust in my wife. Fascinating.)

Eaton changed, too. Since abandoning his sex trade, he let a (not very prominent) tummy replace his previously impeccably lean six-pack. Though, far from me to suggest that he abandoned gyms! His workout nowadays simply concentrates on different muscle groups. His biceps muscles now bulge twice their previous size. Recently, after a protracted absence, during an evening of socializing, Eaton demanded that each Lionheart personally finger his scrotum (I guess an impossible social activity anywhere in the world bar Newlands). He had reason to be proud. After loosing both his natural testicles to a dangerous cancer, the prosthetic ones he sported for a couple of years finally got replaced by fully functional testicles, cloned by MARC scientists.

I'm a bit peeved at my scientists. It's my personal but never loudly stated conviction that Eaton's new testicles happen to appear almost twice the size of the originals, giving his scrotum, now so obviously dangling in front of his powerful buttocks, an undue prominence.

Or, maybe, that size is just some post-surgical swelling, to subside over time?

(Or some necessary by-product of the cloning process? What do I know....)

The ex-porn idol appears inconceivably different in another way. His naked torso supports a harness, holding a baby tightly strapped to his chest. The fifteen months old Ivana Ross – Magnificent, daughter of Eaton and Amanda. Somehow, try as I can, I could never visualize Eaton as a proud father. That is until his daughter was born (she was a product of invitro fertilization, then implanted into Amanda's womb and naturally delivered). That isn't the end, though. Rumor is that Amanda is pregnant again, and that this time, with his new fully functioning testicles, Eaton managed to perform in the most natural of ways.

Ah, horny youngsters (stated by a horny middle-aged man, heh.)

I study the next picture.

President Nemanja Petrović. During one of his rallies.

Politically, 2015 was for me an eyeopener, as I finally had a chance to observe the long process of elections for the office of the President of Newlands and the members of Congress.

Here are two more pictures of Nemanja. Both place him on a stage, one with his soon to depart Vice-president Domenico Barnes, the other with Nina Jones, our Minister of Defense. Both were my good acquaintances.

Maybe you'd expect me to have mostly followed President Petrović and his campaign, him being such an important person in my life. However, I was centering much more on my Li Lian and her public speeches designed to boost chances for presidency of Luis Peres, an able and well-known politician from her Constitutional Party (by now a solid friend of mine, though no sex yet, I'm not even certain if he'd perform man-to-man; also, the most beloved politician of the Lionhearts, not because of his ideas but because of his devastatingly sexy Latino looks). And here they are, together, a dozen digital photos of Li and Luis, from a rally which I attended, held in the "Desert Pearl" open marketplace in Old City.

Blimey, when I think of it, this election folder is already well formed. Why make unnecessary changes? I only need to rename it.... tap, tap, tap.... and drag it to its proper place....

Done.

Well, let's check who else is there.

Ah, of course. An even dozen pictures of Toša Popović, Newlands Atlantis Party's leader (pejoratively dubbed by their opponents the "Newlands Nazis"). The party dedicated to a future which would separate our country from the rest of humanity and see us develop a truly underwater culture, even an underwater empire. Toša is nowadays a friend till death, as well as an occasional lover (mostly in threesomes with Li or other women, such as my Fanta or Alisa). He's earnestly trying to modernize the appearance and goals of his party, without endangering its basic traditions. In 2015, for the first time in our history, a leader of NAP appeared in serious contention for the presidency.

Ah, yes. My election folder also contains the rally photos of John Shelton, Newlands Future Party's leader, and Ivanka Molek, the leader of the good old Demarchy Party. From the very beginning of the 2015 Presidential race, political pundits described their chances as marginal.

They were proven right.

As per Li's prediction, Nemanja won, harnessing in the initial round fifty-one percent of the vote. If compared to the fifty-eight percent he secured in his first campaign in 2010, you might be tempted to conclude that he suffered a popularity drop. Not true, though. In 2010, Nemanja won his first Presidency, and that high rate of approval, only in the runoff voting, securing a modest thirty-five percent in the first round. This time our Electocrats voted him in with their first ballot. Therefore, his second term started in January of 2016, and will end in January of 2021. After

that he won't be eligible for the office of our President ever again (unless Newlands changes its constitution, which appears unlikely).

His party fared a bit worse, though. From an outright two thirds majority during his first term in office, it slipped into a strong minority position in the Congress, albeit remaining its largest caucus. Nemanja and his colleagues decided to form a minority government, counting on support and a loose unofficial coalition with a couple of smaller parties (there including NAP) to keep their government afloat.

Another important event happened during this election. Though NAP, as a party, fared as poorly as usual (receiving around six percent of votes), Toša secured almost every fourth presidential vote, beating Luis Peres by twenty-three to twenty-one percent to secure the second place in this race. The highest score ever for a NAP leader, auguring well for his chances in the 2020 elections when the unbeatable Nemanja Petrović will be out of the picture).

A fleeting, horny thought. Am I an occasional lover of the next President of Newlands? Nemanja and Li definitely think so.

Another aspect of Newlands elections struck me as important, especially when compared to the scandals of the American elections held a year later. The apparent lack of acrimony. And of the American-style Neolithic chest thumping. That a candidate would ask for their opponent to be jailed is impossible here. Nor were there any promises like: "if I win, I'll build a wall or cancel this or that law." Frankly, no President, nor any other politician on Newlands, can claim such powers and make such promises. For this is a real democracy and people rule here. It's the Newlands Electocrats who, with their votes, have the power to build walls, cancel laws, or, for that matter, pass the new ones which might put someone into jail.

Not the President.

Not the Newlands Congress members.

Only the people.

"Bà, bà!" – rings the young voice of my daughter Zhenxiang Hadži-Janković as she runs into my den – "Look, pa! Look what I did!"

Zhen is today with us in Nake, though I haven't seen her interact much with the other children (she's not a fan of football, nor attracted to water, though she can swim well enough; I personally thought her to swim). Though of similar age as most of our sons, she's rather short, at

least a head shorter than Mansy. Short but proportional, very slim and incredibly nimble and dexterous.

And incredibly Chinese, too. To me, Zhen's face is much more Chinese than her mother's. (I often question what impact my half of her genetic inheritance has; certainly, none of it seems to manifest in her appearance.)

And if you wonder what "bà" might stand for, in Chinese it means daddy. My six-year daughter is an incredible polyglot. She already fluently speaks English, Chinese, and Serbo-Croatian, and is now concentrating on learning French, Korean, and German. Unfortunately, she has trouble understanding that other people aren't like her. In her speech, she often mixes all those languages.

Carefully, as if not to disturb her creation, she places a doll on my table.

"She's beautiful, Jenny. She really is."

Early on I started calling my Zhen "Zhenny". Over time, it resembled so much to "Jenny" that I started using her Anglicized nick whenever we happened to be alone. Zhen immediately fell in love with it and accepted her new nick with pride and gratitude. Do the other adults of families Lionheart and Hadži-Janković know about Zhen's special nick? Maybe. Probably. No one ever reproached me for it.

"Are all her clothes your creation?"

"Da! Shì! Shì! All of them! I made them myself!"

I already recognized Zhen's doll as a "Chamellia". For the last thirty years a Newlands favorite, this doll's tradename derives from the word "chameleon" and not the name for a plant. Like its namesake, it can change the color of skin, from Nordic pink to Bantu black, depending on the temperature she's exposed to (different heads, which can be switched around, are provided to represent at least six racial types; auxiliary ones can be acquired separately). Another curious fact: these dolls are sold nude, without any clothing, and are anatomically correct representations of the female body, avoiding extremes. Ample material and instructions are supplied to doll's new owner (or new owner's parents) to create doll's clothes. Though this doll is meant for older owners, starting around nine or ten, Zhen got her Chamellia a year ago as a gift from her socially recognized father Rob Hadži-Janković, and has since created numerous progressively more complicated attires.

Zhen's Chamellia is named Mara. Today, Mara is wearing a translucent dress made of fine white lace (where did Zhen get that lace,

I wonder?) nicely stitched together to accentuate doll's shape. On her head is a complicated pink hat made of.... cardboard and.... plush, I guess. She's wearing velvet knee-high moccasins, each decorated with a tiny Impatiens flower freshly plucked from our garden. Oh, and her skin is milk chocolate.

"You're a real fashionista, Jenny!"

"What's fashionista, bre?" – Zhen appears quite perplexed.

"A designer of haute couture, Jenny my love." – I see her mouth work; I can also almost hear her say: what's haute couture? Therefore, I speed on – "A devoted creator of fashion."

For a moment, Zhen watches me with wonder, her eyes dark and round: - "You speak French, shì shì!"

I grab my daughter around her waist and easily lift her into my embrace.

"I don't, Jenny."

"But haute.... and that other word....

They are French!"

I remain silent and squeeze her a bit more, until her face is right in front of mine. She stops struggling and goes limp in my embrace.

"Kiss, pa."

I plant a ceremonial kiss right onto her lips. As I do, she produces the childish smacking-kissing sound, which I expected. Then she bursts into unstoppable giggling.

"Your thing itches!"

My "thing" is my moustache.

"Tickles, love. Itch is a skin rash."

Zhen's still giggling – "Same as fùqīn!"

If you wonder, that's more Chinese, this time another term for father. Zhen is comparing Rob's and my moustache. For years, his was bigger. Now I'm the champion.

I pivot and grab the platter with broghies.

"Take one, Jenny."

"Méiyǒu, pa, no. Not hunger. I ate."

She's lying, the little devil. Zhen's a very fussy eater. It's difficult to please her with any food.

"Not hungry, love. You have hunger. You're hungry. See?"

"Not hungry!" – shouts Zhen, carefully lifts her doll, and disappears into our garden.

For a couple of long minutes, a smile hovers on my face.

Next pic.

Nanjing.

Modern looking but still dotted with the communist-era rectangular skyscrapers. Leaden skies. And an incredible, sprawling, two-hundred-plus square kilometers research park producing dazzling technological advances.

In February 2016, I finally made it to China, before all hope was lost.... No, no. I won't let my mind dwell on that subject. Not right now.

Think of China.

So, I made it to China. Not as a tourist, but as MANATO's Commander – in – Chief. Luckily for me, Li was free to accompany me. Our daughter Zhenxiang Hadži-Janković, born on July 1st of 2012, was old enough to comfortably remain those two weeks at home, with Rob looking after her (helped by my wives). So was Atlas Hadži-Janković, Li and Rob's younger son, likely born on a July 1st, but in 2014. Incredible parsimony.

I was terrified of this trip. To me, in 2016, China still appeared as mystical and mysterious (and, frankly, alien) as always. Li's presence made the journey one of discovery and intellectually satisfying revelation (lots of sex notwithstanding).

Bit by bit.

Site by site.

One city at the time.

One romantic meal after another.

Chinese officers and politicians wined and dined us all over the country: in Beijing, Shanghai, Hong Kong, and everywhere else in this large land. And under it, since the Chinese, who somehow learned about my passion for diving, took us to the submerged city of Shi Cheng at the bottom of the Qiandao Lake. Finally, close to the end of our journey, we made it to the ancient Chinese capital of Nanjing, three hundred kilometers from Shanghai up the Yangtze River. Nowadays, at eight million inhabitants, trailing far behind the glitzy, internationally prominent coastal cities (though almost equal to the whole population of Newlands), somewhat in political disarray after its strongman mayor Ji Jianye "Bulldozer" got convicted for taking millions of dollars in bribes.

And my eyes popped wide open.

For years MANATO purchased cheap Chinese military hardware, mostly ships and helicopters. The current decision of our CCofGHQ is to change this to buying software and internet technology, no matter its cost. Nanjing's research park harbors companies which are ideal partners for such a switch. Deals which I concluded there (to be later approved in detail by my CCofGHQ and in general by our Electocrats) will chart the course of MANATO's development for a decade.

That whole trip reeked of success.

I probably made good friends with many important Chinese political leaders and officers.

Yet, when I returned home, China still appeared to me as mystical and mysterious and alien as always.

Thom, Nikola and Fran aren't today in Nake. We're still a busy military family, highly involved in MANATO's protective functions. To be factual, more involved (at a higher level) and busier than ever. Too bad. It would have been nice if they were here.

I have many photos of my husbands.

Let's see, maybe these can be transferred to this folder....

I'm proud of my husbands. Thom and Nikola recently became Brigadier Generals. Fran has been a Vice-Admiral since 2016, in practice equally sharing the command of MANATO with me, though not officially.

I'm no less proud of Alisa and Fanta, both risen to the rank of Operations Officers of the Administrative branch of MANATO despite their challenging motherhood to eight unruly boys, with Alisa's rank of the Komodor of Newlands Navy frozen.

I love them all.

Yet....

There's an incurable emptiness in my heart.

A tear drops from my left eye, right into my moustache. I try to brush it away.

Enough!

My cell rings again. Even without checking its caller ID, the dedicated melody informs me it's Fran. This time, it's a MANATO military videocall.

"And?" – I start "in medias res", as I'm waiting for some important info.

"I inspected it, Marka mu."

I'm getting impatient: - "And?"

Fran dallies a bit, absentmindedly twirling the end of his moustache.

"Dave, that prcat house is beautiful. Its layout is beautiful, and its position on top of the Mild Hill is ochen balshoy beautiful too."

Fran was inspecting a home in the "Arbustes" neighborhood of Ceticity, on Rue de la Defense (all streets in that quarter of Ceticity have noble-sounding French names). Much as we're all fond of our small Ceticity apartment on Javorovog lista 15 and the beautiful memories which tie us to it, with our children spending ever more time in the military capital of our archipelago, we're desperate for more space.

"Their advertisement material hinted at that."

I saw some pictures online and studied that home's floor plans. It appeared quite appealing to me.

"Four bedrooms...."

"Ample."

"Orcae ita, as we hoped. Swimming pool with a nice patio, hot tub, a whole mrdat stunning tennis court in the back. Enough bathrooms and other specialized space."

"But?" – somehow, Fran appears somewhat hesitant; therefore, I expect a "but" somewhere along the way.

"Oh, I forgot to mention the ochen balshoy indoor – outdoor kitchen equipped with the most fashionable appliances, sporting a dinning room space with glass wall which can completely be opened to the putz pool patio, weather allowing."

"Neat.... but?"

A sigh from my Fran.

"Two buts. It's more expensive than we expected."

A serious flaw. Well, maybe not so serious. We all earn a lot of money.

"To be discussed (and voted on, in the Electocratic Lionheart way, the whole family present), but I don't believe money will be a problem. Especially if we sell the Nova Britanija apartment, as we planned. What else?"

A bit of hesitation: - "Do we really want to live that close to Colonel Janosh and Yrinne? I mean, permanently (as opposed to occasional socializing, I guess)? Spasitelju, I mean.... should we expose our sons to them so much?"

I pause to muse on my husband's words. Colonel Janosh, of course, is Colonel Boris Janosh, the recently retired Warden of the National Jail of

Newlands. A long time ago he boasted that he would keep working until the day he woke up and couldn't.... eh, copulate with his spouse Yrinne, a glamorous and exciting transvestite, originally from South Africa. I guess that day must have finally arrived. Chuckle, chuckle.

So, why would living near to Janosh and Yrinne, and exposing our sons to them, bother Fran? On two accounts, I guess. Transvestites are still not fully understood and integrated into human society, even here, on Newlands, where they have all the imaginable rights under the sun. The second problem is the incredibly foul language Janosh and Yrinne use to communicate with each other, notwithstanding the presence of anybody else, including children.

"You're not keen on exposing our sons to their linguistic shenanigans?"

"Multitax, right!"

"Our kids are great. I doubt it would be a problem."

"Really, bre? You think so?" – I can see that it appears much more of a problem to Fran; still, after a bit of hesitation, he goes on – "So, do you think I should put down the minimal deposit, legally required at this point? To secure it before somebody else takes it, bre? Marka mu, its hundred percent refundable within the first week. We could schedule our family parliament for the next weekend and decide before that mrdat official deadline."

Yes.

Good plan.

I like that idea.

"Yes, Fran. That's a great notion. Let's grab it. Please put down that deposit."

"OK."

"You have enough (money)?"

A very broad grin under his eternally perfect moustache.

"Right. Saturday or Sunday?"

"No, I can gahba do it today."

"No, I meant, should we meet on Saturday or Sunday?"

"Well....

(Fran's eyes travel to his right and there's some noise, maybe typing on a tablet or a keyboard.)

I'd say Saturday, Marka mu. And it better be AM."

Saturday AM.

Remember.

You better remember, stupid!

Bright idea: write it down this time!

"Where (do we meet)?"

"Definitely here, multitax. Ceticity. We can inspect our potential newest property before making a final decision."

"Another great notion, hub. I'll tell Fanta and Alisa. They are here with me. You tell Thom and Nikola. They are there with you."

Now Fran smiles: - "I ochen balshoy will."

He's beautiful, I state to myself, and I feel the truth of my statement with my whole body. Beautiful, caring, intelligent, inquisitive: - "Something else on your prolific mind?"

Fran chuckles: - "Some new studies. I found out that our demise will arrive twice earlier than predicted, Marka mu."

Our demise? Newlands is in trouble? The archipelago is (finally / again) sinking?

"You make no sense whatsoever."

"Well, sexy CIC, someone's prcat home may get demolished. In two billion years."

"Two.......... billion? Did I hear that right? Fran, what are you talking about?"

"Well, our Astronomical Society published their newest findings. Our Milky Way galaxy is on a collision course with the LMC, bre."

I'm still quite lost.

Something concerning our galaxy.

And LMC, whatever that may be.

"Ochen balshoy, the shape of your moustache informs me that you've no idea what LMC may be."

"How true!"

"It's the Large Magellanic Cloud, ten times smaller than our galaxy, our prcat closest neighbor. Some also call it our satellite galaxy."

My puzzled facial expression must have persisted.

"Well, our prcat galaxy and our satellite galaxy will collide. In about two billion years. They forecast all kinds of horrendous destructions, most stars in the middle of our galaxy will be destroyed or displaced, and the central black hole is apparently going to swell to eight times its current mass, tabarnaque."

"Fran.... but.... you said two BILLION years from now! I don't.... care what will happen in fifty years, not to mention two billion!"

(Not true. I may be dead by then, but what happens in fifty years will affect my children. I better start caring.)

"True, but we now know someone who may be affected. Dixi."

Ball.

The alien being living inside our sun.

"Go on."

"Dave, we never discussed it, but there's a gaping hole in the story Thom Brdar told you."

"There is?"

"Orcae ita, assuredly so."

"Which one?"

"Isn't the premise of the life cycle of those sun-dwelling plasma beings that they reproduce by fission in the moment of explosion of their home star when it goes supernova? Am I right, Marka mu?"

"You are."

"But that's yatsume impossible, my Mo."

Impossible?

How?

Why?

"How? Why?"

"Our sun will never go supernova. As it nowadays appears, its lifetime is predicted to be another five billion years or so, after which, exhausting its fuel, it will start cooling down to become a super concentrated ultra-dense white dwarf. A star the size of our planet, great nature above and around."

"What the fuck?" – for a moment, my emotions rise in a froth of anger, making me forget the impoliteness of using the "f" word. Did Ball and Thom Brdar, or those DFQL aliens (or both), lie to me? Why would they lie? What did they gain by lying?

Paradoxically, Fran chuckles: - "Besides hearing it, I can sense your sudden anger. Multitax, simmer down. It's not what you think."

"What am I thinking?"

"Elementary, sakra. That Thom Brdar or the DFQL priests lied to you...."

"Or both."

"Or both; immaterial, svih mi svetaca. Maybe he didn't. Maybe they didn't."

"They didn't?"

"Ochen balshoy. I'd rather say that the DFQL aliens may have themselves missed that fine point. Alternatively, majke ti, they might know something which they didn't pass on to you."

Indeed, they know a lot which they didn't pass on to me. To us.

"Look, Dave, it's much more complicated than what I stated. As its internal composition is changed by fission, hueles a mierda, a sun like ours, before petering out, passes through a phase of enlargement. Our calculations aren't yet exact, but our sun will inevitably turn into a red giant. Temporarily. Yatsume Mercury and Venus will certainly be consumed. Some scientists say that the sun won't stretch further than half the distance between the orbits of Earth and Venus. Some say it will inevitably engulf Earth. As sun loses its mass in a series of nebula forming pulses, Earth will be migrating further away, so that's another element of uncertainty, bre. I mean, how far away may our Earth escape. Pai, pai, scorched or devoured, our Earth will certainly be toast. This is supposed to happen in about seven to eight billion years. Then, after a short period of time, as judged by the standards of astronomy, our sun will shrink and shrivel away."

"OK. I'm starting to see the light at the end of that particular tunnel. Two billion years till the collision with that cloud.... satellite, whatever. Five billion years till sun goes supernova, as stated by DFQL. Seven to eight billion years till the sun turns your...."

"Red giant."

"Red giant, yes. So, unless two kills us outright, it's the choice between five or seven. Both destinies can't be true. One excludes the other."

"Da. Majke mu, there's more, love."

"Even more?"

"Another collision. Four to five billion years from now, our Milky Way will inevitably impact our nearest neighbor, the Andromeda galaxy. Unfortunately for us, Andromeda is prc twice larger. There's no way our galaxy will survive, but that doesn't mean that every star will be impacted. The models suggest that the two galaxies may recombine into a super-galaxy, with a hugely massive black hole in its center, or two independent black holes. Being peripherally positioned, our sun may very well survive, tabarnaque."

Silence.

I can't square this circle.

"That's what made me wonder. What if DFQL is right, but with a wrong timescale? Your Ball must be perfectly aware of all these facts I just shared with you. After all, Sol is its putz home and the DFQL aliens hinted at a Ball network which spans the Universe. Ii kagen ni shiro, what if your plasma alien possesses means to change our sun in a way which will guarantee that it goes supernova before it gets destroyed in the collisions with the LMC or Andromeda?"

What a colossal idea!

Hair raises on my arms!

Fran is right!

"Labyrinthium!"

"Aha, now we're talking, my Mo!"

"How can Labyrinthium do that?"

A childish thought: can then our Labyrinthium turn the Earth into a supernova?

Not intentionally, but by accident?

No way!

Yet....

"I've no prcat idea. Still, we know but a fraction of what's to be learned about our main energy source. It does consist of many superheavy elements. Anything is possible, tabarnaque."

"Then, nothing will happen seven to eight billion years from now, as the sun would have gone supernova billions of years before."

"And destroyed the whole solar system, while also propelling the neutronium ships of the newly hatched junior plasma aliens into space, towards their new homes. Quite possibly in the adjacent but more stable galaxies, with better survival outlook."

"Colossal idea, Fran! Labyrinthium is the key! You solved it."

Fran keeps a smug silence.

Something still doesn't appear right to me: - "Then, why is it important what happens in two billion years when we hit that satellite?"

"Aha, good question, bre! That's the problem. Right now, all our scientific models predict that the peripheral stars, like our sun, won't be much affected by that cataclysm. But what if they are? Will your Ball have enough time to prepare Sun to become a supernova in only two billion years from now?"

A fantastic idea, certainly. Yet, how to divine that riddle's correct answer?

"Fran, will we ever know for certain? I mean, in our lifetimes?"

"Marka mu, I doubt it."

"Do you see a way to communicate our conclusions to the DFQL aliens or Thom Brdar?"

Fran shakes his head: - "At this moment, nyet."

"Then, let's not lose sleep over it, right?"

Silence.

"You're right, as usual.

(As usual? I'm usually never right! Fran is! That's why he's such a godsend!)

Anything else, my exalted CIC? Something much more down to earth?"

Throughout our video chat, Fran has obviously been carefully ogling me. I can guess which part of my body he's so studiously watching: - "When we meet, hub. All yours."

"Da. You're mine."

Click.

What other pictures need my attention?

I click on the first of a dozen stashed in a folder created last year. It pops up and I freeze, my heart once again pierced by pain.

Rocco Stelle. Major Rocco Stelle. Great movie star Rocco Stelle, the idol of our nation. Alone. In downtown New Belgrade, close to the old GHQ building, now turned into the museum of MANATO. Wearing his alter ego face (moustache only, no goatee), occasionally required by his roles.

Then Rocco with John František. With me. All three of us together.

I sigh.

Rocco's July 15, 2017, death in an Istanbul hotel shocked all Newlanders. He was shot twice. Once in his head, from behind, a weird hit which MANATO pathologists, examining his body after it got returned ten days after the assassination, assured me instantaneously destroyed his brain and killed my friend, then later the second time from up front into his chest, while lying on his back; an overkill, or insurance when his heart wouldn't stop beating.

News was traumatic for our whole nation.

Turkey is a traditional friend of Newlands, and our bilateral cooperation has historically been steady and stable, though unspectacular. For a couple of days, that status quo appeared thoroughly shaken.

Officially, Rocco was in Istanbul for negotiations with some Turkish movie producers about a potential role.

Unofficially (but actually), he was there on behalf of the Newlands Secret Service to track certain people associated with the faltering ISIS. Rocco's mission in Britain, to obtain samples of bacteria with artificially produced DNA, proved a spectacular success. He himself obtained the first samples, then created an ingenious automatic supply chain, devoid of people, which will assure MANATO secretly receiving further English lab discoveries for years to come. His other assignment, to trace those responsible for the 2012 destruction of a MANATO Dornier by a bomb hidden in its tail, which cost us lives of two CCofGHQ officers (my personal friends) and two elite pilots, lingered in limbo for a long while. Then, in 2016, John František obtained fresh information from Syria, which sent Rocco's investigation in a new direction and quickly bore substantial fruit. Finally, we had three names of interest. And their trail led from England through Turkey to Eastern Syria or Western Iraq.

Hence Istanbul.

At first, an aide to the Turkish President Recep Tayyip Erdoğan accused Rocco of being involved in the failed summer 2016 coup d'état, stipulating that he was killed by state agents while resisting arrest.

Our government bristled at that accusation. On the surface of it, that obviously false Turkish position couldn't be maintained. Yet, if Turks persisted in their claims, someone (from one of world's more developed intelligence agencies) might become curious enough to start digging. And if that person, or those persons, dug deep enough, the core secrets of Newlands might get exposed. Furious diplomatic activity ensued, centered around my (and Rocco's) friend John František, MANATO's very own Ambassador.

Finally, the Turkish President Erdoğan appeared on their national TV, with a rare public apology to the people of Newlands, and accolades for our dead actor. It was a case of mistaken identity, he said, involving the National Intelligence Organization, Turkish government's intelligence service. It appeared that some agents wrongly connected Rocco Stelle to Fethullah Gulen, Erdoğan's main opponent, currently living in exile in America, and executed him hastily as a danger to Turkey. (That presumed

connection between Rocco and Gulen was an outright fabrication, as Rocco had no links to the Islamic thinker. MANATO knows; therefore, I know. Our President knows. NSS knows.) In his speech, President Erdoğan offered generous compensation to Rocco's children, as well as any other reimbursement which our country may request, including rendition of the culpable agents.

Our President Nemanja Petrović poured cold water on Newlandeans' burning anger. He avoided any hasty reactions and consulted with all political structures of Newlands (and, behind the scenes, with NSS and MANATO). Finally, three days after Erdoğan's apology, Nemanja delivered a speech on our TV National in English, Serbo-Croatian, and (unprecedently, reading from a special teleprompter script) Turkish itself.

In short, Newlands accepted Turkish President's apology. Our country wished to celebrate the life of our greatest actor and lament his untimely death, excluding any thoughts of revenge. With all pomp imaginable, our government sent one of its planes to bring Rocco's body back, to be later entombed in Pesak in a gigantic (unprecedented) public ceremony. Schools of acting, streets, planes, ships.... were speedily renamed in his honor, both in Turkey and on Newlands. Turkish monetary compensation to the next of kin was praised and accepted. We declined the offer of rendition. "Rocco Stelle Contemporary Film Festival" was established, to be held annually, alternating between Old City and Istanbul. "Rocco Stelle Football Tournament" was to be held yearly in Atlantis or Ankara. A drama contest carrying his name would be yearly held in Sunshine Valley, near the entrance to the Optimus Cave, inspired by Rocco's most celebrated role as Calisto in "The Saga of Atlantis", voted our best movie of all times, followed by two sequels, which netted him multiple accolades and awards. And a giant statue of Rocco Stelle was commissioned, to be placed in the Razorback Park, near one of its downtown observation points my friend cherished in his life.

After a thorough investigation by MANATO's intelligence service, only one fact couldn't be filtered out. Did President Erdoğan personally order Rocco's death (we had solid proof that it was done according to his orders) because he genuinely believed our actor connected to his enemies, or because the secrecy of his work as an agent of Newlands Secret Service got breached?

The close political relationship between Turkey and Newlands survived, though diminished. On the other hand, relations between the

TSK (Turkish Armed Forces) and MANATO radically cooled down (to the great extent because of me; I'll never forgive this Turkish misdeed, committed to protect those ISIS lowlifes).

I will miss my friend. I'll dearly miss him.

Newlands will dearly miss his professional skills and abilities, though not those the average Newlandeans have in mind.

An additional event, the final epilogue of Rocco's death, happened two months later. It's destined to give both me and President Petrović headaches and nightmares far into distant future. Bogdan, President's son, my blood-brother, was accepted as Rocco's replacement in NSS, while keeping his assignment in Swift – 1.

Bogdan and Nikola, now joined in their service in NSS, from the outside supported by Thom.

Beware, you hapless enemies of Newlands, you've no idea what's coming your way!

What a double source of pride.

What a double source of fear.

Tough.

Apparently, our boys got fed up with football (a rare occurrence) and decided to move to the edge of the pool and engage in a diving competition. Sam, Costa, and Stein tried to move one of the lounge chairs closer to pool's edge to serve as a jumping platform. (We're still discussing whether to install real diving boards for our Nake and New Belgrade pools.) Alisa, Fanta, and Eaton reacted fast and prevented that dangerous activity. For a moment, our boys seemed disappointed, but were soon one after another splashing into the pool from its side, amid delighted shrieking and applause.

Happy children.

Thom.

In uniform. SWIFT-1's KGZ camo, nowadays perfectly shielded to avoid exposure to the deadly residual Labyrinthium radiation.

The lord of any tactical battle, probably the best soldier Newlands ever had.

Strong. Fierce. Wise.

Unmovable like a rock.

Unflinching under pressure.

Since his double death and even more improbable double resurrection, his temper has been permanently placed under control of a newly established iron will. After he apparently perished in Benghazi, for a considerable time Thom survived, existed, lived inside two other human beings (Nikola and me). Then he lived inside a machine. And then, inside.... well.... something. A god, you might say. An almost eternal being, immensely wise and immensely different from us. Thom's mind has grown and expanded in ways no human being ever managed to achieve (except Thom Brdar, of course, but I guess that's a completely different story).

Not so his body (the cloned version, of course). It hasn't changed a bit. At forty-five, he still looks the same as when I saw him first, in the National Jail, seven years ago. His muscled frame is still imposing (even slightly larger than before; I know this for a fact because MANATO scientists made his reconstituted cloned body one-point-eight centimeters taller and correspondingly wider); his moustache and scalp hair are still dark, with no trace of grey.

I dare not speculate on that peculiar lack of aging signs on my husband's body, miraculously cloned from his remaining organs and previously stored tissues (which MARC preserved without ever telling us, his family; there was never much of Thom cremated and entombed in Pesak). His mind (essence, aura, soul.... whatever) which sheltered first in my brain, then Nikola's, then in MARC's robotic android contraption, then in Ball, before returning to his reconstituted body, must have greatly suffered. But his body nowadays appears untouched and untouchable by the flow of time. What did my scientists accomplish, really? Another great miracle of Newlands?

What did.... Ball.... accomplish?

For there's no doubt who, or what, was behind that miracle.

Returning to life, Thom faced a challenging year in which he had to be presented to our people and his miraculous survival somehow explained. The full truth was never revealed, nor could ever become public. The gist of the story told to our Electocrats was that MARC kept his body in stasis, in a deep coma, preserving the functioning of his brain while his damaged organs healed or were regrown. The ashes entombed in Pesak were from those organs and body parts which couldn't be saved.

It was a challenging year.

Slowly, inch by inch, Thom's case gained traction (while he was immediately returned to his MANATO duties). At the end, he became

the only citizen in our history to personally withdraw his plaque from the National Graveyard in Pesak, all his privileges regained and returned.

The happiest of all endings imaginable.

Another photo.

Thom and Nikola.

Soldierly serene, serious, armed, deadly, perched on a rock. In uniform, though one of its lighter versions for the (not rare) warm tropical days. Probably during one of Swift-1's training operations. Different, yet the same. Biologically unrelated, yet closer than twins.

Ah.

Then, Nikola alone.

My beautiful teddy bear. A real-life grizzly-sized grizzly-strong and grizzly-deadly (when on an assignment for NSS) teddy.

Forty-five years old, like Thom. But his beard is nowadays half grey (if not more than half). His facial hair started greying in the first couple of weeks after....

No, no. I don't want to dwell on those dark memories.

Not now.

Not today.

With Electocracy deeply rooted in our society, Nikola decided to openly poll soldiers of his Swift – 1 whether a greying officer can still merit, deserve, and retain their full trust, obedience, respect, devotion.... all essential prerequisites for a successful military leader on tactical field of battle (fleetingly reminding me of my discussions within the GHQ whether an impotent officer can command). Their answer was empathic and enthusiastic. Nikola decided to proudly keep his new greying hair and beard, though we tried to convince him to start using any of the omnipresent, everywhere-available cosmetic products which could rejuvenate his looks.

I never openly objected to my wives and husbands' requests, though this new grey-bearded Nikola elicits in me a certain kind of unanticipated erotic lust rarely experienced in my life. Therefore, his choice not to camouflage his greys made me a happy husband.

"Dave, tabarnaque, is everything OK with you?" – this time it's Žana's voice which is interrupting my solitude.

"Certainly, Žana. Why ask?"

Žana enters my den, carrying her cellphone in her hand, her breasts seductively swaying with every step.

"Marka mu, you're here all alone, while we all wait outside...."

"Just work, Žana, nothing worse than that. Work. You know me by now."

Žana produces a temporary sour smile, fleetingly disturbing her soft, pink lips.

"It's Bogisha. Calisse de merde, he says that he can't reach you on your cellphone."

I chuckle.

"Actually, true. My cell is upstairs, in our bedroom, getting charged. I forgot about it."

It got plugged upstairs after I finished my chat with Fran.

I watch Žana, not able to decide what she wants me to do. Maybe take her cellphone and directly talk to my blood brother? She appears undecided, then lifts the cell to her face.

"Boggy, his cell is upstairs.......... prc true. I'll ask." – Žana turns towards me – "He's only asking whether he's still to meet you in Ceticity GHQ tomorrow at nine?"

Yes.

We need to discuss some things.

Like, I was just yesterday notified of his last week's trip to Iraq and Syria. And full success. The two criminals who imbedded that bomb in our Dornier, and their bomb maker, won't kill anyone ever again.

I nod: - "Yes. Tell him that I'll be happy to see him."

Žana blows me a kiss and turns towards the patio door, talking as she's leaving: - "Da, Boggy. Ochen balshoy.......... And he's happy to.........."

David Mann, modern media painter and a close friend of our family, is on this digital picture. With Fanta. David can't be considered a large man under any circumstance, though his figure is perfect. On this photo he appears dwarfed by my wife, somehow all shrunk, sad, and inwardly collapsing.

I remember when this photo was taken. It wasn't a happy occasion.

(Another unhappy one, I'm afraid.)

In 2012, not much after I met his husband Željko Bogdanović - Zex, likewise a painter and photographer of great renown and my famous namesake, showed signs of serious illness. The only remedy was a liver

transplant. A long rehabilitation ensued, but Željko's health steadily improved, to the relief of all friends, acquaintances, and the general Newlander public which thoroughly appreciates his contribution to our art. Despite his improved health, there was an important change in Zex's stance towards life. Often pointing at fate of Apple's creator Steve Jobs, as well as the medical statistics, he figured that he's now living on borrowed time. He became responsible, serious, workaholic; in short time he managed to catalogue and reorganize all his art exhibits, place his works in various galleries and museums (some even on our own walls), and bring order to his legal paperwork. During this time Zex and Dupence (David Mann) became often met friends of family Lionheart, as Željko Bogdanović insisted on as much socializing as possible.

Then, in November of 2014, his health suddenly tanked. Zex's body was massively rejecting his implants. Various other complications were preventing another transplantation, the only realistic cure. Unusual in his behavior to the end, Željko Bogdanović lingered to the last possible moment in a hospital in Paloma, eschewing the possibility of painless assisted suicide, then died at the beginning of March 2015.

This picture of Fanta and Zex's beloved Dupence was taken in front of Pesak's National Graveyard after Zeljko's funeral.

Once Zex was gone, David Mann likewise suffered a transformation. All his flamboyance deserted him. His political activism, itself one of the major impetuses for his art, disappeared too. On the other hand, once alone, he became a close friend of our family, and through us of Robert and Li, often to be seen either in their home or our homes in Nake or Rad. He was supposed to be with us today but was recalled to his gallery to meet a prospecting foreign art dealer.

Click – click.

Ah, a rare one. David Mann, Mansy, and I, on FC Rad's stadium, in our New Belgrade's immediate neighborhood. When I arrived here, FC Rad was a solid team in the Superleague, our major football league. Not anymore. Nowadays FC Rad is competing in the second tier, together with my (still) beloved FC Tom Garrowitz. When that photo was taken, my Tom Garrowitz was visiting. David Mann, too. I impulsively offered to take him and Mansy to the game, and he accepted.

If I remember correctly, Tom Garrowitz won, scoring the single goal of the game just before its end. Still, my team didn't yet manage to climb into the top tier of Newlands football.

Alas.

That picture will now be on its way to a new folder.

Click.

"Ochen balshoy, Dave, would you like me to start preparing for your barbeque?"

In the first instant, Fanta's unexpected words make me all but jump from my sitting ball (a long time ago Alisa replaced all our computer chairs with various ergonometric devices; healthy, but unpleasant to sit on). Then I recognize my wife's voice and turn with alacrity, hoping to mask my moment of perturbed disquiet.

Laughter. Crystal clear, light, and as sparkling as water flowing down Fan park's waterfalls.

"I startled you, tabarnaque!"

"No."

Lie.

Why lie to a person I love so much?

A broad smile lights Fanta's face: - "Yes, I did, bre. Finally!"

"Yes."

Now relieved, I chuckle.

She bends over, kisses me. Her hand searches for the usual handle in my lap and my handle immediately responds.

"Boy, what a gahba horny husband you are!"

"Horny for you, my sexy wife." – my voice is deep, deliberate, and dark. If Fanta goes on like this (I'm talking about the movements of her hand), we might have a bit of sex right here, right now, notwithstanding all those children around us.

"Later, hubby." – she watches me quizzically, as if gaging my arousal and how far I'm prepared to go; then she sighs – "Seriously, hubster, do you want me to start preparing?"

Over the years, Lionhearts developed a special culinary tradition around our barbeque meals. Alisa and Sam were always our best cooks.... until.... Fran and Fanta are wonderful cooks, too, albeit with a limited repertoire. Nikola and Thom can hold their own; they often cook for themselves because their work requires separation from our family and forces them to fix their own meals. Without any doubt whatsoever, I'm the lousiest chef among the Lionhearts.

Except when the barbeques are concerned.

Thus, those barbeques became my exclusive province.

My culinary art of a barbeque chef blossomed and solidified. Prompted by my family, I introduced into my BBQ repertoire numerous new varieties of meat, delicatessen products, and fish: ostrich, kangaroo, venison, deer, buffalo (bison), African antelope meat, farmed tuna, salmon, various European-style sausages, and glass eel (farmed in the Paloma Channel as it's a critically endangered species in the wild). I made mistake after mistake, but with an unusual (for me) tenacity and persistence I never allowed them to stop me. Eventually, I learned how to barbeque those novel foodstuffs, which spices to use, how to marinate them, and which sauces and wines to mate them with.

(Pavel helped with wines; the only wines served during my barbeques are Varina wines.)

Now I'm a barbequing genius.

Heh.

"Fanta, if you wish, take those two fish and sausage trays out of the fridge. Are you guys hungry? I've just a bit left to do. Is it OK if I start barbequing in an hour?"

"The adults are prcat hungry, but we can wait. Soon, the kids will be hungry enough to start complaining. Calisse de merde, you know how unpleasant that can be."

I motion towards my tray with broghies.

"They won't. I already fed some of our boys. Maybe you can offer the remaining broghies to other children. That should last them until dinner. Or, even better, take one for yourself."

"Hey, good idea, bre."

Fanta leans over me and grabs one of my remaining broghies. As she does, her right tit covers my face. I give her nipple a lick, then a fleeting suck.

"Boy, you really are horny!" – Fanta comments while munching – "Can't gahba wait for tonight."

"My work always makes me horny; you know that by now.

(Tsk, tsk, such a lie, I'm not working.)

Until tonight, wife."

Then she's gone, too. And I've got just two broghies left!

As soon as I became the Commander – in – Chief of MANATO, a secondary but very persistent problem manifested itself; that of MANATO

carpool. We possessed all those amazing airplanes, ships, and armored vehicles, but our fleet of ordinary vehicles was nothing to brag about. Since the early nineties, all branches of MANATO relied heavily on the ever-present (imported in large numbers) ubiquitous Hummers and Humvees. They proved so useful because they could easily switch from pavement of our best highways to offroad conditions on the less developed islands. In this land of immensely cheap oil, their fuel consumption was irrelevant. But their Stateside production ended after the 2008 recession, many of our vehicles were old, and spare parts became difficult to obtain. The rest of MANATO's carpool was a mishmash of various cars and SUVs, of multiple unrelated brands, some rather old, others with rather high millage on their odometers.

There was pressure from my colleagues to solve this problem. Through an accidental acquaintance I chanced on the highest executives of Nissan Newlands. And a deal was struck.

On the photo I'm scrutinizing, I'm posing in front of a Nissan Xterra model 2004 with the youthful Chief Warrant Officer Vladimir Ruski on my left and the higher-ranked somber Master Warrant Officer Rosalyn Sussman on my right. I remember that particular Xterra. It was equipped with experimental McLaren airless tires, which proved excellent in our volcanic terrain trials.

Early in 2012, my deal with Nissan got us almost a hundred used Xterras, model 2004. Later that year, Xterras of the newer model 2012 also started being delivered, until all other vehicles in MANATO's carpool got replaced.

Not our Hummers and Humvees, of course. All those which remained in good condition were withdrawn from everyday use and grouped in operational units of MANATO's various services, to be exploited only in tactical military roles (to prolong their useful military service), while those with defects got sent to Titan in Atlantis to be repaired or recycled, boosting our stockpile of spare parts.

Then, in 2017, MANATO chanced on a contract with Chevrolet (luckily before our little spat with Trump). Under our guidance, Titan bought the manufacturing rights to assemble, exclusively for MANATO, hundred eighty units of a new experimental crossover design known as 2018 Chevrolet FNR-X-NL (the Newlandean FNR-X). A month ago, the first three of these vehicles got delivered. In due time, over the next decade, they will replace all aging model 2004 Nissans.

Smile.

Good deal.

Two good deals.

My carpool interventions were certainly successful.

"Dave, are you willing to share your food?"

For the second time in twenty minutes, lost in my revelries, I'm startled by a human voice. This time a man's voice. Today, other than me there's only one man around.

Eaton.

"Sorry for startling you, my friend."

One thing about Eaton never changed. A while ago his job demanded that he totally purifies his speech patterns, eliminating cussing and common Newlandean bywords. Though he changed his profession, he still allows none to creep back into his phraseology. In any of the languages he speaks.

I turn and smile in a friendly way. In the friendliest of ways! Why not? This hunk deserves a friendly smile.

"Hey, buddy! Hungry? I've just these two broghies left. You're welcome to both if you wish."

I offer my remaining snacks.

"I've seen Fanta feed them to children." – Eaton sounds wistful and hungry – "They look delicious."

"They are delicious." – as if I'd know; I haven't tried any!

"I'll take one; thanks."

"All yours, sexy."

Eaton bites into his broghy, unwaveringly watched, from the harness seat, by his daughter Ivana, sporting a ludicrously quizzical expression.

"Very good. Veryyyy good, indeed. Where did you find those? Your local Safeco?"

"Oh, what a thing to accuse us of! You wish to become an enemy of our family? We didn't buy them, mister. This morning Fanta made them from scratch."

"She did? Really?" – genuine surprise manifests on his face – "I must ask for her recipe."

My turn to be surprised. Eaton cooks?

Well, why not! I was as surprised by Eaton being a father. Serves me right. He's a complete, multifaceted person, like everyone else. I should

stop exiling people into exclusive niches (the one for Eaton labeled "sex worker / male whore", however honorable that profession may be here on Newlands).

"Lean over."

"Why?"

Eaton is perplexed but does as asked. I lean towards him, careful not to crowd too much on Ivana. Then I lick some cream off the corner of his stache (thinking that it really tastes delicious). Cream, not his moustache; though, his moustache would taste delicious during sex, I'm certain; I yet have to taste that, too. That line of thinking makes my penis stiffen, and my friend immediately notices. Of course, he would!

I need to cover for my sexual arousal.

(But someone is going to pay for all these recent arousals, and soon! I do feel like.... fucking. Smile.)

"What's new in your new line of work?"

(chuckle, chuckle)

"Well, Pavel is again sending me to China. So, it's China, China, and more China, I can tell you! I've been taking some additional Chinese classes."

I'm surprised. Eaton's Chinese is supposed to be flawless. Even Li is of that opinion.

(Predictably, Li is delighted with Eaton. Did they sleep together? I mean, did they.... well.... fuck? Very, very probably. More tension on my dick!)

"You need lessons in Chinese?"

"My Chinese is perfect for commenting on art or.... (an unapologetically proud expression on his face) seducing a lady into my bed. To sell wine, though, you need some...."

Eaton embarks on explaining the Chinese language intricacies pertaining to a successful wine seller. I listen with a fraction of my attention. After all, it all sounds Chinese to me!

(another smile)

Pavel.

My friend Pavel.

My friend and lover.

Pavel, the head of the Varina vineyards and farms.

On the twenty-ninth of March 2014, Jan Varina was born, son of Cleo, Pavel's wife, and Jiří, Pavel's father, to the acclamations of Pavel's

parents and Pavel's sprawling Varina – Bertoni family (as sprawling as my Lionhearts, or Andrew Lighthouse's family unit).

And, most important of all, ebullient delight of Pavel himself. Privately, I'll never be easy with such sexual freedom, but was among those sincerely happy for my friend, right then passing through another anxious period of recuperation from his chronically recurring ankle injury. In the unique Newlandean way, not possible in any other society I know of, Pavel (who never had a sibling) at the same time became half-brother and socially recognized father of this new Varina boy.

As always in life, balancing yin with yang, tragedy wasn't far. Jiří, who in his old age discovered renewed sexual youth with his predominantly female workforce, died in his early seventies some.... (let me calculate) sixteen months ago. It's rumored that he expired while achieving an orgasm with one of his female employees. It's also rumored that it was one of Bogdan's wives he was having sex with, nowadays all three gainfully employed by the ever-expanding Varina company.

But that's a rumor.

Reality was that for a moment that successful company, the miracle story of Newlands economy, appeared in limbo, without steering, without a steady hand on its tiller. After Jiří's funeral and the socially prescribed length of grieving was over, Pavel and his mother conferred for two long days. And jointly announced on TV National that Pavel is to abandon his coaching job and will be stepping into his father's shoes.

After some months of uncertainty, while Pavel strived to gain a sure footing in his new role, Varina Vineyards took off into the stratosphere of business! And Eaton was undeniably part of that success.

Alone again.

Next picture.

I instantly sober up. The truth is, whichever picture I scrutinize, there's a loss to be remembered. Long ago Fran told me that life itself is an endless list of losses; living is but learning to cope and overcome. Boy, was he right!

One after another, an even dozen photos, from slightly different angles, of a serious group of senior MANATO officers (snapped by our professional photographer), half of us sitting in a semicircle, the other half standing behind the seated officers.

Central Command of MANATO's General Headquarters.

These official photos were taken last year, after we finally moved to our new Ceticity headquarters and the new assembly of CCofGHQ got constituted. In the upper row are standing Admiral of Newlands Navy John Bute, Army General Predrag Nenad, General of Marines Igor Litvinenko, Chief Superintendent of Newlands Police Liam Patrockles, Firefighter Chief Luiggi Tomatelli, Army Brigadier General Salvador Kuul, and my close friend and lover Pukovnik of Newlands Marines Andrew Lighthouse, the newest CIC's Exec (my own). Without any doubt, Andy is the rising star of our group, rapidly advancing in Marines' ranks as well as in his appointments (such as being my new Exec).

I'm sitting in the middle of the bottom row, hemmed in on my right by my husband, Vice-Admiral of Newlands Navy Fran Lionheart, who is also MANATO's Second – in – Command, and on the left by my friend Miki, Airforce General Miodrag Raonić, the Commander of GHQ Intelligence (his face curiously displaying a rarely seen moustache-only appearance and some traces of aging). Left of Miki are Taske (Vice-Admiral of Newlands Navy Zoran Tasić) and Vice-Admiral of Newlands Coastguard Marino Marino. Right of Fran sit Airforce Major General Raj Chahal, Commander of MASP and MALD, and Brigadni General of Newlands Marines Henri Deladin.

Great men.

Great officers.

My men; my officers.

My friends.

My unquestioningly devoted friends.

Yet, yet....

Two faces are missing from those pictures. Not because they were that day, for one reason or another, absent. Those two were permanently taken away.

Retired Fleet Admiral Francis Gonzales isn't on those pictures.

Over the years, he became my closest associate in CCofGHQ and the privilege of five; an ancient intellect, a vault of vast knowledge, a compassionate soul who always stood by my side without any wish for reward, an important and intelligent player who diligently worked from shadows, never stepping into limelight. Though he retired considerably before I arrived here, he remained at his post, as all appeared well with his health. Until the summer of 2015. Then a debilitating disease suddenly struck. MANATO's doctors again and again ascertained that despite the

severity of the onset of that dastardly illness, Francis has been extremely lucky. The first manifestations of his inherited disease, which occurs only in a few families around the globe, were delayed until late in his life. Which is very unusual as it predominantly manifests in middle age. But Gerstmann – Straussler – Scheinker is a terrible affliction. Lack of muscle coordination, clumsiness, unsteadiness, difficulty walking, dementia, slurring of speech, involuntary movements of eyes, rigid muscle tone, and visual disturbances all slammed my friend within the first two weeks after his diagnoses.

For the last time Francis left the GHQ building on August 12, walking with visible difficulty, yet proud enough to eschew help. I visited twice during fall of the same year. By then he was already confined to a specialized care ward of MANATO's Nordporte hospital. Those visits were horrible experiences. Almost nothing of my friend remained. Just an inert living shell, not containing any human spark.

Even today, Francis is still alive.

He breaths and his heart beats. But his mind completely evaporated years ago.

It's only a matter of time now.

Tears form in my eyes. My pain is there for Francis, though he's still alive. Yet, most of it is there for the second person missing from that group of MANATO officers.

My husband.

My love.

The greatest hero of Newlands.

The one who left us forever.

Airforce Major General Sam Roberts – Lionheart.

My Exec.

Sam died on January 3, 2017.

When Alisa finds me, I'm bawling over a photo of Sam in front of his Aurelia. Not many people can immediately recognize our pilot as Sam. True, only his signature dark moustache is visible through the visor of his light-blue helmet, which obscures his other facial features (though dark moustache is a trademark of most MANATO pilots, therefore far from unique). The rest of his body is hidden under the silvery metallic high-G suit.

Yet, for those who know where to look, there are many clues. In its center, above the forehead, Sam's helmet sports our Lionheart family logo, exclusively used only by him. And the silver suit discloses the softened lines of his powerful metallic Terminator-like robotic left arm. Incidentally, his left glove is missing, and his arm's knobby fingers are clearly visible. On his left breast is a sticker with his rank: that of an Airforce Major General. There aren't many Airforce Major Generals walking around.

To be truthful, there was only one.

Only Sam.

"Love, what, bre....?" – Alisa is perplexed by my tears.

I point: - "Sam."

In that one sacred word is packed all my frustration with fate, the injustice of life, the horrible emptiness of the permanent loss.

Oh, god, if you exist.... and you don't, I know, you don't.... I hate you! I still hate you!

She hugs me, without talking.

I hug back.

Though we're naked and our bodies are in full contact, there's nothing erotic about our embrace. Just comfort and empathy.

After a while, my sobbing subsides.

Still embracing the love of my life, I flip through the rest of the pictures in this particular folder. Sam in a Nordporte hangar, still in his metallic suit, talking to a bunch of support personnel. Sam in the mess of Braća Karan base, this time in his full uniform. Then Sam, just in his shorts, playing tennis with Robert Hadži-Janković, Peter Boer, and another pilot I don't immediately recognize. The last photo is of Sam, stark naked, with his Terminator arm adjusting sails of a boat, somewhere on the Atlantic off our coast (I guess Peter Boer's boat).

Peter Boer recently emailed those pictures, taken in the summer of 2015, when life seemed without any worries.

For the Lionhearts, 2016 was the year of greatest pain and tribulations. True, Sam finally surrendered to the inevitable scythe of death just a few days into 2017, but most of his illness developed during the summer and fall of 2016.

I still remember with stark dread the July morning when Sam and I woke up, alone in our Rad home in New Belgrade, and Sam couldn't

stop coughing. It took me an hour to convince him that he must seek help from our excellent MANATO doctors. I never thought it could be a serious problem; probably bronchitis or something similar. Or he inhaled a corrosive substance in one of our hangars. Something like that.... I was peeved at Sam for choosing to endure this coughing in order not to miss a day of flying. Then, suddenly, Sam broke down and confessed. Coughing be damned, he was terrified of what our doctors may tell him. Unbeknown to me, or anyone else, besides his cough, Sam suffered from a week-long headache which wasn't abating no matter which remedy he tried.

That put an end to all further discussion. Instead of both of us proceeding to the airport and MANATO's new Ceti III GHQ, I personally drove Sam to Nordporte, relinquishing for that day command of our mighty force to Henri Deladin. And I sat with Sam through all those tests our doctors found necessary: bloodwork and other sampling, x-rays, MRI, other scanning procedures.

I started our hospital trip with banter and enforced joking, thinking that there's nothing MANATO doctors can't cure. By noon, I was sufficiently in panic to summon Dr Amanda Ross from Paloma. The weirdest thing was, as my panic grew, Sam grew more composed. He received those hammer-blows of perilous life-threatening diagnoses with supernatural calm, as if he expected them and was already prepared for the worst.

Non-Hodgkin lymphoma, mesothelioma of both lungs, glioblastoma.

Boom, boom, boom.

Hammer-blows to the head. But not Sam's. Mine.

Amanda was mindful and full of care. Yet, her verdict was devastating. A month of life at an outside chance. Probably less.

Besides those three terrible cancers, each of them already in a late stage, and each terminal on its own, never mind all three combined, there were signs of other terminal illnesses rearing their ugly heads. The truth was, Sam's body, if not his mind, was rapidly quitting and throwing in a white towel.

There wasn't any doubt what the underlying cause of all this medical havoc was. Sam had accumulated too many exposures to Labyrinthium. The first exposure was when we together performed our Tom Garrowitz–style attack on the enemy submersible trying to destroy one of our Labyrinthium buoys. The second time was when his Aurelia

exploded underneath his bum. And the third time when he discovered the super concentrated, super enriched Labyrinthium deposits. Amanda was certain that, hidden deep in Sam's body, some minute quantity of Labyrinthium persists, somehow sheltered from the eyes of our doctors as well as detection equipment, steadily working over the years on his demise, now plunging my husband into a terminal life-and-death crisis. She invoked all necessary protocols to try to trace the whereabouts of that stray Labyrinthium but wasn't optimistic about locating it.

I was reeling, not knowing what to do. My head ranged with questions like "why is life so unjust?", "why Sam?" or "how did it come to this?".

The useless madness.

It was Sam who rose above all my petty tumult like a giant he was. In a steady voice he acknowledged everything Dr Ross and the other doctors had to say. Then he asked for one thing only. A fighting chance. A chance to fight. Somehow, into that fight, he carried everybody: his doctors, Amanda, and even me (and our whole family).

An exquisite plan was formed. It centered on use of immunologically targeted radiation. MRNA autovaccines were to be concocted for each tumor. Photothermal therapy with gold nanoparticles was to start immediately. Various supportive treatments were to be included. Chemotherapy was to be reduced to a bare minimum, but still used. Apparently (to my utter surprise), on average it killed patients faster than their tumors did. Some experimental anti-cancer medication was to be tried too.

By the evening, there was only one thought in my mind. No surrender.

And Sam didn't surrender.

The very same evening Sam was placed on an indefinite (paid, of course) medical leave. Unfortunately, except for Nordporte, he wasn't destined to ever again step into a MANATO base or facility of any kind. A few key officers were informed of the seriousness of his illness, predominantly those who had to take over his duties and needed to understand that this was a permanent change as Sam wouldn't be returning.

Next day Lionhearts had a powwow. The strangest one we ever had, as there was no Electocracy involved. We all suggested things to be done, but no voting occurred. We simply let Sam choose whatever course he preferred.

Natural remedies.

Absolute change of diet, especially for him. All the rest of us vowed to follow his lead when we're together, but Sam released us from that burden.

Medium difficulty workouts, to maximize his strength and focus, which we should all help him with.

And, above all, no surrender.

No surrender.

Sam's illness brought me into a weeklong confrontation with Dr Irena Panj. MARC's scientists were very early brought into the picture (engaged almost immediately); after all, Sam has for decades been one of their favorite guinea pigs. To my utter surprise, their main contribution was some professed knowledge of obscure experimental drugs and procedures, as well as advice on the improvement of autovaccination protocols.

No miracle solutions offered.

I couldn't understand their passivity. I hounded Dr Panj whenever I could reach her, my frustration boiling over. But our phone conversations followed a single unexpected pattern, as Irena continuously kept her voice low, her sentences short, and for once didn't offer copious scientific explanations.

Sam's needs and my job kept me from flying outright to Ceti II. Day after day, I postponed my visit to the once-upon-the-time GAF. Perversely, during that whole first week, though I was now spending almost all my time on the mainland instead in our new GHQ in Ceticity, Irena seemed not to return home to New Belgrade, continuously working in MARC.

Avoiding me?

Why?

Ridiculous!

MARC's scientists twice saved Thom's life. Firstly, they constructed the android receptacle as a new home for his inner being, then the second time when they cloned his body. All right, I was warned even then that the android construction probably couldn't be repeated. But why not grow a new body, a new home, for Sam's inner being? Isn't the greatest hero of our history worth it?

(I simply disregarded the fact that with no DFQL aliens / Ball around, I/we didn't really know how to accomplish transferring Sam's aura into a new body.)

"Why not?" – I almost shouted.

Dr Panj was brusquely walking next to me. I finally got to corner her in MARC, and we were currently on the famous path by the lake, where so much hidden history of Newlands seems to happen.

"Why not, Marka mu?"

"Yes, damn it, why not?"

"Because we don't know how!"

Her answer shocked me into temporary silence.

MARC doesn't know how (to construct an android or clone an adult human being)?

But then, Thom....

"But.... Thom....?"

"Tabarnaque, General, did you really think that I'm avoiding you because we don't wish to help Sam, calisse de merde?" – words gushed out of Irena's mouth; at the same time, she was impotently wriggling her hands in a thoroughly tortured way. I've never seen her like this, so.... helpless – "I didn't sleep since Sam's diagnosis, reviewing all protocols. I'd give my life to save him! It's all in vain, tabarnaque. We prcat can't do it!"

Words still avoided me.

"What do you see around you, nature the great? Is Newlands this gahba land where humankind finally realized its deepest obsession to abolish death? Where nobody dies, just putz transforms into an android or a cloned copy of their own body? Is it, multitax?"

Of course, it isn't. Newlanders still regularly die, most still unafraid of the final plunge as their peculiar culture prepares them for that last moment throughout their lives.

But Thom was twice brought back from death. That's a fact. And MARC did it; that's also a fact. I never asked if there were any others.... (No, there were none. I'm the CIC around here, I should know. No need for pathetic thoughts, despite Sam's desperate plight.)

Dr Panj now stood in front of me, barring my path, her head turned upwards (as I towered over her, dark as a stormy cloud), her eyes shining like two mighty stars.

"All my staff, me including, worked seven days in a fugue state to fashion Thom's android. That's after weeks of exhaustive preparations. 'Bem ti miša, no records of what was done were ever kept, all blueprints are prc vague, even the electronic ones, and when I later questioned those

who participated, including myself, none could precisely remember what and how we did. Marka mu, no one!”

(I was shocked again. Irena has used a new cuss word, one I never heard before, but still one invoking a shortened form of the word fuck. Using the word fuck, either in English or Serbo-Croatian, is socially proscribed on Newlands. This made it certain; she’s shaken, and this memory is painful.)

When we all took a couple of days of rest and returned to work, tabarnaque, we couldn’t believe our eyes. Spasitelju, the tools which we used during the construction of that android! Why would we need a Fokker-Planck semi-infinite surface plasma container, why we invoked Chapman-Enskog method for the solution of the Boltzmann transport equation, why.... prcat why....

(She was glaring at me, and I must have been glaring at her, too; as far as I was concerned, she lapsed into Chinese.)

.... Why did we need to pay the particular attention....

(she stumbled into a temporary silence, probably grasping the fact that she utterly lost me)

.... To yatsume derivation of diffusion and viscosity transport cross sections....

(a minute passed; Dr Panj’s pupils dilated)

.... Later, later.... when I.... ii kagen ni shiro, when I secretly scanned Thom android’s head while performing other tests, his brain.... his brain.... appeared having a core of....”

A bulb went on in my mind.

“Plasma.” - I finished her sentence, sure of what she was trying to say.

Her pupils dilated even more, almost like cat’s when orienting on prey.

“You knew?”

I didn’t answer but flapped my hand in a vaguely negative way.

“How could you yatsume know?”

I didn’t. It never occurred to me that part of Thom’s android could have been plasma. But it all now made sense.

Ball.

Ball.

An additional small favor I need to be grateful for. Now it all made sense. Thom’s android was so erratic in its behavior because Ball never intended it to permanently shelter Thom’s mind. It was constructed (we

were made – instructed - educated to construct it) as the final ingredient necessary to steer Ball's spaceship from Earth to Sun. From the start, Ball must have planned to displace Thom's mind into a clone.

Two and two are four, dummy!

Out of despair, a new ray of hope. If Dr Panj and her team couldn't reproduce an android, could they develop a full adult human clone?

Wait, didn't she indicate a moment ago that they couldn't do that, either? A tide of black despair flooded back.

Irena froze as she perceived the switch in my thoughts. My appearance, or my posture, must have somehow betrayed the battle of hope and despair in my inner being, informing her that a sudden idea sparked through my thoughts.

"My dear doctor, I didn't know, but it wasn't difficult to guess."

She tried to butt in, but a move of my hand stopped her.

"Irena, I'll make another guess. Your team isn't aware how to build a fully functional adult human clone either?!"

Her eyes bulged: - "Yutz how....?"

I kept quiet, but an echo travelled through the labyrinth of my tortured mind, elated to discover an undeniable truth, at the same time distressed with understanding that there wouldn't be any simple cure for my beloved Sam produced by MARC's miracle scientists. Now I was certain that Thom's clone is also Ball's doing, not just that omnipotent alien exploiting our existing knowledge. It was another parting gift to.... Ball's chosen people, or maybe Ball's chosen.... person (me)?

"You're right, dixi. Sharmoota haygana, you're right."

Dr Panj turned towards the lake; her glance getting lost on its surface: - "We tried. And tried. And experimented. We're good at recreating many organs. Even getting them fully functional. Once all obstacles are cleared, those sakra methods will be employed for everyday transplants in Newlandean hospitals and will help cure thousands of sufferers. But that's not what we need right now, is it? In our tubes, we can grow a living fetus, as you're well aware. Almost all children of yours gestated there, Marka mu."

Instantaneous grasping at straws: - "Couldn't we then transfer.... somehow.... imprint Sam's mind onto a baby born from your tube?"

What an abomination am I suggesting! Wouldn't that forever destroy the natural person inside that child? Yet, if Sam could somehow survive, even that....

We never managed any of those "soul transfers" on our own, either. In the final analysis, it was only with Ball's help that Thom got transferred from his dying body into mine, then from me to Nikola, and later from Nikola to the android. And, of course, Ball transferred Thom's essence from the android into the clone. DFQL aliens also had that knowledge as they downloaded their essences into their humanoid avatars to later upload them again when they needed to leave.

"No, General. Full-grown person's mind can't survive in baby's brain, which still needs years to form essential connections between its neurons; no, sucatum tauri...."

Irena trailed off as I kept silent, all my hopes crushed.

"Dave, you must let me go."

Sam's voice is barely audible, a whisper of the autumn wind among the falling leaves.

We're in the isolation ward of Nordporte Hospital's ICU. Sam is the lone occupant of his room.

Nowadays, he's down to half his bodyweight. No hair remains on his face, grace of various treatments. His nose appears gigantic, protruding like a periscope as he lies on his back. His left eye is bulging out. Another unchecked metastasis is developing right underneath it.

>Don't speak. Don't waste your energy. Somehow, we'll beat your enemy. Watch us! We will!<

Even I don't believe my own words.

Not anymore.

I hope that my despair isn't telepathically transferrable to Sam. (Did any of us in PsiMANATO ever experiment with the transfer of emotions? I can't remember!) After all, though never more than a meagerly successful telepath, Sam is one. I mustn't cause Sam to despair!

During the last week I have been visiting daily and telepathically supporting Sam's life force, replenishing its energy reserves, prolonging his fight. A desperate strategy, which can't last forever.

In reality, it's hugely costly to my own body.

I'm as exhausted as Sam looks.

But I can't let go, I can't let go.

I can't let Sam die.

Sam goes on whispering: - "You must.............

(pause)

Let me..................
(long pause)
Die......................."

The last word is almost inaudible, I'm guessing more than hearing.

>How can I, love? How can I?<

My anguish is so palpable that I can't stop it from overspilling into my words and Sam's mind. I can feel Sam's whole body stiffen. That's a shock, as it has been completely passive and immobile this whole week. (Moribund. No! I can't be thinking ideas like that!)

Sam's whisper increases in volume: - "You deny.........
Relief to me.......
But will........
Kill yourself........
In the process.......
Hub."

>Don't talk, don't talk, please!<

To manage those words, Sam is at an unacceptable rate burning through his tiny remaining energy reserves. I must stop this! I reach out and place my palm on his chest.

And something slams into me.

Not physically, but telepathically.

From Sam's body, Sam's chest, right into my mind.

Like a telepathic dagger!

I feel a presence arise in the room, encircling Sam, encircling me.

Sam's body morphs, changes. Before my very eyes, his face pops up, his diseased eye recedes into its socket, his hair regrows, his moustache bristles again, he regains his muscles, his chest swells, his arms fill up. Both of his natural, biological arms!

(About a month ago doctors disconnected Sam's bionic left arm to treat a metastasis close to its point of insertion. The plan was to connect it back as soon as Sam's again in shape to use it.)

Sam has his left arm back!

How's this possible?

It's Sam as I knew him, in full health, full power, before his Aurelia exploded under his very seat. What miracle is this?

Then all my body hair stands up.

It's not only Sam who's morphing. The presence which slammed into me is morphing too!

It encircles and suffocates me.

The light is suddenly cut off.

It's darkening.

It's black.

It's black on black on black.

Despair.

I recognize it!

I recognize it!

It's not a black tentacle, slowly advancing from a distance towards me! It's all around me! That black tentacle is all around me, encircling me, holding me, transfixing my form.

And there's no escape!

Ball!

Ball!

Ball!

My body relaxes.

My mind opens.

My defenses drop.

There's no point in fighting this superior being.

(A tiny light of hope sparks in my mind, difficult to extinguish. Ball is here! Unlooked for, unhoped for, that eternal being with its inhuman intellect is here! Is there something it can do for Sam that I, and all the assembled doctors and scientists of Newlands, couldn't?)

I move my palm. I need to check. I touch Sam's face. His protruding nose is still there, sticking out of his shriveled, hairless face. Yet, my mind sees it differently! I SEE Sam's massive moustache below my palm, I see it caress my skin, I'm transfixed by his inquisitive shiny eyes which are carefully watching me.

How can that be?

Then another shock, producing a shiver as if someone plugged me into a wall socket.

Sam was always a marginal telepath, managing in dire need to carry his message across (but not much more, even after relentless training with Alan and Andy). But the telepathic presence now touching my mind is hugely powerful, immense. Yet, it's still my old Sam!

>Dave, luv, if you won't listen to me, I have a message you need to hear.<

And, in an instant, Sam's telepathic voice transforms into another one, which years ago I knew so well.

Thom Brdar.

>Sam. Death won't be your ending. This fight is pointless. In this duel, you can't tabarnaque win! Give up. There's no possible recovery for the human flesh. Let go. Let go and let me take care of your future. I'm waiting....<

I blink.

All my hope is crushed.

{There's no possible recovery for the human flesh.}

{There's no possible recovery for the human flesh!}

There's no cure for my Sam?

There's to be no cure for Sam?

No cure.

No hope.

A tear falls from my eye, followed by many more.

Sam's still there, as I knew him all those years ago. Watching me, willing me onward, yet not saying a word.

The black tentacle is still there, surrounding us. But it doesn't appear threatening anymore. It's surrounding us, embracing us, connecting us. A serene presence of someone (or something) almost eternal, divinely powerful.

Then it slowly withdraws.

Dissolves into room's floor.

Dissipates into the walls.

Fades away.

Disappears.

Is gone.

Is it really gone?

A miracle is still manifesting in this room.

Sam remains as he once was, the all-powerful officer of MANATO.

Yet, utterly inert.

No longer watching me.

No longer moving.

His face faces the ceiling.

His arms are limp, by his side.

Only his chest still moves, barely perceptibly lifting and falling.

Up.

Down.

Up.

Down.

My mind surges forward, touches Sam's.

There's almost nothing left there.

No Sam as I knew him.

No Sam.

No life force.

No life.

This is the moment I always awaited to act, to interfere; the moment I would transfer my own life energy into Sam's body to prolong his fight.

{There's no possible recovery for the human flesh.}

But also, {let go and let me take care of your future}.

Is that hope beyond hope?

Is that hope beyond.... The grave?

Not what I wanted to hear, yet a source of wonder.

In front of my eyes, Sam's visibly fading.

It's now or never.

It's now or never.

It's now or....

This time, I take the most hurtful sigh of my whole life, and don't do a thing.

This time, I don't interfere.

Sam's chest still moves, barely perceptibly lifting the thin green sheet wrapping his body.

Up.

Down.

Up.

Down.

Sam's chest moves on, its rhythm slowing.

Up.

Down.

Up.

Down.

Sam's chest expands, then freezes.

For a moment.

Then it deflates.

And inflates again.

Up.
Down.
Up.
Down.
And there it stops.

# FINALE OF THE FINALE

It's Tuesday, the Nineteenth of January 2021. I'm in New Belgrade, sitting in the first row of the Congress Hall auditorium inside the monumental Newlands Master Trade Center. Probably the most fitting position for MANATO's CIC, I guess. Still, throughout my tenure in that exalted position, I never got fully accustomed to pomp and limelight, though it's now been almost a decade since I became MANATO's most prominent officer.

Sigh.

Master Trade Center is a massive building with a curved roof somewhat reminiscent of the undulating ocean waves. On its front side is mounted the largest Newlands flag I've ever seen, hanging superimposed over the glass wall above MTC's main entrance. The Congress Hall itself isn't large. Its steep auditorium can accommodate about five hundred people, much less than many other locations in our capital city. It's Congress Hall's massive multifunctional stage, in my estimate superior to any other in the archipelago, which predestines this venue for the currently unfolding event. At least, that's my guess. I never bothered to check.

The event in question is the transfer of power between the Government of our old President, my adopted father and great friend Nemanja Petrović, and the incoming new President, also my great friend, Toša Popović.

And Nemanja isn't even here! Even though Nemanja and Toša are themselves very good friends and Nemanja for years prophesized Toša's victory in November 2020 general elections, he couldn't attend tonight's ceremony. This morning, in Centralna Bolnica (the Central Hospital), here in New Belgrade, Mary, Nemanja's wife and my socially adopted mother (and likewise a great friend), had to undergo an emergency surgery for a bowel problem, her unexpected, sudden, and urgent illness causing consternation in both families. In our last communication Nemanja sounded positive, quite optimistic. Mary's surgery was a success, the problem solved, her doctors satisfied with the outcome, and she was

currently slowly waking up in hospital's intensive care unit. Yet, with Toša's blessings, my "adopted father" wouldn't leave her side.

Another sigh.

But this time of relief.

Last couple of days proved personally strenuous (though MANATO seems to be ticking along in perfect shape, people here tend to say: "like a Swiss watch", unheeding the personal problems of its personnel, though they may be its Commander-in-Chief).

How peaceful, filled with optimism, civilized, full of goodwill, and uneventful is this political event! Compared to the shock, strife, and bloodshed of the Capitol Hill invasion back in the United States, which occurred a couple of days ago, an almost-insurrection by the American right-wing militias. Here we're attending a political milieu of calm, tranquility, and civilized interactions. And of full.... even absolute transparency of political action.

Actually, there's no possible comparison. No comparison at all.

We are the future.

They are the past.

Those terrible days in the United States since Trump lost his bid for re-election almost made me forego my American citizenship (I was stopped only by Alisa's fierce disapproval and opposition).

A third sigh.

This one of inner mental pain and disquiet.

I stretch a bit, easing my cramped position. My move triggers a similar response from Nikola, who's serenely sitting by my right side. He's even larger than ever, his muscles bulging through the fabric of his KGZ fatigues.

(Nowadays they are made of the properly shielded KGZ, officially abbreviated to sKGZ, to distinguish from the previously unshielded KGZ. However, no one really uses the new sKGZ abbreviation. I shouldn't, either.)

Nikola spent the whole day in my company, in his parade uniform, proudly displaying his Gold and Bronze Stars (he's still wearing the same outfit and the same decorations; I managed to grab a change of clothing, brought by our wives).

And as proudly wearing his shimmering silver-gray facial hair.

Though Sam's death triggered his graying, Nikola turned fully gray in the week following the Wednesday, August 15 of 2018.

The whole process took just a week, maybe just a couple of days!

In that same week he also received his well-earned Gold Star.

On that fateful day Nikola was seated in the rear cabin of the glistening new Boeing 737 Max8 NL-DAB "Plava Obala", belonging to Newlands Airlines. He was on board the flight LN125, from New Belgrade to Edinburgh, on urgent NSS business. Departing New Belgrade Capitol Hill International, "Plava Obala" was routed clockwise around our Main Islands. Unusually so, because in normal circumstances it would have turned the other way around, climbing northwards over the ocean to the east of Old City. That day's heavy incoming traffic from Europe didn't permit this shorter route to be used.

How providential was this change in airliner's flightpath?

Enormously so.

If the plane flew its routine path, it would have been over the ocean when the trouble occurred, with no land in sight.

The first signs of trouble appeared while the sleek, brand-new jet sped above Atlantis, still climbing. Its crew reported that their plane tried autonomously, multiple times, without any input from its pilots, to lower its nose. Much later the investigation attributed this action to the malfunctioning of Boeing's once obscure and suddenly very prominent MCAS anti-stall system relying on the angle of attack sensors mounted just behind stricken airliner's nose. Five minutes later, still circling the southern parts of our Main Islands, the crew declared a full emergency. It proved impossible to return to Atlantis under any semblance of control. Instead, the airplane continued westwards, and its crew decided to attempt an emergency landing at Monty's International Airport in Palomin Most. As the airplane descended towards this airport, another nose lowering episode occurred, resulting in undershooting of its single runway. The Max8's wheels touched down the rocky terrain in front of the large square filled with "engineered materials arresting system" (EMAS), positioned at the beginning of the runway to stop rogue planes, impacting a firetruck whose driver was killed on the spot becoming the sole casualty of this accident. It then lost its landing gear and slid over the rough terrain shredding its belly, to finally stop on the left side of the runway. The fuel tank in its left wing immediately burst into flames (luckily for those on board the central fuselage tank and the right-wing tank delayed their combustion for a few crucial minutes). There were 176 passengers and crew on board, and all escaped alive. Ten passengers and crew suffered

traumatic injuries during the emergency landing and the panicky exit down the slides, albeit none were life-threatening. Seven more passengers suffered burns inside the fuselage, none of them deadly.

That's the short story.

The long story is that of those seven, six were brought to safety by Nikola (him being the seventh burnt person), who carried them one by one out of their fiery entrapment in the tail section of the burning wreck. For his pains he suffered second degree burns on arms and legs (where his KGZ short-sleeve shirt and shorts couldn't protect him).

And secured his Gold Star.

And turned gray.

For us, the Lionhearts, it was time to rejoice in another successful defiance of the ever-present danger of sudden death, this time by the width of a whisker. For the Newlands air industry a few confusing months ensued. With only one casualty, "Plava obala" crash never raised red flags nor aroused much international interest. At home, the investigation lagged; some say because Boeing considerably dragged its feet in providing pertinent answers to the functioning of computer systems on its Max aircraft. Initially, there weren't any consequences for the remaining ill-fated Max airliners in service on Newlands. More than fifty of them kept flying for Paloma Sun, AHS, and Newlands Airlines. There were that many because our airlines were among the first in the world to embrace the new design and start receiving them. Subsequently, after two additional casualty-heavy crashes of the same model in Indonesia and Ethiopia (no Newlanders were lost on those flights), which uncovered the existence of major flaws in Max's design, a prolonged worldwide grounding of all Boeing 737 Max aircraft ensued. In the two years since those events started unfolding, it also meant that various airlines of Newlands, those which bought the Max aircraft, or planned to buy them, started severing ties with the Seattle-based manufacturer.

The repercussions for the air industry of Newlands were clear: Airbus has won here for the foreseeable future, as the most important domestic airlines started converting their fleets to the European models.

But Nikola survived.

And that's what matters the most.

At least, to me.

"Hub, I checked those intelligence reports. Your mrdat Americans are going to pull out of Afghanistan and leave it to the Taliban to rule.

Trump's administration started that process, the next administration won't have any choice but to continue that way."

Nikola's words hurt, though darn if I'm going to show it. I fought in Afghanistan. For years. So many of my friends died or got mutilated physically and psychologically. No, I can't believe our intelligence conclusions nor Cybercommand's intercepts of American military communications. No sane American government would dare pull out of Afghanistan.

"No way, Nikola. After sinking all those billions of dollars into that pitiful land? No sane President would dare do such a dastardly deed; Trump, Biden, or anyone else. The American people would never accept that. Nor would the military."

Nikola shakes his head, obviously disagreeing with my emotional words: - "I believe you almost always right, my hubby, my boss. But not this time; no way Jose! You're khange khodah speaking with emotions, not your rational mind. The Americans had enough and are pulling out of Afghanistan; all political structures the West built will rapidly collapse like a house of cards."

I decide to discontinue this line of conversation. Nikola's opinion is by far not a minority one, nor is this the first time I heard similar words (besides, as a dutiful CIC, I also read all those same reports). Everyone, every single officer of our Cybercommand and the GHQ Intelligence Section, believes their conclusion to be right: the Americans are leaving Afghanistan to the Taliban and the pro-Western government will collapse as soon as the American troops leave.

Suddenly I feel the need to prove to my husband that his statement didn't in any way anger me. Accepting the conclusions of those intelligence reports, he's doing nothing wrong, just his duty. My hand sneaks forward and touches Nikola's left elbow.

He smiles.

I return the smile and, once again, try to concentrate on the proceedings.

Except for one other person, our new President Popović is currently alone on the large stage. That other person is TV National's Hayv Kahraman. Whether upon hearing that name it's immediately obvious or not, Hayv is a middle-aged woman, today the "master of ceremony" of this event, otherwise one of network's less distinguished reporters. At least, in my decade in the archipelago, I never noticed her (and I should

have, since she's so distinctive). My wives sport a different point of view. Alisa told me she likes her. Fanta ascertained that "Hayv's been around", whatever she meant by that statement.

I believe that it's much more significant that Hayv Kahraman is a (rare for Newlands, as her ethnicity is in a very small minority here) black reporter. That special significance is derived from Toša's choice of his ministers (he picked the first two black ministers in the history of Newlands). I believe that TV National, in its turn not wanting to be outdone, decided to pick a black anchor.

Quid pro quo.

Hayv's long dark hair is freely dancing above her shoulders. She's in an ocean gray column-scoop-neck knee-length chiffon cocktail dress with a light lace veil over her shoulders (I'm not even going to try to guess which fashion house produced it; ask Li). Its color is blending well with her milk-chocolate skin, the thin summery material cooling her body and amply accentuating her sizeable curves. Her shoes are trendy and high heeled. (That I may try to guess: Paradise Bird or Monarch? I'll have to check with Alisa. If I remember to, that is....) From my first-row seat I can distinctly hear them click as she moves around the stage.

On any other occasion Hayv might appear supremely confident and professional, but her dark eyes are right now quizzical with unguarded surprise, her tone of voice openly questioning: - "Mister President, are you implying that President Petrović won't be with us tonight for the traditional transfer of the Presidential Wood Branding Iron?"

"No, Hayv, Marka mu, my friend Nemanja Petrović won't be with us. As you maybe know, nature the great, his wife is undergoing urgent surgery in Centralna Bolnica...."

"But, bre, certainly...."

(A wife undergoing surgery compared to the transfer of an obscure, if hallowed object; how could that be compared at all? Still, I understand her consternation. I was told that no Newlands President missed the transfer of Presidential Wood Branding Iron. Ever. If alive for it, that is, as a couple of them here and there died before having a chance to meet their successors. Nemanja will be the first still living one to eschew that hallowed ceremony.)

"I spoke with Nemanja an hour ago, tabarnaque. Mary is doing great; her surgery seems to have gone exceedingly well. No need to worry.

(a wave to the cameras)

I'll now take a moment to send Mary our best wishes for speedy recovery. From the bottom of putz hearts of all of us here."

Applause from the auditorium.

"Still...." - Hayv Kahraman smiles a strained smile and turns towards the cameras – "Dear guests and all who're tonight with us by your screens, wherever you may be, watching the inauguration, I must inform you that this departure from the ancient protocol of this most solemn ceremony wasn't previewed...."

"Nature above, not a problem. It's not a mrdat problem at all, Hayv. Instead of himself being present, Nemanja sent Pedro Goran. As you all know, he was for the last five years our young and, if I may say so, excelling Vice-president and my prc esteemed major competitor in this presidential race. In President Petrović's name, Pedro will conduct the Presidential Wood Branding Iron transfer." – cunningly turning towards the cameras with a sincere smile, Toša spreads his hands in a warm, welcoming manner – "My friends, let's welcome our Vice-president."

A strong applause breaks from the auditorium.

Yet, no movement.

For a moment, nothing happens.

Toša steps towards the rim of the stage close to where I'm sitting, lowers himself on one knee, and extends his right hand downwards: - "Come Pedro, majke ti, take my hand and climb up here."

Two seats to my left, a smallish guy finally stands up. He's short; I'd say five foot seven, yet athletically proportional, with strong chest, sturdy neck, and narrow hips. He's a redhead with a full but neatly trimmed beard and a dazzling white smile. Shirt, tie, the sport blazer, dress pants, and his Browns leather shoes fly about spurned by his energetic moves (though his formal clothes are all crafted of feathery fabrics favored in this tropical country), followed by a quick turn towards the spectators and a slight nod. Pedro Goran takes Toša's professed hand and with ease hops onto the stage.

I first heard of Pedro Goran just prior to November 2015 elections, when Domenico Barnes, the accomplished Vice-president in the first Petrović Administration, whom I enjoyed working with, got diagnosed with a serious medical problem (after prolonged illness, he died last year, greatly saddening all of us who collaborated with him). Plucked by Nemanja out of his party's lesser-known backbencher ranks, young Pedro Goran (then thirty) became the new Vice-president in Nemanja's

second government, expertly using the next five years to create a well recognizable political brand. Born in Atlantis, he happened to be an indifferent student of his hometown's University (UNA) and even less distinguished wannabe sportsman (or so Thom informed me, who is in my family, for some obscure reason, Pedro Goran's strongest critic). Anticipating the constitutionally mandated end of the Petrović decade in power, Newlands Realists (ReoN), Nemanja and Pedro's party, organised their new leadership contest early, exactly a year ago, in January of 2020. With Nemanja about to withdraw from politics, thus also vacating the position of ReoN's leader, Pedro Goran stepped into his shoes by acclamation.

I was fast to develop rapport with the diminutive Vice-president. It's curious to note how many projects can the Commander – in – Chief of MANATO and the Vice-president of Newlands share. Let me immediately tell you: a lot! His youthfulness and glorious looks had something to do with our developing friendship, but also his sincere enthusiasm for every program and activity, however unimportant. A different set of circumstances added to the rapid bridging of gap dividing us. Though young, Pedro Goran already went through three divorces, and had three sons to boast about. In 2016, they were respectively aged ten, six, and three. Over time, one thing led to another, and Pedro's sons met ours. Imagine eleven rowdy boys together! It was easy to notice that they immediately formed a competent football (soccer) team.

Then another surprise arrived to excite the Newlandean social media. In 2017 Vice-president Goran remarried, forming his fourth (still lasting) marital union. This time with a man. With the plurality of sexuality in the Lionheart family, this quirky development just drew Pedro closer to us (up to then everyone, even the social media, considered Pedro an incorrigible heterosexual). Candidly he confided that his husband was his lover since his teenage years and that his marriages were probably just attempts to escape from his homosexuality into the grove of socially standardized aspirations of "normalized" family.

Believing that his five years of good work didn't go unnoticed by our electorate, and that it was fair for him to try to undertake the ultimate step upwards, with great energy and determination Vice-president Goran valiantly battled for the 2021 presidential mandate. In the first round Toša easily fulfilled pundits' predictions and claimed the top spot with 35% of all valid votes. Vice-president Goran followed in the second place,

albeit with only 25% of the vote. Not all was lost, though. Instead of the initial eight candidates, only Pedro and Toša were to face off in the second round. If Vice-president could mobilize voters supporting those defunct candidates....

It wasn't to be. Pedro augmented his final tally by eleven percent, but Toša recorded 61% of votes in his favor, one of the most convincing second round victories on record.

Back to the stage now. As Pedro turns towards Toša, in the process straightening his blazer, I overhear our new President say: - "Pedro, majke ti, don't run away after you hand me that thing."

Interesting.

Something unexpected brewing?

Also, the interesting language: "that thing".

That thing Toša is referring to is the Presidential Wood Branding Iron, firmly enclosed in its carved wooden box which is currently held in Pedro's left hand. I mean, all of us watching must necessarily presume that the sacred object is inside its box. During this ceremony it won't be publicly shown as that's not required by the protocol.

Fran already warned me about that.

A "Presidential Wood Branding Iron"; what a strange object to represent power vested in the office of presidency of the most powerful person on Earth! (Though many Earthlings have no idea how much power the President of Newlands possesses!) In 2011, I arrived just after Nemanja Petrović became the President, so I wasn't aware of the traditional iron and its significance. As Nemanja won the November 2015 re-election, there was no transfer of power in January of 2016, therefore no need to dust up the ancient, revered box and the almost secret sacred object it contains (as much as anything in this secular land can be considered sacred). But, while spending together an evening of binge drinking a couple of weeks after Sam's death, my "adopted father" (attempting to cheer me up and divert my thoughts) told me about its history and even demonstrated the branding iron itself.

Apparently, in the early years of Newlands, paper was scarce and so were means of communication between the far-flung kernels of its future cities. The legendary first President of Newlands, Marko Pavlović, resorted to writing his proclamations on plywood sheets, dispatching them to be posted (I guess nailed) on squares and other locations of communal life. To ascertain that a proclamation really came from the

President himself, he had a branding iron made, able to burn an image of the Newlands Crest into wood it was applied to. To my untrained eye, the instrument itself appeared well preserved, its metal parts shiny and glittering, its handle pristine.

In 1955 President Pavlović resigned as his failing health wouldn't allow him to continue in office, relinquishing his powers to the Congress of Newlands. When the Congress organized the next election, the second President, John Jakes, inherited the wood burning iron along with Marko's other official possessions. By then, communications in the fledgling nation got improved. Its initial road system was completed (one ring each around Anan and Dekan, the two Main Islands), the first ferries were crossing the Paloma Channel, and boats and seaplanes connected all the more distant settled islands. It's certifiable that John Jakes never used the burning iron in any official capacity.

Then the situation repeated itself. Early in his second mandate, John Jakes died in office, Newlands Congress again temporarily reigned supreme, and the third President was elected.

Réné Bomberger.

(Incredibly, I met him in 2012. He still lives in Paloma, nowadays in his hundred and ninth year, outliving many a President who ruled after him!)

This time the Congress wanted to "pomp up" the inaugural ceremony. Someone got the idea to transfer Marko's old wood burning iron to the new President's care with all the ceremony they could muster. And a new tradition was born.

Nemanja told me that it's not just himself, but many previous Presidents as well, who felt that just holding the hallowed iron in their hand somehow connected them to the mythical Father of the Nation.

While I reminisced about the ancient Newlands history, with a couple of succinct comments Hayv Kahraman deftly introduced Pedro Goran to the spectators and announced the transfer ceremony of the Presidential Wood Branding Iron.

"Well, Tošo, I certainly battled hard to retain this object in my hands, but great nature knows that you were unbeatable. I know that Nemanja is greatly disappointed not to be on this stage tonight. Mook kebba, here I am in his stead. And here's our revered Presidential Wood Branding Iron, tabarnaque. It's yours. You're welcome to it."

With a slight nod, Pedro offers the box, openly displayed in both hands, in the same way a samurai sword is traditionally offered. Equally formally Toša accepts, then faces us.

"I am endlessly grateful for this special gift." – he brandishes the box – "So much history is contained within this box. And Hayv, do you mrdat know what I'm going to do right now?"

Taken aback by his rhetorical question, Hayv simply shakes her head.

"Hayv, no ideas?" – he turns towards Pedro – "You, Pedro?" - Toša continues, not waiting for an answer - "I always wondered how the hell that prcat burning iron looks! Didn't you all?"

Accompanied by gasps of surprise, scattered applause, and salves of laughter, in a clear breach of protocol and the traditional ceremony, he pries the box open and produces the sacred object for everyone to see (I guess that the cameras must be zooming it in for our spectators at home).

Toša is turning the brandishing iron from side to side, thoroughly inspecting all details of its make: - "Well, I'll talk to my cabinet; we'll find a way to put this to good use, Marka mu! Everything in my government will be put to good use!"

More laughter and applause. Toša packs the iron back into its box, then motions for quiet.

"Thank you, thank you. As you know, tonight's ceremony is far less formal than...."

I stop listening.

I know what my buddy is going to say. I got informed in advance, not the least by Toša himself. On Newlands, there's not much formality in a presidential inaugural. There's a quick oath, sworn on the Newlands Constitution, but otherwise it's the first chance for the Electocrats to officially glimpse their new President's vision for his cabinet, ministerial positions (still to be approved by the Congress), and the direction he would like to steer the nation into (of course, if approved by the same Electocrats on future referendums). I've encountered some of the politicians who Toša plans to crown as ministers. They are all sitting here, near me, in the very first row, presumedly so they could easily step up to the podium when called forward.

My mind returns to Nikola. Of all Lionhearts, during my decade on Newlands, he changed the least. At least, in my opinion. Yes, his hair turned gray, he advanced in ranks, but Nikola remains Nikola. Thom, his spiritual brother, is the opposite, but who or what he nowadays is I

dare not say. Thom gained in mental and physical stature, becoming the strongest pillar of our family. If he put his heart into achieving the status, he could easily command the whole of MANATO. Yet, he's nowadays always in the background, in the shadows. Sam, we lost, of course (oh Sam, my Sam, you're an incurable wound on my heart). Alisa morphed into a writer, finishing her fifth book. The pattern got set with her Thom Brdar novel. Each book is dedicated to a controversial resident of the National Jail of Newlands. Fanta became an incredibly emphatic mother, tending to our ever-growing boys, occasionally still working in MANATO without any wish for a sustained career. Fran is more thoughtful, logical, and calculated than ever, an amazing second-in-command for MANATO. He makes twice as many decisions as I do. To his consternation and horror, many times I offered to step aside and let him assume the post of CIC. Yet, in the process, he lost his eagerness for field command. I can imagine Fran being the emperor of the world but not the commanding officer of a Newlandean fleet out at sea. Fran also lost any optimism about the future of humanity. He's consuming all kinds of United Nations publications and reports and has become convinced that by 2050 the world is going to face a double whammy: too many inhabitants to feed and no more fertile ground to grow food. He predicts wars for meat (and water), where one group of people fights another not just to capture and eat all their livestock, pets, and wild animals to be found on their territory, but also the opposing soldiers and their civilians. I'm not concerned. By then I predict being safely dead. Our children will have to face that world, true, but Newlands is slowly drifting away from the rest of world, and they will be safe behind our barriers, protected by MANATO, belonging to a true oceanic culture.

I changed, too. Nowadays I'm mostly a figurehead, doing all social media contacts and live appearances for our public relations. A beloved figurehead at that. My great subordinates, Fran, Miki, Andy, Raj, Salvador, Taske, Marino, to name just a few, nowadays carry the burden of command without me having to bother much about actually commanding. I don't even do those regular long GHQ shifts anymore and am free to roam the archipelago at will. I'm often filmed having sex with various people and posted to our intranet social media. This has become such a regular occurrence that I feel that my unofficial porn career is more successful than Rocco's or Ethan's ever were.

Is that sad, or is it providential?

For the life of me I can't decide.

Instead, I concentrate on the trio of impeccably clad industrial managers sitting to the right of Nikola, in whose company my husband and I spent the whole day: the terribly serious (never smiling) bald and bearded Djordje Jan, the CEO of TOC (Titan Old City), the incredibly youthful (is she out of her secondary school yet?) Saška Grey, Titan's production manager responsible for Tesla-Titan vehicles, and the very Japanese (thus for me of unguessable age) Shoaku Takahashi, production manager for 5G technologies. Flown early this morning from Ceticity by our irreplaceable 100$^{th}$ Squadron (Robi Presinac piloting our Dornier with Alex Edwards as his co-pilot), Nikola and I landed on Old City's Platin International only to promptly be whisked off to the Titan Aerospace TOC facilities nested in a far corner of the same airport.

And there we remained for hours.

The all-important satellite production, testing, and launch schedules, crucial to plan the development of our military space program, were to be discussed with Djordje Jan. We also touched on the state of Aurelia and Rudius production lines (equally dwelling into their strengths and weaknesses). There was lot to be demonstrated and observed, requiring walking endless kilometers inside huge assembly complexes (I couldn't fail to conclude that Nikola is in much better physical shape than I am; I definitely must do something about that!). Incidentally, I have been communicating with the CEO Jan for years, via conference calls, emails, text messages, over the phone (you name it, we've done it), but we never met in person. In Djordje Jan I discovered a serious professional who never balked at saying no (whenever my requests proved unreasonable or complaints unfounded), notwithstanding my rank and position (after all, I do command this guy, albeit in an indirect way), then thoroughly explained his reasons for denial until certain that I firmly understood them, as well as ways in which TOC can and is functioning. Which led me to, by the end of the day, come to a startling conclusion: in Djordje Jan I gained an honest friend.

Negotiations with Saška Grey kicked in whenever we exhausted a topic with Djordje Jan. I intentionally let Nikola conduct most of those. From almost a decade ago, I still clearly remember my discussions with the brightest minds of Newlands, in which they prophesized that sitting on an inexhaustible reserve of oil, with the price of gas comparable to Venezuela's, Newlands wouldn't rush into electrification of its carpark.

Not for a long time to come. How wrong those forecasts proved to be! At the end, the Newlanders themselves started fancying the idea of an evergreener tourist offer (except for the inevitable flights or ship journeys; after all, we do live on an archipelago in the Atlantic). Electric vehicles started being imported, with each passing year augmenting in numbers. Our land produces a clear surplus of electricity, thus charging those vehicles remained as cheap as using gas or diesel for propulsion. The trump card was their range. Even the limited range of modern electric vehicles works perfectly fine on Newlands where a single charge can get you to any possible destination. Another wild card was the construction of numerous "en route" high voltage charging stations, all over the archipelago, paralleling the network of existing gas stations (thus keeping the jobs, mostly for our youth). They can charge a standard electric car battery in five to ten minutes: a nice "toilet and snack" stop. Those charging stations are another autonomous domestic design, appearing out of the blue (I wonder; did their designers dream about them?), though rumor is that some of their components were developed in cooperation with Israel.

Finally, crowning the good relations with Elon Musk (who already supplies ideas and research for a future superfast Newlands train system and cooperates with our civilian space program), Titan bought license to assemble four models of his Tesla vehicles. Throughout our history, there existed a tested and tried strategy: from a specific manufacturer Titan would purchase a predetermined number of half-assembled car kits, then finish them in its factories in Atlantis, in the process adjusting those vehicles to Newlander standards (such as adding their CREDIT start mechanism with its NLPS tracking, intranet access, and Newlarmin navigation system). Those cars would then be sold as "domestic", thus avoiding import taxes. In all such enterprises, the name of the original manufacturer was kept behind Titan's own (such as in our "Titan - Ford Territory"). Elon Musk's ego, however, warranted a modification of this practice. All Tesla vehicles on Newlands are now known as Tesla-Titans.

Eh.

My colleagues in the GHQ recently decided that MANATO must follow this new green trend (I did vote against). Understanding the overwhelming importance of battlefield mobility, our Electocrats didn't insist that we do. However, GHQ felt that it's inevitable to embrace the future. At least, we can easily exchange our Main Islands' carpool

gas-powered vehicles for a fleet of electrical cars. Therefore, the pressing necessity of negotiating models, quantities, and delivery dates with Saška Grey. To the last, all Tesla-Titan vehicles will remain on Main Islands, at least until 2025. Titan is already assembling the futuristic Titan-Chevrolet FNR-X-NL for MANATO, albeit only in small series, less than two dozen delivered every year, thus each of those sleek SUVs is for all purposes handcrafted. In everyday military life we call that model "the ax". Equipped with the airless tires and a couple of additional gadgets, those "axes" will be able to replace most of the offroad Nissan SUVs currently in use, as well as the last venerable Hummers. Titan will retrofit them with its eKonT (electric conversion) technology, which will allow them to use their interior combustion engines only when strictly necessary.

Shoaku Takahashi had the least contentious task, as his role was to report on the process of supplementation, conversion, and/or replacement of existing 4G technology with more modern 5G systems throughout MEZ territories (MANATO Exclusion Zone). Frankly, compared to Huawei or Nokia, world's preeminent suppliers, Titan's 5G products are spaceships, years ahead of their competition.

A sudden gasp arises from the fellow spectators around me, followed by some loud commentaries.

What the hell did I now miss?

Look left, look, right, look at the stage.

Toša and Pedro seem to be starring at each other, but there's a glint in their eyes.

Emotional, are they now?

Then Pedro's glance momentarily travels to a man sitting by my left side. There's a question written on his face, a hint of uncertainty and doubt. My peripheral sight detects neighbor's small affirmative nod. Then a customary smile bursts over Pedro Goran's face!

"I do!"

What?

I do?

I do as in "I will marry you"?

Did I just miss Toša openly proposing in public, on stage? He's been invariably single and bisexual. That much I know from my own experience with....

My neighbor jumps to his feet, his arms raised in triumph: - "Yes, ochen balshoy, yes!"

He's giant of a man, towering at almost seven feet. As is often case with people so tall, I was told for hormonal reasons, his hands appear enormous and he has a squarish, large head. Three-day stubble covers his face. A dark moustache dominates under his straight nose. The width of his beefy shoulders is comparable to his height (enormous!), making his hips appear narrow and pinched. You might wonder how he manages to stand upright being so top heavy.

Nikola notices my consternation and correctly guesses that I had a lapse of attention to proceedings: - >Beshoor Toša asked Pedro to continue as Vice-president. To mrdat remain the Vice-president in his government.<

(Since sharing his body with Thom, Nikola is fully telepathic when he wishes to be.)

Toša did, indeed?

Good for him.

The aha moment: do you want to be my Vice-president? Hence, "I do". Now I understand.

Good for the ex-Vice-president as well, now the new Vice-president, I guess.

(Good for me, too; I'll be able to continue our cooperation.)

What a surprise!

Yet maybe not such a surprise, after all. Toša was very coy about whom he planned to offer vice-presidency to. In the last few days that question was the main topic of intrigue on Newter and other local social media. (I'm delighted to disclose that virtually no one considered Pedro a candidate!)

My neighbor carefully packs himself into his seat, definitely too small for his frame.

I know who he is; he's not a stranger. Alisom Winter, Pedro Goran's husband (for a while I figured that I got the spelling of his name wrong, yet I didn't; this is Newlands and there are some strangely spelled names around). We were introduced a while ago, on an event during Nemanja's time in office. I guess that congratulations are in order (and I want to cover for my lack of appropriate astonishment). I profess my right hand: - "Congratulations, sir. That was indeed a surprise."

We shake hands.

"Thank you, General, bre. Dodjavola, Peddy and I.... we hoped for something like that, maybe a ministerial position.... But mrdat Vice-president again? Hijo de mil putas, what a break! It's my Peddy's lucky day, I'm so putz happy! With this mandate, he might still one day become the President."

His voice is the deepest bass you can imagine; any Russian choir singer would go green with jealousy. I smile, but don't comment. The veracity of his statement is self-evident, even for me who's not proficient in political calculations.

"Listen, General. When dust settles and Peddy has a bit more time for private socializing, would you care to pay us a visit, Marka mu? To celebrate this development. Flocci non facio, I know that you and my Pedro work well together, but I never had a chance to get to know you...."

As Alisom elaborates, I smile and nod my agreement. On Newlands, such a visit is a synonym for a sexual invitation. Not that I would mind, not at all.

Then the next scene unfolding on the stage claims our attention and stops my erotic daydreaming. Toša is calling on his government ministers to join him.

All right.

The proposed composition of the new government is of great interest to our Electocrats, but not so much to me. In due time I'll meet all of them (and much sooner than that Fran and Raj will explain all intrigues associated with those appointments).

Once again, I tone down my concentration on the current events, reminiscing instead on those which happened this afternoon.

Early in our discussions, CEO Jan discovered Nikola's childhood devotion to FC Old Fortress. It so happened that today was scheduled the greatest local derby match the city of Old City can boast of. FC Old Fortress versus FC Old City. Behind our backs, mostly during our lunch which all five shared in the exceptional Old City restaurant "The French Tradition", some calls were made, and contacts established. Somehow, without Nikola and I noticing, all three Titan managers coordinated their offer. With our stunning Parisian deserts arrived a printed invitation from FC Old City (the host of today's game) for Nikola and me and up to twenty people in our party to visit the derby. Nikola and I were forced to rush through some furious consultations. By the time we were leaving the restaurant it was all set. The five of us will go to the game, as will Alisa,

Fanta, and all eight of our children. The remaining seats will be filled by Jan's wives, husband, and children.

It proved to be quite an entertaining and competitive game. Early on, Old City scored twice to finish the first half leading 2:1, a solid, well-deserved advantage both on the pitch and in the score. In the second half Old Fortress scored thrice, completely overturning the game. When all appeared lost, an eighty-fifth minute penalty and a last second equalizer saved a point for the hosts.

4:4!

Devoid of concern for standings of either of these teams (the football club I care for, Tom Garrowitz, is currently playing in Second Division, two tiers below the Superleague), and as always thoroughly enjoying my presence on the National Stadium stands (for the first time there since Pavel Varina quit playing), I enjoyed every moment of the game, especially how our sons reacted to its unfolding and dramatic changes in team's fortunes. Yet, I couldn't completely overlook the irony of this moment, how mighty have fallen.

FC Old City is this giant of Newlands football everyone here venerates. In its history it won all soccer trophies winnable on Newlands twice more than the second club on the list (New Belgrade's FC Union, Andy's favorite), including twice becoming Champions of Europe (albeit those international triumphs happened decades ago). Yet, something must be terribly wrong with this year's Old City squad, though it still harbors the largest number of players from the national team of Newlands. As we speak, at the end of the autumn half of competition, FC Old City is sitting just one point above the relegation to the lower tier of competition (logically named "The First Division", don't you dare laugh!). Of course, I had to check, but Nikola was aghast with my question. No, in its history Old City never got relegated; how dared I ask such a sacrilegious question? Some twenty-two games must still be played next spring, so things are far from decided. Yet, for the first time ever, next year's Superleague might not contain the like of FC Old City.

Opposite are current fortunes of today's opponents. After this game, FC Old Fortress sits just a few points behind the leader, firmly pegged to the second place. With so many games yet in play, they can certainly dream of winning this season's championship. Indeed, I understood that the main concern of my TOC hosts was this particular ambition of the "all

green" players (all three of them hoped that Old City would win). For this year's leader in the standings is none other than their very own FC Titan, the football club belonging to the Titan concern they are all working for.

A glance back at the stage. It now appears much more crowded. There are two dozen people on it, and Toša is proceeding from one to the other, presenting to our nation his chosen associates, their tasks, and programs.

And that's it.

The most astounding, most puzzling, totally unbelievable aspect of today.

Strangely absent from the domestic discourse.

Strangely absent from the international discourse.

Am I the only person who can grasp it all, put it in perspective?

I doubt that.

Yet, on this subject, a strange silence reigns supreme.

For today is Tuesday, the Nineteenth of January 2021.

January 2021.

Yet!!!

We unimpededly gather for business.

We unimpededly gather for meals.

We unimpededly gather for sport events.

We unimpededly gather on our beaches.

We unimpededly gather to celebrate our new political leadership.

Think!

Today is Tuesday, the Nineteenth of January 2021.

In the outside world, the panic is widespread, international relationships are unravelling, globalized chains of supply with them, and people are dying. In most countries their residents are sheltering in their homes, isolating by their own will, or forced into quarantine by their authorities. The anti-masker rallies are held and dispersed by police. Schools are closed. So are gyms, swimming pools, restaurants, stadiums, theaters, museums. Foreigners are not even supposed to visit.

And even the Olympic games got postponed by at least a year (we're still not certain if they will happen this summer and even less certain if Newlands is going to send its competitors)!

All over the world, businesses are failing.

It's the Coronavirus pandemic.

COVID-19.

SARS 2.

The China virus.

Call it as you wish.

So far more than two million dead worldwide.

So far.

Soon it will be more, as that number can only grow, never decrease.

Astoundingly, more than four hundred thousand of my fellow Americans dead (including a couple of distant cousins of mine)! How the hell could that happen, be allowed to happen, tabarnaque (as the Newlandeans often say)?

What the hell is Trump's administration doing?

Yet, no one died here, on Newlands.

No one!

Very few got sick or are getting sick.

Even among our tourists!

And we have a medication for that disease; apparently, we had it for a long time.

And we have a vaccine for that disease, too; also, apparently, something that existed for a while, and simply waited for an opportunity to be used.

And there's something about us, our bodies, our land. We seem to have a special level of immunity against this disease, provided by the typical microbiome found in Newlanders and nowhere else in the world.

The first Coronavirus cases on Newlands were registered very soon after China declared the existence of this new disease. There was a bit of furor and consternation. Hospitals were mobilized to the highest level of preparedness (MANATO ones too, coordinating their response was my tiny role in the pandemic). A readjustment of the health system and customs procedures was needed.

Masks were introduced into all facets of everyday life (with an emergency Electocratic vote to affirm the mask mandate). I remember the humor and almost ludicrous merriment with which our population accepted them. Then something else got introduced: the biochemical "mask", a special coating for nostrils which could be introduced in the form of nasal drops. Soon the scientists demonstrated that this coating efficiently prevented Coronavirus from attaching to its primary nasal receptors. I never knew such a thing existed, but apparently it was for decades in use on Newlands.

And no one died.

Here and there, some did catch the disease. Almost inevitably, very soon, it became obvious that an old antiviral medication named "Stantivir", produced by Old City's Stachepharm, for decades successfully used against numerous viral ailments, worked quite well as treatment for the new disease.

And no one died.

By March of 2020, using the genetic code of the offending Coronavirus supplied by China, Neopharma from Pesak produced a 99+% reliable fast test, immediately deployed to our international airports, ports, and all over the nation in general. Everyone who tested positive was promptly isolated and treated.

And no one died.

Soon, no one wore any masks, either, or bothered with nasal drops.

By May 2020, tries of a single-shot vaccine produced by Paloma Research demonstrated above 99% efficacity, after being tested on volunteers who allowed being intentionally infected with the virus. Apparently, this was an older vaccine, designed in early 2000s, a sort of universal antiviral jab (who knew such a thing existed?), simply tweaked to correspond to this new emergency. Its production rapidly ramped up. By the end of July all ten million Newlanders were vaccinated. From the newly born babies to those about to die from advanced age. Six months later, Paloma Research is able to point that their vaccine retains 99% efficacy against all new strains of the virus.

And no one died.

On arrival to Newlands, nowadays all foreign tourists get tested. Those testing positive are treated for free by the Newlands health establishment. Those testing negative can roam our land as always. If belated symptoms of disease develop, they are treated as well. They even return home healthier, temporarily protected by the microbiome acquired while eating our food.

And no one dies.

Seemingly neither does anyone notice that no one is dying.

Not even the WHO! (With which Newlands doesn't cooperate much, nor is a member of, as I learned.)

No one from the outside world asks which treatments are used, what kind of vaccine is applied. All over the world, in the journalistic furor

about development of vaccines, nobody ever mentions that Newlands possesses one, a perfectly reliable shot!

No one asks us to share our knowledge or our patents, nor do we ever profess any.

No one pays heed to the scientific papers our researchers and doctors publish.

But it goes further than that.

Further than that incredible that.

Our media daily reports numbers of infected and dead all over the world. About two million dead by today, the number probably a conservative estimate as many countries seem to be underreporting their casualties. Overall, I'd say that Newlandeans are well informed, maybe better than anyone else in the world. Our government reduced travel to many destinations, or outright banned it (and immediately announced financial help for our airlines and cruise lines).

The European football is in turmoil, impacting on all Newlandean clubs still participating on the international scene; that, more than anything else, tells Newlanders how deep the crises is. Yet, no one suggests we share our knowhow, our medications, or our vaccines.

Two million dead and no Newlander utters one compassionate sentence anywhere, in public, in private, or on our social media.

Nobody.

NOBODY.

Nobody at all.

(Not even a single member of my family. I love them; I know how great they are, how compassionate. Yet....)

Why is the world so indifferent to us?

Why are we so indifferent to the world?

How's that possible?

How's that possible?

How?

How?

Who arranged it all?

And how?

I know.

I know.

For I don't, for a single second, doubt who's to blame (thank) for our good fortune.

What....

Did....

Ball....

Do....

To....

Us....

All?

# APPENDIX

# OTHER CHARACTERS FOR PERCEPTIONS:

Adam Dams, engineer, civilian employed with MANATO Labyrinthium Defense Satellite Control Project.
Adam Ristovski, Master Warrant Officer of MANATO, custodian of GHQ armory
Adnan Kostallari, Centurion, Swift – 1
Adrijan Kerkorian Dr, veterinarian, DolTeam
Agama, one of DolTeam's dolphins
Akiko Hayakawa, ex - First Lieutenant, Japanese Self-defense Force, Honorary First Sergeant – Pilot of Newlands Airforce
Alan Martins Dr, MANATO Nordporte hospital
Aldevant Bradley, Dr, MANATO chief of behavioral analysis.
Alejandro Smith, Constable of Newlands Police, Izvori detachment
Alek Panić, Judge of the Newlands Mobile Judiciary
Alex Blanche, Komodor of the Newlands Navy
Alex DiMarti, Pilot of Newlands Navy
Alex Edwards, son of Alexander Edwards
Alexander Belinski, Newlands Civil Air Administration Accident Inspector
Alina Petrović, wife of Bogdan Petrović, 100th Squadron pilot
Alisom Winter, Pedro Goran's husband
Alliaia, one of DolTeam's dolphins
Ana František, wife of John František
Anita Bradić – Treskić, wife of Andrew Lighthouse
Ante Provalija, pilot of NGAT Embraer ERJ145
Bane Edwards, son of Alexander Edwards
Biljana František, wife of John František
Bleda Kosara, Corporal NLA, prison guard
Bo Gugutka, co-pilot of NGAT Embraer ERJ145
Bob Perkins, Military Constable
Bob Small, Newlandean astronaut
Boris Janosh, Colonel, National Jail Warden
Branislav Kovač, Master Sergeant-Pilot of Newlands Airforce, 100th Squadron
Brian Ford, Field Sergeant of Newlands Army, exec of TP Brigade

Calisto, a person from the old Atlantis
Carlotta Zvezdan, current Minister of Business and Innovation
Cathy Vidak, Newlands Civil Air Administration Accident Inspector
Christoph Sholokovski, First Sergeant-Pilot of Newlands Airforce
Clint Edwards, son of Alexander Edwards
Costa Bertoni, son of Rigoberto Bertoni
Curtis McNeal, Newlands Ambassador to Libya
Dash Ranković, Commander – Pilot of Newlands Airforce
David Lionheart, son of Sam and Fanta
David Mann, a famous painter
David Ratzaff, lawyer
Davit Jighauri, Georgian student who unearths the Atlantis Tablet
Djordje Jan, CEO of Titan Old City
Djordje Janković Professor Dr, one of the pioneers of Labyrinthium lasers, pioneered Cophot's Labyrinthium weapon
Djordje Rosić, anchorman of TV National
Djuro Ebner the Trainer, four-star sex worker
Dolgam, one of DolTeam's dolphins
Domenico Barnes, Vice-president of Newlands in the Petrović administration
Donald Macintyre, Inspector of the Newlands Police
Dracco Rudić "Draco the infantryman", Sub-Captain of Newlands Army
Dragana Edwards, wife of Alexander Edwards
Eaton Magnificent, House Vojnik / Soldier sex worker and escort, best male sex worker of Newlands for 2014
Elon Musk, the American entrepreneur cooperating with Newlands in car production, train design, and space travel
Fanta Gluščević, a renowned Newlands designer
Fifi Baratz, a teen involved in a rape
Francis Gonzales, Fleet Admiral of Newlands Navy (retired), CCofGHQ, Privilege of five
Frank Zawatsky, Pilot of Newlands Airforce
Geoffrey Miclat, Marines Centurion, prison guard
George Papazian Dr, volcanologist
George Petrović, Legionnaire 1st class, TPB
Georges Mrdjenović, Corporal of Newlands Army, one of Swift – 2 quintuplet brothers
Giorgi Okriashvili, Davit Jighauri's relative and his future husband

Giulia Marra, Monitor of Marines, Swift – 2
Goran Treskić, husband of Andrew Lighthouse
Goran Zlatić, Tetrarch, Swift – 1
Gordon Andrews, Mayor of Upplandia East (Uppland Mine and Uppland Village)
Gordon McKinnon, Master Sergeant-Pilot, 100th Squadron
Greg Bielinski, Lieutenant of Newlands Navy, Dave's aid on Cosmodrome
Guillermo Gonzalez, First Sergeant-Pilot of Newlands Airforce
Halea, a person from the old Atlantis
Hayv Kahraman, TV National's anchor
Helen Xu, NL Navy Midshipwoman, DolTeam
Hippolyta Petrović, daughter of Žana and Bogdan Petrović
Ignacio Morales, Grenadier, TPB
Igor Litvinenko, Pukovnik of Newlands Marines, CCofGHQ
Igor Mrdjenović, Corporal of Newlands Army, one of Swift – 2 quintuplet brothers
Ilona Farkaś, High Coordinator of Newlands Secret Service
Ina Trozubac, Porto River's stewardess
Iolanda Rupert, Grenadier of Newlands Army
Irene Bell, Midshipwoman of Newlands Navy
Isaak Garrowitz Dr, veterinarian, DolTeam
Isaak Rabinowicz, High Coordinator of Newlands Secret Service
Ismail Petit, Tetrarch, Swift – 1
Ivanka Marković, Lieutenant Commander, CO of NLD51 *Dark Star River*
Ivanka Molek, leader of Demarchy Party
Jack Mariner, First Sergeant-Pilot of Newlands Airforce, 100 Squadron
Jadranka Janković, Matroz 1st class of Newlands Navy
Jakov Strombopulos, Colonel of Newlands Army, Commanding officer of Swift – 3
Jana Trojka – Bertoni, wife of Rigoberto Bertoni
Jane Georgiou Dr, Volcano Watch volcanologist
Janko Djurišić, Tetrarch, Swift – 1
Janko James, NL Navy Lieutenant, leader of training program
Janosh Zlin, NL Navy Midshipman, DolTeam
Japjit Kaur - Singh, Supreme Court judge
Jason Averill, Newlands Civil Air Administration Senior Accident Inspector
Jason Marx, Corporal of Newlands Army

Jean Ouellette, Centurion, Swift – 1
Jeka Antonijević, a young upcoming artist
Jeremy Larousse, Newlands Army Sub–Captain
Jim Ryan, Captain of Newlands Army
Jiří Varina, father of Pavel Varina and owner of Varina Winery
Jiro Ogata, current minister for police and immigration
John Bernard, Centurion, Swift – 1
John Bute, Admiral, Commander of Home Fleet, CCofGHQ
John Dallas, state prosecutor
John Onduken, leader of Party Zora
John Shalf Dr, head of the Cophot Design Bureau in Paloma Shipyard, COPHOT section
John Shea, Master of science, physician, part of the group which theoretically predicted positions of major ores to be found in Upplandia
John Shelton, leader of Newlands Future Party
John Starbuck (Little John), Poručnik, Swift – 1
Joni Gea, judge
Jose Mrdjenović, Corporal of Newlands Army, one of Swift – 2 quintuplet brothers
Joshua Krüger Master of Science, anthropologist who analyzed the Atlantis tablet
Jovana Glavan, Naval Lieutenant tender NLNAU103 *Main*
Jovanka Bošnjak, judge
Kailani, one of DolTeam's dolphins
Karen Cates Dr, surgeon of MANATO Newlands Hospital in Ceticity
Karl Tutyko Tut, Lieutenant Commander of Newlands Navy
Katrin Matelaux, Major – Pilot of Newlands Airforce
Kim Kamichi, three-star sex worker, best female escort for 2014
Kipp Nelson, Constable of Newlands Police, Team ROKU
Kirk Show, Ensign NLN, prison guard
Kiron, a person from the old Atlantis
Knut Pedersen, Centurion, Swift – 1
Kosta Kuzmanovski Dr, coinventor of deep-tiling process which turned silty plains into arable land
Kristina Gavrilović, wife of Andrew Lighthouse
Kulak, one of DolTeam's dolphins
Lela Bertoni, wife of Rigoberto Bertoni

Lela Raonić, wife of General Miodrag Raonić
Lenny Schmidth Dr, surgeon of MANATO Hospital in Nordporte
Leonid Prokesch, Sub-Sergeant of Newlands Army, Swift – 3
Leopold Marini, MANATO's Chief Space Researcher
Leta Margolin, Naval Lieutenant, CO of tender NLNAU103 *Main*
Li Huei Dr, MANATO geneticist and the guardian of the Vault
Liam Patrockles, Chief Superintendent of Newlands Police, CCofGHQ
Luda, one of DolTeam's dolphins
Luiggi Tomatelli, Firefighter Chief, CCofGHQ
Luis Peres, from the Constitutional Party
Maksim Ognjanić, ex Newlands Marine, Chief of security of the Newlands Embassy in Tripoli
Mansur Lionheart, son of Dave and Alisa
Marc Landau Dr, Head of Volcano Watch Istočno Lipište, cofounder of the group of three
Margita (Gita), the hostess of House Vojnik
Marija Black, the seventh President of Newlands
Marija Bursać Dr, Volcano Watch volcanologist
Marija Bursać, NLRaiL logistics management
Marina Busalo, Centurion of Newlands Marines
Mark Broksville, Rear Admiral of Newlands Navy, Commander of the Military Port of Ceti III, Director of Navy Special School
Marko Strikeland, Sub-Captain of Newlands Army, commanding officer of Swift – 2
Marta Mondavi, Field Sergeant of Newlands Army, 1st Tank Brigade
Martin Minkowski, Sub-Captain, Exec of TP Brigade, husband of Andrew Lighthouse
Mary Petrović, current First Lady of Newlands, wife of President Nemanja Petrović
Matt Arnold, Constable of Newlands Police, Izvori detachment
Matt Fish, Lieutenant Commander, commanding officer DolTeam
Matt Fish, NL Navy Lieutenant Commander, CO DolTeam
Matthew Vandyke, TV National journalist
Max Zvezdanić, Military Police Sergeant
Mbilini oNdini, NL Navy Sub-Lieutenant, DolTeam
Melinda Staples, Decurion of Marines, Swift – 2
Miki Plamen, NL Navy Lieutenant, 2nd in command DolTeam
Milan Mišković, Poručnik of Newlands Marines, Swift – 3

Milan Mladić Dr, MANATO geneticist
Mile Vlak, Constable of Newlands Police, Izvori detachment
Milomir Zdravković, Constable of Newlands Police, Old City traffic department
Mira Macura, Constable of Newlands Police, Old City traffic department
Misha Zec, Master Sergeant-Pilot of Newlands Airforce, 100th Squadron
Mnyamana amaGoda, NL Navy Ensign, DolTeam
Morgan Finlay, Treasury Minister in Petrović Government
Moshe Rabinowitz, Captain-Pilot Newlands Airforce, 100th Squadron's administrative officer
Mumford Steve, a young upcoming artist
Nancy Alvarado, Ensign, propulsion specialist of the patrol boat "514"
Nataša Janković, Constable of Newlands Police, Old City traffic department
Natasha Petrović, wife of Bogdan Petrović
Nathaniel Causgrove Dr, oceanologist who analyzed the Atlantis tablet
Nebojša Lazić, Military Constable
Nela Bertoni, daughter of Rigoberto Bertoni
Nikodim Traubert, Commander–Pilot, Shift Commander of MANATO Nordporte Traffic Air Control
Nina Jones, Minister of Defense in current Newlands Government
Obren Petersen, Ensign, weapons specialist of the patrol boat "514"
Ofer Bar-Yosef Prof Dr, chemistry who analyzed the Atlantis tablet
Olaf Thompson, Poručnik of Newlands Marines, Swift – 3
Olena Slapski – Bertoni, wife of Rigoberto Bertoni
Ozren Radić, Cyber-coder, Team ROKU
Pablo Petkovski, Constable of Military Police
Pam Raonić, wife of General Miodrag Raonić
Paul Elmer, NLRaiL logistics management
Pedro Goran, Vice-president in two Governments of Newlands
Peter Boer, Captain–Pilot of the 31st Newlands Airforce Experimental Squadron "Birds of Prey"
Peter Schneider, Sub-Lieutenant, naval diver
Peter Schweinfurter, Curator of Atlantida Museum in Old City, member of privilege of five
Petra Varina, wife of Jiří Varina
Pietro Lurie, Master of Science, MASP Construction Bureau
Piotr Reszke, Embraer Captain, Newlands Petrol Airlines

Polly Kawkawa, Petty Officer, crew member of the patrol boat "514"
Prajesh Kindberg, Energon truck driver
Predrag Nenad, General of Newlands Army, CCofGHQ
Rada Mastilo, Lieutenant-Pilot, Team ROKU
Radarion, one of DolTeam's dolphins
Ratko Zmajković, Komandir of Newlands Marines, second-in-command Swift – 2
Ravna Motet, one of the first healers of Newlands
Regy McArthur, Centurion of Newlands Marines, Swift – 3
Renata Petrović, daughter of Natasha and Bogdan Petrović
Renata Rukavina, TV National anchor, political channels
Renzo Šćekić, Newlands Coastguard Midshipman
Rhan Mueller, Poručnik of Marines, Swift – 1
Rita Ayesha, Retired Major-Pilot of Fleet Air Arm, first female fighter pilot of Newlands Navy
Rita Steiner, Lieutenant of Newlands Army
Robert Dobrašinović, husband of Zelda
Robert Prosinac, pilot of Newlands Airforce and the 100th GHQ Squadron, PsiMANATO
Roberto da Silva, Major-Pilot of Newlands Airforce from the Golden Eagle squadrons
Roderic Laguarde, a young upcoming artist
Rosalyn Sussman, Master Warrant Officer
Rudi Van der Vyver, NL Navy Lieutenant, DolTeam
Salvador Kuul, CCofGHQ Colonel, GHQ
Sam Perkins Dr, coinventor of deep-till process which turned silty plains into arable land
Samson Krombacher, employee of Atlantida Museum
Saška Grey, Titan's production manager responsible for Tesla-Titan vehicles
Satoshi Mori, Cyber-commander of the Newlands Cybercommand
Shimshon Dudaev, Chief Inspector of Military Police
Shoaku Takahashi, Titan's production manager for 5G technologies
Simon Pasha Dr, Engineering Division of MANATO
Skylar Bor, Field Sergeant of the Newlands Army, 1st Tank Brigade
Slav Norton, Lieutenant of Newlands Army
Slaven Mrdjenović, Corporal of Newlands Army, one of Swift – 2 quintuplet brothers

Slaven Panajotović Dr, Upperland Mines Hospital Uppland Village
Slavko Kondratiev, Constable of the Newlands Police
Slavko Veljković, Constable of Newlands Police, Old City traffic department
Son Merritt, NL Navy Petty Officer, DolTeam
Stanislav Godzuik Dr, surgeon of MANATO Newlands Hospital in Ceticity
Stanko Graovac, Legionnaire 1st class, TPB
Stavros Filikaki, Constable of the Newlands Police
Stephen King Dr, New Belgrade dentist
Takeo Ishihara, Superintendent of Newlands Police
Tamar, one of DolTeam's dolphins
Thom Brdar, telepathic prisoner
Thomas Mrdjenović, Corporal of Newlands Army, one of Swift – 2 quintuplet brothers
Thomas Riley, MASP, head engineer on the Cosmodrome
Tiffany Windsor Dr, veterinarian, DolTeam
Tim Thumb, Reservist Centurion of Newlands Marines
Timothy Jacknife, retired Commander-Pilot of NL Airforce, working for the Old City Airshow
Timothy Tomson, Poručnik of Newlands Marines, Swift – 3
Todor Garrowitz, NL Navy Sub-Lieutenant, DolTeam
Tom Donelson, the current leader of Constitutional Party
Tom Higham, Grenadier, TPB
Tom Smith, husband of Andrew Lighthouse
Triksi, one of DolTeam's dolphins
Trudy Anderson, nurse of MANATO Hospital in Nordporte
Truth Martinez, financial adviser of the National Bank of Newlands
Tylan, one of DolTeam's dolphins
Umwashi Koseki, Cyber-commander of the Newlands Cybercommand
Uroš Rabrenović, Navy Lieutenant, Team ROKU
Urt Rossi, MASP, engineer on the Cosmodrome, head of NL Space program study
Valdemar Kurhonen, Legionnaire 1st class of Newlands Marines, TP Brigade
Valentina Živković – Treskić, wife of Andrew Lighthouse
Vera Budimirović, Newlands Army Corporal, GHQ switchboard, converted to Islam and helped mount a suicide bomb attack on the GHQ

Vinka Peeva, Master Sergeant-Pilot of Newlands Airforce, 100th GHQ Squadron
Violeta Petrović, daughter of Alina and Bogdan Petrović
Vladan Durand, Centurion, Swift – 1
Vladimir Ruski, Chief Warrant Officer
Vladislav Gilberg, Constable of the Highway Patrol
Wade Cooper, the most awarded TV National investigative reporter
Wil Seattle, Minister of Mining in the current Newlands Government
Will Tainer, MASP Construction Bureau
Yrinne – Yrin Janosh, originally Sitshitshili uKhandempemvu, transgender spouse of the National Jail Warden Colonel Boris Janosh
Žana Petrović, wife of Bogdan Petrović
Zara Miočič, Sub-Captain, TPB
Zdravko Thompson, Sergeant-Pilot of Newlands Airforce, 100 Squadron
Zelda Dobrašinović, wife of Robert Dobrašinović
Željko Bogdanović, a famous painter
Željko Mornar, Chief Air Inspector of the Newlands Police
Zeno Dukakis, Centurion of Newlands Marines, second in command Swift – 3
Zhang Sanfeng, DFQL elder
Živka Ping, NL Navy Ensign, DolTeam
Zlatko Zec, NL Navy Midshipman, DolTeam
Zora Perello - Godina, Lieutenant NLA, Forced Labor Team Leader of the National Jail
Zora Zhupanchich, judge
Zoran Živković, son of Andrew Lighthouse

# CENTRAL COMMAND OF GENERAL HEADQUARTERS OF NEWLANDS ARMED FORCES – MANATO

2013

GHQ General (NL Army) David A-H Anderson – Lionheart, Commander-in-Chief of MANATO

GHQ Major General with flight endorsement (NL Airforce) Sam Roberts-Lionheart, Exec of the CIC

GHQ Komodor (NL Navy – Intelligence Branch) Fran Lionheart, GHQ Intelligence

GHQ Admiral (NL Navy) John Bute, Commander of Home Fleet

GHQ General (NL Airforce) Miodrag Raonić, Commander GHQ Intelligence

GHQ Rear-Admiral (NL Navy) Zoran Tasić

GHQ Komodor (NL Coastguard) Marino Marino

GHQ Colonel-Pilot (NL Airforce) Raj Chahal, Commander MASP and MALD

GHQ General (NL Army) Predrag Nenad

GHQ Brigadni General (NL Marines) Igor Litvinenko

GHQ Fleet Admiral – retired (NL Navy) Francis Gonzales

**Associated members:**

Chief Superintendent of Newlands Police Liam Patrockles

Firefighter Chief Luiggi Tomatelli

**New members:**

GHQ Colonel (NL Army) Salvador Kuul, Commanding Officer of 1st Tank Brigade

GHQ Major (NL Marines) Henri Deladin, Overall Commander of TPB

**Deceased:**

GHQ Airforce General – retired (NL Airforce) Robert Magyar

GHQ Brigadni General (NL Marines) Stanko Broz

**Privilege of five members, 2013:**

GHQ General (NL Army) David A-H Anderson – Lionheart, Commander-in-Chief of MANATO

GHQ Fleet Admiral – retired (NL Navy) Francis Gonzales

GHQ Komodor (NL Navy – Intelligence Branch) Fran Lionheart, GHQ Intelligence

Dr. Philip Kieron Pardagh, MANATO historian

President Nemanja Petrović

Curator of Atlantida Museum Peter Schweinfurter

Bundeskanzlerin Angela Merkel, Chancellor of Germany

**New member:**

Conditional Honorary Kapetan Andrew Lighthouse, Tactical Commander of TPB

**Deceased:**

GHQ Airforce General – retired (NL Airforce) Robert Magyar

# FAMILY LIONHEART:

| Family: | | | | |
|---|---|---|---|---|
| | ***Name + change of name during the story*** | ***Date of birth*** | ***Starting rank*** | ***New rank*** |
| 1 | Fran Lionheart | $2^{nd}$ August, 1975 | GHQ Komodor, Newlands Navy Intelligence Branch + GHQ Intelligence | |
| 2 | Fanta Lionheart | $1^{st}$ January, 1980 | Chief Warrant Officer, MANATO | Honorary Practice Manager |
| 3 | Thom Vigo-Lionheart | $3^{rd}$ May, 1973 | Captain, Newlands Army | Major, Newlands Army |
| 4 | Nikola Tomić-Lionheart | $10^{th}$ May, 1973 | Captain, Newlands Army | Major, Newlands Army |
| 5 | Alisa Tomić-Lionheart | $29^{th}$ December, 1980 | Komodor, Newlands Navy Intelligence Branch | |
| 6 | David (Wade) A-H Anderson – Lionheart | $15^{th}$ May, 1977 | GHQ General, Newlands Army | |
| 7 | Sam Roberts-Lionheart | $3^{rd}$ August, 1974 | GHQ Major General with flight endorsement, Newlands Airforce | |

| Children: | | | |
|---|---|---|---|
| 1 | Mansur Lionheart | 1st September, 2011 | Biological parents Alisa and David |
| 2 | David Lionheart | 22nd December, 2011 | Biological parents Fanta and Sam |
| 3 | Vid Lionheart | 22nd August, 2012 | Biological parents Alisa and Robert |
| 4 | Athom Lionheart | 22nd August, 2012 | Biological parents Alisa and Thom |
| 5 | Vuk Lionheart | 22nd August, 2012 | Biological parents Alisa and Thom |
| 6 | Ralf Lionheart | 22nd August, 2012 | Biological parents Alisa and Sam |
| 7 | Stein Lionheart | 22nd August, 2012 | Biological parents Alisa and Fran |
| 8 | Rok Lionheart | 22nd August, 2012 | Biological parents Alisa and Nikola |

# OTHER IMPORTANT FAMILIES:

| *Family of Bogdan Petrović* | | |
|---|---|---|
| Nemanja Petrović | President of Newlands, Bogdan's father | |
| Mary Petrović | First Lady of Newlands, Bogdan's mother | |
| Bogdan Petrović | Newlands Naval Cadet | |
| Natasha Petrović | Bogdan's wife | |
| Žana Petrović | Bogdan's wife | |
| Alina Petrović | Bogdan's wife | |
| Renata Petrović | Daughter of Natasha and Bogdan | October 18, 2011 |
| Hippolyta Petrović | Daughter of Žana and Bogdan | November 10, 2011 |
| Violeta Petrović | Daughter of Alina and Bogdan | November 18, 2011 |
| *Family František* | | |
| John František | Ambassador of Newlands, Ambassador of MANATO | |
| Ana František | Social worker | |
| Biljana František | Electrical engineer | |
| Yakub František | Son of Ana and John | November 28, 2014 |
| Leia František | Daughter of Biljana and John | November 30, 2014 |
| *Family Lian - Hadži-Janković* | | |
| Robert Hadži-Janković | MANATO pilot | |
| Li Lian | 9th President of Newlands | |
| Zhenxiang Hadži-Janković | Daughter of Li and Dave | July 1, 2012 |
| Atlas Hadži-Janković | Son of Li and Robert | July 1, 2014 |
| *Family of Pavel Varina* | | |
| Jiří Varina | Wine producer, Pavel's father | |
| Petra Varina | Wine trader, Pavel's mother | |

| | | |
|---|---|---|
| Pavel Varina | Footballer, trainer, wine producer | |
| Cleo Novotny | Footballer, wine trader | |
| Rigoberto Bertoni (Berto) | Footballer, politician | |
| Olena Bertoni | Party functionary | |
| Lela Travica | Radiologist | |
| Jana Miller | TV playwright | |
| Sam Novotny | Son of Pavel and Cleo | April 30, 2012 |
| Nela Bertoni | Daughter of Berto and Olena | May 1, 2002 |
| Costa Miller - Bertoni | Son of Berto and Jana | June 3, 2010 |
| Jan Varina | Son of Jiří and Cleo | March 29, 2014 |
| Jonni Bertoni | Son of Berto and Cleo | March 22, 2016 |
| Paola Novotny | Daughter of Berto and Cleo | December 2, 2018 |
| ***Family Raonić*** | | |
| Miodrag Raonić (Miki) | Newlands Airforce General | |
| Pam Raonić | Teacher | |
| Lela Raonić | Economist | |
| ***Family Marino*** | | |
| Marino Marino | Komodor of Coastguard | |
| Moira Marino | Energon executive | |
| Anette Marino | Cook | |
| Tara Marino | Platin analyst | |
| Vlad Marino | Son of Marino and Anette | December 1, 1997 |
| ***Family Ross - Magnificent*** | | |
| Amanda Ross - Magnificent | Heart surgeon | |
| Eaton (Dragan Mladenović) Ross - Magnificent | Sex worker, wine trader, actor | |
| Ivana Ross - Magnificent | Daughter | March 6, 2017 |
| Alex Ross - Magnificent | Twin son | June 28, 2019 |
| Alexa Ross - Magnificent | Twin daughter | June 28, 2019 |
| ***Family Gonzalez - Sholokovski*** | | |
| Christoph Sholokovski (Chris) | First Sergeant–Pilot of Newlands Airforce | |

| | | |
|---|---|---|
| Guillermo Gonzalez (Guil) | First Sergeant-Pilot of Newlands Airforce | |
| Akiko Hayakawa | Honorary First Sergeant – Pilot of Newlands Airforce | |
| Tor-Kenji Gonzales - Sholokovski | Biological parents Akiko and Guillermo | May 23, 2012 |
| ***Family Cates - Godzuik*** | | |
| Dr. Karen Cates | MANATO surgeon | |
| Dr. Stanislav Godzuik | MANATO surgeon | |
| Roberta Grande | Egg donor | |
| Nenad Godzuik | Son | December 15, 2012 |
| ***Family of Andrew Lighthouse*** | | |
| Andrew Lighthouse | Newlands Police, TPB, PsiMANATO | |
| Kristina Gavrilović | Architect | |
| Valentina Živković – Treskić | Sanitary worker | |
| Anita Bradić – Treskić | Nutritionist | |
| Zoran Živković | Son of Andrew and Valentina | August 21, 2002 |
| Antwo Bradić | Son of Andrew and Anita | March 25, 2005 |
| Mona Gavrilović | Daughter of Andrew and Kristina | January 26, 2007 |
| Malea Gavrilović | Daughter of Andrew and Kristina | September 30, 2012 |
| Goran Treskić | Valentina's first husband | |
| Tom Smith | Anita's first husband | |
| Gloria Živković – Treskić | Daughter of Tom and Valentina | May 4, 1996 |
| Ana Živković – Treskić | Daughter of Goran and Anita | October 10, 1997 |
| Martin Minkowski | Officer of TPB | |

# STRUCTURE OF PSIMANATO IN 2013:

***PsiOne:***

Dave (Menasor) – intangibility, telepathy, Labyrinthium shield, premonitions

Alisa (Nightbird) – empath

Sam (Devastator) – telepathy

Constable Andrew Lighthouse (Sharkticon) – telepathy and emotional transfer

Inspector Alan Wykes (Soundwave) – telepathy

Robert Prosinac, Pilot of Newlands Airforce (Skywarp) – telekinesis

Gordon McKinnon, Master Sergeant-Pilot (Ramjet) – manipulation of emotions

Mietje Dobrašinović (Galvatron) – telepathy and telepathic interaction with computer systems

Robert Hadži-Janković, Major-Pilot of Newlands Airforce (Buzzsaw) – telepathy

Nedžad Hasanović, Sub-Lieutenant of Newlands Navy (Nenad) – telepathy

Akiko Hayakawa, Honorary First Sergeant – Pilot of Newlands Airforce, formerly of Japanese Self-defense Force (Desutoron) – detection of distant objects

***PsiSupport:***

Jim Ryan, Captain of Newlands Army (RhoPsi)

*Thom (TauPsi) – temporarily considered deceased in 2012*

Nikola (NuPsi)

Henri Deladin, Komandir of Newlands Marines (DeltaPsi)

***Various support:***

Cyber-captain Yoshi Soga (PsiTyr)

Dr. Irena Panj (PsiIng)

Robert Dobrašinović (PsiBorn)

Zelda Dobrašinović (PsiStan)

Dr. Lenko Zdravkov (PsiMan)

Pilot Alex DiMarti (PsiGull)

First Sergeant-Pilot of NLAF Christoph Sholokovski (PsiHawk)
First Sergeant-Pilot of NLAF Guillermo Gonzalez (PsiCondor)

***DolTeam:***
Matt Fish, NL Navy Lieutenant Commander, CO DolTeam (Kirk)
Miki Plamen, NL Navy Lieutenant, 2nd in command DolTeam (Spock)
Janko James, NL Navy Lieutenant, leader of training program (Bashir)
Rudi Van der Vyver, NL Navy Lieutenant (Mudd)
Mbilini oNdini, NL Navy Sub-Lieutenant (Rostov)
Todor Garrowitz, NL Navy Sub-Lieutenant (Chekov)
Živka Ping, NL Navy Ensign (Cutler)
Mnyamana amaGoda, NL Navy Ensign (Dax)
Janosh Zlin, NL Navy Midshipman (Dukat)
Helen Xu, NL Navy Midshipwoman (Uhura)
Zlatko Zec, NL Navy Midshipman (Riker)
Son Merritt, NL Navy Petty Officer (Quark)
Dr. Isaak Garrowitz, veterinarian (McCoy)
Dr. Tiffany Windsor, veterinarian (Data)
Dr. Adrijan Kerkorian, veterinarian (Picard)

**The dolphins** - telepathy:
Dolgam
Agama
Luda
Triksi
Kulak
Tamar
Radarion
Tylan
Alliaia
Kailani

# FAMILY LIONHEART RESIDENCES:

| City | Full address | Details |
|---|---|---|
| Paloma - Stonehill | Stonehill Road 44 / X / 54<br>33350 Paloma | One room rented from Varina family |
| Nova Britanija | "Palmin Raj"<br>Sunshine Way 236 / III / 8<br>96100 Nova Britanija | Fully owned apartment |
| Palomin Most | "B&B Lionheart",<br>Pavlović Avenue 69<br>02440 Palomin Most | Fully owned house turned into a B&B, one room reserved for the family |
| Nake | Fanforrest Avenue 177<br>61850 Nake | Fully owned house<br>The family home |
| New Belgrade - Rad | Martin Street 1312<br>12010 New Belgrade | Fully owned home |
| Ceti III | Javorovog lista 15 / III / 7<br>MP4539 Ceticity | Fully owned apartment |
| Nordporte | Markovo Road 22 / III / 17<br>54000 Nordporte | Fully owned apartment |
| Freedom Ship | FSA09666, 00001 Freedom Ship | Fully owned apartment |

# MANATO SECURITY CLEARANCES

<table>
<tr><th>Civilian</th><th>MANATO</th><th>NSS</th><th>Cybercommand</th></tr>
<tr><td colspan="2">Privilege of five (Po5)</td><td>NSS security clearance (NSSSec)</td><td>Cybercommand security clearance (CySec)</td></tr>
<tr><td>Government security level (GoSecLev)</td><td colspan="3">Privilege of twelve (Po12)</td></tr>
<tr><td>Representatives' security level (RepSecLev)</td><td>Officer security clearance level 1 (OffSec1)</td><td rowspan="5"></td><td>Top Cybercommand employee security clearance (ToCySec)</td></tr>
<tr><td rowspan="4"></td><td>Officer security clearance level 2 (OffSec2)</td><td rowspan="2">High Cybercommand employee security clearance (HiCySec)</td></tr>
<tr><td>Under-officer security clearance level 1 (UnterSec1)</td></tr>
<tr><td>Under-officer security clearance level 2 (UnterSec2)</td><td rowspan="2">Basic Cybercommand employee security clearance (BaCySec)</td></tr>
<tr><td>Basic security clearance (BaSec)</td></tr>
</table>

# SOME COMMON NEWLANDS BYWORDS, CUSS AND SWEAR WORDS:

| Byword - saying | Origin | Use | Circumstance |
|---|---|---|---|
| Aha (Shit) | Arabic | Impolite | Any negative feeling |
| Acta est fabula, plaudite (The drama has been acted out, applaud) | Latin | Polite | Irritation |
| Alea iacta est (The die is cast) | Latin | Polite | Resolution |
| A fronte praecipitium a tergo lupi (A precipice in front, wolves behind) | Latin | Polite | Exasperation |
| Aut vincere aut mori (Conquer or die) | Latin | Polite | Resolve |
| Baszd meg; Vazze bassza meg (May you fuck it; fuck it) | Hungarian | Impolite | To be avoided |
| Bre, more bre (Enough) *similar use to fuck* | Serbo-Croatian | Bad form but not vulgar | Interjection, everyday punctuation |
| Beshoor (No brained) | Persian | Polite | Insulting comment |
| Carpe diem (Seize the day) | Latin | Polite | Optimism |
| Cretin | French | Impolite | Anger, wrath |
| Calisse de merde (Shit) | French | Impolite | Disappointment, pain, unhappiness |
| Dulce bellum inexpertis (War is sweet to those who have never fought) | Latin | Polite | Exasperation |
| Dixi (I have spoken; amen) | Latin | Polite | Definite ending |
| Dum spiro spero (While I breathe, I hope) | Latin | Polite | Hope |
| Dodjavola, do djavola (Go to hell, it goes to hell) | Serbo-Croatian | Polite | Exasperation, disappointment |

| | | | |
|---|---|---|---|
| Dormi mecum (Sleep with me) | Latin | Polite | Affirmative, desire |
| Damn, damned | English | Polite | Surprise |
| Dura lex sed lex (The law is hard, but it is the law) | Latin | Polite | Resignation |
| Exampli gratia (For example) | Latin | Polite | Erudite speech |
| Flocci non facio (I don't give a damn) | Latin | Polite | Scorn |
| Figlio di puttana (Son of a bitch) | Italian | Polite | Generally derogatory |
| Great nature around us, nature the great + any variation | Newlandean | Polite | Surprise, awe, anything a bit outstanding |
| Glavom i bradom (With my head and chin, *stands for:* I, myself) | Serbo-Croatian | Polite | Ascertaining someone's identity |
| Gahba (Bitch; fucking bitch) | Arabic | Impolite | Common expletive |
| Halleluiah chance | Newlandean | Polite | Lucky break |
| Heavy | English | Polite | Disappointment |
| Hutzpa, hutzpah, chutzpah (Balls of nerves) | Hebrew | Polite | Admiration |
| Hiljadu mu mučica (thousand little tortures) *"Hiljadu mu" can be combined with any other noun, such as, for example: hiljadu mu sunaca (thousand suns), hiljadu mu dabrova (thousand beavers) and so on. The word used depends only on speaker's eloquence.* | Newlandean | Polite | Surprise, everyday byword |
| Hijo de mil putas (Son of a thousand bitches) | Spanish | Polite | Surprise, pleasure, admiration |
| Hueles a mierda (You smell like shit) | Spanish | Impolite | Disgust |
| Holly molly | English | Polite | Surprise |

| Ii kagen ni shiro (Stop messing around) | Japanese | Polite | Exasperation, disappointment |
|---|---|---|---|
| Is cuma liom sa diabhal (I don't give a dam) | Irish | Polite | Generally derogatory |
| Irrumatror (Bastard) | Latin | Polite | Disappointment |
| Id est (In other words) | Latin | Polite | Erudite speech |
| Inta shaz (You're a pervert) | Arabic | Impolite | Debasing |
| Kuš, ćut (Shut up) | Serbo-Croatian | Impolite | Anger, opposition |
| Khange khodah (God's screw up) | Persian | Polite | Lament |
| Multitax | Newlandean | Polite | Difficulty, labour |
| Marka mu (By Marko) | Newlandean | Polite | Everyday assertive, to counter disbelief |
| Mo (Abbreviation for a Moroccan)<br>*but also:* | Arabic<br>*Newlandean* | Impolite<br>*Polite* | Derogatory for Moroccan and all Arabs<br>*Mustached man* |
| Malik kahell (Your king is a black) | Arabic | Impolite | Insulting, racist |
| Majke ti, majke mu (Your mother, his mother) | Serbo-Croatian | Impolite | Doubt, everyday byword |
| Mook kebba (Your mother is a whore) | Arabic | Impolite | Generally insulting |
| Mrdat (Fuck) | Czech | Impolite | Derogatory |
| Merde (Shit) | French | Impolite | General unhappiness |
| Nyet (No) | Russian | Polite | General speech |
| No way, Jose | English | Polite | Denial |
| Niko se naučen rodio (Nobody's born all-knowing) | Serbo-Croatian | Polite | Persistence |
| Nod (Fart) | Hebrew | Impolite | Disappointment |
| Non omnis moriar (Not all of me shell die) | Latin | Polite | Hope |
| Oh la vache (Holy cow) | French | Polite | Surprise |
| Over my dd | Newlandean | Impolite | Spite, defensive, wrath |
| Orcae ita (Hell's yeah) | Latin | Polite | Affirmative in everyday speech |

| | | | |
|---|---|---|---|
| Ochen balshoy (Very big, very good) | Russian | Polite | Surprise, pleasure, admiration |
| Pai, pai (Breasts, nipples) | Japanese | Polite | Balancing |
| Putain de bordel de merde (*In use equals:* holy fucking shit) | French | Impolite | Derogatory |
| Pic cocuk (Bastard child) | Turkish | Impolite | Derogatory |
| Prcat (Fuck) | Czech | Impolite | Derogatory |
| Proklet bio / prokleta bila / prokleto bilo *gender specific* (Damn him / her / it) | Serbo-Croatian | Impolite | Anger |
| Putz (Dickhead) | Yiddish | Impolite | Denigration |
| Spasitelju (Saviour) | Serbo-Croatian | Polite | Exasperation, danger |
| Svetitelju (Hail Saint) | Serbo-Croatian | Polite | Surprise, doubt |
| Sotonico (Little devil) | Newlands | Both | Generally derogatory, sarcasm, joking, disappointment |
| Shards | English | Polite | Disappointment |
| Sharmoota haygana (Horny bitch) | Arabic | Impolite | Wish to hurt |
| Sucatum tauri (Bull's shit) | Latin | Polite | Polite form of shit |
| Sakra, sacrament (Christian derivative) | Czech | Polite | Common byword attached to almost any noun |
| Sacré bleu, sakrebleu (*In use equals:* damn it) | French | Polite | Surprise |
| Santa Muerte (Saint Death) | Latino | Polite | Personification of death |
| San Martín y el mendigo (Saint Martin and the beggar) | Spanish | Polite | Variety, exasperation |
| Svih mu svetaca (By all saints) | Serbo-Croatian | Polite | Surprise, persistence, stubbornness |
| Scheisskopf (Dickhead) | German | Impolite | Surprised anger |

| | | | |
|---|---|---|---|
| Tabarnaque (Tabernacle, *in use equals English:* damn or shit) | Quebec French | Polite | Disappointment, pain, unhappiness, general everyday byword |
| Tutto finito (All finished) | Italian | Polite | Everyday byword |
| Über alles (Above all else) | German | Polite | Everyday speech |
| Vamonos (Let's go) | Spanish | Polite | Eagerness |
| Vi bacio tutti (Kiss you all) | Italian | Polite | Everyday speech |
| Verdammt (Damn it) | German | Impolite | Surprise |
| Vai a morire ammazzato (Go and get killed) | Italian | Impolite | Anger, unease, opposition |
| Va te tripoter (Go jerk off) | French | Impolite | Generally derogatory, disagreement |
| Večna im slava i pamet (Eternal glory and remembrance; *same use as:* RIP) | Serbo-Croatian | Polite | Respect |
| Woodla halum (Allah wills it) | Arabic | Polite | Indifference, hope, resignation |
| What the heck | English | Polite | Surprise |
| Yatsume (Unpleasant person) | Japanese | Impolite | Derogatory |
| Yakamashii (Shut up) | Japanese | Impolite | Derogatory |
| Yutz (Asshole) | Yiddish | Impolite | Derogatory |

CPSIA information can be obtained
at www.ICGtesting.com
Printed in the USA
LVHW081515040322
712645LV00024B/1297/J

9 780228 872702